DOMINION

THE IMMORTAL VAMPIRE Counts have ravaged the Old World for many hundreds of years and their undead scourge has left its mark on many generations. Heroes have risen to combat this seemingly unstoppable tide and following the death of vampire lord Vlad von Carstein, the vampires are thrown into disarray. Struggling to rebuild their forces, the insane Konrad von Carstein comes to the fore and his bloodthirsty reign of terror will leave a swathe of destruction across the world...

Steven Savile brings the bloodshed to life in the second novel of this series, which features the rise and fall of Konrad von Carstein.

D1601284

A WARHAMMER NOVEL

BOOK TWO IN THE
VON CARSTEIN TRILOGY

DOMINION

STEVEN SAVILE

For Dave,
For years of friendship and support and being a second father to a
young boy who needed one and was too stubborn to know it.
With love.

A Black Library Publication

First published in Great Britain in 2006 by
BL Publishing,
Games Workshop Ltd.,
Willow Road, Nottingham,
NG7 2WS, UK

10 9 8 7 6 5 4 3 2 1

Cover illustration by John Gravato.
Map by Nuala Kinrade.

A CIP record for this book is available from the British Library.

ISBN 13: 978 1 84416 292 5
ISBN 10: 1 84416 292 3

Distributed in the US by Simon & Schuster
1230 Avenue of the Americas, New York, NY 10020.

Printed and bound in Great Britain by
Bookmarque, Surrey, UK.

See the Black Library on the Internet at
www.blacklibrary.com

Find out more about Games Workshop
and the world of Warhammer at
www.games-workshop.com

THIS IS A DARK age, a bloody age, an age of daemons and of sorcery. It is an age of battle and death, and of the world's ending. Amidst all of the fire, flame and fury it is a time, too, of mighty heroes, of bold deeds and great courage.

AT THE HEART of the Old World sprawls the Empire, the largest and most powerful of the human realms. Known for its engineers, sorcerers, traders and soldiers, it is a land of great mountains, mighty rivers, dark forests and vast cities. It is a land riven by uncertainty, as three pretenders all vye for control of the Imperial throne.

BUT THESE ARE far from civilised times. Across the length and breadth of the Old World, from the knightly palaces of Bretonnia to ice-bound Kislev in the far north, come rumblings of war. In the towering World's Edge Mountains, the orc tribes are gathering for another assault. In the east, the dead do not rest easy, and there are rumours of rats that walk like men emerging from the dark places of the world. From the northern wildernesses there is the ever-present threat of Chaos, of daemons and beastmen corrupted by the foul powers of the Dark Gods. As the time of battle draws ever nearer, the Empire needs heroes like never before.

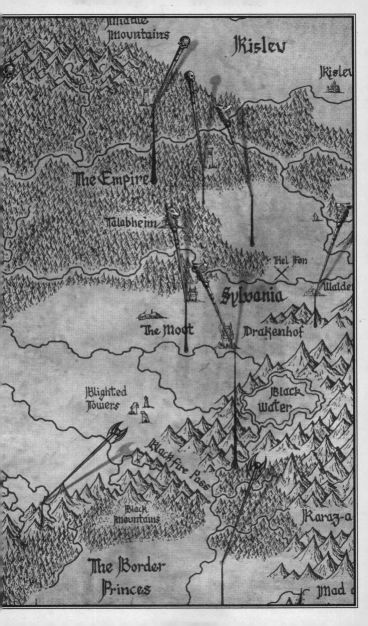

PROLOGUE
The Eye of the Hurricane

GRUNBERG
Late Winter, 2052

IT WAS DESPERATE.

Kallad Stormwarden knew the tide of the battle had turned. Still, the young dwarf prince stood side by side with his father, matching the gruff dwarf blow for blow as Kellus's axe hewed through the swarm of dead storming the walls of Grunberg Keep. The dwarfs of Karak Sadra had chosen to make their last stand against the Vampire Count together with the man-lings.

The walkway was slick with rain.

Kallad slammed the edge of his great axe, Ruinthorn, into the grinning face of a woman with worms where her eyes ought to have been. The blade split her skull cleanly in two. Still the woman came

on, clawing desperately at his face. He staggered back
a step beneath the ferocity of her attack, wrenching
the axe head free. Grunting, he delivered a second,
killer blow. The dead woman staggered and fell life-
lessly from the wall.

He knuckled the rain from his eyes.

There was no blood and the dead didn't scream.
Their silence was more frightening than any of the
many horrors on the field of combat. They surged forwards mercilessly as axes crunched into brittle bones,
splintering shoulders and cracking skulls. They
lurched and lumbered on as arrows thudded into
chest cavities, piercing taut skin and powdering it like
vellum, and still they came on relentlessly as heads
rolled and limbs were severed.

'Grimna!' Kallad bellowed, kicking the woman's
head from the wall. His rallying cry echoed down the
line as the dead shuffled forwards. Grimna. Courage.
It was all they had in the face of death. It was all they
needed. Grimna gave them strength while the stubbornness of the mountain gave them courage. With
strength and courage, and their white-haired king
beside them, they could withstand anything.

There was an air of greatness about Kellus Ironhand.
More than merely prowess or skill, the dwarf embodied the sheer iron will of his people. He was the
mountain, indefatigable, unconquerable, and giant.

And yet there was a chill worming its way deeper
into Kallad Stormwarden's heart.

Only in death did moans escape their broken teeth,
but these weren't real sounds. They weren't battlefield
sounds. They were sussurant whispers. They weren't

human. They weren't alive. They belonged to the gathering storm and they were terrifying in their wrongness.

It didn't matter how hard the defenders fought, how many they killed, they were trapped in a losing battle. The ranks of the undead army were endless, their bloodlust unquenchable.

Bodies surfaced in the moat, rising slowly to the surface, their flesh bloated and their faces stripped away by the leeches that fed on them.

Kallad stared at the tide of corpses as one by one they began to twitch and jerk like loose-limbed puppets, brought violently to life. The first few clawed their way up the side of the dirt embankment. More followed behind them: a seemingly endless swell of death surfacing from beneath the black water.

The futility of fighting hit him hard. It was pointless. Death only swelled the ranks of the enemy. The sons of Karak Sadra would be dining in the Hall of the Ancestors by sunrise.

Kallad slapped the blade of Ruinthorn against his boot and brought it to bear on a one-armed corpse as it lumbered into range. The bottom half of its jaw hung slackly where the skin and muscle had rotted away. Kallad took the miserable wretch's head clean off with a single vicious swing. The fighting was harsh. Despite their greater prowess, the dwarfs were tiring. Defeat was inevitable.

Behind Kallad, someone yelled a warning, and a cauldron of blazing naphtha arced high over the wall, crashing into the ranks of the dead. The fire bit and burned bright as dead flesh seared, tufts of hair shrivelled and bones charred. The pouring rain only intensified the burning, the naphtha reacting violently to the water.

The stench was sickening as the corpses burned.

Kellus brought his axe round in a vicious arc, the rune of Grimna slicing into a dead man's gut. The blow cracked the man's ribcage open. His entrails spilled out like slick loops of grey rope, unravelling in his hands even as he struggled to hold them in. The dead man didn't bleed. His head came up, a look of bewilderment frozen on his features as Kellus put the thing out of its misery.

Kallad moved to stand beside his father.

'There's no better place to die,' he said in all seriousness.

'Aye there is lad, in a bed with a score of grand bairns running around and yapping, and your woman looking down at you lovingly. This here's second best. Not that I'm complaining, mind.'

Three shambling corpses came at them at once, almost dragging Kellus down in their hunger to feast on his brains. Kallad barged one off the walkway and split another stem to sternum with a savage blow from Ruinthorn. He grinned as his father dispatched the third creature. The grin died on his face as down below one of his kin fell to the reaching hands of the dead and was dragged down into the mud of the field where they set about stripping flesh from bone with savage hunger. The dwarf's screams died a moment before he did.

His death spurred the defenders on, firing their blood with a surge of stubborn strength, until the desperation itself became suffocating and closed around their hearts like some black iron fist, squeezing the hope out of them. On the field below, another dwarf fell to the dead. Kallad watched, frozen, as the creatures ripped and tore at his comrade's throat, the fiends choking on his blood in their urgency to slake their vile thirst.

Kallad hawked and spat, wrapping his hands around the thick shaft of Ruinthorn and planting the axe-head between his feet. The last prince of Karak Sadra felt fear then, with the understanding that his wouldn't be a clean death. Whatever honour he won on the walls of Grunberg Keep would be stripped from his bones by von Carstein's vermin. There would be no glory in it.

The rain intensified, matting Kallad's hair flat to his scalp and running between the chinks in his armour and down his back. No one said it was going to be like this. None of the storytellers talked about the reality of dying in combat. They spun tales of honour and heroism, not mud and rain, and the sheer bloody fear of it.

He turned to his father, looking to draw courage from the old king, but Kellus was shivering against the rain and had the deadened look of defeat in his old eyes. There was no comfort to be drawn from him. The mountain was crumbling. It was a humbling experience, to stand at the foot of the mountain and witness the rock crack and fall, nothing more than scree where once the mountain had stood tall and proud. In that one look Kallad saw the death of a legend at its most mundane.

Kallad looked out across the fields where countless hundreds of the dead shuffled and milled aimlessly among the piles of bones, waiting to be manipulated into the fray, and beyond them the black tents of Vlad von Carstein and his pet necromancers. They were the true power behind the dead, the puppet masters. The corpses were nothing more than dead meat. The necromancers were the monsters in every sense of the word. They had abandoned every last trace of humanity and given themselves to the dark magic willingly.

Kallad watched as five more fiends clawed their way up the wall of the keep to the walkway. Would these be the ones who sent him to the Hall of Ancestors?

'They need you down there,' Kellus said, breaking the spell of the creeping dead. 'Get the women and children out of this place. The keep's fallen and with it the city. I'll have no one dying who can be saved. No arguments, lad. Take them through the mountain into the deep mines. I'm counting on you.'

Kallad didn't move. He couldn't abandon his father on the wall; it was as good as murdering him.

'Go!' King Kellus commanded, bringing his own axe around in a savage arc and backhanding its head into the face of the first zombie. The blow brought the creature to its knees. Kellus planted a boot on its chest and wrenched the axe free. The creature slumped sideways and fell from the walkway.

Still Kallad didn't move, even as Kellus risked his balance to slam a fist into his breastplate, staggering him back two steps.

'I am still your king, boy, not just your father. They need you more than I do. I'll not have their deaths on my honour!'

'You can't win… not on your own.'

'And I've got no intention of doing so, lad. I'll be supping ale with your grandfather come sunrise, trading stories of valour with your grandfather's father and boasting about my boy saving hundreds of lives even though he knew to do so would be damning this old dwarf. Now go lad, get the manlings out of here. There's more than one kind of sacrifice. Make me proud, lad, and remember there's honour in death. I'll see you on the other side.' With that, the old dwarf turned his back on Kallad and hurled himself into the thick of the fight with vengeful fury, his first blow splitting a leering skull, the second severing a gangrenous arm as King Kellus, King of Karak Sadra, made his last glorious stand on the walls of Grunberg Keep.

More dead emerged from the moat. It was a nightmarish scene: the creatures moving remorselessly up the embankment, brackish water clinging to their skin. Cauldrons of naphtha ignited on the dark water, blue tinged flames racing across the surface and wreathing the corpses. And still they were silent, even as they charred to ash and bone.

The slick black bodies of hundreds of rats eddied across the blazing water, the rodents racing the bite of flame to dry land.

Kallad turned reluctantly and stomped along the stone walkway. He barrelled down the ramp, slick with rain, and skidded to a halt as the screams of women and children tore the night.

Heart racing, Kallad looked around frantically for the source of the screams. It took him a moment to see past the fighting, but when he did, he found what he was looking for: a petrified woman staggering out of the temple of Sigmar. She clutched a young baby in her arms and cast panicked glances back over her shoulder.

A moment later, the bones of one of Grunberg's long dead emerged from the temple. Dust and cobwebs clung to the bones. It took Kallad a moment to grasp the truth of the situation: their own dead were coming up from the dirt and the cold crypts, and were turning on them. Across the city, the dead were stirring. In cemeteries and tombs loved ones were returning from beyond the veil of death. The effect on those left behind would be devastating. To lose their loved ones once was hard enough, but to be forced to burn or behead them to save your own life... few could live through that kind of horror untouched.

It made sense, now that he could see the pattern of the enemy's logic. The necromancers were content to waste their peons in a useless assault on the walls. It didn't matter. They had all the dead they needed *inside* the city already.

The impossibility of the situation sank in, but instead of giving in to it, Kallad cried, 'To me!' and brandished Ruinthorn above his head.

He would make his father's sacrifice worthwhile, and then, when the women and children of Grunberg were safe, he would avenge the King of Karak Sadra.

The terrified woman saw Kallad and ran towards him, her skirts dragging as she struggled through the mud. The baby's shrieks were muffled as she pressed the poor child's face into her breasts. Kallad stepped between the woman and the skeleton hunter, and slammed a fist into the skull. The sounds of metal on bone and the subsequent crunch of bones breaking were sickening. The blow shattered the hinge on the right side of the fiend's head, making its jaw hang slackly, broken teeth like tombstones. Kallad thundered a second punch into the skeleton's head, his gauntlet caving in the entire left side of the monstrosity's skull. It didn't slow the skeleton so much as a step.

The twin moons, Mannslieb and Morrslieb, hung low in the sky and the combatants were gripped in a curious time between times, neither the true darkness of night nor the first blush of daylight owning the sky. The fusion of the moons' anaemic light cast fitful shadows across the nightmarish scene.

'Are there more in there?' Kallad demanded.

The woman nodded, eyes wide with terror.

Kallad stepped into the temple of Sigmar expecting to find more refugees from the fighting. Instead, he was greeted by the sight of shuffling skeletons in various states of decay and decomposition trying to negotiate the rows of pews between the door down to the crypt and the battle raging outside. He backed up quickly and slammed the door. There was no means of securing it. Why would there be? Kallad thought bitterly. It was never meant to be a prison.

'More *manlings*, woman, not monsters!' he said, bracing himself against the door.

'In the great hall,' she said. The overwhelming relief of her rescue had already begun to mutate into violent tremors as the reality of her situation sank in. There was no salvation.

Kallad grunted.

'Good. What's your name, lass?'

'Gretchen.'

'All right, Gretchen. Fetch one of the naphtha burners and a torch.'

'But... but...' she stammered, understanding exactly what he intended. Her wild-eyed stare betrayed the truth: the thought of razing Sigmar's house to the ground was more horrifying than any of the creatures trapped inside.

'Go!'

A moment later, the dead threw themselves at the door, fists of bone splintering and shattering beneath the sheer ferocity of the assault. The huge doors buckled and bowed. It took every ounce of Kallad's strength to hold the dead back.

'Go!' he rasped, slamming his shoulder up against the wood as fingers crept through the crack in the door that the dead had managed to force open. The door slammed closed on the fingers, crushing the bone to a coarse powder.

Without another word, the woman fled in the direction of the naphtha burners.

Kallad manoeuvred himself around until he braced the huge door with his back, and dug his heels in stubbornly. He could see his father on the wall. The white-haired king matched the enemy blow for savage blow. With his axe shining silver in the moonlight, Kellus might have been immortal, an incarnation of Grimna himself. He fought with an economy of movement, his axe hewing through the corpses with lethal precision. Kellus's sacrifice was buying Kallad precious minutes to lead the women and children of Grunberg to safety. He would not fail. He owed the old dwarf that much.

The dead hammered on the temple door, demanding to be set free.

Gretchen returned with three men, dragging between them a huge black iron cauldron of naphtha. There was a grim stoicism to their actions as the four of them set about dousing the timber frame of the temple in the flammable liquid while Kallad held back the dead. A fourth man set a blazing torch to the temple wall and stepped back as the naphtha ignited in a cold blue flame.

The fires tore around the temple's façade, searing into the timber frame. Amid the screams and the clash of steel on bone, the conflagration caught and the holy temple went up in smoke and flames. It took less than a minute for the building to be consumed by fire. The heat from the blaze drove Kallad back from the door, allowing the dead to spill out of the temple.

The abominations were met with hatchet, axe and spear as the handful of defenders drove them back mercilessly into the flames. It was nothing short of slaughter. Kallad couldn't allow himself the luxury of even a moment's relief – the battle was far from won. His brow was smeared with soot, and his breathing came in ragged gasps, as the heat of the blaze seared into his lungs. Yet, in his heart, he understood that the worst of it was only just beginning.

Kallad grabbed the woman. He yelled over the crackle and hiss of the flames, 'We have to get everyone out of here! The city is falling!'

Gretchen nodded dumbly and stumbled away towards the great hall. The flames spread from the temple, licking up the length of the keep's stone walls, and arcing across the rooftops to ignite the barracks and beyond that the stables. The rain was nowhere near heavy enough to douse the flames. In moments, the straw roof of the stables was ablaze and the timber walls were caving in beneath the blistering heat. The panicked horses bolted, kicking down the stable doors and charging recklessly into the muddy street. The stench of blood coupled with the burning flesh of the dead terrified the animals. Even the quietest of them shied and kicked out at those seeking to calm them.

The dead came through the flames, pouring over the walls in vast numbers, lurching forwards, ablaze as they stumbled to their knees and reached up, clawing the flames from their skin even as the fires consumed their flesh.

Still they came on.

The dead surrounded them on all sides.

The horses kicked out in panic.

The conflagration spread, eating through the timber framed buildings as if the walls were made of nothing more substantial than straw.

Kallad dragged Gretchen towards the central tower of the keep, forcing his way through the horses and the grooms trying to bring the frightened beasts under control. The flames chased along the rooftops. No matter how valiant the defenders' efforts, in a few hours Grunberg would cease to be. The fire they had lit would see to that. The dead wouldn't destroy Grunberg; the living had managed that all by themselves. All that remained was a desperate race to beat the fire.

No direct path to the great hall lay open, although one row of ramshackle buildings appeared to be acting as a kind of temporary firewall. Kallad ran towards the row of houses, racing the flames to the doors at the centre. The hovels of the poor quarter buckled and caved in beneath the heat, and caught like tinder. Kallad was driven towards the three doors in the centre of the street; the intensity of the blaze forced him to skirt the heart of the fire. Only minutes before, the crackling pile of wood before him had been a bakery.

Kallad swallowed a huge lungful of searing air and, taking the middle door, plunged through the collapsing shell of an apothecary's as demijohns of peculiarities cracked and exploded. Gretchen followed behind him, the child silent in her arms.

The lintel over the back door had collapsed under the strain, filling the way out with rubble. Kallad stared hard at the obstacle, hefted Ruinthorn and slammed it into the centre of the debris. Behind them, a ceiling joist groaned. Kallad slammed the axe-head into the guts of the debris again and worked it free. Above them, the groaning joist cracked sharply, the heat pulling it apart. A moment later, the ceiling collapsed, effectively trapping them inside the burning building. Cursing, Kallad redoubled his efforts to hack a path through the debris blocking the back door. He had no time to think. In the minutes it took to chop through the barricade, thick black smoke suffocated the cramped passage. Over and over, he slammed Ruinthorn's keen edge into the clutter of debris, and as chinks of moonlight and fire began to wriggle through, he kicked at the criss-cross of wooden beams. The smoke stung his eyes.

'Cover the child's mouth, woman, and stay low. Lie on your belly. The best air's down by the floor.' The thickening pall of smoke made it impossible to tell if she'd done as she was told.

He backed up two steps and hurled himself at the wooden barrier, breaking through. His momentum carried him sprawling out into the street.

Coughing and retching, Gretchen crawled out of the burning building as the gable collapsed and the roof came down. She cradled the child close to her breast, soothing it as she struggled to swallow a lungful of fresh air. The flames crackled and popped all around them. Inside the apothecary's, a series of small but violent detonations exploded as the cabinets stuffed full of chemicals and curiosities swelled and shattered in the intense heat.

Kallad struggled to his feet. He had been right, the row of buildings acted as a kind of firebreak, holding the flames back from this quarter of the walled city. The respite they offered wouldn't last. All he could do was pray to Grimna that it would last long enough for him to get the women and children out of the great hall.

He ran across the courtyard to the huge iron-banded doors of the keep and beat on them with the butt of his axe until they cracked open an inch and the frightened eyes of a young boy peeked through.

'Come on, lad. We're getting you out of here. Open up.'

A smile spread across the boy's face. It was obvious that he thought the fighting was over. Then, behind Kallad and Gretchen, he saw the fire destroying the shambles of his city. He let go of the heavy door. It swung open on itself, leaving him standing in the doorway, a length of wood in his trembling hand: a toy sword. The lad couldn't have been more than nine or ten summers old, but he had the courage to put himself between the women of Grunberg and the dead. That kind of courage made the dwarf proud to fight beside the manlings; courage could be found in the most unlikely of places.

Kallad clapped the lad on the shoulder, 'Let's fetch the women and children, shall we, lad?'

They followed the boy down a lavish passage, the walls decorated with huge tapestries and impractical weaponry. The hallway opened onto an antechamber where frightened women and children huddled, pressing themselves into the shadows and dark recesses. Kallad wanted to promise them all that they were saved, that everything was going to be all right, but it wasn't. Their city was in ruins. Their husbands and brothers were dead or dying, conquered by the dead. Everything was far from all right.

Instead of lies, he offered them the bitter truth, 'Grunberg's falling. There's nothing anyone can do to save it. The city's ablaze. The dead are swarming over the walls. Your loved ones are out there dying to give you the chance of life. You owe it to them to take that chance.'

'If they are dying, why are you here? You should be out there with them.'

'Aye, I should, but I'm not. I'm here, trying to make their deaths mean something.'

'We can fight alongside our men,' another woman said, standing up.

'Aye, and die alongside them.'

'Let the bastards come, they'll not find us easy to kill.'

One woman reached up, dragging a huge two-handed sword from the wall display. She could barely raise the tip. Another pulled down an ornate breast-plate while a third took gauntlets and a flail. In their hands, these weapons of death looked faintly ridiculous, but the look in their eyes and the set of the jaws was far from comical.

'You can't hope to–'

'You've said that already, we can't hope. Our lives are destroyed, our homes, our families. Give us the choice at least. Let us decide if we are to run like rats from a sinking ship or stand up and be judged by Morr, side by side with our men. Give us that, at least.'

Kallad shook his head. A little girl stood crying beside the woman demanding the right to die. Behind her, a boy barely old enough to walk buried his face in his mother's skirts.

'No,' he said bluntly, 'and no arguments, this isn't a game. Grunberg burns. If we stand here arguing like idiots we'll all be dead in minutes. Look at that girl. Are you prepared to say when she should die? Are you? For all that your men are laying down their lives knowing that in doing so they are saving yours?' Kallad shook his head. 'No. No you're not. We're going to leave here and travel into the mountains. There are caverns that lead into the deep mines and stretch as far away as Axebite Pass. The dead won't follow us there.'

In truth he had no idea if that was the case or not, but it didn't matter, he only needed the women to believe him long enough to get them moving. Safety or the illusion of safety, at that moment it amounted to the same thing. 'Now come on!'

His words galvanized them. They began to stand and gather their things together, tying cloth into bundles and stuffing the bundles with all that remained of their worldly goods. Kallad shook his head, 'There's no time for that! Come ON!'

The boy ran ahead, the toy sword slapping at his leg.

'That stays here,' Kallad said, dipping Ruinthorn's head towards an ornate jewellery box that one woman clutched in her hands. 'The only things leaving this place are living and breathing. Forget your pretty trinkets, they aren't worth dying for. Understood?'

No one argued with him.

He counted heads as they filed out through the wide door: forty-nine women and almost double that number of children. Each one looked at the dwarf as if he was some kind of saviour, sent by Sigmar to deliver them to salvation. Gretchen stood beside him, the child cradled in her arms. She had eased the blanket down from over the child's face, and Kallad saw at last the reason for the child's silence. Its skin bore the bluish cast of death. Still, the woman smoothed its cheek as if hoping to give some of her warmth to her dead baby. Kallad couldn't allow this one small tragedy to affect him – hundreds of people had died today. Hundreds. What was one baby against this senseless massacre? But he knew full well why the sight of the dead child was different. The child was innocent. It hadn't chosen to fight the dead. It represented everything that they had given their lives to save. More than anything else, it showed what a failure their sacrifice had been.

Then, the baby started to move, its small hand wriggling free of the blankets. The child's eyes roved blankly, still trapped in death, even as its body answered the call of the Vampire Count.

Sickness welled in Kallad's gut. The child had to die.

He couldn't do it.

He didn't have a choice. The thing in Gretchen's arms wasn't her baby. It was a shell.

'Give me the baby,' he said, holding out his hands.

Gretchen shook her head, backing up a step as if she understood what he intended, even though she couldn't possibly know. Kallad could barely grasp the thoughts going through his head they were so utterly alien. 'Give me the baby,' he repeated.

She shook her head stubbornly.

'It isn't your child, not any more,' he said, as calmly as he could manage. He took a step closer and took the child from her. The child was a parasite, but despite the wrongness of it, the woman's instinct was still to nurture her baby.

'Go,' Kallad said, unable to look her in the eye. 'You don't need to see this.'

But she wouldn't leave him.

He couldn't do it, not here in the street, not with her watching.

He moved away from her, urging the refugees of Grunberg to follow. He held the child close, its face pressed into the chain links of his mail shirt. Glancing back down the street to the ruin of the stables, Kallad saw the dead gathering, the last of the moonlight bathing their rotten flesh in silver. They had breached the wall and were pouring over in greater and greater numbers. The fire blazed on all sides of them, but they showed neither sense of fear nor understanding of what the flames might do to their dead flesh. The last of the men were lining up in a ragged phalanx to charge the dead. Their spears and shields were pitiful against the ranks of the dead. Even the sun wouldn't rise in time to save them. Like their enemy, they were dead, only Morr had yet to claim their souls.

Kallad led the women and children away; he had no wish for them to see their men fall. The fires made it difficult to navigate the streets. Alleyways dead-ended in sheets of roaring flame. Passageways collapsed beneath the detritus of houses, their shells burned out.

'Look!' One of the women cried, pointing at part of the wall that had collapsed. The dead were clambering slowly over the debris, stumbling and falling, and climbing over the fallen.

'To the mountains!' Kallad shouted over the cries of panic.

Avoiding the pockets of burning heat became ever more difficult as the fire spread, the isolated pockets becoming unbroken walls of flame.

Kallad set off at a run towards the safety of the mountainside and the caverns that led down into the warren of deep mines, across the open ground of the green, and down a narrow alleyway that led to the entrance to the caves. The wriggling child didn't slow him. 'Come on!' he yelled, urging the women to move faster. There would be precious little time to get them all into the caves before the fire claimed the alleyway. 'Come on!' Some dragged their children, others cradled them. None looked back.

'Where do we go?' the young boy asked. He'd drawn his toy sword and looked ready to stab any shadow that moved in the firelight.

'Take the third fork in the central tunnel, lad. Follow it down. It goes deep beneath the mountain. I'll find you. From there, we're going home.'

'This is my home.'

'We're going to my home, lad: Karak Sadra. You'll be safe there.'

The boy nodded grimly and disappeared into the darkness. Kallad counted them all into the caverns. As the last of them disappeared into the tunnels, he turned to look up at the city walls.

Through the dancing flames, he saw the battle still raging. The dead had claimed huge parts of the city, but the manlings were fighting on to the bitter end. He scanned the battlements looking for his father. Then he saw him. Kellus was locked in a mortal struggle. From this distance, it was impossible to tell, but it looked as if his axe was gone. He shifted onto the back foot, the flames licking the stones around him, and was forced further back into the flames as the dead poured over the wall. The last vestiges of Grunberg's defences were breached. The white-haired King of Karak Sadra fought desperately, hurling the dead flesh of mindless zombies from the wall.

A cloaked figure sprang forwards, unbalancing the king. His cloak played around his body like wings in the wind. Kallad knew the beast for what it was, a vampire. Probably not the undead count himself, but one of von Carstein's gets, so close as to be almost identical, but nothing more than a pale imitation at the same time.

The vampire tossed its head back and howled at the moon, exhorting the dead to rise.

For a moment, it seemed to Kallad as if his father could see him through the black smoke and the raging flame. Every bone and every fibre of Kallad's being cried out to run to the old king's aid, but he had been charged with another duty. He had to see these women and children to safety, giving worth to the great king's sacrifice. He couldn't abandon them when he was their only hope. Down there in the deep, they would die as surely as they would have if he had left them in the great hall.

The creature dragged Kellus close in the parody of an embrace and for a moment, it appeared as if the two were kissing. The illusion was shattered as the vampire tossed the dead dwarf aside and leapt gracefully from the high wall.

Kallad turned his back, silent tears rolling down his impassive face.

The babe writhed in his arms. He laid the child on the floor, face down because he couldn't bear the accusation that he imagined he saw in its dead eyes. Sobbing, he took the axe and ended the child's unnatural life.

Smoke, flame and grief stung the dwarf's eyes as he knelt down over the corpse and pressed a coin into the child's mouth, an offering to Morr, the humans' god of death. 'This innocent has suffered enough hell for three lifetimes, Lord of the Dead. Have pity on those you claimed today.'

One day, he promised himself, rising. One day the beast responsible for all this useless suffering will know my name; that will be the day it dies!

CHAPTER ONE
Kaiser, König, Edelmann, Bürger, Bauer, Bettelmann

DRAKENHOF, SYLVANIA
The Cold Heart of Winter, 2055

Two of Konrad's Hamaya dragged the old man into the cell between them. Von Carstein didn't deign to turn. He made the man wait. It was a delicious sensation and he fully intended to savour the final moments before the kill. There was nothing in the world like bringing death where moments before there had been life. It was such a fleeting thing, life: so transient in nature, so fragile.

He smiled as he turned, although there was no humour in his eyes, and nodded.

The Hamaya served as the Vampire Count's personal bodyguard, his most trusted men, his right and left hands depending upon the darkness of the deed he desired done. They released their grip on the

prisoner, kicking him as he sank to his knees so that
he sprawled across the cold stones of the cell floor.
There was no fight left in the old man. He barely had
the strength to hold his head up. He had been beaten
repeatedly and tortured to the extremes of what his
heart would bear. It was so like the cowards to send
an old man to do their dirty work.

'So, are you ready to talk, Herr Köln? Or must we
continue with all this unsavoury nonsense? We both
know the outcome so why subject yourself to the
pain? You will tell me what I want to hear. Your kind
always does. It's one of the many weaknesses of
humanity. No threshold for pain.'

The old man lifted his head, meeting the vampire's
gaze, 'I have nothing to say to you.'

Konrad sighed, 'Very well. Constantin, would you
be so kind as to remind our guest of his manners?'

The Hamaya backhanded Köln across the face,
splitting his already swollen lip. Blood ran into his
beard.

'Thank you, Constantin. Now, Herr Köln, perhaps
we can dispense with the charade? As much as I enjoy
the tang of blood in the air, yours is sadly past its
best. You are the much-vaunted Silver Fox of Bogenhafen, are you not? The *Silberfuchs*, I believe they call
you? I assume your paymaster is Ludwig von
Holzkrug, although where the loyalties of a man like
yourself lie is always up for debate. The Untermensch
witch perhaps? Or maybe some other lesser schemer.
The Empire is so full of petty politickers, one so much
the same as any other that it is difficult to keep track
of who is stabbing whom in the back at any given

time. No matter. You are what you are and what you are is, without question, a spy.'

'Why don't you kill me and have done with it?'

'I could,' the vampire conceded. He circled the old man. It was the act of a predator. He moved slowly, savouring the helplessness of his prisoner. 'But that would hardly do you justice, Herr Köln. The… ah… notoriety of the *Silberfuchs* demands a certain… respect. Your head must be filled with such interesting truths it would be a crying shame to lose them. Act in haste, repent at leisure, no?'

'What would you have me tell you, vampire? That your people love you? That you are worshipped? Adored? You are not. Believe me. You are hated. Your *kingdom* is fit only for robber barons and fools. It is held together by fear. Fear of the Vampire Count, Vlad von Carstein.' The old man smiled. 'You are not loved. You are not even feared. None of that is of any consequence, of course, because, more than anything, you are not your sire. The only fear around you is the fear that drives you. Compared to Vlad you are a pale shadow.'

'Fascinating,' Konrad said. 'Is that what you intended to tell your paymaster? That the von Carstein threat is vanquished? That there is nothing left to fear?'

'I will tell him the truth: that the scum is rising to the surface, as it always does. That everywhere in Sylvania there is disorder, that the fetid stink of corruption clings to the swamps. I will say that the streets crumble while the parasites suck the lifeblood out of the people, that the peasants despise you for the blight that afflicts their farms, that you are loathed for the famine that cripples the livestock, and blamed for the exorbitant rents you demand from them in return for pox-ridden ground. I will tell him that if they fail to please you with tributes you let your cursed Hamaya feast on their carcasses. Oh, I could tell them that and so much more. I could tell them that your so-called court is infested with sharks that would feast on your royal blood. That Drakenhof is a cesspit of liars, thieves, murderers, spies, and worst of all backstabbing sycophants who whisper sweet nothings in your ear while plotting behind your back. That you are loathed by your own kind, and that you are a fool for believing that they love you.'

Konrad's own grin matched the old man's. 'You are indeed enlightened, Herr Köln. Obviously you are privy to the deepest, darkest secrets of my kind. Yes they would have me dead, it is the nature of the beast to seek out weakness and exploit it. They have not brought me down, as you can see. Drakenhof is mine by right of strength and blood. I am von Carstein. I do not merely call myself such, as others do.' He turned his attention to the two Hamaya who had stepped back from the old man and waited silently. 'Take Jerek, for instance, he understands his place. His loyalty is unquestioning. The blood of our father sings in his veins. He is pure, unlike Constantin, who has claimed the name by right of... what was it, Constantin?'

'Conquest,' the Hamaya supplied.

'Conquest, that's right. Conquest is another word for murder in our world. He earned the title von

Carstein by killing another. Our kind survives by strength alone. Strength breeds loyalty. Like Jerek, his loyalty is pure, and yet you have the audacity to tell me that my truth isn't *the* truth? That my world does not work the way I believe? Should I be flattered or furious, Herr Köln?'

'I say what I see. If you do not like what you hear, well, with respect, all you can do is kill me.'

'Not so, killing you is the very least that I can do. I could drag your soul kicking and screaming back from the comfort of Morr's underworld and consign you to the unlife of the living dead, for instance. I could slay you and raise your corpse to dance to my whims like a puppet, or I could leave you to rot. Don't underestimate the torments beyond death that I could inflict on you if I so choose. Now, tell me about the lands you left behind, spy. Tell me about your beloved Empire.'

The old man's head dropped. He lapsed into silence.

'Oh, do speak up while you still can, Herr Köln. The cat hasn't gotten your tongue yet.'

'I am no traitor.'

'But I think you will be before the sun rises on the new morning, if that is any consolation? I think you'll be delighted to spill your guts. Jerek and Constantin will no doubt be sick of the sound of your voice.'

Konrad stopped his pacing, drawing his sword, a blade of bone with a skeletal wyrm carved into its hilt, from its sheath. The blade's edge whickered as it slid free. Konrad rested it against Deitmar Köln's left ear.

The old man screamed as the vampire sliced his ear off with a single smooth stroke. Blood flowed freely through Köln's fingers as he clutched at the ragged hole in the side of his head. He didn't stop screaming as Konrad raised the severed ear to his lips and sucked the blood from it.

The vampire tossed the ruined ear aside.

'Now, where were we? Oh yes, you were telling me nothing I didn't already know, how those around me are untrustworthy. How I have surrounded myself with fools and traitors and those who are loyal now could be traitors tomorrow. How loyalty can be bought with fear. How fear can inspire treachery. You speak in vagaries meant to inspire paranoia. I am nobody's fool, Herr Köln. How does anyone know whom to trust or who to kill? Tell me that, *Silberfuchs*, and then, when you are through answering the unanswerable, tell me all about dear old Ludwig and the squabbles of the Empire. I yearn for a good story and it would be an honour to hear the Silver Fox of Bogenhafen's last lament.'

The old man slumped against the wall, his bloody hand pressed up against the side of his head. What remained of his life could be counted out in moments, and yet despite the sure and certain knowledge of his fate, he tapped some inner well of strength that allowed him dignity in death.

Konrad resumed his pacing, his slow, measured footsteps echoing hollowly on the stone floor. He didn't say a word, but a smile twitched at his lips as the old man suffered.

'Do we really have to take this to its logical conclusion, Herr Köln? I had hoped you would see sense before my patience finally wore thin. It seems I was wrong.' With that Konrad lashed out a second time with the bone sword, cutting deep into the hand Köln threw up before his face to ward off the blow. Bone cleaved bone, although Konrad pulled the blow before it completely severed the old man's wrist, leaving the hand hanging uselessly by a single tendon. Blood pumped from the ragged wound, at first it came in a huge gush that sprayed like a fountain, but it quickly dwindled as shock set in.

The old man gibbered through the pain, his eyes glazed over. It was doubtful whether a single coherent word would escape his lips before his body finally succumbed to the shock, and he died.

Konrad knelt, taking the old man's chin in his hand and tilting his head until their eyes met. Köln tried to say something. His lips moved and sounds gurgled out of his mouth, but Konrad couldn't make any sense out of them.

'Is this the way it ends? Not with a bang but with a whimper? Tragic, utterly tragic, but so be it.'

Konrad rose, lifting the wyrm-hilted blade above his head, poised to grant death and end the old man's torment. Instead, very deliberately and very slowly, he sheathed the sword and hoisted Deitmar Köln to his feet. The old man's legs refused to hold him. Konrad nodded to his two Hamaya, who peeled away from the shadows to support the spy between them. His body sagged as if he was being crucified.

Konrad slammed a fist into his gut. The old man folded in on himself until the Hamaya straightened him up. Konrad hit him again.

'I could tell you that this hurts me more than it hurts you. I would, of course, be lying. This doesn't hurt me at all. Between you and me, I quite enjoy it actually. Now, before I get carried away, I'm going to offer you one last chance to spill your guts before I spill them for you. Do we understand each other, Herr Köln?'

Deitmar Köln lifted his head. Blood smeared across his face and into his mouth. His eyes were glazed and his skin had taken on a sickly grey cast. The old man's tongue licked along his lips as he tried to form a word. Konrad allowed himself a self-indulgent smirk. 'They all talk eventually,' he said, leaning in close to hear what the dying man had to confess.

Köln spat in his face.

An elbow in the base of the neck from the Hamaya Constantin drove the old man to his knees.

Konrad kicked him in the face. It was brutal. The sound of bone and cartilage breaking was sickening. He kicked the old man over and over until Jerek's reassuring voice cut through the fugue that violence had wrapped around him.

'It's over.'

It was. The Silver Fox of Bogenhafen was dead, his secrets taken to the grave.

Konrad's fury dissipated, leaving him standing over the bloody corpse of the old man, none the wiser, and ruing the cost of giving in to his anger.

'Fool,' he muttered, toeing the dead man under the chin to bring his sightless eyes up to meet his gaze. 'All you had to do was talk. The feuding of the would-be emperors is common knowledge. A few choice comments about the Sigmarites sparring with the self-proclaimed Emperor Ludwig could have bought your life, or at least your death.' He turned to Constantin.

'Still, waste not want not. Take him down to Immoliah Fey. I am sure she will appreciate the gift.'

'As you wish, lord.' The Hamaya gathered the dead man into his arms as if he weighed nothing and carried him out of the cell, leaving Konrad and Jerek von Carstein alone.

'Walk with me a while, my friend. This place brings depresses me.'

'It is understandable,' Jerek said. 'Being trapped in this cloying dark is no way to live.'

The pair wandered the labyrinthine halls of Drakenhof Castle, working their way slowly toward the rooftops. The castle was a curious mix of decay and renewal: certain corridors were wreathed in cobwebs and dank with mildew, and one entire wing of the castle had been abandoned to the ghosts of the dead and was buried by dust. Some warmer chambers in what had once been the van Drak tower were darkened by thick velvet drapes, and danced to the shadows of guttering torches and freshly laid fires.

The tower itself had suffered the most complete transformation, to the extent of owning a new name. Vlad's birds had overrun the spire of the old tower, transforming it into the Rookery. Gone was the opulence of Vlad's reign. Konrad and the new breed of von Carsteins offered austerity; their world was one of decay. There was no place for the redeeming love of beauty Vlad cherished.

'We owe our lives to you, Wolf, don't think that I have forgotten,' Konrad said, finally. He pushed open a heavy wooden door and stepped out into the night. The winds cradled him, wrapping his cloak around his thin frame. He breathed deeply of the night air as he looked around the battlements. Only, of course, they weren't battlements anymore. This place had become a haven for Vlad's birds. Even the servants called it the Rookery now. He took solace in the company of the birds.

'Nonsense,' Jerek said.

'Don't be so quick to dismiss the importance of what you did. When others lost their heads and surrendered to bloodlust, you kept yours. You didn't give in to panic. You didn't flee in mindless terror. You thought a way out of death. You brought us back from the point of extinction, but more than that, you brought us home. We are here now because of you, my friend. You are a good man.'

'Hardly,' Jerek grunted, uncomfortable with the vampire's praise. Vlad's ravens scattered as he walked among them. 'I'm not a good man. Perhaps I was once, it is difficult to remember now, but whatever I was in life, I'm not even a shadow of it in death. I have changed to the point that I don't even know who I am. I have cravings that I don't understand, longings and desires that even a few years ago would have disgusted me, and yet somehow I have become a "good man"? No. I am not a good man. Everything has changed. The sun no longer shines for me, lord. I miss that more than anything.'

'You speak as if you are not who you were. That is a lie. We are all who we were, but we are all more complicated than simply being good men or bad men. We all have countless identities inside us. We have the savage who would rip out a man's heart and feed on it greedily, we have the friend whose nobility of heart is pure, we have the lover who sings to us the sins of the flesh and worships the pale alabaster skin of our woman, we have the child we once were, the lad whose fears have never left him, and we have the man we might have become.

'All these and more live inside our skin, my friend. We listen to all their voices when they cry out. We are truly the sum of our life, of who we were. That is who we are, not some newborn dead thing. We are in every way ourselves, and yet we are more than that. We remember all the fears, all the dreams we shared, we remember and they make us stronger. They do not simply disappear. We carry the joys we knew in life, the compassion, and the love – if we were blessed enough to know it – and equally we carry the hatred and horrors of our existence. The difference is that now we draw pleasure from both aspects of our twin souls. You are still the White Wolf of Middenheim, but you are so much more as well. You find yourself enjoying death in a way that you never did before, but my friend, believe me, that capacity for joy was always within you.'

'Perhaps you are right, although I cannot find myself in here anymore, Konrad. I am selfish. I would live in the sun once more. That is the truth of it.'

'Ah, but the truth is like an expensive whore, Jerek. She comes dressed in many pretty dresses and will bend over for any with the money to pamper her. Your truth is not my truth and my truth was not Vlad's. We each shape the world as we walk through it. We write the "truth" with our actions, if we are victorious, then others come to accept our truth, whereas if we are defeated those same people will vilify our truth as damnable lies. Do not overcomplicate life with the search for one unifying truth, it does not exist, my friend.'

'Concubine, courtesan, whore, they're all words that mean the same thing, she lies with anyone with the coin to have her.'

Konrad knelt to cradle a beady-eyed raven in his hand. The bird didn't react to his touch. 'My point exactly. Now, I think we've done this dance long enough. What is bothering you?'

Jerek stared out over the moonlight town far below, imagining the laughter and life around the hearths, and the simple delight those unseen people found in their pitiful existence. He envied them their ignorance. He envied them their happiness. A mass of black winged birds took flight, banking high in the sky to block out the moon as they circled as one.

'An omen?'

'Birds are always an omen, Jerek. It is whether we chose to pay them heed or not that is important. The psychopomps deliver their messages of foreboding, it is why they exist; they are nothing more than playthings of the gods. We see them now, but, tell me, should we take heed of their warning?'

Jerek turned his back on the birds.

'Do you trust me, Konrad?'

It was a simple question and deserved a simple answer, despite the fact that the answer itself was far from simple. 'Yes,' Konrad said, resting a hand on Jerek's muscular shoulder. 'Yes, I do.'

Jerek nodded, 'Which makes what I am going to say easier and more difficult at the same time.'

'Speak freely.'

'Ah, if only it were that easy. I fear there is a traitor amongst us, my lord.'

Konrad laughed. 'I am surrounded by traitors and assassins, my friend. That is why I bid you gather the Hamaya, the best of the best, the most trusted. With them as a shield, I am at least protected from the more overt manipulations of my kin. They have saved me once from my beloved kin's back-stabbing knives, they will no doubt save me again.'

'That is why the betrayal hurts the most. I believe the traitor lies within the ranks of your bodyguard and feeds information to one or more of Vlad's gets, conspiring against your leadership.'

'A traitor in the Hamaya? Are you sure?'

'No,' Jerek admitted, 'not sure, but suspicious.'

'Then I must trust your suspicions, my friend. I would be a fool to ignore you and the birds. The vultures are cycling, it would seem, and as ever they are hungry to feed on weakness. I am not weak. There will be blood in the water, much blood, but it will not be mine. Their fall from grace will be a lesson to all. No one crosses me. Find the traitor, Jerek. Find them, skin them and roast them on a spit until only their ashes remain. I want everyone to know the cost of betrayal.'

CHAPTER TWO
Shadow of the Vampire

THE SIGMARITE CATHEDRAL, ALTDORF
The Bleak Midwinter, 2055

KALLAD STORMWARDEN HAD been in Altdorf for three soul-destroying weeks. This wasn't his home. He missed the mountains. The cold stone of the buildings was soulless stuff. He dreamed at nights of the stone halls of Karak Sadra.

He was here because of the vampires of Grunberg. As long as the vampires lived, his own life had but a single purpose: retribution.

The path of vengeance had led to Altdorf before it had cracked and broken, and finally died out.

The war of the Vampire Count had taken a heavy toll. Cities live, and like people, cities die. The pulse of Altdorf had weakened and become erratic, the life choked out of the place. It was a shadow of its former glorious self, although the inhabitants did their damnedest to carry on their everyday lives as if nothing had happened. The dwarf found it fascinating and tragic at the same time. Denial it seemed was the primary characteristic of the human condition.

Not for the first time, he wondered how they could do it. There was no miracle to it though; it was a case of necessity. They had to foster denial, or they would drown in self-pity and be as dead as if the Vampire Count had sucked them dry. That would have been the biggest tragedy of all: for the survivors to give up living because of the high price of victory. Their stubborn determination was a way of honouring those who had paid the ultimate price for their freedom.

In truth, there was little difference between this and the way Kallad lived his life. The memory of Grunberg and those who had fallen there overshadowed each day he lived. Days and weeks, and months could pass, it didn't matter, the passage of time had lost its meaning to the dwarf.

If anything, the Altdorfers losing themselves in the mundane tasks of rebuilding their lives was healthier than the grudge he nursed. They at least were looking to the future, not living in the past where the anger only festered.

'When they're dead,' he promised himself, 'and honour's served, then we start living again, right lad?'

Beside him, Sammy Krauss, the butcher's boy, sat whittling at a curiously shaped stick with his bone-handled knife. Sammy was simpleminded. They had been almost constant companions since his arrival in the city. The boy, it seemed, had taken a shine to him.

Kallad didn't mind. He enjoyed the company. It had been too long since he'd enjoyed the simple pleasure of conversation. Given the city's recent history, it wasn't hard to imagine why the boy had attached himself to the dwarf. It wasn't for his rapier wit and philosophical insight: the finely crafted gromril discs beneath the chain links of mail and his double-headed axe, Ruinthorn, were far more reassuring. Kallad was a fighter. With his parents dead, that was what the boy truly needed.

'Do you really remember where all them dents come from?' Sammy asked, marvelling at the idea that each dent told a story.

'Aye,' Kallad said with a reassuring grin. 'This one here,' he tapped one of the layered discs covering his left side, above his fourth rib, 'was a spear thrust from a skaven. It was a long time ago. I wasn't much older than you. Do you know what skaven are, lad?'

Sammy shook his head, wide-eyed with wonder, 'No. I never heard of him.'

'Rats as tall as you. Vicious things, they are.'

Sammy thought for a moment. 'But rats are small, even big ones.'

'Not all rats, Sammy, some can walk and talk.'

'You mean like them from fairy tales?'

Kallad grinned, 'That's the ones. Ugly little bleeders, giant rats that walk like men. They're tainted creatures, for sure. Well, there were four of them ganged up on me. One didn't stand a chance, and two, well it still wouldn't have been a fair fight. Cursed by Chaos or not, the devils weren't stupid. They knew they'd need to take me by surprise to stand even half a chance.

Cunning little beasts they are. Vermin. Would have had me for sure but for the armour. See lad, that's why I remember each dent and ding in these old plates, because without them, well, who's to say I'd even be here today?'

'You mean them dents kept you alive?' The awe in Sammy's voice was unmistakable.

Kallad smiled and patted the dented gromril disc. 'That's exactly what I mean, lad. This metal is tough, tougher than almost anything except gomril.'

'Blimey. You mean if'n the Vampire Count'd had your armour he might still be alive?' Sammy shuddered visibly at the thought.

'Ah, no lad, even my armour couldn't have kept that monster alive. It was his time to die, see. A lot of good people gave their lives to make sure his evil ended here. That makes this city special, lad. This is the place the Vampire Count fell.'

'I saw it, you know. I saw the priest fighting 'im on the wall. I wasn't supposed to. Ma had made us all go down to the cellars, but it was frightening down there so I snuck back upstairs and hid in my room. I could see the wall from my window. It was scary because of all the fires and the explosions, but it wasn't scary like the cellar, because it wasn't dark. I don't like the dark, see. Ma says I'm a big boy and I shoulda grown up out of it by now, but I ain't.'

'There's nothing wrong with being afraid of the dark, lad. All our fears come from there. Did you know that? Everything we're frightened of comes to life in the dark, see. That's why we use torches and light fires, to drive the dark back, because deep down it *still* frightens us. That's why in the backwaters so many revere the sun and the moon. The sun drives away the night. It brings renewal, rebirth. It gives us hope. So don't you worry about what your Ma says, we're all a little bit afraid of the dark, it's good for us.'

'Well I'm a *big* bit afraid.' Sammy said, grinning lopsidedly.

'I'll let you in on a secret… me too.' Kallad said.

'It was a different kind of scary watching through the window. People who come into Pa's shop fell off the wall and didn't get up again. Strangers too. I kept looking at 'em, waiting for them to get up again, but they didn't. And the bad men were throwing things over the wall and making fires and explosions, and I didn't think it was ever going to end.'

'You shouldn't have had to see something like that, lad. No one should. But you know what?'

'What?'

'It's over now and life, well life is going on as normal, isn't it? People still come into your Pa's shop for meat, don't they?'

'Well yes, but we ain't got much meat to sell 'em.'

'Not yet, but you will have. Life goes on. Look around you. Everyone is putting their life back together bit by bit.'

'Not everyone,' Sammy Krauss said solemnly. 'Not the priest, he died. Not the soldiers.'

And that was the truth of it. Those left behind struggled to hold the pieces of their fractured lives together, trying to fill the spaces left by their loved ones who had fallen protecting the once great city. How could he explain that to a boy like Sammy? He couldn't, so he didn't try.

'Come on, lad, time to go for a wander.'

Kallad hauled himself up. He didn't know where he was going to go, but he couldn't just sit on the steps waiting for the answers to come and find him. If he wanted to find the monster that slaughtered Grunberg, he would have to walk in the shadow of the vampire, retracing the fiend's every bloody step.

'Show me where the priest's buried, would you lad? I'd like to pay my respects, one fighter to another.'

Sammy nodded and jumped to his feet, eager to be of use. 'He's in the cathedral. It ain't far. I know the way.'

'I'm sure you do, lad, that's why I asked.'

'I could be your guide, an' if I'm really good at it, maybe I could be your squire, you know?'

'Ah but I'm not a knight, Sammy. I don't need a squire.' The youngster looked crestfallen. 'But you know, you could be my friend, that's a much more important job.'

'I can do that!'

'Excellent, now let's go pay our respects shall we, my friend?'

Grinning, Sammy led the way through the narrow warren of streets. Women washed their sheets and beat the dust from heavy rugs with paddles, young children clinging to their ankles. Washing was hung up to dry on lines that strung buildings together.

The boy loved to smile. It was one of the things the dwarf liked most about the lad.

Altdorf was a city rediscovering its own identity. The moneylenders and pawnbrokers were out on street corners, promising shillings now in return for a few extra pfennigs later. They made Kallad sick, profiting from the hardship of ordinary decent people. It was immoral. It went against the idea of people pulling together in times of trouble. Across the old square, queues of hungry people lined up, soup bowls in hand for handouts from the church. Poverty was a new thing to a lot of these people, but the look of quiet desperation in so many eyes proved that even the proudest man could grow accustomed to taking handouts when it was the difference between going hungry or not.

In the long line, Kallad saw a woman weeping in despair, no bravery left in her eyes, only sadness. He didn't want to think what great loss had brought her to this sad fate. The city had drowned in the hate of the Vampire Count. It was amazing that any of them had the fight to face another day without food, alone, reminded of what they had lost, in the happiness of strangers who could still do the simplest of things like beat the dust out of their rugs with their children clinging to their legs. It was people like her who hurt the most, people for whom there was no escape, even in the most mundane acts of every day living.

The militia patrolled the streets in gangs of six and eight, their presence enough to keep order in the more run down districts of the city.

Few spared the unlikely pair a second glance as Kallad and Sammy skirted the fringe of Reiksport. The smell of brine stung Kallad's nostrils. Large stretches of water weren't something he ever wanted to become accustomed to. It was unnatural. It was hard to imagine that people actually enjoyed having the world constantly tilting and rolling beneath them. He shook his head. It had its uses, he couldn't deny that, but given a choice, he'd always keep a few mountains between himself and the sea. The ships were in, bringing with them much needed produce, but even with the influx of food the city was still slowly starving to death. It would be years before things returned to normal. Von Carstein's undead army was a scourge on the landscape. They left sickness and blight in their wake. Calves and lambs were stillborn, cheeses curdled, and grain stores rotted. The dead were more deadly to the land than a plague. The superstitious blamed the dead; the more practically minded cursed and blamed the living for their failings, while knowing that apportioning blame was a pointless activity. It wouldn't feed anyone.

Kallad and Sammy stood on the dockside, watching the Marshall of the Waters guide the unloading of a huge six rigger. His crew wrestled with ropes and guidelines as they hauled crates out of the ship's hold, climbing nimbly up and down the ropes, hanging from the yardarm and dangling perilously in the rigging. They moved like a colony of ants, busy with purpose and yet completely independent of one another. It was fascinating to see. Indeed, Kallad and Sammy were not alone in their interest. People gathered around, curious as to what the ships were bringing in, desperate to discover that it was, indeed, food.

One of the sailors tossed a small orange ball the size of his clenched fist to the marshall, who looked at it quizzically.

'What am I supposed to do with this?'

'Eat it, what do you think?'

The marshall shrugged, sank his teeth into the orange fruit and spat a mouthful of rind and bits of pulp out. 'It's disgusting!' The marshall wiped his mouth, spitting and rubbing at his tongue to try and get rid of the taste. 'How can you eat something like this? I think I'd rather starve.'

'Not like that. You peel the skin off and eat the fruit. It's good,' the sailor explained, miming the act of stripping the orange's thick skin. The marshall looked uncertain. Seeing Sammy and Kallad loitering on the dockside, he tossed the orange to Sammy underarm. The lad skipped forwards and caught it.

'What do you say?' Kallad asked.

'Thank you, sir!' Sammy shouted. His fingers were already wet with the juice of the fruit as he dug them into the soft flesh.

The sailor laughed and saluted Sammy, 'Take all the skin off, lad, and then tear it into segments. It's like nothing you ever tasted before.'

'I won't argue with *that*,' the Marshall of the Waters said with a wry smile, 'but then so's dung, and happy as flies are to eat the stuff, well it ain't necessarily a delicacy if you know what I mean.'

Sammy moaned with pleasure as he crammed the segments of orange into his mouth, sucking the juice off his fingers. 'Good,' he said around a mouthful of food. 'It's good.'

'Told you!' the sailor called down.

'I'll take your word for it, sonny,' the marshall said dubiously. 'Give me a nice sweet cake of oatmeal dripping with honey and a nice warm bitter ale, and I'm a happy man.'

'It's really good.' Sammy repeated, cramming two wedges of orange into his already full mouth.

Kallad nodded his thanks to the sailor and the marshall. It was good to see the ships back in the Reiksport. Even a couple of weeks without them had turned the dockside into a ghost town. Little by little, the ships promised a return to some semblance of normality. The people needed it. A few exotic fruits wouldn't do much in practical terms, but they would do wonders for morale. The captain of that ship was a canny man, Kallad realised, for understanding the value of a few luxuries over necessities that would run out soon enough.

Sammy Krauss, for instance, would remember his first orange all his life. It was hard to imagine that something as simple as a piece of fruit had made today an extraordinary day for the boy, but it had. That extraordinary day would keep him alive ten times as long as a bowl of grain would. It was all about hope.

Of course, the ships would bring more than produce with them, they would bring sailors, and sailors brought coin and a healthy dose of lust that the local establishments were more than happy to cater for. After a long time at sea, a sailor and his coins were easily parted, and there were places aplenty around the Reiksport that catered for every conceivable desire a sailor on shore leave could need sating. It was a mutually parasitic relationship – the sailors came with their pent-up frustration, needing girls, drink and games of chance to throw their hard-earned money away on, and the city needed the sailors with their drunken lusts every bit as much.

Sammy smacked his lips and licked his fingers all the way to the Sigmarite cathedral. The gates to the grounds were closed. Something about that disturbed Kallad more than the food queues and the moneylenders. The door of Sigmar was always open, or at least it was supposed to be. He hammered on the wrought iron railings until an acolyte came to answer the clanging.

'The world has changed for the worse, it seems,' Kallad said. 'When the House of Sigmar takes to locking itself up like a prison come nightfall it is a sorry state of affairs.'

'Indeed,' the young acolyte said smoothly, 'the world has changed, master dwarf. That is its nature. To stand still is to stagnate. To stagnate is to die. Change is the only way to survive. So, how can we be of service to you?'

'We have come to pay our respects to the priest that fell saving this city.'

The young man nodded thoughtfully. 'As an ambassador of the dwarf folk you are more than welcome to post a vigil at Grand Theogonist Wilhelm III's graveside. It would be our honour. It might be best, however, if your companion waits elsewhere. There can be little of interest for the boy at an old man's tomb.'

'Aye, but then it might be best if the lad can say his thanks to the man as well. After all, it was for boys like Sammy that your priest gave his life, wasn't it?'

'Indeed,' the young acolyte agreed, with a slight nod. 'You are *both* welcome to hold vigil. Will there be anything you need?'

'Shouldn't think so, lad.'

'Then please, follow me.' The acolyte opened the gate and led them through a neatly tended rose garden to a secluded grove on the far side of the cathedral, where the shadows of a weeping willow touched the simple stone of the holy man's grave. A second, smaller gate led through the wall to the street. The dwarf and the boy stood beneath the trailing willow branches. The grave was nothing more than a simple headstone that had already begun to seed over with lichen where the shadows of the willow lingered. A white rose bush grew beside the headstone, the thorns scraping against the words of the prayer carved into the stone.

The acolyte withdrew a step, but didn't leave them.

Kallad whispered a quiet prayer to Grimna before he knelt beside the Grand Theogonist's grave and pressed a small metallic disc into the dirt. The disc was carved with a protective rune of blessing meant to ward off the evil spirits. It was a relic from his home, Karak Sadra. How apt that name was now: Sorrow's Stone. His father, Kellus, had crafted the rune himself in the days before the march from the stronghold beneath Axebite Pass to Grunberg, and had given it to Kallad. The token had kept him alive during the slaughter of that city. Perhaps it would offer some protection to the priest's spirit in death.

'What's that?' Sammy asked, curious.

'My father gave it to me. It's a charm meant to protect the wearer from evil.'

The young acolyte nodded his approval at the offering. 'A suitable token,' he said quietly, making the sign of Sigmar across his heart.

'There are ninety-seven windows in this side of the cathedral,' Sammy said suddenly. 'I counted them. Ninety-seven and only one has someone in it.' The non-sequitur threw Kallad, but he followed the direction in which the boy's hand pointed. A pale face stared down from one of the highest windows. The boy was right: every other window was empty. Curious, Kallad moved to get a better look at the high window where the sun didn't reflect off the glass. The watcher didn't shrink back from the window, despite the fact that he was obviously aware he had been seen. Instead, he matched the dwarf's scrutiny with a detached study of his own.

Kallad turned to the acolyte. 'Who's that?'

The young priest looked up at the face in the window. 'That's the thief,' he said with obvious distaste.

'The thief?'

'Felix Mann, a thoroughly dislikeable man, if you ask me.'

'Aye? An' yet he finds himself inside the cathedral of Sigmar when the gates are locked? I have to say I find that a mite interesting, considering how difficult it is for a normal person to come pay his respects to your god.'

'His presence is… tolerated,' the young acolyte said, grudgingly.

'You could be tempted to wonder if your man is a guest or a prisoner,' the dwarf said.

The young priest didn't have an answer to that, at least not one he could give in words. His eyes shifted involuntarily towards the headstone. People with something to hide tended to give their secrets away with the stupidest of tells. The thief wasn't a prisoner, at least not in the traditional sense, even if the four walls of the cathedral had become his dungeon. There was only one reasonable explanation for why the priests had offered the protection of the temple to a thief: he had friends.

'The edicts of our god require us to tend to the weak and needy, and to protect those that cannot protect themselves. The thief would be dead without us. He cannot so much as fend for himself. He wouldn't last a week on the streets.'

Kallad didn't buy into the priest's rationalisation. It was too convenient by far. Plenty of other people were starving and barely living at a subsistence level, with no homes after the siege, no husbands, and no hope of life ever really returning to normal. Broth lines and prayers for broken souls were not the same as offering Felix Mann sanctuary.

'Neither would a thousand others. They aren't surviving, so what makes Mann special?'

'The thief's curse,' the acolyte said. Seeing the dwarf didn't understand he elaborated, 'No hands.'

That aspect at least made sense: it was a vindictive punishment for petty crimes. Admittedly, it was barbaric and taking both hands was almost unheard of, but what didn't make sense was why the Sigmarites had taken an interest in the thief, instead of just turning him over to the almoners or leaving him to beg? It wasn't as if the city didn't have its share of cripples and beggars, panhandling in the streets for scraps of food and the odd coin that might come their way. There were beggars on every street corner, each with a tale more wretched than the last. That the priests of Sigmar had singled this one out meant that he was marked in some way. He had done something to deserve their charity beyond simply being crippled.

'That's not what makes him special, priest, you and I both know it. Why not turn him over to the almoners?'

'He ahh well his affliction… shall we say that some feel he was maimed in the service of the church, and as such we carry the weight of guilt, which is, of course, preposterous.'

'A thief losing his hands in the service of Sigmar? Are you being serious?'

'Not at all,' the priest assured him.

As if sensing that he was the topic of conversation, the man finally moved away from the window.

A few minutes later, the huge iron banded doors flew open and Felix Mann staggered out of the temple gasping and out of breath from running through the vast cathedral. He was not in a good way. His face had begun to collapse in on itself, his cheeks and eyes waxy sunken hollows, his nose sharp and angular. He was gaunt beyond the point of malnutrition. The waste of a man was shocking to see. What remained were the remnants of Felix Mann. He was less than human.

The thief staggered forwards on shaky legs and debased himself at Kallad's feet, the bandaged stumps of his wrists up in front of his face. Kallad had to imagine the ghosts of hands clenched, begging.

'Just put me out of my damned misery, dwarf! Do it! Crush my skull. Cut my head off my shoulders. Slice my throat, open my gizzards, just do something to finish it, please. I… I don't want to live like this anymore. I don't want to be a prisoner, a freak fed and watered and forced to give thanks for being a cripple to a god who hasn't done a damned thing for me except see to it that I wound up like this. Have pity on me, dwarf. Finish what the vampire started. Do that for me. Do that!'

'You are not a prisoner here. Far from it,' the acolyte said coldly. 'We have made you welcome, fed and cared for you. You could have been left to beg in the gutter like a common criminal. You are free to leave at any time. Remember that before you call us your gaolers.'

'I am not free. If I were there would not be men outside my door at night.'

'We would not have you harm yourself. Sadness over your, ahhh, affliction, might undo reason. We seek only to help you.'

Sammy had backed away behind Kallad, and the acolyte looked distinctly disappointed at the thief's ravings.

'Stand up, man.'

'Look at me. I'm a cripple.'

'Aye, but it ain't the end of the world. I ain't one for judging a man by his looks or his name, better to judge him by what he does. He can curl up an' die or he can get up an' start living again. So stand up.'

'Damn you,' Felix Mann said, but there was no strength in his curse. He spat in the priest's direction and then sagged and folded in on himself, beaten.

'I already am,' Kallad said calmly. 'I am Kallad Stormwarden, the last dwarf of Karak Sadra. The vampires destroyed my people.'

'Then you understand,' Mann said flatly.

'No, I don't. I took their beating and I stood up again. Now, I hunt them. I will not rest until every last vampire is purged from the face of the Empire.'

'Then you'll be joining your people wherever your dead go. You cannot win.'

'Don't grieve for me just yet.'

Felix Mann shook his head violently, 'You don't get it, do you? You're dead already, you just don't know it. I've seen the daemon you are stalking. He did this to me.' Felix held up the stumps where his hands had been severed. 'You can't beat it. It can hide in plain sight. It lives in the shadows. You can't fight it, because you can't *see* it.' His voice took on a hysterical quality, the words beginning to tumble into each other in their rush to be out of his mouth. 'You can't beat it. It isn't alive. It's immortal. It's got the ring. It can't die. It can't die, dwarf. It can't die. Do you understand that? You can hunt it, but you can't kill it. Cut off its head and it will come back. Cut out its heart and it will come back. Burn it and it will rise from the ashes. It will come back and it will keep coming back. Do you understand that? Do you?'

Mann's daemons were like no vampires Kallad had ever heard of, invisible, invincible, they sounded like something invented to scare children. However fanciful, the thief's hysteria had the ring of truth to it. Something had driven the thief to the point of madness. It wasn't hard to imagine that something being the same monster behind the unnecessary evil of the slaughter of Grunberg. That made Felix Mann's story the first real lead Kallad had found since coming to Altdorf, and by necessity that made Felix Mann the missing link that he had been searching so long to find. He just had to bring him back from the edge.

'Rubbish,' the acolyte sneered. 'You're fully of fanciful nonsense. Down to the trauma, no doubt. The Grand Theogonist himself laid down his life to save us from these daemons you rave on about. The threat is gone.'

He was one crucial step closer to finding the fiend that had butchered his people.

'I understand,' Kallad said, 'that the thing has frightened the life out of you, and I understand why the priests have taken pity on you. All I can say is, that way lies madness. This is no way to live.'

'Don't mock me, dwarf,' Mann said, the edge of reason creeping back into his voice. 'Kill me or be done with it and leave me to rot in peace would you?'

Kallad shook his head.

'That's not the way it's going to happen. If you want to live again, help me to kill the beast. If not, well maybe I should crack your skull and put you out of your misery.'

Felix Mann held up his ruined wrist stumps. 'What can I do?' and again, this time more a question than a statement of uselessness: 'What can I do?'

'I can help you, thief, if you are willing to help yourself. Given a forge to work in I can craft hands. Well not real hands. They'll be more like gauntlets than real hands and they'll have to fasten to some kind of shoulder brace. They won't be pretty, and they won't move or have any kind of grip, but they'll be better than nothing. I'm no master smith, but I can make one like it's holding a cup and give the other a kind of hook attachment. They'll give you your life back. You'll be able to feed yourself and start living again. The rest is up to you.'

Silence hung between man and dwarf.

'Why?'

'Because you fought it and you lived.'

'Only because it let me.'

'That doesn't matter. You know it. I'll give you your hands back and in return I want you to talk. Tell me everything you can remember about the vampires. Everything. A good hunter knows his prey. There are less surprises and they die easier that way.'

'They just don't *stay* dead,' Felix Mann said, bleakly.

'This one will,' Kallad promised. 'Believe me, this one will.'

CHAPTER THREE
Voice of Shadows

BENEATH THE SIGMARITE CATHEDRAL, ALTDORF
The Bleak Midwinter, 2055

JON SKELLAN SNEERED as the soldier's fist thundered into his face. He spat blood. He was beyond pain. They could beat him, burn him and brand him, but they couldn't break him. They cuffed him with silver bonds that seared into his flesh, burning it raw. It didn't matter. He was immune.

'Is that all you've got, soldier?' Skellan mocked. The soldier backhanded him twice, hard, knocking the wind out of him. Skellan rolled his head with the blows.

At first his captors' abuse had verged on the inhumane, but as the days had faded into weeks and the weeks into months so their appetite for his suffering had faded. The beatings became more mundane. They lacked imagination. They lacked the hatred that made torture so terrible. They weren't cold or emotionless. They were… benign. Skellan drew strength from the fact that they toyed with him, testing the limits of his endurance. Day after day they beat him savagely, but it only served to make him stronger. He lived. They didn't dare kill him, but they suffered no such restraint when it came to beating him bloody. Skellan was no fool. If the Sigmarites had wanted him dead they could have killed him on any number of occasions. He was under no illusions. He was at their mercy. No, the simple truth was that they wanted him alive.

That meant they needed him.

For all the taunts, for all the experiments with devices of torture meant to break him, they needed their pet vampire.

It gave him the strength to resist them.

Behind the bars of his cage Skellan had few comforts. Soiled reeds were spread across the floor to insulate it from the cold and damp, and he had a blanket. Rats kept him company, creeping in through the cracks in the stone walls and working their way up from the subterranean sewers of the capital as the rains came, flooding out their lairs. Those he could catch, he killed and fed off. It was no way to live, but it was fresh blood, and blood renewed him.

The soldier moved around behind him and delivered a crushing blow to the back of Skellan's neck. The force of it sent the vampire sprawling across the reeds. With his hands cuffed, he had no way to catch himself as he fell. Skellan lay on his stomach as the soldier delivered a solid kick to his ribs. The kick was savage enough to lift him six inches off the ground. Gasping, Skellan drew his knees up towards his chest. Jagged strands of reed dug into his face.

'Better?'

The soldier said nothing.

The vampire wasn't worth his words.

Skellan knew what they thought of him.

He crawled towards the small mound of dried reeds that he had gathered to form a crude mattress. His gaolers had taken his chair away after Skellan had broken the leg off and beaten one of his captors to death with it in an attempt to provoke his own death in return. They let him live, but stripped his cell, leaving him a pot to relieve himself in and little else. The pot was useless, of course. His body didn't process the usual liquids or toxins as a living man's did.

The worst thing, by far, was that knowing he needed blood to survive, the priests brought it to him.

They fed him with it as they would a suckling babe.

They bled themselves and brought it down to his cellar dungeon, still warm, but already congealing as the heat left it. The blood was vital, but had little restorative value after being drawn from the donor. Little was better than none. Although it only took a few minutes for it to lose the life that Skellan needed to survive, the priests didn't trust their prisoner to feed off the living – with good reason.

His pitiful diet meant that hunger tormented him constantly. The need to feed drove Skellan to the verge of madness and hallucination. He began to believe that he could smell the Sigmarites' lifeblood pulsing through their veins as they prowled the corridors beyond his prison.

In the darkness, he closed his eyes and sent his mind out, imagining that he could actually hear each and every distinctive pulse that filled the chambers of the cathedral above him, despite the layers of stone and mortar. He savoured the rhythmic dub-dub beat of a hundred hearts in a hundred bodies that knelt in prayer; the way they missed an occasional beat or raced as the emotions demanded. In the darkest hours, Skellan allowed himself the fantasy of feeding properly. He played with images of white flesh and blue veins rising to the surface of the pale skin as he sucked hungrily at the throats of the priests.

There was nothing like fresh blood drawn from the still living. It was ambrosia. Skellan fantasised himself running amok in the cathedral, draining the priests one by one in a mindless orgy of blood, paying them back for every last one of the torments they had inflicted since his capture.

It was a sweet fantasy, and it would be fulfilled. He promised himself that.

They would age and weaken. He wouldn't.

He would live, and one day he would be free. When that day came they would know the nature of the beast they caged in their cellars, until then he would suffer their beatings.

The bolt on the door slid back and Reynard Grimm, Guard Captain of Altdorf, entered Skellan's prison. The man was a curious contradiction. Trapped in his skin were two distinct men, one a brutal sadist and the other a weaselly sycophant who clung to the Sigmarite gospels as an excuse for his cruelty. Grimm drew far too much pleasure from the pains he inflicted on his captive to be the guardian of righteousness his swaggering pretended.

The shadows shifted curiously around Grimm as he pushed the door closed, as if something hid within them, invisible to the naked eye. Skellan followed the peculiar blur as it merged into the darkness in the corner of the cell. It must be was a trick of the guttering light. There was nothing there. He turned his attention to the soldier.

'Nothing better to do with your life, Grimm?' Skellan asked. The fear was gone. An uneasy contempt rested in its place. The reverse, however, was not true. The Grimm Skellan had come to know was a coward.

'What could be better than listening to you scream, vampire?'

'Oh, I can think of any number of things, but then, I have an imagination. It is both a blessing and a curse, believe me,' Skellan said, letting the corner of his lips curl into a derisive smile.

'Save your breath, vampire, you'll need it to scream soon enough.'

Skellan shook his head. 'You still don't understand do you, Grimm? I don't have breath to hold. I don't have a heart that beats. I don't have those weak human emotions like love and fear. I am kin to the damned. I am a vampire. I am purged of all the weaknesses of your kind. I shall walk amongst the living long after *you* have become dust and slipped from memory. But you, Grimm, you are nothing, less than nothing. You are a child in a man's skin. You are afraid. You fear me. I can smell it. Your cowardice clings to your skin, it infects your sweat. It cries out to every predator in creation: Kill me! Kill me!'

Behind Grimm's shoulder, the cell door opened once more. The Lector looked troubled as he walked into the small prison cell.

'I begged you, guard captain, no more torture. I speak with Sigmar's mouth, do his words mean nothing to you?' the Lector laid a hand on Grimm's shoulder.

'Shut up, priest.' Grimm shook the priest's hand off.

A ripple of movement in the shadows behind the Lector caught Skellan's eye. He was about to dismiss it when he saw it again, a few feet away from where he had first seen it, much closer to the Lector now: a crease in the shadows, a slight blurring of the wall as something passed in front of it. He wouldn't have been able to see it if he hadn't been looking for it, but now he knew what to look for it was not particularly difficult to follow. There was someone – or something – in the shadows, creeping up behind his two captors.

Skellan forced himself up from the reeds, to kneel before his jailors. It was anything but a gesture of subservience. He was defying them. He met Grimm's eye. The soldier was demented. There was no rationale in his gaze, no thought. He hated Skellan, not for who he was, but for what he was. The guard captain had lived through the Siege of Altdorf. He had seen friends and comrades die at the hands of the vampires. He had reason to fear and reason to hate all that Skellan represented. Those reasons drove the man. He was avenging ghosts every time he laid a hand on Skellan. And every time Skellan dragged himself back to his feet he was mocking the man, reminding him that his dead were still dead and that there could be no revenge for the living.

Grimm lashed out, but his blow never connected.

The outline of a tall, thin man gathered substance within the shimmering dark. The stranger threw back his hood and grabbed Grimm by the hair, tugging back hard on his scalp to unbalance him. The surprise and sudden ferocity of the attack meant that Grimm fell back into the stranger's deadly embrace. He was utterly helpless. In the moment before the stranger sank his teeth into Reynard Grimm's throat, his eyes met Skellan's. Recognition passed between them sending a shiver soul deep. For the first time, Skellan believed he was truly insane. He wanted desperately to believe that Vlad von Carstein had materialised out of the shadows to save him, but it was impossible. The Vampire Count was beyond resurrection, and yet Skellan saw the Count's eyes. They were ancient, knowing, and so, so cold. They stripped away the layers of lies and identity, and delved deep into the core of who he was. They *knew* him.

The stranger sank his teeth into the soldier's throat, pinning his arms to his side as he kicked out helplessly. He drank hungrily and then snapped Grimm's neck with a sickening economy of movement.

Grimm's body crumpled and collapsed on the floor in a lifeless heap.

Skellan sprang forward, launching himself from his knees like a cannonball. He arched his back and used the full momentum of his body to hammer his forehead into the Lector's chin. He connected with a sickening crunch of bone, his weight bowling the priest off his feet. The priest sprawled across the floor, insensate.

The stranger, Vlad, smacked his lips as he toed Grimm's unmoving corpse. 'Rather like drinking vinegar when rich Bretonnian claret is so near by, but it slakes the thirst. Still, we'll sample some of that vintage before we make good our escape. No doubt you have a debt or two to settle with the priests.' He saw the way Skellan was looking at him, partly in awe, partly in fear and with unmistakable recognition. 'I'm not him,' he said.

'But you look–'

'Similar,' the stranger conceded. 'We are, after all, similar monsters, are we not?'

'But you are his aren't you? I can smell him inside you.'

'I am von Carstein, if that is what you mean. There is some of him in me, as there is some of your sire in you. Vlad brought me into this life. It was a long time ago, longer than I care to remember, and a long way from this ruined burg. He saw something in me he liked, a ghost of himself perhaps? Only he could say for sure. He may not have loved me the most – that honour I feel sure went to Isabella – but he most certainly loved me longest. Now feed, and then we leave.'

'What about these?' Skellan held up his manacled hands. The silver had cut deep wounds into his flesh.

The stranger nodded once and spun on his heel, drawing the cloak around his head and disappearing into the shadows. The cell door opened and closed on nothing as the vampire slipped out. A moment later, the stifled cry of a guard echoed back to Skellan as he knelt over the Lector's corpse, his chin slick with the priest's blood. The killing had begun.

When he looked up, the stranger stood in the doorway, holding the key to his manacles.

'Care to join me in a feast?'

Skellan nodded. 'I will taste their blood,' he said, simply.

'Good. Hold out your hands.'

The stranger manipulated the key in the tiny lock mechanism until it sprang and the silver cuffs fell to the floor.

Skellan rubbed at his ruined wrists. 'Who are you?'

'Come with me and find out.' The stranger turned his back and disappeared through the door.

Skellan had no choice but to follow him.

CHAPTER FOUR
The Night of the Daemon

THE SIGMARITE CATHEDRAL, ALTDORF
The Bleak Midwinter, 2055

SCREAMING PRIESTS SHATTERED the peace of the secluded graveyard.

For a moment, none of them moved, frozen by the arcane magic of the unexpected scream, unwilling to believe it was actually a scream and not some distant memory, risen to haunt them – a ghost of the past or some revenant shade stirred by their presence amongst the graves. They had all heard enough screams and seen enough horrors for such a basic trick of the mind to unnerve them. It was a curse of the age. This, however, *was* a blood-curdling scream that clawed out of the confines of the cathedral's underbelly. It wasn't the imagination playing tricks. More powerful than any of the eight winds, the scream drew its strength from the most primitive of sources, that primal fear deep in every man. It held the priest, the thief, the dwarf and the simpleton wrapped in its fragile spell. Then the spell shattered as a second scream strangled off into wretched silence.

Whatever had caused the first scream had silenced the second.

Kallad felt the chill touch of premonition as his hands closed around the leather-wrapped shaft of Ruinthorn.

Felix Mann was the first to react. His face crumbled, his newfound resolve short-lived. 'See… see…' he moaned. 'They won't die… they won't die. They won't.'

'Quit your blithering, man.' Kallad Stormwarden dragged Ruinthorn clear and hoisted it over his shoulder. He hadn't gone two steps towards the doors of the temple before the young acolyte grabbed at his shoulder.

'No!' The dwarf spun around. 'For Sigmar's sake, no weapons in the house of our god!'

'With all due respect, you stick with your prayers for comfort and I'll stick with Ruinthorn. Sammy, get out of here.'

The youngster shook his head.

'We're friends.'

That said it all.

Kallad nodded. There was no argument. The lad had used his own words back at him.

'Aye, we are lad, but I can't be worrying about you in a fight. You do as you're told.'

Sammy Krauss bunched up his knuckles, ready to fight, and stubbornly refused to move. 'I can fight.'

None of them had time for an argument. There had been no more screams in the last few seconds, but that didn't mean dying wasn't still going on inside the cathedral. In Kallad's experience, death was silent more often than not.

'Come on, priest,' Kallad urged. Ruinthorn was a reassuring weight in his calloused hands. 'This is your house, let's go find out what all the ruckus is about.'

Like Mann, the acolyte looked more than simply shocked by the screams: his eyes were filled with growing terror. The pair knew something he didn't, that much was obvious, and what they knew troubled them deeply.

The acolyte was hesitant to enter the cathedral.

Kallad gave him a none too gentle shove and followed him in.

At first, the smell reminded Kallad of the deep mines beneath Karak Sadra, the tang of iron sharp in the foetid air, but the priests burned incense and an assortment of powders to take away the reek of unwashed bodies. Blood smelled like iron. What they smelled as they entered the cathedral was blood. It was a cloying out of place stench, acrid against the closed-in musk of the priests.

It didn't bode well.

Kallad kissed the mark of Grimna on Ruinthorn's head and stepped into what he feared would be a charnel house of slaughter.

There were no more screams.

He felt his gorge rise as he walked down the narrow passage. It was quiet: too quiet.

'Something's wrong here. This place stinks of death. What do you know, priest? What are you hiding from me?' Kallad growled at the acolyte. The young priest shuddered and made the sign of Sigmar in the air before him. The man was a nervous wreck.

Kallad pushed past him. The corridor divided into three, a truncated passageway that led to two massive oak doors, and two longer passages that curled left and right. Kallad sniffed the air. The reek of blood was redolent. It was impossible to tell where the concentration was strongest. He listened, but there was nothing, no sign of life within the great cathedral. A hundred priests and countless penitents should have been inside the cathedral's walls. There shouldn't be any place for silence among so many souls. It sent a bone deep chill through the dwarf.

'Taal's teeth, I don't like this,' Felix Mann said, behind him. 'It's too damned quiet. Where is everyone?' The thief had a gift for stating the obvious. 'It's out, isn't it?'

Kallad turned to see that Mann had pushed the young acolyte up against the wall and was forcing the ruined stub of his wrist into the man's throat.

'You let it escape. You fools. You bloody stupid fools!' His voice escalated into hysteria. His accusation echoed through the passageway, the word 'fool' folding in on itself over and over again.

Kallad dropped his axe, grabbed Mann by the shoulder and pulled the pair apart. He slammed the thief up against the wall. Mann's breath leaked out of him in a slow moan. His eyes were wild and wide with terror. Kallad had no idea what the thief was seeing in the dark, but whatever it was clearly had the man frightened.

'You let it escape,' Mann repeated, his voice flat and subdued. He was trembling violently.

'What?' Kallad pressed. 'Let *what* escape?'

'The thing in the cellar.'

'No,' the acolyte whimpered. 'No. They couldn't... it couldn't escape.'

They all heard it: the sound of running feet. For a moment, Kallad believed that the sound belonged to the ghosts of this place, the dead locked in a never-ending cycle of flight and death. He shook his head, trying to dislodge the uncomfortable malaise that had settled about him since entering the cathedral.

He pressed Mann up against the wall. 'Let *what* escape?'

He didn't need the thief to answer. He knew. It made a sick kind of sense. The Sigmarites had taken one of von Carstein's brood prisoner after the siege, it was the only reasonable explanation for their fear. Now the beast was free and they had nothing to restrain it with. The holier-than-thou idiots believed that their god would protect them come what may. That kind of blind faith was dangerous.

'You didn't... tell me you didn't try to cage a vampire down there. Don't you people ever learn? Look at what the creatures did to your city–' Kallad was almost knocked from his feet by a frightened-faced priest as he came hurtling out of the kitchens. The priest's ceremonial robes were up around his knees and his sandalled feet slapped on the cold stone floor. The man looked as if he had come face to face with every daemon his faith had ever imagined into being. For a fleeting moment, Kallad pitied the fool, before he remembered that they had done it to themselves.

'The beast is free! Run! Run for your lives!'

Kallad bent down and picked up his axe. Ruinthorn was an extension of his soul, not merely a weapon. With it in his hands, Kallad Stormwarden was complete. Anger surged through his veins. The fools had tried to harness a daemon. The arrogance of manlings never ceased to amaze him.

He turned his back on the thief and the priest, and loosing a mighty war cry charged in the direction the frightened-faced priest had come from. He didn't care if the others followed him or not. A vampire was loose in the cathedral. One of the stinking creatures that had slain his family was within spitting distance. His thoughts glazed over with a veil of hatred. He would find the creature and he would rip its dead heart out with his bare hands and ram it down its gaping throat.

He stalked down the chill corridor, listening, but only hearing the echo of his own footsteps. The entrance to the vaults would, he reasoned, be off the main chapel, assuming that the vaults were part of the crypt or could be reached through the mausoleum. The other logical choice was the kitchens, since they would no doubt have access to either cold storage or a wine cellar. Either of these might link into the vaults. There was no guarantee of course. With these old buildings, the vaults could actually be some long forgotten dungeon with a secluded stairwell hidden away somewhere. He stopped at a corner as a whiff of cider and roses hit him, but laid over it was the unmistakable tang of blood. He followed his nose and found the kitchens. Knives had been abandoned in the middle of cutting a succulent shank of ham. Pots of vegetables stewed on the fire. There was no starvation in the house of this god. More importantly, he found a staircase leading down to the depths of the cathedral's cold stone heart: the cellars.

From there, he followed a narrow passage down until he found a fork that offered two choices, one to the depths of the crypts and the makeshift dungeons, the other back up to the House of Sigmar. The staircase down was thick with dust. Although it had been disturbed recently, it was definitely the path less travelled. He took the stairs down.

The air grew noticeably colder as he descended, prickling Kallad's skin. There was a peculiar quality about it. It wasn't like the air of the deep mines, there was no vitality to it. It was starved.

The smell of blood hung heavy in the air, richer and stronger than anywhere else in the cathedral.

It was a slaughterhouse reek.

The torches along the walls were dead, burned out. Kallad paused at the bottom of the stairs, listening. He could hear moans from deeper in the darkness. He followed the sounds through a maze of passages until he saw an open door.

Two priests were huddled over the dead bodies when he walked into the cell. He couldn't make out what they were saying – some kind of last rites for the dead, perhaps.

'Where is it?' Kallad asked, making sure the holy men saw Ruinthorn and were left in no doubt as to the meaning of his question.

Sammy Krauss stepped into the cell behind him. Neither Mann nor the Sigmarite had followed. Sammy looked scared but resolute. The lad had guts. Kallad hoped he'd get to keep them after the day was out.

'It's daylight,' Kallad pressed. 'The creature can't be far. Talk to me, damn it!'

He looked at the two bodies sprawled out across the floor, and the silver cuffs laid almost ceremoniously between them: one soldier, one priest. He couldn't understand how the beast had slipped its bonds, but it didn't matter. The creature was free and at least two men were dead for their foolishness.

The dead priest's robes were different to those worn by the others, marking him as special. His head hung back unnaturally on his broken neck, exposing puncture wounds where the beast had drained every last ounce of blood from his body. A crust had dried around the wounds. The soldier had shared a similarly grisly fate of a broken neck and bloody punctures.

Death was death, ugly and dirty no matter whom it befell. There was no special sanitised death for the devout. They bled and soiled themselves exactly the same as the thieves, whores and beggars. When it came, death was the greatest of all levellers. All men left the world equal no matter their station in life.

The tableau of butchery confirmed Kallad's worst fears. Instead of frightening him, the knowledge galvanised the dwarf.

The elder of the two priests looked up from ministering to the dead, the fallen priest's hand cupped in his. 'The beast is free.' His voice was as dead as the men sprawled out at his feet.

'Tell me,' Kallad urged.

'There is nothing to tell you, dwarf. The Lector believed he could trap a daemon. He was wrong. He paid for his error with his life. Now the beast is free and others will pay the same price, Sigmar save their souls.' The way that last, part plea part prayer, came out of the priest's mouth left Kallad in no doubt that the man's faith had been deeply shaken. Violence had a way of making weak men lose their religion and strong men find theirs.

'What are you doing here?' the second priest challenged, finally looking up. His eyes were red-rimmed with tears, his young face deeply scarred from the pox or some such youthful disease.

'Saving your life. Now, help me, instead of asking stupid questions.'

The sound of breathless running had them all looking towards the door as Felix Mann stumbled through it. 'It's killed dozens up there, dwarf. Bodies are everywhere.'

'Is it still here?'

'How the hell should I know? I came to find you because you've got an axe. The way I see things, you're my best chance of making it out of here alive so I am sticking about two steps behind you.'

'Show me,' Kallad said.

Kallad followed him through the vaults, up to the cellar and finally into the main floor of the cathedral. Neither spoke.

It was true. The pews were strewn with broken bodies, necks snapped and hanging impossibly, throats opened, blood congealing in the gaping wounds. Kallad counted twenty corpses littering the aisles of the great domed cathedral. The naked savagery of the attack was shocking. That it should have happened in the House of Sigmar made it doubly so.

They found fifteen more corpses scattered around the many rooms of the cathedral, left where they had fallen, necks broken, flesh tinged blue where the blood had been drained from them.

'How could one creature do this?' Mann asked, looking down at another ruined corpse. In death, the brothers of Sigmar looked distressingly alike, rigor ridding their features of any individuality.

Kallad didn't have a chance to answer, but like the thief, there was something about the scale of the slaughter that disturbed him. He couldn't see how one creature could wreak so much devastation unchecked. Surely someone should have raised an alarm. Nothing about the escape rang true. It was too... clinical.

A cold stone of certainty sank in Kallad's gut.

The creature wasn't alone.

Its escape wasn't some spur of the moment opportunity. Someone, or something, had freed the beast.

That led to the disturbing possibility that there was a traitor inside the cathedral.

Who could he trust? Could he trust *anyone*?

The answer was no. He couldn't trust anyone.

Kallad searched the library. The same instinct that told him the escape was not some random happening nagged him when he looked at the chaos that had been the cathedral's library. He picked up one of the damaged tomes, reading the words off the spine as best he could.

The frightened young acolyte that had met them at the gate found them in the library. The place was a mess. It had been ransacked, books ripped open, spines torn, pages scattered across the table. The librarian sat at the head of the table, his head lolling impossibly on his broken neck. Impossibly, well, impossibly for the living, not for the dead it seemed. The killer had taken the time to mock them, putting a book in the dead man's hands. The beast had gouged the old librarian's eyes out to complete the irony.

The young acolyte slumped into a chair across the table from the dead librarian, his head in his hands.

'They were my friends,' he said simply.

'They were fools for thinking that they could cage a vampire and make it dance to their tune.'

'It wasn't like that.'

'No?'

'No. The Lector thought that if we could study the beast we could learn its weaknesses. You can't beat an enemy you don't know, that's what he said.'

'Well the man was an idiot. Believe me, you can fight anything and anything can fight you, and only a complete idiot would let a blood-sucking monster into his home and not expect it to cause bloody murder.'

'But he–'

'Ain't no buts about it. How long was the thing here?'

'Since the siege.'

'But that was *years* ago.'

The young acolyte nodded.

'But you'd have had to feed it... blood.'

The young acolyte nodded again.

'Grimna's balls, man. Didn't you see what it was doing? Just by being here it was turning you all into monsters. You fed the thing blood?'

'Our own. We bled ourselves to feed the thing.'

'You gave it a taste for your own blood? Your own blood? And you kept the thing caged less than fifty feet beneath you as you just prayed to your precious god. Listen to yourself, even Sammy here wouldn't be naïve enough to think that was a good idea. Now you're paying the price for your stupidity. Ask yourself if it was worth it. When the beast is breaking your neck to get at the big fat vein pulsing in your throat, ask yourself if it was worth it.'

Silence stretched out between them, the truth of the dwarf's words heavy in the air. You couldn't cage a beast forever. At some point it would break free.

The young acolyte walked around behind the dead librarian, treading on pages of ancient texts. Kallad looked at the earnest young man. The light spilling in from the vast stained glass window of the library's far wall fragmented his face into yellows, reds and greens, and vast hues of sickly colours between.

Tears stood out in his eyes when he spoke.

'Kill it,' he said, simply. 'Find the monster and kill it. We have money. We can pay you. Find it and kill it before it causes more death.'

'Aye, that I will, but not for your coin. your money's no good to me. I want four good swords, reliable men, not the kind who lose their heads to panic in a tight spot and some kind of mage or sorcerer, and I'm thinkin' four clerics of Sigmar. We'll set out at dawn and have all day to hunt the beasts. They can't get far.'

'A sorcerer? We couldn't. Magic… it is outlawed. We couldn't sanction such a flagrant sin. It cannot be the only way, surely?'

'Do you want to catch the beast, man? We need magic, and I don't care a whit about your sensibilities. Without a magician we could be chasing round like blue-arsed flies, there's a huge world out there with places to hide, but any dead thing leaves the reek of corruption in the air. It ain't natural, see. What happens is the world cries out against it. Now, a good magician can smell the stink of a vampire on the winds of magic as the beast passes. With a magician, we can track the beasts from their own stench, and holy men are better for fighting the dead than even the best swordsmen. They've got faith *and* weapons.'

The young acolyte nodded sickly. His eyes were haunted. His hand hovered an inch above the librarian's shoulder, unable to rest on the dead man's shell. It was painfully obvious that he was remembering the countless times he had spent with the old man, talking, learning, and thinking about a better world. The events of the last hour had corroded a part of his soul. He would never be the same again. Kallad knew full well what was happening to the priest, it was the forge of life, he was being tempered by the evils of the world. He would either shatter or come out of the fire hardened and able to deal with the very worst the world had to throw at him.

'Nevin Kantor,' the acolyte said at last, turning his back on the others. 'The church holds his life forfeit for the abomination of petty magics. He is due to be executed by Grimm's guards I believe. Perhaps I can barter his freedom in return for him serving you? No promises, dwarf. Be ready at dawn. I will do what I can.'

When he had gone, Mann dragged out a chair and sank into it. 'The vampire wasn't alone.'

'No, he wasn't.' Kallad agreed. 'Someone helped the beast to escape.'

'Who would do such a thing?'

'Or what?' And that was what disturbed the dwarf. The violence was inhuman.

'You think another one of them did it?'

'Tell me, thief, could you deliver someone you hated to this kind of death? I mean truly hated, not just disliked. Feel the blackness of it in your gut and tell me, could you do this?'

Mann thought about it for a moment and shook his head. 'No. There's no humanity in it.'

'Exactly. Manlings may kill, no denying that. They're inventive when it comes to death. Sometimes they dress it up an' make like it is all noble, with rituals and duels, and sometimes it is vindictive, a knife in the night driven home by spite. But this, well I don't know about you, but this goes beyond any notion of spite I've ever known. Makes me think that maybe there's something to that story of yours, truth be told.'

Slowly, all trace of colour drained from the thief's face. He cast a fretful glance at the blinded corpse of the librarian as he laid his wrists on the table. 'You think it is him, don't you?'

Kallad Stormwarden nodded. 'Aye, I think it's him.'

'He's come to finish me because I know about the ring. Oh, sweet Sigmar!'

'Don't look to your god. This is your chance to reclaim your life. Stand up and fight or roll over and play dead, it's your choice and only you can make it. You're alive now, even when all these others aren't. That means it's not about you, not this time. Now, I'll only ask once, come with us in the morning. Slay the beast and get your life back.'

Mann stared at the dwarf, and even before he opened his mouth Kallad could hear the excuses shaping on his tongue.

'But what can I do? I'm a cripple, not some hero. I can't even wipe my own... How can I slay a vampire? Tell me what I can do.'

'Anything you want. Anything you want. Think about it.'

With the invitation hanging between them, Kallad left the library.

The priests had done a sweep of the cathedral, in every chamber, every storeroom, through the mausoleums and the crypts, even up in the vaults and on the rooftops. The beast was gone.

The long process of gathering the dead had begun. Grimm's guards had been summoned and word of the murders was out. Every bustle of movement was tinged with panic. It would take a long time for these people to recover from this invasive death. It was one thing to experience death, after all, Morr came for everyone eventually, but it was quite another to experience this kind of slaughter. Hardened soldiers weren't expected to face a cathedral more akin to a charnel house, and those that did lived with nightmares for the rest of their lives. Simple men like these would never be the same again. They had lost more than their brothers to the butchery, they had lost a part of themselves: their innocence.

That night could easily have been any of many nights from the dark days of the siege. The shadow of the vampires hung over the city once more, a grim shade that dredged up the worst and most painful memories of those desperate times. Kallad wasn't immune. He sat alone, removed from the soldiers as they fought to impose order over the panic of the clerics, remembering Grunberg.

'Will I never be free of these daemons?' he asked himself, staring at the dancing flames of the bonfire. The soldiers were burning the dead men's clothes.

'None of us will, dwarf,' the thief said, coming up to stand beside him. 'Our dreams will never be as empty again. We will never know the love of a good woman or the companionship of good friends. Our love now is vengeance, our friends: hatchet, axe and sword.'

'You are not as thoughtless as you would have others believe, are you, thief?'

'It would seem not. I'll not be coming with you, dwarf. Our roads go in different directions come dawn. That doesn't mean I intend to give up on life. There is something I need to do. Who knows, perhaps our roads will cross once more, some place far from here.'

'That saddens me, manling. Intelligent company is hard to come by. Still, I hope you find what you're looking for at the road's end.'

'Personally, I hope I never find the road's end. That's where we differ, dwarf. I'm not looking for the end. I thought I was. I thought I was looking for an end to life, because I didn't want to live it. What I should have been looking for was a turning point, a fork stuck in the road to show me where my new life began. There are so many directions we can go. We don't need to be in a hurry to get where we are going. Sometimes we need to remember that the journey itself is as important as getting to the destination.'

'And you're ready to start travelling again?'

'I'm ready to start travelling again.'

'And you're not just running away because your daemons scare you?'

'Of course I am, dwarf.' Felix Mann smiled. 'I'm getting the hell out of here and running as far away as I can, any half-wit would. If I am lucky I'll find somewhere I can start living again without being reminded of the beast every waking moment of every god-damned day. I want to die old and happy, dwarf. Metal hands or not, if I come with you that won't happen. Think of it as self-preservation.'

Kallad nodded, the flames reflected in his eyes. A soldier cast a bloodstained robe into the fire.

'Sometimes all we need to do is forget. Thing is, we can burn every last memory and we still can't manage it. Some old ghosts don't like to be laid to rest. You do what you have to. Anything's better than being left here to rot. May your god go with you, manling.'

'And yours, you.'

'Aye, I'll be needing all the help I can get.'

The priests left Kallad alone. Word had spread among them that he was leaving in the morning to hunt the vampire that had shattered the serenity of their cathedral. It hadn't turned him into their hero. There were no hearty slaps on the back, no unending flagons of ale to dampen his fears and wish him well on his way. Their looks left him in no doubt as to how they judged him. To them, he was a killer, just as the beast he hunted was a killer: there was no intrinsic difference in their eyes. He was the second bringer of death to walk the passageways of their home that day. It didn't so much puzzle him as sadden him.

Kallad *was* a killer, he knew that, he had killed many many times in his life, but he slew monsters. He protected those that couldn't protect themselves, people like the priests of Sigmar. He avenged those who had fallen, people like the priests of Sigmar. His kind of death was no arbitrary thing. Only the young acolyte was different, he was the only one that saw that Kallad wasn't a monster.

'Not yet, at least.' Kallad said to himself.

There was always the possibility, however, that a killer like Kallad could cross the line without ever realising it, becoming judge, jury and father confessor to the damned. It was a thin dark line to tread, with either side falling away into madness. The dwarf knew that. He was intensely aware that Ruinthorn brought death, and fiercely determined that it should only deliver to those deserving it. He had, after all, earned the name Stormwarden. It wasn't his people's way to easily grant names.

Kallad didn't want to be around the priests and the soldiers as they buried their own, so he retreated into the cathedral in search of an empty cell. A few hours sleep would do him good.

There was a chill about the place that hadn't been there during the day, as if the soul of the place had iced over come sundown. He found a room with a simple cot and blanket, and lay down to catch a few hours' sleep.

The thief had the right of it: the chance of Kallad growing old was slim at best. It was never something he had worried unduly over. He had sworn an oath to avenge his people. He would do that or die trying. From the moment he had stepped into the tunnels that led into the mountains around Grunberg he had ceased to be his own person and become an instrument of fate. On nights like these he felt the weight of it, but it was his burden to carry, and carry it he would.

Too tired to care, Kallad climbed into the cot fully clothed, drawing the blanket up over his chest, and closing his eyes. Despite his exhaustion, sleep was slow in coming, and when it did, it was fitful and disturbed. Scattered dreams were plagued with memories of Grunberg, the woman Gretchen and her baby. He dreamed of them often, wracked by guilt over his own actions. Even now, he was unable to come to terms with the fact that he had killed a child – even though the child was dead and turned, and was nothing more than a parasite feeding on its mother's tit. It didn't matter that he had had no choice. It didn't matter that it had become a monster. When he slept, he saw only a child, an innocent baby, dead at his feet, his axe bloody in his clenched fists. Kallad tossed and turned, Gretchen's screams bringing him back to jarring consciousness. Only they weren't Gretchen's screams. A priest somewhere in the labyrinth of the cathedral wept while another cried out, and another keened for the dead while others chanted, their lament far more unnerving than any tears. Together, the sounds had become the screams of his dream. He listened to the outpouring of grief. These people would never be the same again.

Long before the night was out, he gave up trying to sleep and went to sit in the secluded grove beside the Grand Theogonist's grave.

There, at last, he found peace.

The token he had pressed into the dirt reflected the twin glows of Morrslieb and Mannslieb.

'Peace be with you, brothers,' he said to the ghosts of the dead, knowing that their souls would have begun the long journey to Morr's underworld.

Come the first blush of dawn, the acolyte found the dwarf sitting beneath the weeping tree, eyes closed, Ruinthorn balanced across his lap. The young priest wasn't alone. Two more nervous-looking Sigmarites accompanied him.

'I talked to my brothers after prayers last night, urging them to help. It seems my request fell on deaf ears, or frightened ones. I could not get your fighters. However, we would come with you, master dwarf. These are my brothers, Joachim Akeman and Korin Reth.' The two men nodded to the dwarf. 'And my name is Reimer Schmidt. I have been assured that three of Captain Grimm's guards will meet us at the postern gate.

Here at least I have not failed you. I am told the guards are most eager to avenge their leader. These are good men, brave, unflinching in battle, veterans of the siege. They know what they are hunting better than most.'

'And what of the mage?' Kallad asked without opening his eyes.

'His parole has been agreed, on condition.'

'I don't like the sounds of that.'

'No, I didn't imagine you would. The magician's life is forfeit, but the witch hunter Helmut van Hal has agreed that the freak can serve your quest as it feeds the greater good, but in return, when his usefulness to the quest is over he is to be... neutralised.'

'I don't kill in cold blood. It's what separates me from the monsters I hunt.'

'Then Kantor will stay here and die as is fitting for a soul touched by Chaos.'

'It must be good to be you, priest, content in your world of absolutes,' Felix Mann muttered, coming up behind the priests. He was packed to travel, a small satchel slung over his shoulder. 'Personally, I couldn't care less what happens to the magician. I'm pretty damned sure it's his fault that I ever ended up in this mess, so I can't pretend that it would worry me unduly if he fell off the end of the world in some tragic accident.'

'Are you coming with us, thief?' the young acolyte, Reimer Schmidt, asked. Kallad grinned at the holy man's discomfort. Travelling with killers *and* thieves was probably more than his principles could bear.

'Hardly. Only a fool would follow the dwarf where he's going, and I stopped being a fool sometime last night. What can I say? Better a live cripple than a dead hero.'

'You disgust me, thief.'

'I'm rather proud of him, myself,' Kallad said. 'Well men, let's wish Herr Mann well on his journeys, wherever the road might take him, and go fetch us a magician, shall we?'

'So you agree to the terms of his release?'

'I never said that. It's a long road and things can happen, let's leave it at that shall we?'

'Then van Hal won't release him into your custody.'

'We'll cross that bridge when we come to it, eh? Me and Ruinthorn here can be *very* persuasive when we have to be.'

CHAPTER FIVE
The Curse of the White Wolf

THE CITY OF THE WHITE WOLF, MIDDENHEIM
The Dead of Winter, 2055

IT WAS AN impossible task.

Jerek von Carstein knew it the moment that Konrad had confided in him, but the new Count would not be dissuaded. Konrad could not deny that the vampire nation needed rebuilding if it was to survive the scourge that was mankind, but the humans were hardly the sole enemy of the dead. They were their own worst enemies. The truth of it was all around him. The livestock around the castle were pitifully weak, drained to the point of anaemic uselessness by the few surviving vampires that had made it back to Drakenhof – restraint was not in their nature. They fed as they needed to feed. These were the last of their kind. Gone was the noblesse of Vlad von Carstein, and with it the wisdom of the Vampire Count. Vlad had known better than to exhaust the fresh blood around his castle. He cultivated the cattle, raising them for food, not slaughter.

Not so this new breed.

They understood only the most basic of urges. They hungered, so they fed. They didn't care that they were killing more and more humans, they were only cattle after all. They didn't care that there were none to replace the dead. There would always be more humans. That was their purpose: to be slaughtered for food to sate the never-ending hunger of the beast. Their lives were inconsequential.

Jerek had walked amongst them during the nights that followed Konrad's visit. It took no great wisdom to see that the remaining cattle would not make strong vampires. He had argued passionately with the new Count, trying to make him see how unsound his reasoning was. Better the few vampires that they had than swelling their ranks with the dregs of humanity. The weak would always fail, it was in their nature. A weak human would become a weak vampire. Weakening the bloodline was a mistake.

Konrad listened, but in listening twisted everything Jerek said to fit his own idea. All he succeeded in doing was convincing Konrad that the Hamaya must go abroad in search of new blood, blood worthy of being sired into the unlife. Each of the five Hamaya must seek out and sire five gets.

Jerek had argued against it because it would weaken the vampires, but Konrad had insisted. He had a vision of a new breed: the deadliest of the species come together as his people. That in turn demanded that their choices be careful ones. Konrad was right: these new gets were the future of their people. In turn, every new get would be forced to sire five of their own, and so on, making unlife a plague amongst the living once more. He couldn't deny that the plan had strategic merits.

The Hamaya were hand-picked from the survivors of Altdorf, the best of the best, most loyal to Konrad's claim to the title Count, strategists and bladesmen forged into an elite band of brothers. The bond between them was as close, Jerek swore, as any he had experienced in his other life as the White Wolf of Middenheim. They were not simply ruthless killers devoid of conscience and scruple. They were not undisciplined beasts driven by the base needs of their kin. They were more than that. They still had something – a spark of humanity that made them so much more than simply mindless beasts.

Jerek had picked them himself for exactly that reason. He knew that left to his own devices Konrad would have simply culled a handful of the most ruthless creatures from within his menagerie of monsters and erected a cordon of fangs around himself, hoping it was enough to ward off the inevitable. That was by far the biggest difference between the two: where Konrad saw weakness in humanity Jerek saw strength. That, perhaps, said more about the Wolf than it did about his master.

'Every leader needs one truth speaker amongst the gaggle of flatterers. Never be afraid to speak your mind, my friend,' Konrad had said. Never be afraid to speak your mind. They were easy words to say, but far from easy ones to live by in the court of the new Vampire Count. 'Few have the courage to stand behind their own words. I am no fool, Wolf. I know I have my share of flatterers, but I would be a fool if I ignored my one truth speaker.'

Therefore, Jerek had bent the knee and sworn always to offer his lord the truth as he saw it, not wrapped up in pretty words meant to flatter into deception. Even as he made the pledge, he knew that he would come to regret it.

With that promise spoken, he had returned to his home and taken to haunting the survivors he had left behind. At night, he roamed the Palast District, hugging the shadows along the north wall of the city. He prowled the Middenpalaz and its warren of buildings crowded in around the Graf's palace, he even stole into the ducal mausoleum to stare at the tombs of the men he had served in life.

He watched ladies walk beside their beaux in the Konigsgarten, and when he could put it off no more, he returned to the Square of Martials, descending the small flight of stairs into the great square to sit on the wooden benches and remember the days when he had drilled his men beneath the watchful gaze of Gunther Todbringer's statue. Sitting there brought back more ghosts than he cared to remember. This cobbled square was as much his home as any place in the world. He heard them all, the clatter of hammers, the buckling of shields, the curses and the cheers, and over and over the chant: 'Ulric! Ulric! Ulric!'

It was that memory that took him to the great bronze statue on the corner of West Weg and Sudentenweg.

'How did you find the strength to do it?' he asked the man of bronze. He didn't expect an answer, because there were no answers. Two children balanced on the statue's broad shoulders and a broken-backed rat was crushed beneath its foot. At the height of the Black Plague, Graf Gunthar had sealed the city gates for six long months, condemning thousands to die. It must have taken incredible fortitude to resist the temptation to open the gates when so many innocent people were dying, but Gunthar had had no choice, the gates had to stay closed to save Middenheim. It was an old story, but one worth remembering: from great sacrifices, great victories are born.

Jerek bowed his head and turned to enter the spectacular Temple of Ulric, the very heart of the city itself. Doubt touched him. Could the creature he had become walk into a holy place? Did enough of his self, enough of the White Wolf, remain to allow him to enter? He steeled himself.

This was it, his last farewell to the person he had been. It was true what they said, you could not go home again. It was only to be expected that a city changed, moved on. Like Graf Gunthar, Jerek was a thing of the past. Few, if any, would remember him. It was one thing for a child to return home a man and find that the streets he knew had grown smaller, but it was quite another for a dead man to return to a city only to find it so fragile and mortal. Everything about the place, even the stone walls that had seemed so resolute and unchanging, owned an air of transience, as if they knew their time was fleeting.

'I am a man,' he told himself, 'beloved of Ulric. That is what I am, not the beast von Carstein made me.'

He believed it, and his belief was so sincere that he stepped through the doors and stood still beneath the vast vaulted roof, amazed once more at the architecture that defied gravity's pull. He wasn't struck down for his temerity. In the centre of the temple, the sacred flame burned brightly. This was why he had returned home: a final test of himself.

He felt an unfamiliar sickness gnawing at his belly as knelt before the eternal flame. In his mind, he held the thought that had been with him since Konrad first issued the order for the Hamaya to breed.

The god had prophesied that so long as the flame burned the city would endure. The flame still burned and the city had withstood plague and the ravages of the Vampire Count's undead host, so perhaps there was an element of truth to the legend. If that was the case, then perhaps more of the old stories held true. One in particular rose in Jerek's mind: the sacred flame would not harm a true follower of Ulric.

Twisting the words of Magnus the Pious, Jerek whispered, 'If I am wrong then the flames will surely consume me,' and thrust his hand into the fire.

He stared at the flame and his flesh, feeling the agonising heat as it seared at his hand, but the flame did not burn him. Jerek withdrew his unblemished hand.

'Then perhaps I am not damned,' he said, turning his hand over to examine the perfect skin.

Despite the sickness in his gut, Jerek left the temple convinced that the Wolf God had given his blessing.

THE SIGN OF a hangman's gibbet and noose swung in the night breeze. The Last Drop was not the kind of establishment that Jerek Kruger had frequented in life. In death, it was made for Jerek von Carstein. Its iniquities were many and varied, and for that reason soldiers and thieves alike loved it. Jerek pushed open the door and stepped into the thick pall of smoke and stale ale that filled the taproom.

No one looked up; no one challenged him. The Last Drop was that kind of place. Patrons kept themselves to themselves. There was nothing to be gained by idle curiosity, but there was everything to lose.

Roth Mehlinger sat alone beside the fire, his gnarled hand closed around a tankard. Five years had worn hard on the soldier. After all that he had seen, it was no surprise he had sought solace in his cups. Jerek sat himself at the table beside the man who had, in life, been his right hand, the Grand Master's Shadow.

Mehlinger had always been a loner, dour and taciturn.

The man's guilt at their failure was etched deep into his face. Black hair hung lank and greasy over his eyes. The Knights of the White Wolf had failed him, or he had failed them. It didn't matter. He was alone, and as Jerek had drummed into them over and over, alone they were weak, only when they stood together were they giants.

It was difficult to see the man like this.

'Hello, old friend.'

Mehlinger looked up from his drink. He didn't seem unduly surprised to see the dead man. 'Come to haunt me have you, Wolf?' He raised the tankard in a toast, 'Here's to the dead who won't stay dead, eh?'

The man was drunk. Jerek pitied him. It wasn't an emotion he was used to feeling. Indeed its wrongness only reinforced the message of the sacred flame – his humanity had not yet been expunged. There was some good in him, enough, at least, to feel pity for a friend.

'It doesn't have to be this way,' Jerek said.

'No? You mean I don't have to live through it day after day, drinking myself into oblivion and *still* unable to escape my damned daemons? You think I come here for fun?' Mehlinger waved expansively, his gesture taking in the whole taproom. 'You think these people are my new friends? I don't and they aren't. I come here to drink myself to death, maybe then I can escape, eh? Maybe then...' The irony of his own words was lost on the drunk Mehlinger.

'Come with me, Roth. Be my shadow once more.'

'Nah, got good drinking still to be done. You go haunt one of the others for a while, leave me in peace.'

'Come with me,' Jerek said again, pushing his chair back and standing.

'Can you make it all go away? Can you make it disappear? Can you take the things I lived through from my head and make me forget them?'

'I can,' Jerek promised.

'Ah, what the hell,' Mehlinger muttered, dragging his chair back. He staggered and almost fell, but Jerek reached out and steadied him. 'Let's go then. Look at me, going for a walk with my ghosts and leaving half a tankard of ale on the table to boot. Must be losing my mind.'

They left the alehouse together, Mehlinger leaning heavily on Jerek's shoulder for support. He led the old soldier away from the front door and the softly sighing sign, and down a narrow alleyway. Jerek pushed the soldier up against the wall, hard, and forced his head back to expose the pulsing vein at his throat. He sank his teeth in, drinking hungrily from his last living friend, gorging himself until Mehlinger was seconds from succumbing to death, and then he relinquished his bite, the soldier sagging in his arms.

'Join me, Roth. Feed on me.'

They shared the Blood Kiss.

He had fed on humans before, but this was different. This was intoxicating. This was exhilarating, but even as he felt his tainted blood mingle with Mehlinger's, he tasted the last shreds of vibrancy that had been the man's life. As it faded his gut twisted and clenched, the last vestiges of his humanity rebelling against the siring. Jerek gagged, coughing up Mehlinger's blood, but it was too late. The kiss had been shared.

In that instant, Jerek von Carstein hated the man that had been Kruger and Jerek Kruger loathed the beast that had become von Carstein.

'Why?' Mehlinger gasped, the vampire's blood running from his mouth. 'Why did you do this to me?' Hatred blazed in his eyes as he sank to his knees, dying.

Jerek couldn't answer him, but he knew then that he couldn't do it, he couldn't sire another soul into this unlife he lived.

'I am sorry,' he whispered into his friend's ear as the last breath of life escaped his lips. 'I am so sorry. I will be here when you wake,' he promised.

He saw out the night cradling the dead man in his arms. He hated the thing von Carstein had made him, but that was who he was now: the Wolf was dead and in his place walked a monster.

An hour before dawn, Mehlinger awoke.

CHAPTER SIX
All On A Summer's Night

NULN
The Dog Days of Summer, 2056

A NATURAL BALANCE asserted itself between Skellan and the stranger as they travelled. By night, they ran as wolves, sharing their kills and feeding off the beasts of the field, but the blood of the lamb and fox and deer was no substitute for the blood of virgins or whores.

The hunger for real blood, the thick, intoxicating stuff of life, lured them into the villages and towns along the roadside.

The richness of it was impossible to resist.

It was in their nature to hunt and feed, but both revelled in the bringing of death and the intimacy of feeding. Any flesh, any blood, would have sufficed, but the pair developed a preference when it came to their kills. They liked them young and ripe for the taking, not soiled old hags. So they hunted the daughters and sisters, coming up on them in the dark, dragging them down into the dirt, tearing at their skirts as they kicked and struggled. Their desperation heightened the thrill of the kill. It didn't matter if they were farmer's daughters or the porcelain-skinned brats of the aristocracy, they begged and pleaded just the same as the vampires sank their teeth into them and they tasted every bit as delicious.

In Kemperbad they feasted on the blood of sixteen virgins in the shrine of the goddess Shallya while the statue of the goddess herself wept her perpetual stony tears.

They delighted in the profanity of it, defiling a holy place, ravaging the little mothers of the shrine while they cried out. It was more than death, more than merely taking lives. It was a ritual. It was a twisted glorification of all things beautiful, since they took only those closest to perfection, those who exemplified the feminine ideal. They dined on exquisite corpses. They sated their hunger on innocent meat, and they worshipped at the divine altar of sex, with passion.

They didn't just kill: they devoured.

They discarded the dead one by one, tossing them aside as they moved on to the next. The dead women sprawled across the cold stone floor, arms and legs akimbo, necks broken, the only colour on their otherwise alabaster-pure complexion the twin rivulets of blood that dribbled from the puncture wounds in their throats.

They became a plague on the countryside, leaving a trail of death in their wake.

In Striessen they savoured the kills, taking several nights to seek out the few jewels in the town's crown: three girls, the daughter of a pawnbroker, the sister of the silversmith and the young wife of a chandler. They were by far the most delicious of Striessen's offerings. Where Skellan was hungry for the kill the stranger urged him to take it slowly and savour it.

'Anticipation serves to heighten the sweetness of the feast,' he explained, standing on a street corner beneath the chandler's sign. A candle burned in the window above invitingly.

'Let me take her.'

'No, my eager young friend, we wait. We draw it out slowly, ounce by precious ounce, tasting it as it drips down our throats like the sweetest elixir.'

'I am hungry.'

'And you will be hungry again tomorrow. We wait. We are not savages. There should be beauty in all that we do, even killing.'

'You sound like *him*.'

'In many ways he was the best of us all, anyone who would be ruler of the vampire nation would do well to study his philosophies.'

'He was weak. At the death, when it came down to it, he was weak.'

The stranger shook his head, like a teacher disappointed in an otherwise apt pupil.

'It takes great strength to rule wisely. All it needs is a hint of weakness to succumb to your most base desires. Think on it.'

'I will, and you know what else? Tonight I will feed.'

With that, Skellan had scaled the outside of the building, climbing the clematis and other vines that clung to the façade of the old house, and tapped at the window.

His smile had opened the window. Her screams had been heard across the town.

The following night, he had claimed the silversmith's sister. This time they had sat on the thatch of her roof, deliberating the effect the chandler's wife's death had had on the small town. Skellan savoured the panic it had injected, while the stranger saw it as the death knell on their brief sojourn amongst the cattle. They would have to move on instead of being left alone to graze selectively for weeks and months more.

The girl's death was a bloody affair. She died in the window, shattered glass digging into her breast even as she sank down onto the wooden frame, the life leaking out of her as Skellan fed.

The pawnbroker's daughter was the last of the true beauties of Striessen to die.

'This one is mine,' had the stranger said as Skellan stood on the threshold.

'Is she now?'

'Yes.' And the way he said it left Skellan in no doubt that he was serious. 'Wait outside. Go find a goat or something.'

He left Skellan at the bottom of the stairs. The girl didn't scream once, although she was far from silent. By the sound of it, she gave herself willingly to the stranger, urging him to take her life.

It was too easy.

They left Striessen before dawn. The stranger urged caution, but Skellan was buoyed up on the adrenaline of the feast and argued for one last stop on the way home: Nuln.

They had to wait before they could enter the old capital. The wooden bridge had been drawn up to allow a three-mast schooner passage down the Reik. In places, the wall that ringed the city was low enough so that raiders would only need carts to scale them, not ladders.

It was easy to see why Nuln had fallen at the feet of Vlad von Carstein, where Altdorf had stood in stubborn defiance. The cities were not comparable. Nuln itself was a city within a city, an ancient core at the heart of the new city, still ringed by the crumbling walls that marked the boundary of Nuln's old town. The old streets of the Old City were so narrow that the two could barely walk side by side, so naturally, this was the busiest district of the city. The place was a curious hodgepodge of architecture. Each new generation had crowded in its own peculiar buildings, cramming them into spaces where there weren't really spaces, making the streets claustrophobic and unpleasant. Even as night gathered, the air was thick with the smoke of blacksmith's fires and the acrid tang of the tanner's newly treated hides.

Women of dubious repute congregated around the streets between the Merchants Gate and the City Gate, calling out to passers-by who looked as if they had coin to spare on a bit of rough and tumble.

Skellan drank in the many and varied pleasures of Nuln with relish. The lure of the big city called to him.

On every corner there was a feast to devour. Every night for two weeks, Skellan stepped out, walking amongst the prostitutes as they worked the streets, feeding in the dark alleys before dawn, and disappearing into the remnants of the night while the stranger watched, biding his time, being careful to select the finest blood rather than the vinegar that Skellan drank so greedily.

It was no surprise that the spires of the great city inspired the pair to new heights of cruelty.

In the course of a single night, they changed the city forever. The ruling family, Liebowitz, was more than merely ousted, it was defenestrated, despoiled and degraded. Their deaths became the thing of legend.

'The Family Liebowitz will mourn this night for centuries to come.'

'You give the cattle credit for a long memory. In my experience, they fart, roll over and forget it ever happened,' Skellan said. They stood in the centre of Reiks Platz, listening to the chestnut vendor struggling to sell the last of his wares. The smell of caramelised sugar was a tantalising counterpoint to the all-pervading reek of leather.

'That, my friend, is because you do not give them something worth remembering. It's all petty pain with you. Back alleys, brothels, and smoke houses. It lacks any panache. Who cares if a prostitute dies? Who cares if some fool strung out on laudanum winds up dead in a gutter? Tonight, we walk into the houses of the rich and the beautiful, bringing death to the fore. We show the city that no one is safe, not even in their own home. The death we offer can find them anywhere.

That is how you make them remember. You make death visible. You make it *frightening.*'

'I still don't see what they have done to deserve such thorough extermination? In every other killing you preach caution, but now you would have us throw it to the wind.'

'It is personal, a debt to be repaid, in full. I will say no more on it. Tonight, we sup on the blood of the aristocracy and see if it is truly blue. No more back street whores. The Family Liebowitz may rule the city for a few hours more, but their fall will be spectacular, and the people of Nuln will remember this night like no other. Tonight, we dine in a style befitting who we are, my friend.'

And they did. They killed both men and women, but they only fed on the women.

Two men died in their beds, fat with the gluttony of the truly rich, another had his neck broken and was thrown down the stairs, two more were given lessons in flight that they failed to master and died sprawled out across the cobbled streets.

The dead were not left to rot.

Together, Skellan and the stranger hauled them up to the rooftops where they impaled the corpses on thatching spikes and lightning rods, making scarecrows out of them. Seventeen more men died that night, only to be mounted like stuffed animals along the rooftops of the old town, but it wasn't about the men. The women suffered fates worse than death and degradation.

In all, they dined on eleven Liebowitz women.

As with their men, the corpses were stripped and impaled, upside down, through the mouth and down the throat, and left to feed the birds on the rooftops, but not before the pair had savoured their flesh to the fullest.

Even in the grip of the blood frenzy, the stranger was ruthlessly selective in his treatment of the cattle. He took only the best meat for himself, leaving Skellan to please himself with his cast-offs even as he moved on in search of better game.

Skellan followed him into the last house, the one the stranger had claimed for himself, into the woman's bed-chamber, to where she lay beneath the sumptuous scarlet covers of her divan. The stranger moved silently to the bedside and knelt, whispering something in her ear that caused her lips to part and a forlorn sigh to slip between them.

Skellan lurked in the shadows, tasting his own blood as he bit into his lip. The stranger captivated him as he guided the woman, little by little, towards a willing death, until she finally loosed a single primal scream as the vampire's teeth found her pulse and penetrated her supple flesh.

The woman's blood fresh on his lips, the stranger held her beautiful corpse in his arms, and turned to where Skellan lurked in the shadows. His smile was cold. He touched his fingers to her blood where it ran down his chin and began to daub his name, in her blood, on the wall above her bed.

Three words, written in blood: Mannfred von Carstein.

In that moment, Skellan understood the nature of the stranger's power and the terror that this hidden message would inspire, claiming ownership of the slaughter as it did.

She was the one they didn't carry up to the roof. Instead they arranged her corpse so that it looked as if she merely slept deeply. It was a fragile illusion destroyed by the blood on the wall above her head.

Part of Skellan resented the way the vampire treated him like some stupid lackey, but a bigger part of him admired the stranger's economy of slaughter and the ritual aspect of it. The cattle would wake in the morning to find thirty-three naked corpses impaled on the rooftops of Nuln. It was a message that would be impossible to ignore.

As Skellan walked away from the last of the Liebowitz houses, he wondered how many of the onlookers would understand the full irony of the message: that these deaths mirrored the fall of Vlad himself. It was not only savage: it was beautiful.

The stranger was right: the cattle of Nuln would remember this night.

The stranger. He had to stop thinking of him as that.

The stranger had a name now: Mannfred von Carstein.

Mannfred, Vlad's firstborn.

The moons were still high in the sky, shining their silver on the streets as Skellan and Mannfred shifted into lupine form and bounded away from the city. After the frenzy of blood, the fresh air was intoxicating. They ran on into the night, taking shelter before dawn in a hermit's cave once they made certain the old man had no more use for it.

They slept the whole day through, only waking deep into the following night. Despite the feast, they were both starving and cold.

Skellan banked up a bundle of dry sticks and lit a small fire in the mouth of the cave. Outside, wolves howled, insects preened, their mating calls another layer to the music of the night, and bats flitted about the treeline.

'I know who you are,' Skellan said, turning his back on the night.

'I never tried to hide it,' Mannfred said, toying with the ring that he wore on his right hand. It was his only concession to adornment; he wore no other jewellery, no chains or broaches or other trinkets, only this solitary ring, which, Skellan had noticed, whenever he grew pensive he toyed with.

'But you never told me.'

'Oh, but I did, my young friend. I did. I told you many times, but you were not listening. I was his first, I said. He may not have loved me most, but he loved me longest, I said. I never hid who I was.'

Skellan poked at the flames with a stick. He watched as the ashes scattered, conjuring a short-lived flame sprite. Finally he said what was on his mind.

'Why are you here? Why are you hunting with me? Why aren't you in Drakenhof claiming your kingdom? It's rightfully yours.'

'Indeed it is. I am here because there is nowhere else at this moment that I would rather be. I am not embroiled in a bitter war with our own kind because it is not time yet. Believe me, there is a time for everything.'

Skellan looked sceptical.

'You have spent time in the form of a wolf, I know, but how much time have you actually spent as a wolf?'

'Is there a difference?'

'Oh yes, in the form of a wolf, you shroud yourself in wolf's clothing – it is merely for appearance's sake. If you surrender yourself, relinquish your grip on your identity and truly *become* a wolf, the petty concerns of this life cease to be important. You live to hunt and feed. You cease to be you and in turn take on the identity of the pack.'

Skellan nodded.

'What happens when the alpha male dies and the pack is left leaderless?'

'The survivors fight for dominance.'

Mannfred nodded. 'They fight amongst themselves, the contenders asserting their right to rule by strength and cunning. What some don't realise is that sometimes the fight needs more cunning than it does brute strength. Remember that every wolf is potentially deadly, even the runt of the litter. They circle and circle, looking for a moment to strike, and when that weakness arises they are bloodthirsty and brutal. They descend as one, bringing the opposition down, and pick the corpse clean. In any pack, the fight for leadership is bitter, and make no mistake, it could easily cripple the pack if too many males lock themselves into the fight for dominance.'

'Is that what you are doing? Using your cunning instead of your strength?'

'Fights are won by strength of arms, young bucks lock horns, it is all about bravado, swaggering and intimidating your enemy, but wars aren't won that way. Wars are a long game won by strategy. Answer me this: why wrestle all of my brothers, Pieter, Hans, Fritz and Konrad, when I need only fight one of them? The others will have weakened that one. You see, my friend, there are times when it is better to stand back and watch them struggle, and then challenge the winner when the others are dead and gone, don't you think?'

Skellan couldn't fault the logic.

'It makes sense. So while you sit by idly, they give in to the wolf and strive for dominance, not for a moment suspecting that you are waiting in the wings to dethrone the victor.'

'Something like that, yes.'

'It sounds exactly like that.'

'Only I have no intention of waiting idly in the wings, as you so elegantly put it. There are things I must do, preparations that involve me going away for a while. They will be occupied, no doubt, chasing their own tails.' Mannfred reached inside his pack, drew out an oilskin-wrapped package and began loosening the ties that bound it together. Tenderly, he peeled back the skin to reveal a book. Laying it on the ground between them, he turned to the first page.

Skellan couldn't read the scratchy symbols that scrawled across the top sheet – the ink had faded, soaking into whatever it was the book's maker had used for paper. It wasn't parchment, that much Skellan *could* tell.

Mannfred traced his finger over the crude design, lingering almost lovingly over the tail of what appeared to be a comet drawn in the centre of the page.

'There is power in this. More power than a fool like Konrad or an oaf like Pieter could ever dream of.

While they strut and preen, and try to impress the lesser breed, let *us* learn from those long since departed. It was in this book, and in nine others like it, that Vlad found his strength. The wisdom of this book is unparalleled, but then its author was a genius. This is a distillation of power. The glimpse these pages give into the Dark Arts is unlike anything you can imagine, Skellan. With these words alone Vlad raised an army from the bowels of the earth: words, not swords. Words.'

'And you would use them?'

'I'd be a fool not to, and I may be many things, but I am no man's fool. These are only the tip, like a berg of ice. These incantations offer a hint of the power that lies below the waterline. It is intoxicating, my friend, and I admit, I want it all, but I am not ready for it, not yet. I'd drown before I'd even tapped an ounce of this power.'

'Then what good are they? All the spells in the world and you can't use them.'

'Oh I could use them, I could raise a great nation of the dead, I could despoil the lands of the living, turning it into a vast waste. With this power, I could shape the world to my whim, but in the process, I would lose myself. With great power comes far greater danger. Already I crave the power these offer. The temptation is huge to simply absorb all they have to offer and avenge our people, becoming a scourge on the Empire. It is already a canker in my unbeating heart. The thirst is unquenchable. I could destroy them. I could raise a glorious army with myself at its head. I could be worshipped and feared. The cattle would bow down at my feet and my enemies would tremble at my might. I want all of this and more – so much more. I dream of it at the height of day, and I dream of it as the shadows stretch towards dusk, I dream of it and I taste it, so real are my dreams. This world is mine, Skellan, mine for the taking. In my dreams I hold dominion. I rule.

'But, I am no fool. This power would consume me. I couldn't hope to contain it, not as I am. A wise man knows his limitations and weighs them against his ambitions. I know mine. I am no match for the maker of this book or the dark wisdom he imparted. Not yet, but I will be… I will be.'

'I believe you,' Skellan said, and he did.

'And yet, you have no idea what it is you see before you. Blind faith. Well, my blind friend, let me open your eyes: these incantations were crafted by the first and greatest of the necromancers, the supreme lord of the dead himself. Now do you see?'

'Nagash,' Skellan hissed through clenched teeth, the name as ephemeral as a dying breath as it faded into the flames.

'Nagash,' Mannfred agreed. 'With this power I could rule the world of the living, metamorphosing it into a land of the dead. With this power I would be unstoppable. However, with this power, I would condemn the thing I am, I would banish whatever it is that passes for my soul, and become *him*. I have seen how his magic works, seen the traps woven into the spells to draw the reader deeper and deeper into the darkness until it is too dark for him to find his way back to himself. I would not sacrifice myself for all the power in the world.'

'We have no souls. We are empty.'

'Do you believe that? Do you feel empty?'

Skellan didn't have an answer for that. He stirred the fire again, thinking about it. The power for revenge, for dominion over the Empire of the Cattle was there, before them, ripe for the taking. All he had to do was reach out and take it, but he couldn't.

As much as he wanted to, he couldn't bring himself to accept the gifts that the book promised.

'Then the book is useless,' he said, casting the stick into the heart of the flames.

'Today, yes, but who knows about tomorrow? Our paths, for the moment, lie in different directions, but they will merge again, of that I have no doubt. At dusk, I will leave you.' He raised his hand as if to forestall any argument. 'I must walk this road alone. While I am gone, though, I would have your help. I will need eyes and ears in the court of the Vampire Count so that when the time comes I will be able to claim what is rightfully mine.'

'You would have me be your spy?'

'Not only my spy, but so much more than that. The new Count will need friends. I would have you be one of them. I would have you get close to him, close enough to feed his uncertainty and bolster his ego. We have hunted together, Skellan. I know you as I know all of my brothers. Play to your strengths, make yourself indispensable and you'll have the pack dancing to your tune.'

'What is to stop me, then, from turning my back on you, using this influence to betray the surviving von Carstein's and taking the pack for myself? They know me. They have fought beside me. They have hunted with me, but, more than anything, they fear me because I have none of their weakness.'

'Yet, you were captured and they run free. You may not have their weaknesses, but you have your own, believe me. What stops you from claiming the pack? Two things: first, the sure and certain knowledge that when I return from the Lands of the Dead you will have to face me. I suffer no compunction when killing to get what I want, even when I have hunted with the victim. Second, the fear that will eat away at you that when I do return I will be both the Mannfred you know, and so much more. That will suffice. Be my instrument in the Court of the Blood Count. Be the voice in the night that drives my enemies to madness or be my enemy. It is your choice, Skellan.'

CHAPTER SEVEN
In The Court of the Crimson Count

DRAKENHOF, SYLVANIA
The Dying Light of Autumn, 2056

KONRAD VON CARSTEIN had surrounded himself with sycophants and fools, and he knew as much, but his need for platitudes and praise outweighed his need for forthright speaking. For that he had Jerek and his Hamaya. For everything else, he had the fools with their forked tongues.

He understood the nature of battle. He understood the need for wise council and truth speakers. He understood the need for strength and the need for cunning, but most of all, he understood that he was alone, and could trust no one.

He had seen men die – he had killed them. There was a natural order to it: the wolves slaughtered the lambs. It had always been that way, and it always would be that way. It was a simple philosophy, but its simplicity made it no less telling. Konrad knew better than most that the difference between life and death was a single heartbeat. He knew that the others would bring him down if they could, if they thought for a moment that he was a lamb. It was the nature of the beast: the strongest survived, and in strength became godlike, forcing those weaker to bow and scrape before them.

He felt the stirrings of fear as he prowled the passages of the castle. There were reminders of his heritage everywhere, of who he was, and what he was. The portraits of Vlad and Isabella had been vandalised, slashed with knives, the gilt frames bent out of shape. Some lay splintered on the floor while others hung on the wall still, a gallery of tattered canvases mocking the dead. He took no pride in being Vlad's get. Vlad had failed. He had succumbed to the most basic of all human weaknesses: love. It had been his undoing. Konrad would not fail. That was the only promise he made to himself. He would not fail.

Fear was good, it gave strength to the man who held it in his heart. It was a peculiar truth. He often heard others talk of fear as weakness, and every time, found himself believing the speaker to be a fool. A lack of fear was as potentially lethal as, say, panic or arrogance. Panic undermined a fighter, leaching away at the warrior's muscles, whereas arrogance left the warrior open to carelessness. No, no matter what they said, there was no shame in fear.

Konrad stared at the ruined face of his progenitor hanging from a broken frame. The knife had sliced through the canvas in a vicious X, dividing the face into four broken diamonds. In his vanity, Vlad had surrounded himself with his own likeness, needing the oils to remind him that he existed. They were not the same beast. Vlad had worn his cold arrogance like a shroud, but at the last, faced with the taunting of a simple mortal, he had surrendered to rage, and that anger had been his undoing. The dead Count had forgotten the simple lesson of fear. Had he harboured even an ounce of it for his enemy, he would never have fallen to the Grand Theogonist. His cardinal sin was in believing himself immortal. It was his vanity that led to it. He allowed himself to believe that he was special.

He had forgotten the truth: even the dead could die, and true death, *that* was worthy of fear.

Konrad turned his back on the man and continued on his lonely rounds of the ancient castle.

There were ghosts, of course, trace memories that lingered. He fancied he heard the laughter of Vlad's minions echoing from more than one chamber, only to open the door on an empty room and dust – so much dust. The sounds of women giggling and lusty calls of men in heat faded to nothing as he closed the doors and moved on.

He was alone, yes, but never truly alone. The ghosts of the conquered resided still in the old castle, clinging to the stones they had called home. Of course, people also surrounded him almost constantly, servants and sycophants ready to bend and scrape to his every whim.

It was a curious dichotomy. Konrad craved the very company that left him feeling so isolated and alone.

Then there were the cattle with their petty problems. They crawled like lice out of the woodwork, looking to him for salvation.

He was no one's saviour.

So, while they begged for mercy and petitioned for his wisdom to settle disputed land rights and grazing, or sought redress for the stupid thefts of loaves of bread and milk, he felt himself going slowly mad. He didn't care about them or their problems. They were cattle. They existed to be fed upon.

Why Vlad had thought them worthy of his time, Konrad had no idea. Perhaps it amused the dead Count to play lord and master? Konrad found no such amusement in the game, at least not when it was played straight. Changing the rules offered some possibilities. Improvisation was the secret to entertainment. Many of the petitioners he simply had thrown to the wolves, not caring if they were the wronged party or the wrongdoers. Their deaths were poor sport. They fell on their knees and begged and wept, a few even put up a fight, but in the end their bare hands were no match for the wolves' teeth. He saved a few special victims as treats for his necromancers to experiment on. It would teach the others a lesson: not to bother him with trifles.

Konrad savoured his reputation as a cruel count, even cultivated it: it kept the cattle in their place and sent out a clear message of dominance to his kin.

Konrad swept down the marble stairs of the grand staircase and through the great hall with its crush of penitents, ignoring the pleas and grubbing hands that reached out to touch him. He was in no mood for the smell of unwashed cattle – they stank and they made his home reek of bodily fluids. He paused, halfway through the hall, imagining the place aflame, the cattle burning away to nothing. There was something to be said for a cleansing fire. Smiling, he continued on his way.

The room he was looking for was buried deep within the bones of the old castle, beneath the cellars and the dungeons, even beneath the crypts. Once, it might have been a treasure house, but now it was a macabre gallery of sorts. The heads of thirty dead men, in various states of decay, were set on three, tiered rows of spikes. He knew every one of them, or had known every one of them well enough to kill them. Over the years, he had taken to collecting, as trophies, the heads of those that wronged him. It gave him grim satisfaction to know that in death they were his.

He visited the room regularly, using the captive audience to talk through his thoughts, looking for flaws in his reasoning. Talking aloud helped, and having an audience made the talking easier.

Only recently, they had started talking back to him.

It was nothing more than a word or two at first, little enough that he had doubted he had heard it in the first place. However, those precious few words soon grew into full sentences. He stopped hearing whispers of: 'murderer' and 'fiend' and found himself eavesdropping on conversations of treachery and betrayal as the heads argued amongst themselves.

'Still alive then?' the head of Johannes Schafer asked.

'Yes,' Konrad said, closing the door.

'We're surprised, considering,' the skull of Bernholdt Brecht mocked. Brecht was the oldest, his skin stretched like leather and smooth where the burns had taken his life. 'We hear things, you know, even down here.'

'You keep us locked in the dark, but we still hear whispers.'

The voices were a maddening chorus, their words interchangeable, their voices insubstantial and indistinct as they blurred around one another. Konrad could barely tell them apart as they became more animated.

'We know the darkest secrets of those around you.'

'You surround yourself with people who say what you want to hear, but behind your back they plot and scheme away, planning your downfall.'

'You place too much trust in those who say what you want them to say instead of giving you good council. You love the flatterers and ignore those who would serve you well. It will bring about your end.'

'You will not walk so tall then, dead man. Oh no, you'll be like us, stuck on a spike and left to rot, Morr take your soul to keep.'

'He already has it,' Konrad said, no hint of irony in his voice.

'No, it walks the long dark road searching for rest. It is locked in eternal torment, trapped between waking and sleep. There can be no rest, not for the killer in you, not for the boy in you or the man in you. Your soul withers in denial. The boy you were burns. The man you were burns. It never ends. The fire never ends. It consumes all that you were and all that you could have been.' The voices were in such a rush to talk that their words tumbled into a single demented voice, losing all separation and identity as they filtered through the thickness of Morr's veil.

'You aren't real. You think I don't know this? You are all in my head.'

'And you are in all of ours.'

'All of ours.'

'Yes. In all of ours.'

'If we are in your head our words must be the truth as you believe it to be. Welcome to your truth, Konrad. Welcome to your truth, a soul damned to the fires of hell, no rest for you, not when they send you on your way. Oh no. Not when the knife in the night cuts out your rotten heart and feeds it to you. No rest for you. Trust no one, not even your closest. Oh no, in the land of the blind, who can see the invisible threat? Who will remember you when you are gone and turned to dust? They circle around you, they are looking for a weakness to exploit, and they will find it. They will, because you are weak.'

'I am not weak.' Konrad lashed out, taking the head clean off the spike and sending it rolling across the floor.

The others laughed, a horrible mocking sound that threatened to deafen him.

He kicked the head viciously into the wet stone wall and walked down the line, hand drawn back to strike any head that goaded him.

'He will be first,' the last head said.

'Who will be?'

'The golden one, the one that shines brightest, the one that burns. All that glitters is fakery to lull the fool. To trust him is to die.'

Konrad paced the small chamber, clutching at his head as he tried to clear it, to think straight. The heads had never let him down before, in that regard their council was not easily discarded.

'How can I know?'

'Look in the mirror and see the lies reflected in the glass.'

Konrad laughed bitterly. 'I am surrounded by lies and liars, and none of them cast reflections. That is your wisdom? It is the curse of our kind to be invisible.'

'The invisible threat is the one that the wise man fears most, because they are like you. They are weak and their weakness drives them. They are not to be trusted, like snakes. Snakes, yes. They are snakes, not to be trusted. Oh no, not to be trusted.'

Konrad knelt, gathering the fallen head in his hands. Slowly and deliberately he impaled it back on its spike.

'This is insanity.'

'These are your thoughts, aren't they? This is your wisdom, spoken aloud. Trust no one. That is the wisdom we offer you. Heed it. You should. It could save your life.'

The voices fell silent as one.

There was nothing left to say.

Someone would betray him, someone close to him. Someone he thought of as a friend: the Golden One.

Konrad walked along the line of faces, studying them one at a time.

None spoke.

He prodded them with a finger, poked them, held either side of their jaws and tried to force them to speak, but they had nothing to say.

They had imparted their wisdom.

He wanted to dismiss what they had said, but he couldn't. They knew things they couldn't know. They knew things *he* didn't know.

And still they came to pass.

He sat a while in silence, thinking about what they had said. There was no great trick to it. All men of power surround themselves with advisors of ambition and hunger. Treachery is a part of their hearts. Few who strive for power are pure. To say that the seeds of his downfall were all around him was nothing more than his own paranoia talking, sowing the seeds of doubt.

Yet even the paranoid man can have good reason to fear those around him.

He was not von Carstein's only heir, but for now, he had the support that gave him power enough to hold off the threat of the others.

That might not always be the case. He would have to be a complete fool to think otherwise. Loyalties shifted. People could be bought and sold.

He was playing the long game. He needed to cement his power, become the undeniable master of the vampire nation.

While the others lived there was always the threat of usurpation. They were strong, among the strongest of Vlad's remaining kin. They were von Carsteins. The legacy of Vlad's tainted blood flowed in their veins.

The irony was that he needed to build up the strength of his people, yet his paranoia would have him tear out the heart of them to save his own skin. Given the chance, they would kill him. He knew that. He couldn't allow them the chance.

However, before the game played out, he would have to deal with them.

It was the only reasonable solution.

Konrad left the room of heads. He found Constantin in the library. In another life, the vampire had been a scholar with an uncanny grasp on the histories of the Old World.

'How goes it?'

'It goes,' Constantin said, scratching the back of his head with ink-stained fingers. Papers were spread out on the desk before him.

Konrad settled into a chair beside the first of his own gets. He felt an acute bond with Constantin. It was almost fatherly in nature, and like any father, he had high expectations and higher hopes for his son. He steepled his fingers and feigned interest in the peculiar sigils scrawled across the papers laid out in front of him.

The new library was just a small part of Konrad's legacy, but it was a vital part. With knowledge came power. By surrounding himself with great knowledge gathered from the four corners of the world, Konrad hoped to secure even greater power. He ached when he thought of the wealth of knowledge that his sire had lost in his folly. No doubt the damned Sigmarites had burned everything and Nagash's genius was lost to the world forever. It was a sickening thought. With a single spell, Vlad had raised an army from the dirt. What could he, Konrad, have done with that power at his disposal? That was Vlad's other sin: he had lacked imagination. Power existed to be unleashed.

'I see you are making progress.' Konrad gestured at the spread of papers.

'Cataloguing this would take twice my lifespan,' the scholar said, and then seemed to remember that his world had changed and he had time enough at last to read all of the books in this vast library, and then more. 'I suppose you are most interested in the histories?'

With Constantin's care, Konrad's library would rival any house of learning across the world when it came to tomes of magic and ancient knowledge. The histories were Konrad's own addition. With the scholar's aid, a new version of his life was being fed into the history of the old world. It didn't matter if the stories were lies, given time they would merge into truth. Konrad could create his own dynasty, tracing his blood back to Vashanesh, the first great vampire, and eventually enough people would believe the lies and the lies would become accepted truth. That was the wonder of knowledge; it was fluid, malleable.

Konrad had studied the history of the Empire as much as father, mother and circumstance forced upon any aristocratic boy – it didn't do to be ignorant amongst your peers. He knew of the plagues and the wars, the triumphs of spirit and the darkest days when all, it seemed, would come to an end. The dates and details had lost their clarity, but it didn't matter. With Constantin, he was slowly rewriting the world, one page at a time.

'And the... ah... other matters?'

Konrad had no gift for the arcane and so, of course, found himself utterly fascinated by it. He sought to learn everything he could from the likes of Constantin who had a natural grasp of it, but the more they explained, the less he understood.

'When documents of interest surface they are taken down to Immoliah Fey. She is most grateful for your sponsorship, my lord, and hopes to repay your trust when the time is most pressing.'

There was that word again: trust.

'Indeed, nothing in this world is given freely, Constantin. She knows that I expect something in return for my generosity. The day will come when I extract my price, whatever it may be. There is no trust involved in our relationship. I command her, master to servant. Tell me Constantin, is there trust in our relationship?'

'My lord?'

'Do you trust me, and more to the point, should I trust you?'

The scholar thought about it for a moment, which pleased Konrad. It wasn't an automatic response. He wasn't kow-towing to his lord. He was weighing up the various aspects of their relationship. If that was not a sign of trust, what was?

'No, my lord. I fear there is little or no trust between us. For my part, I live in fear that I shall displease you and suffer the fate so many others have. You brought me into this life, and blood aside, this life is not such a bad place to be, but there is no trust there, only fear. For your part, I suspect that you covet that which you do not have, in this case, that would be knowledge.

You see these papers and you despise the fact that they mean nothing to you. You hate the weakness that highlights in you. It means, despite your strength, that you are the lesser man in at least one regard, so, you intend to leach out what you can, and then crush me when you have bled me dry. There is no trust there, only bitterness.'

'You are a perceptive man, Constantin.'

'For all the good it does me, my lord.'

'Ah, but you see, ours is a healthy relationship, is it not? We have a respect for one another, founded on fear perhaps, but it is a mutual respect. We need each other.'

'One day my usefulness will come to an end,' Constantin said, picking up his quill and dipping it in the inkwell beside the open book, 'and that is the day that I die.'

'Then it is up to you to make yourself useful, is it not?'

'I try, my lord,' Constantin said.

'I would have you write a ballad, something heroic. It would be good to have troubadours singing of my triumphs, don't you think?'

'It shall be done,' Constantin said. 'Your legend shall be sung across the land.'

'You are a good man, Constantin. I hope you will always be as useful to me.'

'As do I, my lord.'

Konrad pushed his chair back and rose, pausing midway as if struck by an impromptu thought. He nodded to himself. 'At tonight's feast I would have you join the top table.'

'It would be an honour, my lord.'

'See if you can't have something to perform, there's a good man.'

'As you wish, my lord, although it may be a little… ah… hurried.'

'I have full confidence in you, Constantin. You won't let me down.'

The scholar began to scratch hastily at the page in front of him, only to score out the line he had written. Konrad left him to work in peace.

THE FEAST ITSELF was a drab affair, unlike the banquets he had enjoyed in life. The Hamaya had selected ten lucky penitents to be the centrepiece of the feast. They were stripped and bled slowly, one by one, their thick red blood decanted into goblets and passed among the creatures at the top table, still warm. Jongleurs juggled and took pratfalls, but it was all rather dull. Konrad was bored by the whole affair. He gave a lazy wave and the performers were dragged from the stage, joining the delicacies on offer. Their deaths raised a smile from the Vampire Count.

'Some entertainment at last,' he said, leaning over to Pieter.

His brother grunted.

'You always were easily entertained.'

Pieter had been changed by his days in the Drak Wald. They all had, but Pieter more so than the rest of his twisted mockery of a family. He had regressed, become almost animalistic in his mannerisms, and he fed as though every meal might be his last. It was disgusting.

He had made his play for power in the forest, challenging Jerek's right to lead them to safety. The Wolf had slapped down the challenge, effectively emasculating Pieter. He was by far the weakest of them now, reduced to sneaking around, sniffing for victims in the dark like some low hunter, a ferret or a stoat, or some such animal used to living in the filth of humankind.

Emmanuelle, Pieter's wife, was a different monster altogether. He could see why Pieter had chosen to sire her. It was not for beauty; she was interesting more than attractive and the angles of her face were all slightly askew. No, Pieter had sired her for the woman she had been. Even now, the mortal shone through, eclipsing the immortal. With her lips rouged by fresh blood and her eyes wells of lost souls, it was easy to see that in life the woman must have been enchanting. In death, she was magnificent.

Beside her, Hans looked less than amused. Of them all, he was perhaps most like his sire. There was an edge of detachment about him, but it cracked easily beneath his vile temper.

Jerek lurked in the shadows, not joining them at the top table. He never did. Hans could not stand the Wolf. He made no secret of his disgust that Vlad should have soiled the bloodline with a brute like Jerek. In mock deference, Jerek chose to put himself as close to Hans as he could at any given time, stoking the embers of the vampire's temper. He would serve as Hans's personal bodyguard at feasts, knowing it riled Hans. He felt, Konrad was certain, that his own place in the family was threatened by the last of Vlad's gets. It was difficult for Hans to be the bigger man. At

times, he was curiously childish, like a brat that had
been spoiled and subsequently found it maddening
not to get his own way.

Fritz, the last of the brothers, sat beside Constantin;
he was the sun to Hans's moon. Where Hans was
sullen and took to brooding, Fritz was gregarious and
garrulous. He surrounded himself with a coven of
gets, seven glorious women who crawled all over each
other to satisfy even his most basic whim. In life he
had been a hedonist, in death he satisfied his every
desire, no matter how extreme.

Lesser vampires sat at benches around the walls,
where they satisfied themselves with some of the
local meat.

'Bring on the dancing girls,' Fritz said, clapping his
hands. His seven gets moved to centre stage, dancing
with veils of finest silk, their movements supple and
erotic as they danced for their father-in-death. Fritz
crossed his hands across his belly and sat back to
enjoy the show.

Konrad stared at the women. They made him
uncomfortable with their provocative dance. He saw
his mother's disapproving shade behind them, her
twisted face shattering the frisson of intensity for
him. Still, he watched as they moved, bringing out
curved swords that they placed on the floor and
adopted into the dance, bringing a dangerous edge
to the sensuality of their movements.

Breathless, Konrad watched as the swords flashed
and the skin tantalised, and then it was over and the
seven women threw themselves to the floor to the
rapturous applause of Fritz. Others joined in as the

women rose, and soon the great hall was full of appreciative applause. Konrad stood, bringing his hand down for silence. His control over the crowd was complete. He nodded.

'I think it is time we partook of another delight, having stuffed our faces with fresh meat, and satisfied our eyes with these young ladies. It is time to look to the future. After that, I believe young Constantin wants to treat us to a ballad of his own creation. First though, the soothsayer, please.'

Two of Konrad's Hamaya escorted a filthy little man between them. He led a goat on a rope up to the top table and bowed stiffly. The goat was little more than skin and bones, and its master looked no healthier.

Pieter stifled his giggles.

Hans shook his head in disgust.

Fritz clapped delightedly, while Constantin, at the end of the table, looked decidedly uncomfortable.

Emmanuelle was looking at Konrad, not the curious little man and his goat. He found it impossible to look away. Was it wrong to covet his brother's get? He was sure it was, but then, so much of the very best things in life were wrong. That didn't stop him from wanting them.

'My dark lord,' the soothsayer muttered, trying to claim Konrad's attention. 'Speak what you would know, and we will consult the omens.' He pulled a slim, gem-studded ceremonial dagger from the rope band cinched around his waist. He brought it to his lips and kissed the blade's edge. 'What is it to be, lord? What questions burn in your heart?'

The word 'burn' jarred in Konrad's head. It seemed to haunt him today. He turned to take in the little man. His skin was dark, although it was dirt not tan that muddied it, he was thinning on top and his beard was scraggy.

'I would know the future for House von Carstein, fortuneteller. Speak to me, man. You have us all on tenterhooks. What is the wisdom of the gods?'

Two of Konrad's loyal Hamaya lifted the goat onto the central table and held the beast by the scruff of the neck, covering its eyes with a hand until it calmed. The animal was understandably skittish. The thick tang of blood was heavy in the air.

'Hear our words, oh goddesses of discord, oh gods of dissension, show what the fates have in store for this great house, peel back the dark shadows, illuminate the path to wisdom, show us the clefts where failure lurks in wait, we ask this of you. Show us.' With that, the little man thrust the ceremonial dagger deep into the goat's belly, tugging on the blade until the animal's guts spilled out across the table, black and bloody as they slopped over the diners and their food, and spilled down onto the floor. The goat convulsed in his arms, its hooves kicking and sliding through the reeking string of guts. When the beast's death throes subsided, the soothsayer dumped its carcass on the floor and knelt to study the omens offered up by the animal's entrails still smeared across the table.

The soothsayer looked up, fear written bold in his ugly face. 'The omens are not good, lord.'

'Not good?' Konrad said, raising an eyebrow. 'Explain.'

The little man swallowed and rose to his feet. Even standing, he was no match for the Vampire Count. 'The guts are rotten, lord. The beast's flesh is putrid. This is a bad omen.'

'Indeed, perhaps we have another beast to hand that you can divine some mystical insight from its disembowelling.'

'This is ludicrous,' Hans objected. 'Must we sit through this chicanery? I for one have better things to do.'

'You will sit down,' Konrad said calmly.

Hans stood.

'I said you will sit down,' Konrad repeated, an edge creeping into his voice as he rose to meet Hans.

'I will do no such thing.'

'Brothers, brothers, let's just enjoy the show, shall we. Look, they're bringing in a sheep to gut. This ought to prove most entertaining, as our frightened little soothsayer looks to predict a glorious future to save his own skin.' Fritz stood between the pair. 'This really is unnecessary. Show some decorum, please.'

Grunting, Hans sank back into his seat. He made a show of teasing off his gloves one finger at a time and cleaning his nails with the tip of his knife, studiously not looking at the soothsayer as he gutted the sheep.

The animal's entrails were putrid.

Terrified, the little man looked up at the row of vampires sitting at the table before him. His tongue cleaved to the roof of his mouth as he struggled to speak the doom he read in the spilled guts.

'Betrayal lurks on every corner. Betrayal will be your downfall. Friends cannot be trusted.'

'Give me your knife, man,' Konrad said, coming round from behind the table.

He held out his hand.

'Now.'

The little man passed the vampire his thin-bladed knife, his eyes alert, darting with fear. Konrad enjoyed the momentary thrill of power that coursed through his body as he drove the point of the knife into the soothsayer's stomach. He opened the man up, even as the soothsayer screamed and tried to hold in the ropes of blue intestine as they spilled between his fingers.

'Now, I am no magician, but I suspect, looking at the signs here, that the future is bright for House von Carstein. Very bright indeed.' He kicked the dead man. 'I am equally sure that if he could speak, our soothsayer would agree. Alas, it seems the divination took rather a lot out of him.'

'Oh, this is preposterous,' Hans said, in disgust. He rose, picking up the leather gloves from the table. 'You are a disgrace to the family. Everything about you is vile. You are an aberration. You strut and pose, and act as if you are superior. You act as if you are *him*, but I have news for you, brother: you are not him. You are not worthy of his name. You are a disgrace. You always have been, you always will be. The soothsayer is right, if we follow you, we march willingly to our own doom!'

'How dare you,' Konrad said.

No one else moved as Hans came around the table and slapped Konrad across the face with one of the gloves.

'A duel!' Fritz cried out delightedly.

No one listened to him.

Still holding the bloody knife, Konrad, sneered and pressed the keen edge of the blade up against Hans's cheek. 'I could gut you here and now,' he rasped. He applied pressure to the blade, enough to cut the skin. It drew no blood. Konrad licked at the blade, tasting the soothsayer's blood. His smile was filled with predatory cunning.

'You could try,' Hans said coldly.

'Our brother is right, you have called me out. Your bloody sense of honour will be served in the last minutes before first light. We will settle this once and for all, *brother*. I will give you a few hours to regret the rashness of your actions, and then I will meet you in the duelling hall where your gets can watch me cut your heart out. Now get out of my sight.'

It was Fritz's idea to add fire to the spectacle.

They banked timbers up along both sides of the duelling hall and doused it in oil. As the duellists faced off, they would apply a torch to the wood and make things interesting.

'This is all so childish,' Emmanuelle said, taking her seat in the gallery. For all that she obviously disapproved, she was more than happy to partake in the proceedings.

'On the contrary,' Constantin said, leaning in to talk quietly. The duelling hall had odd acoustics. Words had a way of carrying further and louder than intended. 'A duel of honour is the last bastion of civilization, my lady. The situation might be contrived, but it is designed to maximise fairness of combat. It is likely that either Hans or Konrad will die in just a few moments, and in their death will prove the right of the victor. Scholars call it the last resort of law. It is a fascinating process.'

'It is barbaric.'

'On the surface, perhaps,' Constantin conceded, 'as all forms of war are, but beneath the surface it is immensely cultured. Consider the phrase "throwing down the gauntlet". This comes from the ritual of the duel. One accepts the challenge by picking up the gauntlet or glove, and there are, of course, many alternatives that could provide satisfaction. First blood, which of course means the first man to bleed would lose, but given our nature that is rather inappropriate, I am sure you would agree. Hans could of course have chosen to demand the ultimate price, to the death, in which there is no satisfaction until the other party is mortally wounded. He would equally have been within his rights to cease the duel when either of them is incapacitated, albeit not yet fatally.'

'You know a lot about fighting for a man who locks himself away with his books day and night.'

'It is precisely for that reason, my lady. There are things of interest in every book. The word "duel", for instance, could have derived from the old Imperial word for war, "duellum"; but it could equally have originated from the word "duo", giving new meaning to one-to-one combat. My personal favourite is actually much older, coming from Reikspiel, "teona": "to burn", "to destroy". The gauntlet of fire is a fitting addition to the proceedings. It certainly adds an element of danger to both participants. Only the strongest of our kind can resist fire. Many peasants still believe the way to destroy a vampire is to burn it.'

On the duelling floor, Konrad turned to stare at the pair in the gallery. Constantin lapsed into silence, assuming his constant chatter had disturbed his sire's preparation.

Grinning, Fritz leaned in from behind the pair. 'You know, Constantin, you really do need to get out more. I could send some of my girls to your library to… ah… help you forget about those books of yours for a while if you like? If nothing else, they could most certainly offer you a unique avenue of study for a while.'

'Fritz, you are incorrigible. Now, stop trying to corrupt young Constantin.'

'Yes, sister-mine. You take all the fun out of life, Emmanuelle, do you know that?'

On the floor, Konrad ran through a series of stretching exercises, both with and without his daemon sword in his hand. He moved with the grace of a natural gymnast, supple and lithe in the way he shifted from pose to pose. His balance complemented his graceful movement. The speed with which he ran through the exercises turned them into a beautiful kind of dance. The fluidity of the dance was hypnotic. There was an arrogance to it that was almost brutal. He took a silk cloth, tossing it into the air, and spun, bringing the sword to bear. The silk parted into two on either side of the blade and fell to the floor as Konrad sheathed the sword.

He looked up as Hans entered the duelling hall.

'I had begun to think you had come to your senses, brother. I am glad to see that I was mistaken. I will give you a moment to prepare. I would hate to be accused of foul play.'

Hans rolled his shoulders and then turned to bow to the gallery. He turned back to Konrad.

'You are an insufferable windbag, Konrad. It's time you were cut down to size.'

'Ah, but are you the man to do it, brother?' Konrad sneered. 'Personally, I think not. We shall see, soon enough. Seconds, light the fires, if you would.'

Two of Konrad's Hamaya touched their torches to the oil soaked wood, and a tunnel of fire was born.

The heat was staggering.

At either side of the duelling hall, a necromancer tapped the winds of magic, channelling the flame to make sure it didn't rage out of control. A single word from either of them would douse the conflagration before it could spread further into the castle.

Konrad drew his sword and stepped into the tunnel of flame.

At the other end, Hans matched him, his own sword a slim, slightly curved, blade that was unique to his native land. He touched the sword to his lips and stepped into the flames.

The duel was not graceful.

Hans launched a reckless lunge, the flames pressing in around his shoulders, which Konrad easily side-stepped and countered with a cuff from the pommel of the daemonic blade, and with an easy laugh meant purely to goad Hans into even more recklessness. It succeeded.

Konrad swatted aside two more thrusts from his brother, his smile broadening with each.

The only sounds in the duelling hall were the clash of blade on blade and the snap and crackle of the flames building into a genuine blaze.

Konrad allowed Hans a moment's respite, trading parries before he countered with his first serious attack. Hans was no match for either Konrad's reflexes or his swordsmanship. He had no intention of allowing his brother dignity in true death. He wanted the vampires in the gallery to see him for what he was: their better. He took three steps forwards, and rather than launch a feinted move, a combination of blows ending in a high cut, which Hans would have expected, he thrust hard, driving the daemonic blade into his opponent's upper arm. The blade pierced deep into the muscle, causing Hans to lose his grip on his own blade. The curved sword clattered to the floor. In that moment, Hans knew that he was dead.

Konrad showed no mercy.

Untouched by the flames licking around his feet, Konrad stepped in close, drawing Hans into a deadly embrace.

'You're dead,' he rasped, and then pushed his foe back so that he stumbled trying to catch his balance. With dizzying speed, the daemonic blade swept around in a vicious arc, cleaving Hans's head from his shoulders in a single cut.

Konrad didn't stop there.

He cut his fallen brother up, and piece by piece fed him to the flames, while the others looked on.

'He who burns brightest…' Konrad said, laughing. 'So much for the Golden One.' With the fire blazing around him, Konrad walked from the hall.

In the gallery, Fritz rose to his feet and applauded.

'That, my friends, is a true von Carstein.'

'That,' Emmanuelle said, 'you idiot, is a true monster.'

'One and the same, my dear: one and the same.'

'Your ignorance is dazzling, Fritz. Don't tell me you can't see what just happened.'

'Hans was a fool. He allowed himself to be manipulated into a fight that he had no hope of winning.'

'And next time it could be you, or Pieter, or me, or whoever, dear Konrad believes is a threat to his blessed reign.'

'I am no fool, sister-mine.'

'Oh, I think you have just proved that you are, Fritz.'

CHAPTER EIGHT
Slouching Towards Sylvania

THE BORDERLANDS OF SYLVANIA
The First Kiss of Snow, Winter, 2056

THERE WAS SOMETHING about the magician that made Kallad Stormwarden distinctly uncomfortable.

He was not like other manlings he had encountered. It wasn't that he was distracted and seemed to spend most of his waking hours lost inside his own head. It was not that the man was unreadable where most manlings wore their allegiances proudly, like badges of honour. It was not that the man spoke in cryptic rhymes of things that made little or no sense to the dwarf.

It was much more simple than that. Kallad did not *like* Nevin Kantor.

Still, he was necessary. Without the sorcerer, their pursuit would have been next to impossible. Kantor paused on the rise just ahead, apparently sniffing the air. The dwarf knew that the unnatural passage of the dead left a stink on the winds of magic, rich enough to be followed by a deaf, dumb and blind adept. Kantor had explained it to them on that first night, so many moons ago. The dead were an abomination and as such were reviled by nature. The winds were sensitive to the nuances of the world they flowed over, and picked up traces of nature's revulsion, fashioning a tainted ribbon that could, in theory, be tracked on Shyish, the sixth wind, all the way to the beasts themselves.

Kantor disappeared over the rise without looking back to see if the rest of the party followed.

Grunting, Kallad shouldered his pack and set off after the magician.

Kantor was tall, even for his kind, although it seemed that he possessed no more flesh than the soldiers that journeyed with them, which left him looking gaunt and emaciated by comparison. His hair was drawn up in a topknot and the sides had been shaved high above his ears, in the fashion of the corsairs.

The magician had led them to Nuln as the month slipped into Vorhexen. The butcheries of the vampire, Jon Skellan, were all too apparent inside the walls of the old town. The streets teemed with gossipmongers, and charlatans offering protection from the vampires with their gewgaws and talismans. The charms were of course useless, but the peasants were willing accomplices in the trickery, needing to believe that they offered some form of protection. Every other person they met in the streets wore the sigil of Sigmar on a chain around his neck. The rest carried more practical forms of defence: stakes, garlic cloves, bloodwort, wolfsbane, vials of water blessed from the temple fonts of their chosen deities, and silver. Merchants traded their share of the season's harvest for the silver to fashion into daggers and amulets. Superstitious fear gripped the city.

The conversations on every street corner returned again and again to the bloody fate of the ruling family, the Liebowitzes. Their bodies had been buried in the family mausoleum, face down, their coffins sealed over with huge slabs of stone.

No one was prepared to risk their return.

They had stayed in the city for four days, learning what they could from the gossips, but it was next to useless. Reports varied from Vlad von Carstein himself having returned to savage their city, to a vast horde of the undead descending in a single night's depravity. There were stories that informers working with the beasts had walked through the city during the day marking the houses for slaughter and making sure that members of the blue-blooded aristocracy were singled out.

In a peculiar way, the locals had come to think of the beasts as liberators as well as monsters.

This was a revelation to Kallad.

Nuln had a marked effect on the others. The sense of urgency that had gradually dwindled during the long weeks of walking returned. Memories of the butchery of the priests in the cathedral were fresh in the mind once more. Even Sammy, who had been a continuous chatterer, grew solemn and withdrew into himself during the days they spent in the old town. It gave Kallad another reason to hate the beasts they stalked.

They left Nuln with renewed purpose.

What none of them had expected was for the magician to tell them that the spoor he followed divided into two. It confirmed Kallad's greatest fear – they were tracking two vampires, not one: Skellan and the creature that had rescued him from the depths of the Sigmarite cathedral.

'The spoors are different,' Kantor explained. 'One is much more potent than the other. It is impossible to say which is our creature, meaning the one imprisoned by the priests, but of the two, the greater evil took the path leading south. The other, I would hazard, is returning to Sylvania.'

'So we have a choice,' Reimer Schmidt said, the young acolyte obviously not liking either of the options they faced. 'We track one beast back to its lair, where more of its kind will undoubtedly be waiting, or we follow the other south, wherever its path may lead. The other being the obvious master of the pair.'

'That's no choice at all,' Joachim Akeman said quite matter-of-factly. It was obvious that the cleric was resigned to meeting Morr along whichever road he travelled.

'We could return home,' Nevin Kantor suggested. 'We have seen what the beasts are capable of. What chance do we stand? We few against monsters capable of such savagery?'

'Aye, you could all run off home like cowards with your tails stuck between your legs. There's nothing stopping you, but I won't.' Kallad said. 'The only thing evil like this needs to flourish is for good men like us to do nothing. You can go home and hide if you like, but I won't. I'll walk into the belly of the beast if I have to. I'm killing that creature, or it's killing me. Make no bones about it.'

Korin Reth nodded. 'I'm in no great rush to meet my maker, but the dwarf has the right of it. I'll stand with him wherever he leads us.'

'Good man,' Kallad said. 'And' what about the rest of you?'

'I'm with you,' Akeman said.

'Me too,' said Reimer Schmidt.

Grimm's soldiers nodded one after the other, pledging themselves to the hunt.

'And what about you, magician?'

'One death is much the same as another,' Nevin Kantor said, without enthusiasm.

'Then it's settled. We go on. It dies, or we do. There's no going home. So tell us what you can, magician.'

'Not much more to tell, dwarf. The greater evil has taken the path south, the lesser monster has turned for home. Both, as far as I can tell, travel alone.'

'Well, that's something. Now then, we've got us two roads to choose from. Magician, what's your gut say? Which way did *our* vampire go?'

The sallow-faced mage gathered up a handful of grass and tossed it into the air. The blades fanned out and drifted on the breeze, each one following its own unique path.

'Pick a blade of grass, dwarf, any one, and toss it into the air. Then do it again, and again, and one last time, just to make the point.'

Kallad did as he was told. His green stems followed yet more trajectories. 'I'm guessing there's some kind of wisdom in the demonstration?'

'Indeed. How can we tell which way the next blade of grass will blow?'

'We can't.'

'Obviously. Each blade takes its own path. Like destiny, if you like. It is fated to fall precisely so, but we can predict its path, to an extent. We can test the wind,' Kantor moistened his finger and held it in the air for a moment. 'Wind's coming from the south-south-east, so there's a better than average chance that our blade of grass will drift this way.' He sketched a rough path with his finger. 'The wind isn't strong, but the grass is light, so it could well travel further than we'd expect. I'd guess it'll land around… here.' He marked out a spot with a small white stone. 'Another stem, if you would, dwarf.'

'What's this got to do with anything?' Korin Reth asked.

'Patience, priest. You'll see soon enough.'

Kallad tossed the stem into the air. It caught on the breeze and twisted, landing less than a hand span from the sorcerer's stone.

'Impressive,' Kallad conceded. 'So how does this help us, because I assume it does?'

'Oh, it does. It most certainly does. You see, we can apply the same logic to determining which path we should take.'

'What? Throw ourselves in the air and see which way we are blown?'

Reimer Schmidt chuckled.

'Not quite, if we assume that Skellan is the weaker of the pair, we can deduce that he was the one who returned to the safety of that cursed country.'

'And why would we assume Skellan is the weak one?'

'Because he was caged for the best part of two years, whereas the other one has been at liberty all this time, feeding properly and building its strength. From the disturbance in the winds, it is obvious that the stronger of the beasts went south. It isn't random at all, it is logic.'

'So you're sure the creature that killed them priests went across the border into Sylvania?'

'As sure as I can be, yes.'

'Then we head south.'

That surprised them.

'You mean east, surely?'

'No, I mean south. We don't want the runt of the litter, we want the master.'

'But if Skellan went east—'

'We go south,' Kallad insisted. 'Your man's right. Skellan must have been near helpless when the other one rescued him. That means the other one has to have been behind most of the killing in the cathedral. Stands to reason.' It wasn't a convincing reasoning, however, and Kallad knew it.

He had his own reasons for wanting to head south.

He knew that Skellan was a link between him and his father's killer, but he wasn't the murderer. Kallad's gut told him that this newcomer was more important to his continuing search, which meant going south.

It was a matter of strength; it always was with wild animals. These beasts were no different.

'Like I said, one death is as terminal as another, dwarf. You say we go south, we go south,' Nevin Kantor said, picking up the white pebble and drop-kicking it into the distance.

Now, almost a month after that parting of the ways, they were close to exhaustion, short on rations and water, and a long way from home. The animals were tired and they were reduced to taking turns riding in the cart.

Kantor led, as he had done every day since they had left Altdorf. Kallad and the others trudged along ten paces behind the sorcerer.

They had long since dispensed with the idle chatter of the road. Now, they walked on in silence. It had been that way for weeks. They had nothing left to talk about so they fixated instead on the road as it opened up ahead of them. Sammy trudged on at the dwarf's side without complaint, but it was obvious that he was missing the familiar streets of Altdorf, even without his parents there to take care of him.

As Kallad crested the rise, he saw that the sorcerer had stopped a short distance ahead. It was obvious something bothered him. Kallad turned and gestured for the others to hurry up.

'I can smell him.'

'How close?'

'As close as we've ever been, dwarf. It's less than a day since he came through here, the stink is *that* strong.'

'That would mean he bedded down somewhere around here.'

Kantor nodded towards a stand of trees less than a mile distant. It was dense enough to provide cover from the sun. 'That's my guess, right there.'

Kallad squinted as he surveyed the landscape that stretched out before them. He couldn't fault the sorcerer's reasoning.

They were close.

After all this time, they were close.

Sunset was still a good hour away, meaning that the vampire had nowhere to run. All they had to do was flush it out into the sun and the beast would burn.

'This is it, we've got it cornered.' He shouldered Ruinthorn. 'The bastard's down there and he's got nowhere to run, and if he so much as steps outta the trees the sun'll fry 'im.'

'Are you willing to risk your life on an old wives' tale, dwarf?' Kantor asked, pointing up at the setting sun. 'There's nothing to say he *will* burn except stories. I'd rather have something more substantial if I am going to be staking my life on its veracity.'

'Doesn't matter, last thing we want to do is flush him out. If we're lucky, he'll be sleepin' the sleep of the damned an' we'll be right on top of him before he even opens his eyes.'

'Or he's wide awake and waiting for us to walk into a trap,' Reth said, staring at the trees as if by sheer force of will he might see right through them to the dark heart of the wood where the vampire waited.

'Or he's wide awake and waiting for us,' Kallad agreed. 'Either way, it ends here.'

It wasn't a reassuring thought.

After months of searching there was no time left to prepare. They all knew what they had to do. There were only so many ways you could kill a vampire: beheading, burning, cutting its black heart out or dismembering the beast. It would be a bloody struggle, Kallad knew, and given the strength of the enemy, more than one of them would fall before the day was through.

It was a price he was willing to pay if it brought some satisfaction for the victims of Grunberg. The beast was accumulating a huge life-debt. Grunberg, the Sigmarite priests, the thief. Too many had suffered. Kallad thought of the thief, Felix Mann, and the courage he had shown facing up to his crippling. It was humbling in a way, to see such courage. It was almost easy to face death on a battlefield, to run headlong toward it matching skill for skill with the enemy but to leave the safety of the cathedral and try to find a new place for himself within the world was bravery beyond measure. Kallad wondered how the thief would cope without being reduced to begging; he had faith the thief would find a way. His resourcefulness would be tested, for sure, but Mann was a survivor. His encounter with the beast proved that.

It was time to start repaying the life-debt.

He set off across the field to the trees. The others followed.

With Ruinthorn in his hands he felt whole. On another day it might have disturbed him that he needed his axe to feel complete. Today it felt natural.

The vampire sat on an upturned stump of tree, waiting for them as they stepped into the clearing. There was no doubting that it *was* a vampire. The creature's face was aquiline, its features sharp, hard, but it was the eyes that gave the lie to the creature's vile nature. They were utterly soulless.

The vampire rose with deceptive grace and inclined his head towards Kallad.

'You were looking for me?'

'Aye, if you're the one responsible for the dead priests, we're looking for you.'

'Well, it seems that you have found me, dwarf. Now what do you and your merry band of misfits intend to do about it?'

Kallad bristled. The creature's arrogance was aimed at goading him into doing something stupid, he knew that, but knowing it didn't stop him from wanting to gut the fiend with his bare hands. He brought his axe to bear.

As one, the three soldiers from Grimm's guard drew their swords. The metal sang as it slid free of the sheaths.

'Eight against one, hardly a fair fight.' The vampire said, a wry smile playing over his lips. 'Let's do something to redress the balance shall we?' He bent, and in one fluid motion drew two wickedly pointed daggers from sheaths concealed in his left boot, and sent them end over end into two of the soldiers' throats. The men were dead before they hit the ground. The vampire tumbled to the left and came up on his right leg, flinging a third dagger into the eye of the last soldier. 'Now, that's better,' he said, rising smoothly.

In that moment Kallad froze.

The young acolyte, Reimer Schmidt, reacted first, hurling himself across the clearing at the vampire.

The creature didn't move as the young man brought his fist around and smashed a vial of blessed water from the font in the Sigmarite cathedral. The glass cut into the creature's cheek, but the water did nothing except wet his face.

'Your faith is weak, priest. You don't believe, do you?' Before the young acolyte could answer, the vampire had him in a deadly embrace and snapped his neck savagely. He tossed Reimer Schmidt's body aside and launched himself at the dwarf.

Kallad barely managed to block the creature's first strike, bringing the butt of Ruinthorn up and slamming it into the vampire's jaw as the beast sank his fangs into his forearm. The blow sent the vampire reeling and bought Kallad a few precious seconds.

The naked savagery of the beast was staggering. It had torn through them in seconds. Kallad stood side by side with Sammy Krauss, Joachim Akeman and Korin Reth. Behind them, Kantor screamed. It was a sound of pure, wretched, panic.

It was over before it had even begun. Despair threatened to overwhelm Kallad. This was it. He had failed. There would be no avenging the tragedies of Grunberg, no satisfaction for his people, and no rest.

The magician turned and fled the clearing.

Kallad let him go. He wouldn't get far if the beast chose to hunt him down, that much was obvious.

It was over for all of them and the vampire hadn't even drawn its blade.

'Well, well,' the beast said, rubbing a hand across its jaw, 'I think I should save you until last, don't you, dwarf? Let you see your friends die.' The vampire dropped into a tight crouch, its body seeming to contort and stretch, tearing its clothes from its back as its body elongated. The leather of its sword belt snapped and the sheathed blade fell to the floor. The thing – because it wasn't a vampire anymore, it was something between human and wolf – threw back its head and howled before it sprang forward, huge jaws tearing at the throats of the terrified Sigmarites as the vampire's form shifted into that of a massive dire wolf.

Kallad hurled Ruinthorn. The axe flew end over end and embedded itself in the beast's arched back. The vampire roared in pain, and fell, sprawling in the dirt. It drew itself back to its feet, face contorted in rage as it turned. Ruinthorn had hurt the thing, but not badly enough, nowhere near badly enough. It was too late for Akeman and Reth. The creature had torn the flesh out of their throats. Their blood soaked its muzzle as the wolf turned on Sammy.

It came forward cautiously, protecting its wounded side. Even wounded, the beast was lethal.

'Run, boy!' Kallad yelled at Sammy, but Sammy stood rooted to the spot, too frightened to move. 'Run!'

The spell holding Sammy shattered and suddenly the boy screamed, stumbled back a step, tripped, and fell, sprawling across the dirt.

The wolf was on top on him in a second, huge teeth tearing at the flesh of his arms as he threw them up to defend himself. His screams were terrible as the wolf took off half of his face with one savage bite.

Then the screaming stopped, and the silence was twice as terrible.

Kallad threw himself at the creature, trying to wrench his axe from its back, but the beast twisted and threw him across the clearing. Somehow, Kallad kept his grip on Ruinthorn, tearing the axe from the beast's back. He scrambled to his feet.

The wolf circled him cautiously.

Despite the massive wound in the beast's arched back there was no blood.

For a moment, he wondered what it would take to kill the creature – but he knew. Less than a quarter of an hour ago he had told the men exactly what they needed to do to slay the vampire, in whatever form it took: burning, beheading, dismembering. There was no fire, but Ruinthorn was more than capable of meting out the other deaths.

The creature was hurting, that much was obvious by the way it moved.

It wasn't invincible.

'Time to die, vampire,' Kallad said through gritted teeth.

The wolf growled deep in its throat, keeping a distance between itself and the dwarf's axe.

Kallad took a single step back, rocking on his heel and raising Ruinthorn above his head. Loosing a savage cry, he launched himself into a spinning step forwards. The momentum of the axe carried him through the arc faster than any normal blow, but it missed its mark. The wolf's head was still planted firmly on its shoulders.

The massive swing left Kallad dangerously open, but the wolf failed to take advantage of the opportunity that Kallad's miss had gifted it.

The dwarf surged forwards again, swinging wildly. There was no finesse or subtlety to the attack, but it was as brutal as it was ugly. The wolf went up on its hind legs as the axe thundered into its side. Bone crunched, splintering under the impact. The dwarf's momentum sent them both tumbling and rolling across the dirt floor. The wolf's jaws snapped at Kallad's face, scoring deep cuts down his left cheek and biting clean through half of his ear.

His head swam. The pain was blinding.

The clearing blurred in and out of focus.

He tried to stay focused on the dark shape of the wolf prowling in front of him.

The wolf growled low in its throat and lunged. Kallad sidestepped and slammed a gauntleted fist into the side of the beast's head. The wolf's teeth sank into his shoulder.

Can the beast feed in this form? The thought flashed through his head as they rolled together, locked in a deadly embrace.

He broke the beast's hold, but only for a moment. The wolf's teeth bit into Kallad's forearm. The surge of pain as the fangs sank into his flesh was excruciating, and was made much worse as Kallad yanked his arm forwards, dragging the wolf close enough for him to thunder his forehead into the beast's muzzle.

Snarling, the wolf rolled away from him.

Kallad scrambled to his knees, planted the axe in the dirt and hauled himself to his feet.

The world swam dangerously.

Kallad stumbled back two steps and righted himself. When he looked up, the wolf had begun to change.

'Fun,' the vampire growled, caught halfway between his own form and that of the wolf. The beast stood on two legs once more, its skeletal structure hideously malformed. Two huge wounds gaped in his torso, one in his side, the other scored deeply along the line of his spine. The beast's skin writhed with unnatural life as beneath it the bones cracked and reshaped until the metamorphosis was complete. 'But not so much that I want it to last all night.'

'Then stop your yapping and finish it.'

'My pleasure.' The vampire dropped into a crouch, its face twisting with rage as it sprang sideways, rolling and coming up with the discarded sword belt in its left hand. It drew the blade, and threw the scabbard aside. The blade sang as it rasped free. The vampire brought it round in a vicious arc, cutting low and high in a single sweep before returning to guard.

Kallad stepped in to meet the beast's attack when it came.

He stumbled, tripping over Sammy Krauss's out-stretched arm, and in that instant the vampire was on him.

Kallad felt a searing pain across his chest as the vampire's blade plunged into his side, working its way up between the dented discs beneath his mail, seeking out his heart.

The world faded into black. The last thing he saw: the cold eyes of the vampire. The last thought: that he had failed his people. That the grudge would go to the grave with him.

Then he slipped into the blackness.

CHAPTER NINE
The Left Hand of Darkness

THE BORDERLANDS OF SYLVANIA
The First Kiss of Snow, Winter, 2056

MANNFRED STOOD OVER the dwarf.

The wounds in his back and side were deep, the pain debilitating, but far from lethal for one of his kind. Even so, he owed the dwarf a more painful death than he was able to offer. He left him to bleed out into the dirt.

He opened himself up and breathed in the winds.

It was as he thought: the magician had opened himself up to Shyish, the death wind. That was how they had tracked him. It would be the fool's undoing. Only the strongest sorcerer could bear any kind of exposure to Shyish without being blackened by it. The man was already doomed. It would be eating away at his immortal soul even now, burrowing its way into every crease and fold of his humanity and stamping it out.

Mannfred reached out, touching Shyish.

The wind was invigorating. He savoured it as he drew it into himself.

'I'm coming for you, little man,' he said, knowing that Shyish would carry the taunt to his victim's ears no matter how far away he had managed to flee. It wasn't far enough. 'Run, run as fast as you can. It isn't fast enough. I will find you. Maybe today, maybe tomorrow, but someday, I promise, and it will be the end of your life. So run, coward, while your comrades rot.'

He walked amongst the dead, but there was no sustenance to be had from them. Their blood had already begun to lose its vitality. It was about the life-essences in the blood, not the blood itself. To drink now would be poison. Pity, because thanks to the damned dwarf he needed to feed.

They carried nothing of worth, a few petty trinkets and holy marks of Sigmar, hammers and swords. By far the most interesting thing was the dwarf's hammer, but he had no intention of touching it. He could feel the silver threads that the dwarf had had woven into the leather grip. It was a fine weapon, a match for any axe he had ever seen.

What he needed was clothing. His own clothes were left in tatters after the transformation.

He stripped the dead, taking what would fit.

The wound in his side troubled him. He could feel it burn where it had opened up. It would take time to knit. In the meantime, it made walking uncomfortable where the raw flesh rubbed.

He had time.

Mannfred returned to the tree stump and sat. He found himself toying with the ring he wore on his left hand, turning it around his middle finger.

The wound in his side was really beginning to burn. He touched it with curious fingers, feeling out the true extent of the damage, and he found that it was much smaller than he had at first thought. The sides of the gash were hot, which explained the fire he felt. He reached around awkwardly, probing the deep cut that ran parallel to his spine. Only it wasn't deep anymore. It was a shallow cut.

Neither wound was as damaging as he had first thought, although both burned with a hellish fury.

A sudden jag of pain lanced from his side into his heart. Mannfred cried out against it, sinking to his knees. He threw his head back and roared.

As the black agony subsided, Mannfred touched the wound in his side, dreading what he might discover.

The gash had almost sealed. Already the burning was beginning to ease.

It made no sense, until he thought of the times, when, with his own eyes, he had seen Vlad fall only to return, rejuvenated. He looked at the signet ring, the plain little trinket that he had claimed as his inheritance from the thief, Felix Mann, and began, finally, to understand.

'Thank you, father,' he said, standing.

He dressed himself in the dead men's clothes. There were no boots that fit, so he resigned himself to going barefoot as he set off after the magician.

Mannfred moved carefully, but the wounds had already healed over. After a few minutes, he broke into an easy ground-eating lope. The magician was easy to follow. He had blazed a panicked trail that even a blind man could have followed.

He caught up with the man in the middle of the open field. The man scrabbled about in the dirt, begging for his life. It was quite pitiful.

Mannfred could smell Chaos taint on the magician, already. He had tasted Shyish, and now he was addicted.

'Spare me,' the magician begged. 'Please, sweet Sigmar save me.' It was a pathetic whimper.

Mannfred smiled coldly, his face shifting as he released the beast within, and reached towards him.

CHAPTER TEN
The Unforgettable Fire

THE SUBTERRANEAN CATHEDRAL,
BENEATH DRAKENHOF, SYLVANIA
The Darkling Buds of Pflugzeit, Spring, 2057

MIESHA'S WORDS HAUNTED him, even now.

She may have been Hans's get, but she was also Hamaya, chosen by Jerek for her loyalty to the vampire nation. With her sire dead, she had suffered. It had taken every ounce of her will to reclaim some sense of herself, and with it she had become stronger.

For that, he had promised her a commendation, an elevation in the ranks of the Hamaya. She would be rewarded.

Whether he wanted to or not, Konrad believed her when she said that his brothers Pieter and Fritz were scheming behind his back. He had always known they would.

The fact that they had chosen to band together to see him beaten, however, was like a stake through the heart. Although he was loath to admit it, the fact that they could hate and fear him so much was curiously gratifying.

Konrad had always known what he would have to do, but their petty scheming had forced his hand far sooner than he would have liked.

He stood on the stone dais, his brothers flanking him on either side. Behind them, Konrad's loyal Hamaya had arranged themselves in a tight cordon.

They were nearly a mile beneath the surface, in the subterranean cathedral that his thralls had mined out of the very earth itself. Down here, they were immune to the whims of the sun and the moon, and other such inconveniences. Around the vast cathedral with its ceiling of stalactites as a warren of cells and chambers that made up the war rooms and Immoliah Fey's vault. The necromancer had built a sprawling underground kingdom for her research into the dark arts, including a black library that far exceeded anything from the rooms above. She had assembled treasures dating back to Nehekhara, and perhaps even Neferata herself, holy books and unholy ones, artefacts of power, masks, some renditions of familiar animal faces and other far stranger creatures, charms, icons, rods, staves, wands, and a vast arsenal of weapons.

There was even a caged pit for gladiatorial death matches, all in the name of amusement. The cage fights were brutal and bloody, with the new vampires thirsting to be a part of the kill as they looked on.

Death was good for morale.

In the galleries, a thousand flickering torches illuminated the upturned faces of his new vampires. Their faces were tainted a sickly green by the luminescence given off by the lichen that grew on the walls. Some wore expressions of idolisation, others outright hatred. Both were vital to the future of his people.

There were hundreds of them, all tied in some way to the bloodline. These were *his* people: he was their father-in-death, their lord, their master, their god.

He turned to Miesha.

'Come forward, girl,' he said, quietly. Then louder, to the gallery: 'Hear me, my family.' His voice carried easily, the acoustics of the domed vault amplifying his words. 'Our people have suffered since the fall of our beloved father-in-death. We were beaten, forced into submission, the lands around us stripped and useless, our cattle drained and our spirit broken.

'It is not so now. In each and every one of you we have been reborn. In ways that the living cannot comprehend, we are kindred. We are merely the beginning. We stood against the might of the Empire in the war and we suffered years of loss as a result, struggling merely to subsist. As our people slept, so did their dreams of dominion. Now, take a look at the faces around you. Do you see the hunger there? Do you see the fire to take back what is rightfully ours? Has it woken in the face of each and every one of you?

'You are servants of the vampires, but you alone are nothing. As part of the organic whole you are everything.'

Konrad paused, giving his words a moment to sink in.

'We are one, you and I. Nothing separates us. If you suffer hurts, I suffer with you, and if I suffer hurts, you, in turn, will suffer with me.

'Miesha, my love, kneel.'

She came forward and knelt at Konrad's feet, her smile one of satisfaction. Her loyalty was being rewarded, her position of influence cemented. She bowed her head, going along with Konrad's mockery of the knighting ceremony, and waited.

'If one amongst us betrays one of us, they betray all of us. If one harbours deceit in their heart, if one would scheme for their own gain, understand that they are scheming against all of us, understand that they are lying to all of us, and believe me, I will not stand for that.'

He drew his sword.

'Miesha, one of my trusted Hamaya came to me. She spoke of my brothers, my beloved brothers Pieter and Fritz,' he gestured with the sword towards first Pieter, and then Fritz. 'She claimed that they plotted treachery behind my back. I know my brothers, they would do no such thing, for like me, they have only the best interests of the vampire nation in their hearts. So why would Miesha do such a thing? Because she sought to profit from it.'

Konrad nodded to the flanking Hamaya, and one, Onursal, a dark-skinned giant, stepped forwards, laying a hand on Miesha's shoulder, claws sinking into her flesh and holding her in place.

She looked up at Konrad, and the first flickerings of fear registered in her eyes.

'There can be no other reason. She came to me with outright lies about my brothers. So here, my people, I make an example of those who conspire against *my* rule.'

Konrad brought the blade down with an executioner's precision, cleaving the woman's head from her body in a single smooth blow. Her body held its position for a moment before collapsing in nervous convulsions. Konrad sheathed his sword. Miesha's head rolled across the dais, the look of shock frozen on her face as it came to a stop.

He turned and bowed to each of his brothers.

They understood the point of the demonstration. It was not for the assembly of vampires, it was for them.

The message was plain: those who stand against me can expect no less a fate. The ruthlessness of it was shocking.

He had sacrificed one of his own to reinforce the point.

'Let us speak of this no more. We have more important things to consider by far. Together we stand before you, brothers, united.

'You,' he spread his arms wide to encompass the entire gallery, 'are the results of my desire to rebuild our great nation. You are here because of *my* will. I have a vision for our people. You were but the first stage of that great vision. It is time now to put the second stage into practice.

'Some of you may say: "He has brought us another plan. When he had completed the first, why couldn't he leave us in peace to feed and grow at our own rate? Why the haste, why run before we can walk?"

'The truth is our enemies do not stagnate, they move forwards every day.

'Now that we are restored, it is time to take the fight to our enemy's door. They shall tremble once more as they peer out into the darkness, knowing that we walk in the night. It will be a war fought on three fronts, the first a guerrilla assault on their societal structure. You are to go abroad in search of those with peculiar gifts. You are to scour the land for any with even the slightest aptitude for magic, not just known practitioners, but folk with unusual luck, men surrounded by uncanny stories. You will seek out midwifes who have never lost a child, soldiers who have survived terrible campaigns and tell tales of their fortune while other suffered, and people, who might, in some way, have touched one of the Eight Winds. They are to be brought back here to Immoliah Fey, who will drain them of their talents, creating a second tier of what will be our unstoppable force: a corps of magicians skilled in the Lore of Death.

'To show how little store I put in the gossiping of that traitor,' he inclined his head towards Miesha's corpse, 'the second assault, a force of purebloods led by my brother Pieter, will sack Nuln, spreading discord amongst the humans. We will not give them the luxury of sleeping easily in their beds. The third, a force of equal measure, will be under the command of my brother, Fritz. I trust him to make Middenheim bend its knee before the year is out.

'It is time for us to reclaim the night and teach these humans the true meaning of fear.'

It was done. He had trapped his brothers into exile whilst making them into heroes. In sending them away, he had shown the assembly who was in charge, and made it difficult, if not impossible for Fritz and Pieter to continue to plot his downfall in tandem. He had meant what he said; alone they were nothing. He smiled coldly as he turned to face them.

Their exile was only his first move in a long and drawn out dance of death.

A part of him looked forward to their response. It would keep life interesting.

'The fate of our people is in your hands, my brothers, do not fail us.'

With that he dismissed the assembly, bidding his brothers take their pick of whichever subordinates they would take into battle.

He looked down at poor Miesha. He was proud of her, and proud of himself for giving her death meaning.

'Stay,' he said to Jerek as the Hamaya turned to leave. 'All of you, stay.'

The six took up positions around their master.

'What would you have us do with her body?' Onursal asked.

'Dispose of it as befits a traitor.'

The vampire nodded. The fate of a traitor in the new vampire nation was gruesome. The corpse was spitted and roasted, and then stripped, and the meat was fed to the birds up in the Rookery.

'I find it hard to believe.' The Wolf's gaze drifted towards Miesha's corpse. Konrad had known Jerek would take her death personally. He had chosen her.

He had helped her through the insanity that threatened to overwhelm her in the wake of Hans's death. Seeing her die branded a traitor must have galled him.

'It is not so hard to believe, my friend,' Konrad said, smoothly. 'The madness had obviously rooted itself deeper than you were able to reach. Without question she was still spoiled by her master's evil. You cannot hold yourself responsible. You did all that you could, but we always knew there was a chance she would not come back to us.'

Jerek remained unconvinced.

'She had weathered the worst of the withdrawal.' He shook his head. 'She was getting stronger and stronger. It makes no sense.'

'Then perhaps she had a relapse,' Konrad said, his irritation flashing through. 'I suggest, my friend, that you let it go.'

He refused to allow himself to get worked up during his hour of victory. No, this was a moment to be savoured, not lost in a blur of anger. Konrad took a moment to compose himself.

'There is someone I would have you meet. He came to me last night, having escaped from the belly of the beast itself. Vlad placed great store in his talents. Wolf, I believe you and he are acquainted?'

Konrad gestured for the newcomer to join them.

All eyes turned to see Jon Skellan step out of the shadows. He came to stand beside Konrad.

'With the… ah… sudden vacancy, I have asked Skellan to join us. He has unique skills. Now, there is something I have no wish to talk of, but alas must. Despite our best efforts, I believe that at least one of you is loyal to my brothers. This pains me greatly. I do not ask much from those around me, only loyalty. In return you are privileged above all others. This is my reward, to learn that there are vipers in my nest.'

No one argued with him. No one claimed that he was wrong. They knew better than to try to dissuade him when he had his mind set on something.

'Well, my little schemers, take this to your masters, and let them stew on it. They aren't coming home.'

He looked at them all, one by one, judging them. Then he gave the assassination orders for Fritz and Pieter.

CHAPTER ELEVEN
The Ravens Left The Tower

KONRAD'S TOWER, DRAKENHOF, SYLVANIA
The Long Dark Night of the Soul, Spring, 2057

HE KNEW THEY would come for him. It was only a matter of time. That was why he had challenged them so openly, proclaiming their death sentence before the Hamaya.

He had expected it to goad either Pieter or Fritz into some rash action, some obvious treason that he could punish with impunity.

He had taken measures to protect himself, of course. He was no fool.

Konrad no longer slept in his own coffin. While it was empty, the coffin was set up to look as if the new Count slumbered within. Instead of the coffin, Konrad preferred the solitude of the rooftops when Morrslieb and Mannslieb held sway, or the subterranean seclusion of the cathedral when the sun was at its zenith. This night, he held a lonely vigil on the balcony outside his bedchamber.

The armies had gathered, billeting the city below.

The differences between Konrad's new army and the last army that had marched to the banner of the von Carsteins were marked. Where Vlad had enjoyed the portability of tents, Konrad chose to stamp his authority on the land, claiming ownership of houses and leaving families begging for scraps. For him, there were no banners or pennons snapping in the wind, no black pavilions for the marshals, and no supply wagons. The dead had no need of such accoutrements. There was movement, however: black coaches rumbled through the streets bearing the seal of the von Carsteins.

Hundreds of small fires burned in the fields between the castle and the city. He didn't look directly at them, knowing their dance would slowly mesmerise him. He needed to be alert, watchful. He kept his gaze moving over the countryside without allowing it to settle on anything for too long. Every once in a while, he glanced up towards the green aura of Morrslieb and the brighter silver corona of Mannslieb; it all served to break up the monotony of waiting for the inevitable.

He listened to the nocturnal chorus: the insects, the hoot of an owl, the mournful cry of a wolf, and the wind in the gutters of the tower.

Ravens gathered along the balustrade, their beady eyes surveying the night world. At times like these the birds kept him company. Their presence also held the ghosts at bay.

The chamber door creaked open. The wait was over. They had come for him.

With the torches lit, the room was fully illuminated, although the glass between them effectively rendered Konrad invisible. He watched as the three men, wrapped in dark cloaks, crept up on the coffin, standing at the head and on either side of the wooden box. It was a measure of how little his brothers regarded him. Three assassins. Three humans. Insult aside, it was fascinating to see his own murder taking place, or what they thought would be his murder.

The attack when it came was shocking in its savagery. The body in the coffin was butchered.

He suffered a curious sense of disassociation, watching his would-be murderers hacking away at the corpse in the coffin. It was like watching his own death through the eyes of a stranger.

He would have to thank Immoliah Fey for the corpse, and for the glamour that disguised it.

Konrad watched until their frenzied cutting subsided into exhaustion, and then pushed open the balcony door and walked into his bedroom.

'Sorry to disappoint you, but it seems I am still very much alive.'

One of the assassins dropped his blade in fright. It clattered on the floor.

'You, on the other hand, well, forgive me if I am wrong, but I think you could very well be dead.'

He came at them in a vengeful fury, his fist bursting through the ribcage of the first assassin and wrenching the dead man's heart out of his chest with one vicious tug. Spinning on his heel, he lunged out with his hand extended and rammed clawed fingers into the second assassin's throat, rupturing his windpipe. The man dropped his sword, gagging, and stumbled back, clutching at his throat as he suffocated.

Konrad turned on the last assassin.

'Which of my brothers sent you?'

The man said nothing.

Konrad moved in closer. He reached out. His hand closed around the man's jaw.

'I'll ask you again, which of my brother's sent you?'

He squeezed, hard.

'Fritz.'

He had got what he wanted. Not what he expected, but what he wanted. He still didn't relent, even as he felt the bone crush beneath his fingers. The man's screams were silenced abruptly as Konrad snapped his neck.

He stripped the dead man of his hood. He recognised him. It was one of his own. He stared at the man's twisted face. The recognition was galling.

Quickly, Konrad stripped the hoods from the remaining assassins. Again, both were, or had been, his own thralls. They should have been bound to him, and as such incapable of rising against him. They should have been subservient, existing solely to do his bidding. The evidence to the contrary lay dead at his feet.

Somehow, Fritz had turned them against him. That fact was more disturbing than the botched assassination attempt. Fritz had found a way to break his hold on his own servants.

Konrad had been sure that the fop was only interested in his hedonistic pursuit of pleasure, but obviously, the whole harmless philanderer persona was an act, one he played perfectly. He surrounded himself with whores and doxies to help keep up the act, but obviously the Fritz he thought he knew was not who Fritz really was. This would bear thinking about.

In that moment, cold-blooded fury overwhelmed him. All rational thought burned up within his anger. Had he been his sire, he would have dragged their souls back from the abyss, kicking and screaming, and raised them again, as mindless zombies. He wasn't his sire, however, and his impotence maddened him all the more.

He lashed out, splintering the side of his coffin with his fist.

He upturned the box, spilling parts of the dismembered corpse across the bloody floor. He tore down the portraits from the wall. He splintered the back of the chair on the open door and, raging, pulled the books from the shelves. He shredded the spines and ripped out the pages, scattering them around him like confetti. Blood soaked into the pages where they fell around the bodies.

His rage consumed him. It was blinding. Then, as quickly as it had come, it was spent. All that remained was slow smouldering fury.

He looked at the assassins with thinly veiled hatred. He *would* extract his price for this insult. Fritz would pay.

He stood in the doorway, calling for a servant to fetch the Hamaya.

'I want these,' he gestured at the bodies, 'delivered to my brother Fritz's chambers immediately.'

Onursal bowed. The Hamaya betrayed no expression upon seeing the devastation that Konrad had wrought in his own chamber. 'It will be done.'

He gathered the body of the last assassin in his arms.

'I know this man. He was no assassin.'

'Until today,' Konrad said, the implication obvious. Something had turned the man into a hopeless assassin. Onursal was no fool, the fact that he was being asked to deliver the bodies to Fritz was a clear indication of where the responsibility for the man's conversion lay.

Jerek von Carstein stood in the doorway.

'Are you sure this is wise, Konrad?'

'Are you questioning me, Wolf?'

Jerek shook his head. 'Not at all, just urging caution. Once you deliver these to Fritz's door there can be no turning back. You know that.'

'Take one of the damned bodies, Jerek. You are not my conscience, so stop acting like it. I'll carry the third myself. I want to see his face when his filth washes up on his own doorstep.'

Only he didn't carry the third, he beheaded it and carried the head by a bloody tangle of hair.

Together, they swept through the cold passages of the castle, climbing the hundreds of stairs to Fritz's high chamber. Konrad threw the door open and sneered at Fritz's surprise as he bowled the assassin's head into the room. The head cracked off the doorway as he threw it. It landed at his brother's feet.

Konrad stepped into the room. The Hamaya didn't cross the threshold.

'What do you have to say for yourself, *brother-mine*?' Konrad asked, cruelly mimicking Fritz's intonation.

'If you want something done right, do it yourself would seem to be appropriate.'

'Indeed, that would be why I am here.'

Konrad drew his daemon blade, feeling the vibrations course through him as the blade sang out, demanding blood.

Fritz was unarmed.

'It seems you have me at a disadvantage,' Fritz said, stalling. He cast his gaze left and right, looking for something that could be used as an impromptu weapon. There was nothing.

'I don't really care, brother,' Konrad said, moving closer, 'but more to the point, I don't see why I should.'

'We're family,' Fritz offered, a smile spreading across his face as he spread his arms.

The smile incensed Konrad, as he knew it was calculated to. He did his best to stifle the anger he felt building, but it was difficult.

The need of the daemon blade sang in his tainted blood. It demanded a death, demanded sating. It fed off the heat of his rage, stoking it even as he battled for control.

Slowly and deliberately, Konrad brought the dark blade to his lips and kissed it before shifting into a fighting stance.

'So be it, brother-mine.' Fritz clapped his hands sharply, twice. Doors on either side of his chamber opened, and his women entered, hunkering down and giving themselves over to the form of she-wolves.

They circled around Konrad, jowls curled back in feral snarls. 'Seven angry young women, Konrad, I would call this an even match.'

'You've miscalculated, brother. I don't need to kill them, only you. They can snap and snarl all they like. It doesn't matter. They are all tied to you. Your death will be enough to put an end to any threat they might pose, pretty though they might be with their shiny pelts. I would have thought swords would have been more your style, Fritz. They are so terribly... suggestive, after all. Now, I am taking what is mine, by eternal right. Say your goodbyes. I am sure your bitches will miss you.'

Kicking a wolf aside, Konrad launched a blistering attack, the sheer ferocity of it driving Fritz towards the window. He ignored the howling wolves as they snapped at him. They were insects, annoying, but inconsequential. He only had eyes for Fritz. The traitor would pay.

Lunging, he buried the bone blade deep in Fritz's stomach. The sheer momentum of the attack carried the pair out through the huge window, spraying glass everywhere, and for a moment, they were falling, locked together by the daemonic sword. Their black cloaks wrapped around the pair as they wrestled then flared out wildly as the wind ripped them away. For a moment, they became the silhouette of vast black wings as Konrad lost his grip on the sword and Fritz fell away, the sword still impaled in his gut.

He fell soundlessly, threw his arms wide and burst upwards suddenly, his body going through a hideous transformation, the cloak fusing to his arms like leathery wings, his bones breaking and metamorphosing into the shape and form of a huge black bat.

The sword tumbled away harmlessly, chased by the black ghost of Fritz's shed clothing.

Konrad spread his arms wide, focusing on the form of a bat in his head. He gave himself to it, feeling his body respond. He stopped freefalling, and was flying.

As a bat, he was blind.

He reached out with his remaining senses, using the displacement of the air caused by the panicked flapping of his brother's wings to build a picture in his mind, and chased Fritz out into the darkness.

They banked high, arcing back towards Konrad's Tower – what used to be called the Raven Tower in Vlad's day – and swooped low along the castellations, scattering the birds. He lost Fritz in the chaos of wings.

Konrad scoured the sky for a quarter of an hour, but what seemed like thousands of the black birds had taken flight, blinding him in the sheer volume of wing beats and caws.

Cursing himself for a fool, he went to ground, dressed and collected his sword. Its hunger was far from sated, but its longing would be answered before the night was over.

He could, at last, sleep. There would be no more attacks tonight. Fritz was beaten, and Emmanuelle would prevent Pieter from giving in to any kind of rash stupidity.

First, he had one thing to do.

He climbed the several hundred stairs to Fritz's chamber and, revelling in their screams, butchered his brother's harem while Jerek and Onursal looked on dispassionately. He didn't care that their true deaths weakened the vampires as a whole. Losing seven gets in a single night would virtually cripple Fritz, which was what mattered.

He left the corpses littering the floor for Fritz to find if he was foolish enough to return.

That would not be for a long time yet.

The link between sire and get was a powerful one, and Konrad knew that Fritz would be lying somewhere in a gutter, stinking with fear, and sure, beyond a shadow of a doubt, that he was dying.

'He will not cross me again,' Konrad said to the Hamaya as they returned to his tower.

'He would be a fool to,' Onursal said, opening the heavy wooden door.

'We will stand guard at your door tonight, all the same.' Jerek said as Konrad entered the chamber. The room looked as if a tornado had blown through it. Jerek stooped and righted the toppled coffin. The side of the box was splintered where Konrad had hit it, but it would do for a few hours more. 'Sleep well, my lord.'

And sleep he did, the sleep of the damned.

He dreamed he was walking the streets of the city below, loitering in the seedier districts of Drakenhof. On a corner, he saw the indistinct shape of a woman, blurred as is the nature of dreams.

SHE LURKS IN the darker shadows of the alleyway. He can see that she is wearing an exquisite gown of flowing silks and a veil that covers the lower half of her face. Even so, he knows that she is beautiful.

'Do you think I am beautiful?' she asks, as he approaches.

All he knows is that he must possess her.

Up close, she is even more attractive.

She reminds him, in almost every way, of his sire's bride, Isabella.

'Of course you are,' he says.

'Liar!' she screams, tearing away the veil that covers her mutilation. Her mouth has been ripped open, her unnatural smile spreading from ear to ear, her tongue lolling horribly through the gash. 'Tell me again, now that you see me, am I beautiful?'

Konrad stares at the ruin of Vlad von Carstein's bride, screams and tries to flee, but she is too fast. She snares him in claws that he cannot escape and draws him up close to whisper: 'I want to do to you what was done to me,' in his ear as she pulls a sharpened stake from the many folds of her gown and plunges it into his heart.

As he dies in her arms, her face blurred, losing focus and form, shifting into the face of Jerek, into the face of Vlad, into the face of Skellan, of Miesha, of Pieter, of Hans, of Fritz, Onursal, Immoliah Fey, Constantin, Emmanuelle.

The faces of those he once called friends.

HE AWOKE IN a cold sweat, trapped inside the confines of his coffin. He lashed out, hammering at the wooden lid until it shattered, and surged out of the wooden box, gasping even though he had tasted his last breath more than a century earlier.

He rose, trembling, as Jerek and Onursal burst into the room. Their expressions said they expected the worst. Konrad was not about to confess his dream.

'Leave me.' The manner in which he said it brooked no argument. The Hamaya backed out of the room.

He didn't know who he could trust.

Trust, he laughed bitterly. The truth was that he could trust no one.

He couldn't stand to be cooped up in the castle anymore. He needed to feel the wind on his face, to feel the illusion at least of freedom. He wondered if this was how Vlad had felt. Thinking of his sire made him think of the hundreds of nights when the ancient vampire had haunted the rooftops of this very tower. That decided it for him. He gathered his cloak up, fastening the gold chain around his throat, and swept out of the chamber and past the Hamaya.

'Stay!' he commanded, as if he was talking to a pair of dogs.

He climbed the stairs to the roof at a run, taking them two and three at a time in his need to be out beneath the bruise purple sky.

He pushed open the door.

The wind sucked and pulled at his cloak, folding it around him and billowing it out behind him in turns as it funnelled around the rooftop. Konrad strode right out to the edge, standing on the brick-work of the castellation itself, nothing between him and a fall of a thousand feet.

He looked down.

For a moment, it was as if he was suspended out in the black heart of the night. It was breathtaking, that sense of liberation.

The rush of vertigo was dizzying, but there was no fear.

He could willingly have given himself to the fall if he had wanted to, even one thousand feet was not enough to kill him.

Indeed, he wanted to jump, to fly free in the sky.

The ravens gathered around his feet, pecking at his toes and worrying at the leather of his boots. He let them.

'He's not the only one,' the largest of the ravens said, its voice a raucous caw as it craned its neck to peer up at him with its beady yellow eyes.

'I know,' Konrad said, still looking out over the world below.

'They all want you dead,' the creature's voice cut deep into his nerves, the words like nails on glass, as it coughed them up.

'I know.'

'There are enemies on every corner.'

'I know.'

'Your brothers would rise in your place.'

'I know all of this, bird.'

'You do, you do, but know you Pieter? That he plots your downfall? That he dreams of dominion?'

'Then I shall have to see that his dreams become nightmares.'

'Oh yes, yes, yes, nightmares. Before he dies – nightmares. Kill them, Konrad. Kill them. They would kill you.'

Konrad looked down at the carrion bird. It looked positively enraptured by the prospect of more death in the old castle.

'You are your master's creature, aren't you, bird?'

'Oh, yesss.'

'There will be more blood, take that message to your master in whatever Hell he is in.'

'Yes, yes, yes, yes,' the raven cawed. 'Trick Pieter, see him dead, before he tricks you. They scheme and scheme, your lying kin, they would see you rot, cut you into pieces and feed you to us birds, yes they would, yes, yes, yes.'

'Then perhaps that is what I should do for them. Make their dreams come true. Call it my gift. Konrad, the Blood Count.'

'Bringer of death, this immortal,' quoth the raven.

Konrad heard movement on the stairs and retreated quickly into the shadows thrown by one of the tower's many gables, dark enough and deep enough to conceal him.

Jon Skellan walked out onto the rooftop. Bending, he began to feed a few of the birds with small strings of meat. They ate out of his hand.

Konrad watched the spectacle with growing curiosity, gradually becoming certain that the birds were talking to the new Hamaya, even though he wasn't close enough to make out what they were saying.

'So, they talk to you as well?' he asked, stepping out of the shadows.

Skellan scattered the ravens, cawing and flapping his arms to drive them off, and turned to face his master. 'They make good companions,' he said, a sly grin spreading across his face. 'They ask no questions, and tell no lies. What more can you ask for from a friend?'

'Yes,' Konrad agreed. 'There is something almost noble about them, isn't there?'

'Unlike your brothers,' Skellan said.

The frankness of his words surprised Konrad. He was unaccustomed to his servants being so bold. It made a refreshing change. He knew he had chosen well in Skellan. Like Jerek, he was a truth speaker. Konrad had had enough of sycophants to last him several lifetimes. 'From what I have seen of the pair, they lack any semblance of nobility.'

'Guttersnipes, the pair of them,' Konrad agreed. A raven settled by his feet. Utterly unafraid of them, it pecked and scuffed at the scraps of meat that Skellan had dropped.

'Yet they hold great power in your court, and you honour them by giving them command of your forces going to war on the morrow. One would think they have some hold over you. A fop and a whore-whipped fool, not the greatest of vampires ever sired.'

'Well, if any of the gods are paying the blindest bit of notice, we'll both be honouring their gravesides before the war is out.'

'Keep your friends close, and your brothers closer, eh?' Skellan said.

'Or send them away and hope they drop off the end of the world.'

Konrad felt a kinship with this vampire, one that he had not felt with any of Vlad's gets. Perhaps it was because he knew his place in the hierarchy, that as

Posner's get he could never rival a true von Carstein for power, perhaps it was his plain speaking, perhaps it was just a remnant of that foul dream. He didn't know, but he felt an affinity between them. It was something he had little experience of. Throughout his life, he had been forced to fight for everything he had. Even before, in his old life, he had had no true friends. Mother had seen to that. Now, he knew, people sought him out for their own interests. Skellan was different. He was like Konrad. They were both outsiders. They didn't fit comfortably into this world of the dead, and they both carried their ghosts close to their chest.

'Of course, it never hurts to give them a push,' Skellan said.

'Indeed, we owe it to ourselves to weed out the weak. In death, as in life, only the strongest should survive.'

'Couldn't agree more.'

'In which case, my new friend, I have a task for you.'

'I am yours to command.' Skellan's smile was predatory in the extreme.

'Travel with Fritz. Become his shadow. See that he does not return to Drakenhof.' Even in his own ears, Konrad could hear the echo of the raven's broken-up cadences.

'You can trust me,' Skellan said, no hint of irony in his voice.

Konrad felt a great peace settle around his shoulders. Yes, yes he could trust Skellan.

CHAPTER TWELVE
Up From The Ashes, In Flames

THE BORDERLANDS, SYLVANIA
The Last Rites of Spring, 2057

THE BEAST HAD left him for dead.

It was a mistake the fiend would come to rue, Kallad vowed, even as his world was consumed with pain and he slipped into darkness once more.

He had no way of knowing how long he had been unconscious.

Awareness returned, the world revealing itself in hallucinatory fragments: the caw of the carrion birds, the rustle of leaves, the smell of blood thick on the breeze, and with them came the pains of his wounds, but for the most part the world was a meaningless wash of colour. He couldn't focus.

He was lying on his back. He didn't have the strength to move.

I am not going to die.

He felt the muscles in his left arm quiver. He was burning up from the inside out.

Despite his determination to live, he knew he was dying, and that there was nothing he could do to change the fact.

Gritting his teeth against the sudden flare of pain, he tried to move. Blackness rose up to claim him.

When he came to again he was alone. The vampire had disappeared into the trees. Kallad bit down on his lip, beads of perspiration running down into his eyes as he tried again to force his body to move. He succeeded in craning his head enough to see that the vampire had stripped the dead of anything it could use.

The slight movement caused his vision to swim, blur and dissolve into a blackness of agony.

He was alone. He couldn't move, couldn't think.

He knew that death was close. The splotches of light leaking through the trees lay like silver coins scattered across the ground. His dead were offering Morr the price of his passage. There silver was no good to him. He lay in the dirt, staring at the canopy of leaves blocking out the sky, and imagined what it would be like.

Who would come to guide him to the Hall of Ancestors? His father? He had failed his people so he had no right to a hero's welcome. Perhaps there would be no emissary. Would that be the ultimate price he paid for his failure? Being left to find his own way home?

'I am not going to die.' His defiance was less than a whisper, but he meant it. He wasn't going to die – not yet.

He still had breath in his lungs. He focused on the pain, used it to remember that he was still alive.

Across the clearing, carrion birds picked at the corpses of Sammy and the soldiers.

Kallad Stormwarden lay in the dirt. He would have laughed, but there was little of amusement in his predicament. He had lost a lot of blood and even his prodigious strength was failing. The arrogance of the vampire rankled. The beast hadn't bothered to finish him off, instead choosing to allow this slow lingering death. 'Well, I'll not give you the satisfaction,' Kallad rasped, biting back on the pain as he finally managed to roll onto his side and push himself up against a tree bole. He screamed in agony as he worked himself into the sitting position. He slumped against the tree, counting the minutes until the pain finally ebbed.

The worst of the pain was in his shoulder and left side, where he had taken two deep cuts. A slow fire burned in the wounds. He had almost no manoeuvrability in his arm. The slightest change of position sent a sharp dagger of pain lancing through him.

He felt out the wounds. Blood had dried into his armour where the rings and plates had been broken and dug into the gaping wounds left by the vampire's blade. The blood had congealed around the metal, fusing skin and armour together. Kallad was going to have to separate it, and not kill himself in the process, if he was going to have any hope of making it out of the clearing.

His screams ought to have been enough to raise the dead.

The dwarf clung stubbornly to consciousness, focusing on the bodies of the dead, and the fact that they had been stripped, and were nothing more than food for the crows. He was determined not to go the same way.

The wound in his side began to bleed again where he had torn it open, but at least it was clean of the stink of gangrene. It was a small mercy. How long it would stay that way if he didn't clean it and tend to it, well that was a different matter. He had seen too many good men die from infected wounds. While he burned, he knew that his body was still fighting off whatever sickness the wounds had caused. He needed to tend to the wounds before he blacked out again.

Forcing himself into action, Kallad shrugged off his pack and took out his water flask.

He took a swallow, and then biting back against the sheer agony of movement, drew the mail shirt off over his head, and dribbled a little of the water onto the wound, wincing against the sting. He tore a strip of cloth from the muslin wrapping around his rations and used it to tenderly flake away the blood that had crusted around the wounds. They were worse than he had thought. Cleaning the gash was agonisingly slow, and used most of the water in his canteen, but it had to be done.

He clung to consciousness as he poked and prodded the wounds to be sure that they were free of anything that might cause infection. He wished he had some liquor, the alcohol would had been excellent for killing any lingering bacteria that might have gotten into the wound, but if he was going to waste his time lingering over wishes like that then he might as well wish for bigger miracles. He could wish that Nagash's black books had been destroyed before they fell into the Vampire Count's hands, or for his father to have slain the beast on the Grunberg's wall and not fallen. He could wish for his clan to be beside him now, instead of these few dead boys. There were bigger miracles worth wishing for.

Next, he rummaged around in the pack for the thin needle of bone and the seamstress's thread wrapped around it. He threaded the needle and, drawing the lips of the gash together, pushed the tip of the needle through the flap of skin and began to sew the wound shut. It was basic field surgery. It wasn't pretty, but it would hold until he could get to a chirurgeon. More importantly, it would give him a chance to heal.

Twice during the stitching Kallad found his focus swimming and the world tilting beneath him, but he stubbornly refused to give in to it. The thread burned as he drew it through his flesh, but he welcomed the pain as a reminder that he was alive.

Only when he was finished did the dwarf allow himself to slump against the tree trunk and give in to unconsciousness.

A none too gentle boot in the side brought him sharply back around.

Kallad's head came up. In his disorientation he still half-expected to see some emissary of the dead come to escort him to the Halls. Instead, he saw a young dirt-smeared face grinning down at him. The grin disappeared as the boy realised that Kallad was still in the land of the living. Flustered, he stuffed his hands in his pockets, obviously trying to hide whatever he had taken from the bodies of the dead.

Kallad grunted and reached out, trying to grab the boy. The exertion had the world swimming out of focus again. As it settled, he saw that the boy held a blunt-edged knife in his trembling hand, and was obviously torn between helping him up and sticking the knife in his gut to finish him off.

Biting down on the pain, Kallad grabbed the boy's hand and pulled him close enough to taste his sour breath. 'Don't make me kill you, boy.'

The boy nodded quickly, trying to pull away.

Despite the fire in his shoulder Kallad's grip was iron.

'Wouldn't dream of it. I'm rather fond of breathing.'

'I'm glad to hear it. Now, tell me your name.'

'Allie du Bek.'

'And where are you from, Allie du Bek?'

'Vierstein.'

'Well Allie du Bek from Vierstein, just between the two of us, there'll be no easy pickings from the dead, if you take my meaning?' Kallad inclined his head towards the boy's hands where they were stuffed in his trouser pockets. 'Empty 'em, there's a good lad.'

Du Bek turned out his pockets. He had taken two rings and a Sigmarite talisman. The silver hammer was tied on a leather thong. It had belonged to the young acolyte, Reimer Schmidt. He had no more use for it where he was.

'Put the rings back, but if you want to wear the hammer, I don't think the priest would begrudge you.'

Du Bek fastened the talisman around his neck before returning the rings to the dead.

Kallad watched him. He moved awkwardly, favouring his left side as if his hip had dropped or some such skeletal deformity hampered him. He coped well with it though, proving once again the resilience of youth.

He really didn't want to get the boy involved, not after what had happened to Sammy, but he didn't see that he had a choice. Kallad promised himself that he wouldn't let Allie du Bek get too close. Part of him actually hoped that the lad would just run off and not come back, even if that meant his own chances of survival dwindled considerably. He was a fighter. He would make it. He wouldn't have more deaths on his conscience.

'When you're done, bring me some food from one of the packs, and then go find someone from that village of yours to help me. Your father, maybe. Another night out here in the dirt doesn't appeal. Those birds might just get fed up of waiting.'

Du Bek nodded and crouched beside Korin Reth's body. He pulled the pack out from beneath the fallen holy man and rifled through it. He rescued a muslin-wrapped chunk of pumpernickel bread, a browning apple and a hunk of pungent cheese, and gave them to Kallad.

Allie du Bek touched the talisman at his throat and grinned. 'I'll go fetch me pa, he's a border warden,' he said, and ran off into the trees, leaving Kallad alone with the dead.

* * *

THE HEALING PROCESS was frustratingly slow.

Every morning, Kallad woke in agony, fearful of exploring his wounds in case the tenderness of the day before had succumbed to infection during the night. For the first few weeks, even his own light touch was enough to make him wince.

The village of Vierstein was barely bigger than the four stones its name suggested – a double row of buildings clustered close along the sides of a brackish river. The villagers made him welcome, although many stared openly as he went through his gentle morning exercises, trying to recapture some of the strength and manoeuvrability his wounds had cost him. They had never seen a dwarf before so he bore their curiosity with good grace. Kallad chopped wood and moved grain, and laboured, stretching his endurance daily, until his strength began to return.

LOTHAR DU BEK, Allie's father, was a good man. He helped Kallad by burying the bones of his comrades, and saw to it that Kallad was fed and had a roof over his head for the weeks he needed to recover.

He didn't know how to tell the dwarf the magician had not been among the dead.

The border warden was skilled at reading the play of a battle out of the dirt, discerning the signs and getting a mental picture of how the fight had unfolded. He had followed the magician to the point where the vampire had overwhelmed him, but there had been no corpse. There *had* been a one-sided struggle. The lack of a body had disturbed both the border warden and the dwarf. Was the magician the vampire's prisoner? Was he lying dead in a ditch somewhere?

If he was the beast's captive then, day by day, the magician was getting further and further away from them.

Less than a month had passed since he had vowed that there would be no more deaths on his conscience.

Kantor was turning it into an impossible promise to keep.

Kallad and the border warden talked often at daybreak when Lothar returned from his nightly patrols. The hinterland was becoming more dangerous by the day. Lothar talked regularly about huge black wolves the size of men prowling in the dark, picking off game. He regularly found the carcasses of deer and venison, mauled, throats ripped out, hides torn open, ribs cracked apart, and the innards gone, having served as a feast for the beasts.

The black wolves disturbed du Bek, not only because they were unnaturally large, or because they were more powerful than any wolf he'd been forced to hunt in his life as a border warden, but because they showed no fear of him. They didn't retreat from his scent. They howled into the night, as if they were talking to one another, and circled him, shepherding him away from wherever they fed. The animals showed surprising cunning, and truly were pack creatures. They were never alone.

Du Bek sat down heavily at the table and pulled his gloves off. 'I killed one,' he told the dwarf. They had discussed the unnatural creatures often enough for Kallad to know what du Bek meant. 'I caught it shadowing me, I don't know if it was trying to draw me away from something or lead me to somewhere. It didn't feel right. My skin crawled whenever I felt its gaze upon me. I couldn't shake the feeling that it was *hunting* me. I couldn't have that. I brought it down with a silver-tipped arrow through the throat.'

The border wardens had taken to using silver-tipped arrows during the time of the first vampire wars when Vlad von Carstein had tormented the settlements along the River Stir. They had seen a lot of unnatural things, including loved ones rising from the grave to terrorise the night. In defence they clutched every superstition they knew, including silver and garlic, white roses, relics and blessed water.

Tinkers and vagabonds were still doing a brisk trade in pseudo-religious artefacts. It was all about faith. People wanted to believe, so people were gulled out of their money. It gave them a warm, false sense of protection.

'I saw it go down with my own eyes, dwarf, but when I went over to reclaim the shaft the beast's carcass was gone. The corpse of a naked man lay sprawled out in the dirt, Kallad. There was no wolf! As Morr is my witness, there was no trace of blood on the arrow's tip as I pulled it out of the fallen man. He didn't bleed, not a drop. I tell you, dark things are gathering over there,' Lothar du Bek said, shaking his head as he tore off a chunk of bread and dipped it into the steaming bowl of broth that his wife had ladled out a few moments earlier.

The dwarf wasn't about to argue. He had seen enough to know that evil was abroad once more. Lothar's stories of strangers travelling only at night, black coaches on the highways, restless wildlife, and now huge dire wolves that were really men stalking the borderlands, didn't leave much to the imagination. After years of relative quiet, the enemy was amassing its forces once more.

'You did well, my friend.'

'But to what end? Every night there are more of them. What is one death amongst their number? A nuisance, no more, surely. They are like a black wave of death ready to bear down on the country, and all that stands between them and the honest decent ordinary folk of the Empire are a few border wardens and men like you.'

'Well, I'm no man, but I'll forgive you. I get your meaning, but you're wrong. We aren't alone, far from it. Every one of those ordinary decent folk will take up arms against the beast. Don't sell them short, they're good people.'

'Aye, and good people die, Kallad, and much more easily than those beasts, at that. You know that as well as I do. Andreas returned last night. That accursed land has changed him. He used to laugh, but not yesterday. All he would say was that he had seen things no living man was meant to see. I didn't want to force him, he'll talk when he's ready. The little that he did share though was grim indeed. A woman was taken by force. A black carriage bearing the crest of von Carstein came into her village and three men snatched her. The day before, strangers had been asking about folk in the village, peculiar questions.'

'Such as?'

'If anyone had unusual luck, say was always lucky at cards, or dice.'

'I see.'

'The woman was the midwife. She'd saved several babes, including more than one breech where the child came out upside down.'

'What would the Vampire Count want with her? It isn't as if the dead fall pregnant.'

'This isn't the first time the black coaches have taken someone from around here. It's happening more and more, as if someone, or something, is collecting people like her: people who have a certain something about them, something that sets them apart, be it luck, a gift or a talent. It don't bode well, mark my words.'

KALLAD LAY ON his back in the dirt straining to press a sack stuffed with rocks and scraps of metal and other rubbish off his chest. His arms shook with violent tremors as he strained against the weight of it, forcing his elbows to lock. He gasped out a count of ten and slowly brought the sack back down to rest on his chest, counted once again to ten, and then repeated the press, forcing a scream between his clenched teeth as he lifted the huge weight.

His shoulder, back and sides burned, but for the first time in months, the pain was brought on by honest exertion, not his wounds. He still favoured his left side a little, taking the extra strain on his right, but he was mending, finally, and he was strong enough to help out around the farms, doing manual labour for those in need, in return for food and lodging.

Sweat beaded on his forehead and gathered in the valley where his throat met his torso.

Allie du Bek sat cross-legged on the floor, hefting a smaller stone, first in his right hand, five times, and then repeating the exercise with his left. The boy was fascinated by Kallad's stubborn refusal to bow to his wounds.

'What news have you got for me?' Kallad asked, heaving the sack aside and sitting up. He towelled the sweat off with a rag.

'None good, Kallad,' Allie said, tossing the stone over his shoulder. It hit the wooden wall of the wood shack and bounced away.

'Tell me anyway.'

Kallad walked over to the barrel that collected rainwater as it ran from the wood shack's guttering, and sank his head and shoulders into it. He came up spluttering, gasped three times, drawing deep breaths, and plunged his head back into the water again.

He was under for a long time.

Allie counted to twenty before Kallad came up for air.

'More of the same, really: three reports of kidnappings in the last week, lots of sightings of the black coaches, a few rumbles of the sleeping sickness striking some of the younger girls up and down the border. Father's been hellishly busy with the border wardens. He gave me a message for you: the wardens have killed three more wolves, and each one went the same way as the last one he told you about. He said you'd know what that meant.'

Of course, he did – wolves that died as men.

'Keep talking, lad,' Kallad said, hefting his axe and burying it in a chunk of wood. He split it in half on the chopping block, and then in half again, and tossed the quarters onto the grass up against the side of the wood shack. He grabbed another piece, and split it, rolling his shoulders afterwards. It was good to feel the blood circulating again. He felt stronger than he had in months.

'Father's gone out hunting with Jared and Klein. Why does it have to be this way?'

That was something that Kallad didn't have an answer for. He wasn't comfortable trying to pass off evil as some part of nature, and wasn't any more at peace with the idea that the world needed evil to attain balance within itself. Telling Allie that good men and women died just because, well that was no answer at all. So he let his silence answer for him.

'Father says that ignorance breeds fear,' the boy said after a while.

'He's right, but in this case, even knowing your enemy won't help lessen the fear. The more you know about the monster, the more frightening it becomes. These things are like parasites that crawl into the mattress of your bed at night and hide there quietly, coming out when you are asleep, to feed on you, bloating themselves on your blood. They need you to survive, and yet their very nature is obsessed with destruction. They are their own worst enemies, but it's still right to be frightened of them. Let the fear give you strength, but don't allow it to overwhelm you. That's the trick.'

Kallad swung his axe again, slamming it into the log on the chopping block and splitting it clean in two.

With each stroke his determination to heal intensified. The monsters could not be left to ravage the countryside. Good people were dying. They didn't deserve to disappear into the bowels of Drakenhof to feed the vampire's bloody hunger.

He wiped off his sweat, and planted the double-headed axe at his feet.

'Come on, boy. It's time I said my goodbyes to some old friends. I've put it off long enough.'

Allie du Bek hopped down from his perch and skipped towards the trees. He waved for Kallad to follow.

Splitting logs and pressing sacks of coal only took him so far towards regaining mastery of his limbs. The simplest of things, walking, lying down, still caused incendiary pains to flare if he moved even slightly awkwardly. It galled Kallad that while he struggled like some newly hatched bird, the vampire moved further and further away from him. He was not used to feeling so utterly helpless. He was Kallad Stormwarden, the last survivor of Karak Sadra. He was not about to roll over and play dead. Instead, he stubbornly drove the feeling off, and trudged after Allie as he plunged into the forest.

They were going to the graves.

He had always known that the day would come when he was strong enough to move on, and this small respite would be over. Kallad had struggled to convince himself that that was the reason why he hadn't made his peace with the dead. It wasn't, of course. It was guilt.

Guilt had prevented him from returning to the clearing where they had fallen, although he went there when he slept, traitorous dreams dragging him back night after night to relive his failure.

TIME HAD DESTROYED every last physical reminder of the fight with the vampire. The grove was pitted with the shallow graves of a few good men. Nature had already begun the slow process of reclaiming the slight mounds that marked their final resting places.

None of them were marked. They deserved better. Every soldier who died fighting evil did.

Kallad bent his head and offered a prayer to the God of the Underworld to look after the souls of his travelling companions, and took the time to remember them one at a time: Sammy Krauss, Joachim Akeman, Reimer Schmidt, Korin Reth, the renegade magician, Nevin Kantor and the three soldiers from Grimm's guard.

His eyes were red-rimmed with tears when he looked up. He breathed in deeply, ready to turn his back on the dead, when it stuck him – there weren't eight shallow graves in the clearing, there were seven.

'Where's your father?'

'I told you, he's gone out hunting with Jared and Klein. Why?'

'Because something's wrong here, boy, the numbers don't add up. There's a grave missing.'

'We buried all the dead, I helped him.'

'I believe you, but I need to talk to your father.'

'He won't be home 'til sunrise at the earliest.'

'Grimna's balls... You saw the dead?'

'Yes.'

'All right, now think, boy. This is important. Did one of the corpses have its hair drawn up in a top-knot, the sides shaved high above its ears?'

'Like a corsair?'

'Exactly like that, yes.'

Allie du Bek shook his head.

Kallad cursed himself for a fool. It had never even occurred to him that Kantor wouldn't be amongst the dead. He looked back in the direction that the magician had fled all those months ago. It was impossible to tell which way he had gone. An all too familiar wave of helplessness rose up to engulf Kallad. The dwarf needed more than just a skilled tracker, he needed a miracle worker. Whatever tracks the magician had blazed in his panicked flight were long gone.

'I need your father and I need him *now*.'

'But it's getting dark.'

For a second, Kallad felt the cold hand of doubt close around his heart. He brushed it off.

'Find him.'

Allie du Bek nodded nervously.

'I don't know where he is, not really, he could be anywhere along the ranges.'

'It doesn't matter how long it takes, I'll be here.'

IT WAS LONG into the night when Allie returned with his father and the two other border wardens.

That they had been in a lethal fight against the dark hunters was obvious.

Lothar had long raking scratches down the side of his face where claws had dug in, and his shirt was torn at the shoulder and soaked black with dried blood.

He'd ripped one sleeve off and wadded it up to staunch the wound, but it was obvious, even ill-lit by the moonlight, that he had lost a lot of blood and was ghastly pale.

Both Klein and Jared bore wounds of their own, but none as substantial as du Bek's.

The man moved awkwardly, favouring his wounded side. It was no surprise that it had taken Allie the better part of the night to return with them.

'It's worse than it looks,' Lothar said, grinning and almost simultaneously wincing.

'Aye, I don't doubt you.'

'The boy said that you think someone survived, or at least isn't buried here.'

Kallad nodded. 'A magician, he turned coward and ran when the fighting began.'

'Then he must have run like the wind, because believe me these beasts can *move*. If he made it, he's long gone, dwarf, you know that.'

'Aye, but that'd also make him my only link to the vampires. If he's alive, I need to find him, Lothar.'

'The trail will be dead by now.'

'I know. After a couple of days it's almost impossible to follow a trail. There won't be footprints to follow, but maybe he got clumsy. It happens. Like as not nothing made it through the winter, but I can't leave it like that, not when there might be a hint somewhere that'd at least point me in the right direction.'

'Well if there is, it's nothing that we'll find in the dark.'

'Good job it took you the best part of the night to get here then, eh?'

The border warden turned gingerly to scan the glade. The sun was beginning to rise redly through the trees, but the darkness remained fiercely determined to keep its secrets close to its heart for a while longer. He had been right, there was little to see.

'What do you remember of the fight, Kallad?'

'Too much, truth be told. Kantor, the magician, ran off that way.' He pointed towards a break in the trees. 'That was the last time I saw him.'

'Then that would be a good place to start, but, understand, after we step through the trees every step is guesswork. No promises, dwarf. Most likely, he's long gone, or we'll find a corpse that we missed first time.'

Kallad nodded.

It was a slow, painstaking search, the three wardens pausing often to examine the ground, or the break of a fine branch that had gone rotten over the winter, but which could, conceivably, have been a sign of the magician's flight. He had no idea how they could do it. To the dwarf, a snapped twig was a snapped twig. There was no distinguishable difference between any of the many bits of deadfall they negotiated, and a leaf trodden into the dirt was nothing more than nature taking its course.

'Here,' Jared called. He'd split off from the others and was running a parallel path off the beaten track. They fought their way through the undergrowth to join him. Bracken and some kind of nettled fruit bushes had grown up around the mossy tree trunks, building a natural wall that stung and pulled at their skin and clothing as they beat a path through it.

Kallad couldn't tell what he was supposed to be looking at, but Lothar and Klein became quite animated,
kneeling to examine the dirt and the broken branches.

'There was a fight here,' Jared explained.

'Not much of one, either,' Klein said.

'How can you tell?' Kallad couldn't see anything that
could possibly indicate that a fight had taken place.

Lothar knelt, examining something trodden into the
ground. He took a phial from his pocket and dripped a
dribble of clear liquid onto it. There was a sizzle and a
small wisp of smoke, and then it was gone. 'Good find,
Jared. I'd stake my life on the fact that this is where the
beast caught up with your magician,' Lothar du Bek
said. 'The good news is that there's no body.'

'So he's alive?' Kallad asked. He had no idea what the
warden had just done, and he didn't really want to
know what magic it was, either. If it served to make du
Bek certain that the magician had survived, he wasn't
going to waste time arguing.

'Well, the signs of the fight are all but gone, but there
most definitely was a struggle here, and my guess is that
two people walked away from it.'

'So the vampire has the magician?'

'I didn't say that. I said two people walked away from
this fight.'

'What do you mean?'

'They didn't leave together. The tracks have all but
been obliterated, but my gut feeling is that one set leads
off in the direction of the blasted ruins that mark the
border with Sylvania, you can see what looks like a heel
print pressed into the hardened mulch of the dead
leaves, it isn't much, but it is something. The other

heads south, into halfling territory. This one is easier to follow.'

'We followed the vampire south.'

'Then it is reasonably safe to assume that the beast carried on its merry way without your magician. That doesn't explain why it let him live, or why he chose to head into Sylvania alone, but those are riddles that can't be solved by me. You know the magician, dwarf. Is he the kind of man to walk alone into the belly of the beast?'

'Not unless the coward found his courage,' Kallad said, shaking his head.

'Frightened men do peculiar things,' Klein observed. 'It is conceivable that he could have made some kind of pact with the creature, striking a bargain to save his life.'

Jared shook his head. 'Unlikely, what does a magician have to offer a vampire lord? The beasts aren't inclined to strike bargains.'

'True,' Lothar agreed. 'You either get lucky or you die. For some reason he's alive, or at least lived long enough to walk out of this forest. It's likely the beast left him for dead, as he did you, Kallad, only we didn't find him. He could be lying twenty feet away, rotting.'

'Or he could be halfway across the world,' Kallad said. 'If he drove the beast off where we failed, well, who knows, eh? The only thing that makes any sense to me is that he's running. He knows that his life is forfeit if he stays in the Empire. That was a condition of his release by the Sigmarites. He was to serve the quest, and when his usefulness was done, so was his time for breathing.'

'Are you sure he knew this?' Lothar asked.

'He would have been a fool if he didn't. The witch hunters don't give up their prisoners lightly.'

'Well then, I think you're right and we have at least one answer to the riddles we've found this morning. The man is running for his life, in the only direction he can – into von Carstein's foul realm. So, he's beaten, perhaps close to death, and he comes to. His instinct is to run. He can't go back to the Empire, so he has to go forwards. It's likely he'll keep on running 'til he falls off the world.'

'Perhaps he hopes to redeem himself by slaying the beast in his lair, after all, he faced one vampire and lived to tell the tale, which is more than can be said for most men. If it was me, I know I'd be trying to find a way to go home. You can't run forever.'

'I have to find him,' Kallad said, knowing it was the truth. Together, his axe and the magician's sorcery stood a chance against the fell beasts.

Alone they were doomed.

'Then we best return home for supplies and make ready to hunt down this magician of yours.'

'We?'

'No offence, Kallad, but you couldn't find your arse with a map and a mirror. So yes, we. Jared and Klein are more than capable of patrolling the border for a few nights without me, and Allie will keep his mother company. It'll keep the boy out of trouble.'

'What about?' He gestured towards the blood and the ragged cuts.

'They should slow me down enough to move at your pace for a while,' Lothar du Bek chuckled.

CHAPTER THIRTEEN
Vado Mori

MIDDENHEIM, CITY OF THE WHITE WOLF
The Blistering Heart of Summer, 2057

THE WALLS OF Middenheim couldn't hope to withstand them. The city would fall.

Hope, they said, was the last thing to die.

They were wrong. Hope died long before desperation, pain and fear had relinquished their hold on the living.

Even then, death was no escape: not when the dead could be pulled out of the earth and puppeted by the malicious finger of a necromancer like Immoliah Fey.

Skellan watched as Fey drew the dead out of the dirt. She lacked the grace of Vlad von Carstein, but what she lacked in grace, she more than made up for with power. The winds of magic howled around her, the air itself crackling with the intensity of the magic she

wove. The incantations tripped off her tongue, staining the air around her with the putrescence of death.
The necromancer revelled in it, throwing her head
back, her voice spiralling in a discordant chorus as the
dead danced at her beck and call.

He had seen this before, but it still unnerved him.
With Vlad, it had been an awesome display of his
strength and mastery over the nations of the living
and the nations of the dead. He commanded the skies
and the dirt, and both jerked around readily to his
whims. With Fey it was different. Her magic lacked the
ferocity of Vlad's. It was subtle, toying with the fabric
of the universe and cajoling it to respond to her
demands. In some ways it was more unnatural.

They came slowly at first, bones clawing out of the
dirt, broken and rotting, emerging in a second bizarre
birth into the unlife. Then, with increasing regularity,
they were drawn from the earth's shallow graves and
ditches where they had been left to rot.

Skellan could not abide the woman, but her usefulness was undeniable. As a magician, she was hardly
the equal of Vlad, but what had started as a fledgling
army almost certainly destined to fail, had grown into
an unstoppable force of nature, because of the necromancer.

Fritz von Carstein stood two paces behind Fey, his
eyes aglow with the fire of hunger. Skellan had a
grudging admiration for Fritz. The vampire cultivated
the image of the carefree Lothario with his harem of
nubile young vixens, but Skellan had quickly come to
realise that it was all an elaborate act. Beneath the fop-
pish exterior lurked a cold ruthless cunning that

outstripped anything Skellan had seen in the unstable Konrad or the earnest Pieter. Fritz was an enigma. He played the fool beautifully, so well in fact, that it became second nature, a mask to be drawn down, that rarely slipped, but for all his talk of decadence and decay there was an underlying current of dark wisdom and steely determination to Fritz that betrayed the act. Skellan harboured no illusions: the vampire played the fool to encourage those around him to underestimate him. It was a useful ploy, one that no doubt had considerable mileage in it.

Fritz was playing the long game. His plans were subtle and would no doubt have been successful, if left to root and fester.

Which is what made the assassination attempt on Konrad so out of character for the cautious Fritz. It was reckless. Three thralls against a vampire of Konrad's strength was blatant stupidity. Fritz couldn't have expected it to succeed, which meant that the scheme had another aim, something that wasn't readily apparent to Skellan.

What did Fritz have to gain from driving Konrad into a murderous frenzy?

Nothing – or perhaps everything.

After Konrad's assault, Skellan hadn't expected to see Fritz again, but as Konrad blustered and strutted with all the pomposity of a man possessed, dishing out orders for the gathered men, Fritz had walked calmly in through the castle gates to claim his place at the front of his army. It was all Konrad could do to restrain himself. This petty act of defiance was the best laugh Skellan had had in months. He thought Konrad

had been about to burst a blood vessel; the vampire
was apoplectic. The wolf, Jerek, had laid a restraining
hand on Konrad's shoulder and, surprisingly, rather
than brushing it off von Carstein had succumbed to it.

'You made it, I see.'

'Nothing could have kept me away, brother-mine.
This is a great honour, and I intend to see your faith
in me repaid manifold.'

Skellan had almost laughed out loud at that. It was
a subtle threat, but it was a threat nonetheless. It was
a pity that Fritz had to die, because it could have been
interesting to see their little power play run its course.
It would have been entertaining, if nothing else. So little of life – death – offered any amusement.

In one sly act of defiance, Fritz had turned his banishment into a not so silent act of rebellion, and a
promise of retribution.

That was something Skellan could respect.

He had come to know the vampire over the months
they had travelled together. The transformation was
subtly stunning as Fritz came out of his brother's
shadow. He was everything Konrad was not. He was
articulate, thoughtful and ruthless without the callous
cruelty of his kin. Villages fell at their feet, but where
Konrad would have razed them to the ground and revelled in a blood feast, Fritz used death to inspire fear.
He farmed the women, bleeding them a little at a
time, taking them prisoner and exerting a curious
mesmerism over them, so that they willingly pan-
dered to his whims and came to him night after night
to satisfy his hungers. He kept the most beautiful for
himself, rebuilding his harem one beauty at a time.

All but a few of the men, he had put down, with a few survivors encouraged to flee for their lives, thus ensuring that the horrors of the vampiric horde would spread like flames across the parched countryside.

The dead were coming. There would be no mercy. None could resist.

Long before their arrival, word had reached Middenheim, ensuring that the City of the White Wolf knew fear, and that those dark imaginings had had time to fester and grow. Its inhabitants remembered the time before, when the dead had all but destroyed the city, ghosts, wraiths, wights and other ethereal dreads descending on its cobbled streets.

Unlike his father-in-death, Fritz took no great joy in the destruction. It was merely a means to an end, and that end was his ascension to power.

Mannfred was right to be wary of Fritz.

It was Fritz who had taught Skellan the greatest of truths – that sunlight need hold no fear. He hadn't believed the older vampire at first, not until he had reached out into the sunlight itself, turning his hand slowly left and right, offering the palm and back to the sun's glare. Even with the evidence of his own eyes, Skellan couldn't get past the probability that it was some kind of trick, and that if he tried to replicate Fritz's casual exposure, he would burn.

'It's in the mind,' Fritz had assured him, stepping out into the light. 'Only the weak need fear the sun. The strongest of us can move abroad even under a full sun.'

'But–'

Fritz tilted his head up to face the sun, relishing its warm kiss.

'Are you afraid, Jon Skellan?'

'Of nothing,' Skellan said, joining von Carstein in the light. It felt peculiar at first, more intense than he remembered it ever being when he was alive. His skin prickled and he felt sure that he was about to be consumed by unholy fire.

'Concentrate. You have nothing to fear. Focus on the feelings spreading through your skin and dampen them down. Do it now.'

Skellan held his hand before his face. The skin had turned an ugly red.

'What's happening to me?'

'You are burning from the inside out, now concentrate.'

'Or?' The angry red blush had spread the length of his arm. He could feel the intensity of the fire swelling beneath his skin.

'Or you burn.' The brutal matter-of-factness of von Carstein's answer was all he needed. Skellan focused on the searing heat beneath his skin and willed it to subside.

For a moment, he feared the worst as he felt a sudden flare in the glands beneath his arms and between his legs. Then there was nothing, no sense of feeling at all. The fire had died.

'You see?' Fritz asked.

'Can we all do this?'

'Our kind? Yes, we all have the power to master the heat. Few choose to, though, drawing comfort from the shadow world of night.'

'I pity the fools.'

'Don't. Pity is something to be left behind in your old life, Skellan. Savour this triumph and know that the day holds nothing worth fearing. Let that knowledge set you free.'

It had, in more ways than von Carstein could ever have imagined.

Still, as Fritz had said they would, the others clung to the darkness when they could have walked proudly through the day. It disgusted him.

Immoliah Fey brought her hands down and slumped, exhaustion taking its toll. Five hundred corpses in various states of decay and wholeness crowded around the necromancer, bugs crawled over strips of rotten flesh and flies swarmed around the corpses, drawn to the filth of the grave. They shambled and lurched to Fey's danse macabre.

Very soon, the people of Middenheim would know the true meaning of the word fear. Theirs would be a painful lesson, learned in the hardest of ways. Then, with the White Wolves humbled, the vampires would descend with bloody fury.

'Ready?' Skellan asked the dark-skinned man at his side.

'I was born ready.'

'A shame you weren't ready when you died, eh?' Skellan said without a hint of irony. 'We go in the second wave, behind the corpses. Torch the temples and meeting halls to drive out the living. Kill the men and any children that get in the way, but leave the women for von Carstein.'

'As you wish.'

'It isn't as I wish. If it were, I'd loose the beast within and have us go in with a vengeance. Just this once, I would give the vampires free rein. Let the world know what it is like when the aristocracy of the night feed.'

His dark-skinned companion smiled a cold smile.

'Indeed. Such cruel wonders we could unleash. Pity the cattle, then.'

'Pity? No, no, no.' Skellan said, echoing von Carstein's admonition. 'Why waste your time with something so… banal? Pity is for the life you left behind. Focus on yourself, feed on the joy their suffering brings.'

Pressed up against the portcullis, her face pale with fear, Skellan saw a woman clutching a child to her breast. From this distance, she bore an uncanny resemblance to Lizbet. The similarity didn't touch him. When the time for it came, she would burn like his dead wife had. It mattered nothing to him.

THE BATTLE WAS brutal and bloody.

The White Wolves sallied forth, hooves sparking on the cobbled street as they passed beneath the keystone of the massive arch that housed the city gates, two and three at a time. War horns bugled a fanfare. The White Wolves fanned out across the plain into a rolling wall of death as their war cries sang out. This was combat at its most primal. Pennons snapped in the air. Horses stamped, impatient, smelling blood on the air.

The bugle sounded again, a single short violent bray, and the Wolves charged.

The young wolf at the head of the riders threw back his head and howled, his flame-red hair streaming out behind him in the wind as he raised his warhammer above his head and whipped it around in a savage arc.

They hit the dead at full glorious gallop, splintering their ranks, and the battle was joined. The iron heads of warhammers cracked the brittle bones of the dead.

Immoliah Fey puppetted her corpses expertly, sacrificing them beneath the hooves of the Wolves' horses, causing the beasts to shy and fall. Blood spilled, the vampires unleashed the beasts within, and joined the battle.

Infantry followed the charging horses, dogs loping at their sides.

Arrows rained down from the walls of the city, cutting down friend and foe alike. The archers possessed no particular skills, but what skills were necessary to fill the sky with a rain of death? What was important was that the deadly rain never ceased.

Even with their forces bolstered by Fey's zombies, the battle was hard on the forces of the dead. The White Wolves fought with the desperation of the condemned. They knew they stood to lose more than their lives if they failed. They knew that they were fighting for the lives – and deaths – of every one sheltering behind the towering walls of the City of the White Wolf. The intimacy of the battle added steely determination to their fearsome combat rage. This was their fight, their home, and they would not fail this time. They owed the dead that much.

Skellan fought like a daemon, taking the fight to the Wolves. His blade cut and cleaved and stabbed, opening guts and slicing throats indiscriminately, while he kept Fritz von Carstein in his line of sight as the vampire waged his own bloody war on the living of Middenheim. Whether drawn by recognition or merely sensing that the man had risen to replace Jerek and therefore held a pivotal position amid the ranks of the enemy, Fritz fought his way mercilessly towards the Hamaya's kin. Blades clashed on bone. Men screamed. It was carnage.

Then the two met, the young wolf and the immortal beast, and it was over before it could become a fight, the shaft of an arrow jutted from his horse, bringing the beast down and crushing its rider's legs, pinning the young wolf helplessly in the mud of the battle-field.

Von Carstein leaned in close enough to breathe foetid breath into the rider's face as his hands closed around his neck.

Skellan moved quickly, disengaging the soldier he faced, shifting his weight onto his back leg and pivoting, bringing his sword around in a low arc that hamstrung his opponent, and rolling away, ducking beneath a wildly swinging hammer and coming to his feet. A thrust gutted the only soldier between him, and Fritz and the young wolf. He slipped in the mud, but still managed to cover the ground between himself and von Carstein in the time it would have taken a living man's heart to beat once – and for the young wolf trapped beneath his dead horse that single beat was the difference between life and death.

It had to be now.

Skellan came up behind the gloating Fritz, and in one smooth move drew the arrow from the dead horse's neck and rammed its silver tip into the vampire's neck. The bloodless tip punched out of Fritz's throat and suddenly, instead of strangling the young wolf, the vampire's hands were at his own throat, clawing at the silver arrowhead that had killed him, even as the unlife spilled out of his body.

There was no dignity in Fritz's second death.

Skellan leaned in close and, not caring that the young wolf overheard, whispered in von Carstein's ear, 'A gift from Mannfred. Nothing personal, you understand, but there can be only one heir to Vlad. Your continued existence was an irritant. It complicated things. So you see, we couldn't allow you to live. Not that it matters any, but I liked you, Fritz. Of all of them, you were perhaps the most dangerous, the most worthy. Such is life, my friend.' Fritz's eyes had begun to glaze over as the unnatural ties binding him to the land of the living severed one by one. 'Soon, your brothers will be rotting in the underworld beside you. Take some comfort in that last thought, eh? You won't be alone for long.'

Fritz tried to speak. His mouth opened and closed uselessly. He managed a pathetic gurgle before he slumped forward over the young wolf's horse and died.

'Our lord has fallen!' Skellan cried, brandishing his sword over his head. 'Retreat! Sound the retreat!' The news of von Carstein's death spread across the battlefield like wildfire. These vampires had not stood beside the first Vampire Count, they harboured no illusions that their immortality was in fact true immortality. That their leader had fallen sent shockwaves through the survivors, crippling them with panic.

It was all Skellan could have hoped for, and more.

Fey's zombies collapsed where they stood as panic undermined the necromancer's hold on them. She fled, while the vampires surrendered the field, leaving the White Wolves with nothing left to slay.

Skellan loitered on the field, watching from a distance as, freed from beneath his dead horse, the young wolf hosted up Fritz's corpse, preparing it to be dismembered. The man cut Fritz von Carstein's dead heart from his chest and tossed it to the dogs at his feet.

Smiling to himself, Skellan turned away from the slaughter.

CHAPTER FOURTEEN
Victis Honor

NULN BESIEGED
The Blistering Heart of Summer, 2057

JEREK VON CARSTEIN'S HUMANITY refused to be snuffed out.

It lingered, haunting him, a living ghost in the kingdom of the dead. The irony was repulsive.

Instead of revelling in the dark world of unlife, Jerek found himself clinging to the tatters of memory that belonged to his life before. Inconsequential things that hadn't mattered then, but had become more and more vital since his fall from Middenheim spire. He found himself remembering the faces of people he had barely known. They came to him in sudden flashes, accompanied by hints of what they had meant at the time, scents, accents and tiny hallucinations that drew him back towards the man he had been.

Worst of all, he welcomed them. He welcomed the pain that came with remembering. He welcomed the guilt that threatened to consume him. He welcomed the anger that smouldered beneath the memories. He welcomed them all because they were all reminders that he might be a monster, but that he hadn't surrendered his soul. Some tiny spark of it still flickered within him. He hadn't surrendered to the darkness and the cold. He found no comfort in pain. He took no joy in suffering.

The companionship of the dead repelled him.

Instead, he clung to his living ghost, knowing that to do so was to invite madness.

In Roth Mehlinger he saw all the world's sickness made flesh. Even in the few months since his siring, Mehlinger had completely surrendered to the beast within. He savoured the hunt and the kill, and being Jerek's first, he was strong, stronger than he had any right to be. He walked abroad in daylight without any fear of the sun. He infiltrated the city, not caring about the high walls and the iron gates meant to keep the wolves from the door. He took wing, metamorphosing into a ravenlike black bird. No walls ever constructed could bar a bird. Mehlinger came and went as he pleased, feeding on the young and beautiful of the city – and stupidly the peasants suspected nothing, because Mehlinger had a taste for young men and cared nothing for the pretty little bakers' daughters or the temptations of the more worldly barmaids.

He haunted the slums, taking pleasure in the screams of otherwise strong men as he forced them to submit bodily to him, and then he fed.

In death, Mehlinger was everything the man had hated in life.

'You made me, father,' Mehlinger had sneered, seeing Jerek's distaste for the first time. 'Never forget that. I was happily drinking myself to death before you decided to play god and do this to me. Every death is on your hands as surely as if you had killed them yourself, only this way is more fun for me. For once, I don't have to be content to live half a life in your shadow. I can be my own man, Jerek, and you know what? I like the man I have become.'

'You stopped being a man a long time ago, Roth. What you are now, well, that is not a man.'

'I'm whatever the hell I want to be, wolf. I don't need your permission anymore. You did that much for me when you took my life.'

'I'm sorry, Roth, more than you can ever know.'

'Don't be. This death is not such a bad place to be.'

Mehlinger was drawn to Pieter von Carstein. They were similar beasts, ruthless, callous, deadly, and suffered no compunction in killing for fun and amusement. They hunted together at night, Mehlinger feeding while Pieter played with his food. Von Carstein did not share Mehlinger's passion for boys, but he more than made up for it by creatively torturing the cattle before offering the succulent flesh up for Mehlinger to suck greedily on. Their relationship was parasitic. They fed off each other's sickness, exacerbating it, driving each other to acts of fouler and fouler depravity.

Jerek had turned his back on his get.

The thought of putting Mehlinger down had crossed his mind, taking responsibility for the monster he had sired and finishing what he started, but it wasn't easy. Their bond was stronger than sire and get. There was all that went before: the wolf and his right hand. They had a history.

That he couldn't turn his back on that history was another sign that Jerek von Carstein was still, in part, Jerek Kruger, the White Wolf. So, Mehlinger lived on, his corruption growing more and more complete by the day.

Together with Pieter, Mehlinger had rejoiced as one of Konrad's pet necromancers, Katja von Seirt, had touched the winds of magic, drawing on Shyish, the sixth wind, to raise a horde of dead that counted in the tens of thousands. The taint of Chaos hung over their conquering army. It was the ultimate vampiric essence, bleeding the land dry as it swarmed towards Nuln, devastation trailing in its wake. The blight inflicted by Pieter's army rivalled anything caused by his sire, Vlad. The sickness that had for so long afflicted Sylvania seeped into the Empire. Nature itself, the greens and golds of summer, withered and died, trampled beneath the shuffling feet of the dead.

In many ways, Jerek knew, an army was like a snake. It depended upon cunning against greater foes, and its body was impotent against enemies if its fangs were not kept sharp. Pieter was the head of this army, the necromancer Katja von Seirt and the wolf, Jerek, its fangs. Von Seirt was venomous, certainly, but her bites were proving ineffective because of von Carstein's ineptitude. The vampire was no tactician. He had little grasp of the art of war. He was nothing more than a pale forgery, replicating things that he had seen done before, but without the ruthlessness that had made them successful. Like all classically insecure leaders, he ignored Jerek's battle-hardened wisdom in favour of his own council. The siege of Nuln had lasted four months already, rendering the most basic of their weapons, fear, redundant. The citizens of the city had grown familiar with the dead at their door. They were inured to the fear that such a force ought to have inspired.

Without fear to undermine the enemy, they needed to resort to deviousness. Unfortunately, Pieter took to posturing before the city walls, demanding the living bow down before him or die, but he lacked the wherewithal to follow through. His words were little more than empty threats, or so it seemed. The corpses surged at the walls, only to be beaten back with flames and oil.

The defenders did not surrender meekly. They met his demands of servitude with jeers, throwing rotten fruit and vegetables from the battlements, which in turn only served to cause Pieter's anger to spiral out of control. The vampire ranted and raved, cursing all humanity for the vile scum that they were, unable to distance himself from the haranguing. He spat curses as the defenders threw refuse from the walls. Three farmers struggled with the rotten carcass of a dead cow, sending it toppling from the high wall. The animal fell, stiff with rigor.

'HAVE YOU THOUGHT more about my puzzle, Katja?' Jerek asked the necromancer.

'I have thought of little else, wolf. So much so that I have come to think of it more as a curse than a question, it haunts me so.'

'Have you come to any conclusions?'

'Many and none, if that makes a blind bit of sense.'

'Not in the slightest.'

'There is nothing to prove the veracity of your assumption that your sire's power lay in his signet ring.'

'I know it to be true, the cattle talk. The ring was stolen through treachery.' He had heard the story in Middenheim as he hunted Mehlinger. The Sigmarites had turned to thievery to bring about the fall of Vlad von Carstein. In desperate times, humanity was capable of stooping to the most desperate of measures. How they could have known of the ring's restorative magic he had no idea, but he didn't doubt for a moment that they were right. It explained his sire's irrational anger as he had thrown everything he had at Altdorf in an uncharacteristic rage, and it explained why he had fallen.

The ring was the key to it all. He had to find it, Find it and destroy it before others could possess it. He had long since begun to suspect that the ring's existence was the reason for his lingering humanity. It had become a smouldering obsession. He thought of Mehlinger, the callousness of the monster he had become, the pure blooded vampire, and of Pieter with his all-consuming hatred for the living, even Konrad with his capricious whims and fragile instability. Any one of them with the ring on his finger could rise as the ultimate dark lord. The thought chilled Jerek to the marrow.

'Indeed, in which case a magic greater than mine has fused within it some form of regenerative magic. This would not, in theory, be impossible, but it would be beyond the ken of any adept of magic that I have ever encountered.'

'So you couldn't replicate it?'

'Forge a new ring to make you truly immortal? No.'

'That is some small mercy,' Jerek said. 'Do you know anyone capable of it?'

'As I said, I've yet to encounter a sorcerer with the kind of mastery necessary to craft such an artefact. Fey, perhaps, but I doubt it. This is old magic, wolf. Such knowledge has slipped into darkness. The von Carstein ring is irreplaceable, and lost.'

'If Pieter has his way we march on, to Altdorf. He intends to tear the city apart looking for the ring.'

'He's a fool.'

'Worse, he's a desperate fool.'

'Does he imagine that the Sigmarites have buried the old Count with it still on his finger? The ring's gone. Destroyed.'

'Who knows what he thinks – if he actually thinks. It's a mess,' Jerek said to the necromancer, von Seirt. 'The man makes fools of us all.'

'So, what would you have me do, wolf?'

'Humble the fool.'

'The living are doing a fine job of that from where I am standing.'

'This cannot be allowed to continue, woman. They are making a mockery of us. It is a shambles.' He looked up at the wall where a man mimicked Pieter's posturing, strutting backwards and forwards along the wall walk. 'They even have a fool pretending to be descended from the vampire slayer, van Hal. They need to learn humility. They need to remember fear.'

'And how do you propose to teach those lessons, wolf?'

'It is not my place to propose, Pieter has made that plain enough.'

'Rubbish, you are Hamaya. You answer only to the new Count. If you will it, I will have my dead tear the walls apart, stone by stone and feast on the living. You need only say the word and it will be done.'

'And if *I* say the word?' Pieter von Carstein came up behind them, Roth Mehlinger at his side like some fawning lapdog. His honeyed voice dripped with loathing. 'Tell me, I am curious, magician. Would you show me the same loyalty you afford this grizzled old fool?'

'I serve but one master,' Katja said coldly.

'Ah, yes, my beloved brother, we shall have to see about that. Now, answer my question, would you have your dead tear the walls down stone by blessed stone if *I* willed it?'

'Unquestionably.'

'I don't believe you, magician,' Pieter sneered.

'Then ask me, my lord, and find out for yourself.' The necromancer inclined her head slightly, a condescending gesture meant to rile Pieter.

'Perhaps I will.'

'Do it,' Mehlinger said, a sly smiling spreading across his hateful face, 'and then take a leaf from the old wolf's book and turn the vampires loose, let them feed, all of them. Let them drink their fill. No more hiding behind the zombies. Unleash the beasts, Pieter. You know you want to.'

Von Carstein's grin was truly repulsive. He looked beyond them, to the man on the wall, the one who claimed to be Helmut van Hal. 'You will know suffering like no other mortal,' he promised, not caring that the man couldn't hear him, 'and when you are finally dead and think yourself safe from pain, I will bring you back and kill you all over again.' He turned to Katja. 'Come, sister in shadow, there are things I would know before I turn you loose.'

'You need only ask.'

'Ah yes, ask my little dark deceiver. That is exactly what I intend to do, although I doubt that I will enjoy your answers.'

'The truth is seldom uttered for the sake of enjoyment, lord.'

Jerek watched the pair leave, von Carstein linking arms with the necromancer. It was an intimate gesture that spoke of lovers not enemies. Jerek noticed Mehlinger's discomfort at the sight.

'Jealousy doesn't become you,' he said, turning his back on his old friend. Pieter and Katja had neared the wall. Jerek moved close enough to hear the vampire call up to the defenders:

'Your determination to die is impressive, mortal. However, your prancing and preening has lost its edge of entertainment. Frankly, it has become boorish. So, little man, I am here to tell you that you've won, but before all your stupid followers start getting excited, what I mean to say is that I will grant your wish. Tonight you die, all of you. Every last man, woman and child, unless you bow down to serve me, in life, or death. There will be no mercy!' This last Pieter screamed at the top of his lungs, his voice dissolving into hysteria.

The man on the wall smiled, which was not at all what Jerek had expected from a man hearing his own death sentence being delivered. He assayed a theatrical bow, seemingly oblivious to the undead host amassed at his door. This was a blind, Jerek realised, a ruse, misdirection. Pieter was being goaded into making an even bigger idiot of himself than he already was. The gambit put the wolf in mind of a sideshow trickster's misdirection. They wanted von Carstein's eyes fixed firmly on the wall, so what was it they weren't supposed to be seeing? Where was the real threat?

He contented himself with the knowledge that he would know soon enough, and if Pieter and Mehlinger suffered as a result, well, he wouldn't mourn either one of them. He was conflicted. Von Seirt was right, he was Hamaya, but he was also human, or at least some small part of him was. As Hamaya, he served a different master, and had no loyalty to Pieter, Konrad wanted him disposed of, after all, and as a human, he found himself praying for the same outcome, but for very different reasons.

Pieter von Carstein was dangerous.

The men on the walls knew that, the living hiding behind them most certainly did. Their game was obviously intended to blind the vampire to the obvious, like a scorpion backed into a corner, the humans were at their most dangerous when they appeared trapped.

The next few hours would be fascinating for the impartial observer, Jerek knew. Pieter's tactical naiveté and his horde of the damned, matched up against the posturings of the man on the wall and the puppeteer playing his strings. Given the desperation of the situation, few could claim to be impartial. Both factions had a vested interest in the other's failure. It was fascinating to Jerek, who found himself looking for the sting in the tail. It had to be there. What did the defenders have to gain by driving Pieter into a fury?

Apart from the obvious, that mad men don't think straight, he could see no great advantage to incensing the enemy.

Instead, Jerek turned his attention closer to home. He studied Pieter and the woman at his side. Were the two lovers? He thought perhaps they were. There was an intimacy between them, a familiarity of movements, of bodies used to being close together, but there was no obvious affection. He suspected that neither cared very much for the other. For Mehlinger, their easy proximity was like a stake through the heart. The vampire's seething was almost palpable.

Mehlinger's rise amongst the aristocracy of the night would no doubt be spectacular. He embodied the darkness.

A flicker of movement drew Jerek's gaze to the top of the high wall. More men had joined van Hal. They stood beside him on the wall walk, their numbers swelling, fifty, sixty, then a hundred, and more, until finally the wall was crammed with soldiers, who all turned their backs on Pieter von Carstein. Puzzled, Jerek watched as, as one, the defenders of Nuln pulled down their trousers.

The old wolf burst out laughing.

He found himself liking these unknown men. They were his kind of people. They had guts. They were real soldiers. Good men, not shambling corpses dancing to the tune of some madman. They didn't deserve to die any more than anyone else did, but this petty act of defiance had sealed their fate. Forgiveness was not a von Carstein family trait.

THEY WERE DEAD before dawn.

Von Carstein unleashed the beasts, ordering his vampires over the walls. They had no ladders to climb, those were for the lumbering dead that von Seirt had swarming over one another, making ladders out of their own corpses, until they breached the walls in thirty places, bringing them down one stone at a time, just as the necromancer had promised. A cloud of bats filled the night, flitting and darting high over the streets of the city, their song an unbearable chorus of excitement and hunger. The creatures settled on rooftops and gutters, transforming as they did into their feral forms, the beast within released and ready to feast.

Nuln fell in a frenzy of feeding.

The screams were sickening. The creatures chased the living through the streets, hunting them down, tearing the clothes from their victims' backs even as they tore flesh from the bones, and gorged themselves on so much fresh meat.

Jerek took no part in the slaughter.

He walked through the streets strewn with broken bodies and cobbles slick with blood, detached from it all.

Whatever it was the men of Nuln had hoped to achieve by angering Pieter had obviously failed. In a matter of hours, the city had become a necropolis. Death walked the streets of the Imperial city, and stalked the living, welcoming them into Morr's dark embrace. Age, creed, colour, it didn't matter, all were reduced to one single absolute: they were meat for the beasts.

They wallowed in the splendour of the city. They dined in the palaces and in the paupers' hovels, and each meal tasted divine. Virgins offered up their throats and legs, and crones crawled on the floor, bleeding and dying as they debased themselves for the vampires.

It went beyond war. It went beyond death. It was an orgy of blood lust and depravity. It was sickening in the extent of its thoroughness. The vampires drove the living out of their hiding places, torching houses, and smoking them out of the temples where they had clustered begging their gods for salvation. Only there was no salvation from the dead. There was no light to guide or save them. The darkness was all consuming, the creatures of the dark invincible.

Sated, finally, after hours of gorging themselves, the vampires fell into a kind of drunken slumber. Jerek saw them lying side by side with the corpses that they had drained so that it was impossible to tell them apart from their victims. He stepped over them and walked around them. He looked up at the sky. The sun would be rising soon, not that it mattered to the inhabitants of this once great city. Light, dark, it was all the same to the dead. Come dusk, the ranks of von Seirt's horde would swell by the thousands and Nuln would be left to the rats. It beggared belief.

He hadn't done this. He hadn't been a part of it. There was no blood on his hands, but that didn't matter. It didn't absolve him of the slaughter. He was a beast now. Even the smell of the blood had his heart racing and his mouth salivating with disgusting hunger. He wanted to feed, to join in the killing, and that was enough to damn him in his own mind.

The depravity of it revolted the wolf. The sheer scale of the killing was incredible. It outstripped anything he had ever experienced, every battlefield he had ever fought on, it was worse, even, than the fall of Middenheim, because this was different: this was inhuman, monstrous. It was butchery. The dead weren't soldiers, they were women and children, they hadn't taken up arms or bared their arses, they hadn't made the fight their own, it had been forced down their throats until it choked them to death.

After months of seeming impotence, the dead surrounding the city in a lake of rotting flesh, it had become a war of attrition. The living needed to feed, so the dead choked off their farmland and their livestock, polluted their water and waited, seemingly content to let disease and starvation have their way before they stormed the walls. Then suddenly this.

There was no honour in this victory.

It sickened Jerek.

Carrion birds settled on the rooftops and window ledges, drawn to the stink of the slaughter. They were legion.

They came down to feed, even as the sun began to rise slowly, red on the dead city.

Hating himself, hating the need he felt settling on his shoulders and the surety that he *would* succumb to it and feed, Jerek walked out of the killing ground in time to see the trap sprung.

JEREK SAW THE men hunched low and moving swiftly across the ground. Even from a distance he recognised the front man as the supposed descendent of van Hal. He gesticulated wildly, directing men left and right. It was all done silently. They split into smaller groups with impressive discipline, three clusters of ten apiece angling back towards the city, two more groups of ten fanning out across the undead camp, making for the black pavilions of Pieter and his loyal vampires – the same vampires who had gorged themselves senseless in the city and lay in sated slumber like stuffed pigs.

Jerek dropped down on all fours and gave himself over to the change. Focusing on the wolf inside his skin, the lupine form, the grace and power of the beast, he felt himself changing, his curiosity giving way to the most basic, primal, instincts: preservation and hunger. The bones in his shoulders broke and remoulded themselves, larger and more powerful, as the vertebrae of his spine stretched and arched, his wild mane becoming a pelt.

The wolf moved carefully across the field, his easy lope silent beneath the crackling and spitting of the burning city. The smoke masked the pungent reek of fear, but it didn't bury it away. The soldiers stank of it: fear and faeces. Moving close to Pieter's pavilion, he saw the red-rimmed eyes of the lookout and realised what they had done. They had traded their own, gambling that the sacrifice would be worth it, that it would give these last few men the chance to slay the beasts. It was the supreme sacrifice: not their own lives, but the lives of everyone they knew and loved. There was no way that these fifty men would be able to live with themselves come sunrise. Then, inevitably, the blood of more good men would stain the field.

Van Hal emerged from the pavilion, clutching a blackened heart in his hand: Pieter's.

He saw the wolf and nodded, throwing the beast the dead meat.

Jerek fed.

A second soldier stepped out through the tent flaps, the fingers of his left hand tangled in Roth Mehlinger's hair. A stump of white bone jutted out of the ragged flesh where the neck should have met the body. The vampire's face was frozen into a death mask of ridiculous surprise.

'The beasts are dead,' van Hal said, his voice empty. There was no triumph in his victory. The cost had been too high. 'Now we pray for our brothers. May Sigmar guide their swords, for tomorrow, we die.'

Behind him, moving like the ghosts they truly were, the three groups of soldiers re-entered the city through the main gates. With von Carstein's so-called protectors wallowing in the afterglow of murder, these thirty would be more than enough to cut out the canker that was the undead in their city.

Jerek sensed movement, a shape rising beside the canvas pavilion. He knew that the fight was not over for these few, not while von Seirt had breath to command the dead. The wolf tensed and sprang, bowling aside the soldier clutching Mehlinger's severed head. A moment later, they saw what he had seen: the dead rising. Steel rang out as the defenders of Nuln drew their swords, ready, eager, to die now that their final die was cast, the game played out.

The wolf tossed back his head, sniffing out the necromancer's reek, her bodily fluids, the sickly sweet tang of her secretions that were so uniquely female, and then he found traces of her on the wind. She was close. He followed the smell of her. Death aroused her, making it easy.

She had taken refuge amid the cages where von Carstein kept the kidnapped villagers that he used to sate his vampire's thirst. She was pretending to be one of them.

Jerek bounded into the enclosed circle of wagons, his momentum taking him through the wooden bars of the cage, splintering them and cutting him in the process. Snarling and feral, his teeth snapped and tore at the necromancer's throat as she tried to ward off the attack, but the sheer ferocity of the wolf's assault drove her back further into the corner of the cage.

Her screams were desperate, but her death was no more savage than she deserved.

Jerek tore Katja von Seirt's throat out and fed on her.

Her corpse jerked and spasmed beneath him as her nerves fired off random triggers before relaxing into death. Still, Jerek drank greedily, savouring the rank corruption of the necromancer's lifeblood as it trickled down his throat.

When the soldiers came to free the prisoners, he had returned to his human form. Van Hal stood at the broken wooden bars of the cage, peering into the darkness within. He saw Jerek, naked, standing over the woman's corpse.

They shared a moment of mutual recognition. The soldier understood.

'I should kill you,' van Hal said.

'And I should kill you, but I have no desire to, soldier. You have paid enough this day for a hundred lifetimes.'

'Indeed, but I cannot let you leave.'

'You can,' Jerek said. 'This woman,' he toed the corpse of von Seirt with his bare foot, 'would have killed you all. The dead collapsed did they not, even as they rose up to strike you down?'

Van Hal nodded.

'Her hold over them died as she did.'

'You're the wolf I fed?'

'I am, but more importantly I was, once, the wolf. Now I am not sure what I am, but I am not one of *them.*'

'Nor are you one of us.'

'No, but we, I think, want the same thing.'

'I want the beasts destroyed. I want the dead driven back to the hell they came from. I want my family back. I want my world to know peace.'

'Then we are not so different, soldier.'

'Here's what's going to happen, I am going to leave to check on the other prisoners. When I return in a quarter of an hour, I am going to put you out of your misery. Use these fifteen minutes to make your peace with your god.'

'Thank you, soldier.'

'Don't thank me, wolf, I am tired of being thanked for doing the wrong thing.'

With that van Hal left.

Jerek was gone long before he returned.

CHAPTER FIFTEEN
The Sins of the Father

DRAKENHOF, SYLVANIA
The Drawn-out Dog Days of Autumn, 2057

JARED AND KLEIN left them at the border.

Twice, they had encountered the huge dire wolves hunting, and twice they had slain the beasts. Lothar du Bek was a dichotomy in battle. While his eyes blazed with righteous fury, his every action was calm to the point of detachment. He nocked the silver tipped arrows and drew back on the bowstring, holding, waiting, judging the wind, the distance, and keeping the beast in his sight before loosing shaft after shaft with skill and precision. The arrows took the beasts between the eyes, in the throat and heart. It was over quickly.

'You're a dangerous man, Lothar,' Kallad had observed, shouldering his axe as they stood over the corpse of a man who had, moments before, been a huge wolf.

'These are dangerous times, my friend. I am nothing more than a child of the times.'

Kallad and Lothar du Bek travelled on through the barren lands of Sylvania. The folks they passed wore the same harsh signs of malnutrition and superstition, bellies distended, bones pressed out starkly against emaciated skin. They were the physical embodiment of the land they lived in with its dead trees and infertile soil. These were haunted people. They huddled on the sides of the road as the pair passed, clutching their talismans and casting frightened gazes over their shoulders to see that they had moved on down the road. They didn't talk. Kallad was used to trading information about the road with fellow travellers met on the journey, but not so in this hellish place. They kept themselves very much to themselves. They had no time for others.

A signpost on the roadside marked another two miles to the next village.

With night drawing in, the pair would need to find somewhere to sleep. The village would no doubt have a tavern or inn, and hopefully a room to spare, or a common room where they could bed down for the night. The cold nights were drawing in and bivouacking down on the roadside was becoming less and less appealing. A night in a warm bed sounded good to both of them.

'Let's push on,' Lothar suggested. 'Right now I'd trade another half an hour on the road for a night by a warm fire, a minstrel and a jug of mulled wine.'

'Aye, reckon I'd trade half an hour on the road for a decent bite to eat.'

'Fed up of my cooking already, eh, dwarf?'

'Oh aye.'

A mile outside the village they past three cairns piled up by the roadside, the stone mounds marked with the sign of Morr. One of the cairns was considerably smaller than the others, and obviously covered a young child.

They paused for a moment to pay their respects to the dead before walking down into the village.

The windows of every house they passed were shuttered, although glimmers of warm light seeped through the cracks. The doors were likewise closed. There was no livestock in the fields, and no dogs or cats running wild.

It felt to Kallad as if they had walked into the village of the damned.

'I've got a bad feeling about this place.'

'Couldn't agree more. It feels like the life's been sucked out of it.'

'Aye, that's it exactly. It's been drained dry.'

The tavern was no different from any of the other buildings. The windows had been shuttered and barred, although smoke drifted lazily from the chimney, evidence at least that there was life inside. The door, however, was locked.

Kallad rapped on the door. No one answered.

He looked at the border warden, who shrugged, and banged again, hammering on the wood with his gauntleted fist.

'Do we have to batter the damned door down?' Kallad shouted.

'Go away,' a voice answered. 'We don't want your sort here.'

'Open the door, man.'

'Go away,' the voice repeated stubbornly.

'Grimna's balls, just open the damned door before I kick it in and start pounding on your head instead.'

He slammed his fist into a wooden panel above the brace, once, twice, three times, causing the wood to splinter.

'For pity's sake!' the voice behind the door pleaded. 'Leave us be.'

'This is ridiculous, dwarf. Let's just leave these people alone. They've obviously got a good reason for not opening the door. We can sleep in the stable,' Lothar du Bek said.

'All I want is a warm meal and a place to lay my bones. It doesn't seem too much to ask from an inn.'

They heard the sound of a bolt being drawn back.

The door cracked open an inch.

'You're not one of them?'

'What're you blatherin' on about, man?'

'You're not...' he peered out at the dwarf and the hulking figure of the warden beside him. 'No, you're obviously not. Inside, quickly.' The innkeeper threw open the door and ushered the pair in. No sooner had they crossed the threshold than he was slamming and bolting the door behind them.

The taproom was dead. A small fire burned in the hearth. There were no other customers.

'Business is boomin', eh? Not a surprise if you won't let people in, I reckon.'

'People don't want to be outside, not after dark, not if they know what's good for them,' the innkeeper said, locking the final bolt into place. 'Now, we ain't got much in the way of food, but there's some broth, a bit of yesterday's bread left and ale enough to get you blind drunk, if that's what you're hankering for.'

'Sounds like a feast compared to what we've been living off for the last few weeks.'

'Well then, you're welcome to it. I'll see to the drink first. Sit yourselves by the fire.'

'My thanks.' Kallad drew off his gauntlet and held out his right hand. 'I'm Kallad Stormwarden, and this lanky fellow is Lothar.'

The innkeeper shook hands with the dwarf. 'Mathias Gesner. Make yourself at home, Kallad Stormwarden.'

'Are you alone here, Mathias?' Lothar asked, unclasping the hasp of his travel cloak and draping it over the back of a threadbare armchair beside the fire. He sank into the seat and planted his feet on the footstool.

'Yes.' The pain of loss was etched into Mathias Gesner's plain face. He was obviously a simple man, not given to lying. He wore his hurt on his sleeve, as the old Reikspiel saying went. It didn't take any great intelligence to know that it hadn't always been this way. At some point not so very long ago, this inn had no doubt been the heart of a thriving village. Things changed quickly in this godforsaken country. That, at least, accounted for the bolts and the shuttered windows. Kallad remembered the cairns on the roadside. He had been right in thinking that they had stumbled into a village of the damned. These people were living in the dark through fear: fear that the light would draw attention to them, and with it, more death would come their way. They had given up believing that the light would keep the monsters at bay, such were the depths of their despair.

The food, when it came, was far from delicious, but it filled a hole. Mathias joined them at the fire. They ate a while in silence, all three men locked away with their own thoughts. The bread was hard, the broth bland, but after travel fare it smelled almost heavenly. The ale was good, better than it had any right to be in this out of the way corner of Sylvania.

Lothar smacked his lips appreciatively as he banged the tankard down on the table.

'Not bad at all.'

'Aye, it's a tasty drop, for sure,' the dwarf agreed, foam thick in his beard. He backhanded his mouth dry and smacked his lips appreciatively.

'We brew it here, me and…' the innkeeper stopped mid sentence.

Kallad didn't press him. He knew where the sentence had been going: into the territory of the dead.

Outside, a howling wolf greeted the gibbous moon.

It was a sad lament.

The cry was taken up somewhere in the distance, a faint and haunting, familiar response.

Knowing what he knew of the beasts abroad, it chilled Kallad's blood.

Beside him, Mathias had gone pale. His hand trembled. 'Soon,' he said, closing his eyes.

As if in response to the innkeeper's prediction, the door rattled in its frame and a moment later, whoever it was out there was hammering and pleading in a pitiful voice:

'Open up, gods alive man, open up! Please.'

Lothar began to rise, but Gesner stayed the warden with a firm hand and a single shake of the head.

'Please! For pity's sake, please. I'm begging you, man. Please.'

'Sit,' Gesner said, his face blank. 'It isn't what you think.'

'But–'

'I said sit.' The steel in Gesner's voice was surprising.

'Oh, sweet Morr, they're coming! I can see them! Open the door! Please, I beg you! Open the door.'

Then the begging ceased. It was replaced by thick cackling laughter. 'Next time, father! Next time!'

For the next few minutes the only sound was the snap and crackle of the fire in the hearth.

'My son,' Mathias Gesner said finally, his eyes red with unshed tears. 'They took him two moons ago. I buried him with my own hands, alongside his mother, Rahel, and our little girl, Elsa. He returns every night, banging on the damned door to be let in as if he thinks that this time I might unbar the door and he'll be saved.'

'I'm sorry,' Kallad said.

'It's all rubbish,' Gesner continued. 'He's one of them now. He'd feed off me just as contentedly as he would a whore. He's right though, one day I will be too tired to keep him out and the whole charade will be over once and for all.'

'Aye, it's easy enough to die if'n that's what you want,' Kallad said.

'What else is there, really?'

'Life,' Kallad said. 'That's all there ever is.'

'Sometimes it isn't enough.'

'I won't argue with you there, Mathias, but when it comes to this, the beasts turning father against son, well, this is where good men have to draw the line.'

'What do you mean?' The innkeeper sniffed, the first tears salty on his cheek.

'I mean it ends now, here, tonight,' Kallad promised.

He stood up, shouldering Ruinthorn, and strode over to the door. He pulled back the bolts one at a time and raised the bar.

The door burst open before he could get out of the way. It knocked him back, spinning him into du Bek. Kallad barely had the time to turn before Gesner's son was through the door and on them. 'Hello father, I'm home!' The beast mocked, hurling himself at the dwarf. 'Did you miss me?'

Kallad saw his own weakness reflected in the creature's lifeless eyes: his failure to protect his companions from the vampire they hunted, his inability to save Sammy Kraus, his inability to save his own people, and his guilt at his father's death on the wall. In that moment, Kallad Stormwarden knew hatred.

He thundered the butt of Ruinthorn into creature's gut and then reversed the blow, bringing the butterfly head of the axe around in a brutal arc that came within a whisker of decapitating the beast. Gesner's son moved with lupine grace, rolling beneath the axe-head, back arched to the point of breaking, and then flipped, planting the flat of his hand on the floor and springing up off it. He clapped his hands delightedly as he landed.

Kallad hurled himself forwards, matching the beast's grace with stubborn determination. He planted his feet and let Ruinthorn do his dancing for him. The twin-headed blade sliced through the air, once, twice, three times, four, blurring into insubstantiality as it pared the air. The beast mocked him, moving aside from Ruinthorn as easily as if he was dodging a drunk's wildly swinging blows. The blade of the axe cut close to the vampire's skin twice, drawing the thinnest tears in the fabric of his grubby shirt. The beast raised an eye, and Kallad put it out, slamming the butt of Ruinthorn into the vampire's face, the silver hook he had screwed into the shaft ripping up the monster's cheek and splitting its eye wetly.

Gesner's son howled, but the old man didn't move.

Kallad delivered a second and a third crunching blow, bringing the creature to its knees. Then, with one mighty blow, he sheared the vampire's head from its shoulders, and stood over the twitching corpse as true death claimed it.

'Turn away,' he told Gesner, and waited until the innkeeper had done just that before he split the fiend's ribcage with the sharp end of his axe and cracked open its chest to pull the beast's rotten heart out.

Kallad tossed the blackened organ into the flames of the fire and watched it spit and hiss as it shrivelled in the heat.

'Come first light, bury your son, Mathias. He won't rise again. You have my word on that.'

The innkeeper didn't say a word. He shuffled forwards and knelt, cradling the dead boy's body in his arms.

Kallad left him alone to grieve.

Du Bek followed him upstairs. They closed the door on a small bedroom to shut out Gesner's stifled sobs.

'Why did you do it?' Lothar asked, still at the door. Kallad didn't have an easy answer for him. 'We could have slept the night out in the safety of the room and moved on in the morning. You didn't have to make this your fight, Kallad. So why? Why risk everything for an old man in a damned village?'

'It's in my blood, laddy. What would have happened if we'd gone on our way tomorrow, eh? Gesner would be dead. Hell, the whole village would be nowt more than food for the bloodsucking parasites. By moving on, we'd have condemned every living soul in this place as thoroughly and completely as if we'd driven the stake through them ourselves. Could you live with that?'

'No,' du Bek admitted.

'No, me neither. So there was no choice, not really, see? It became our fight the moment the lad started banging on the door.'

The border warden nodded thoughtfully.

'But that's not it, is it? That's not the truth. It's noble and it's the right thing to say, but it isn't the truth, is it? I mean, it's like saying the fight was yours the moment you opened the door. It's right, but it isn't the truth. So tell me.'

Kallad was silent for a moment. He turned away from du Bek, unable to meet the warden's eye. He stared out through the window, at the darkness and the mirror of their room reflected on it in the glass.

'No,' he said at last. 'It's not the truth.'

'What is?'

Kallad grunted. 'The truth. What can I tell you? All that evil needs to flourish is for good men to do nothing. Every fight is my fight. They killed my father. Cut him down in cold blood as he fought to save wives and children in Grunberg. They killed my people, not just one or two: all of them. I'm the last dwarf of Karak Sadra, the last. My family died fighting for humans, in a fight that wasn't theirs, but they did it, 'cause that's our way. We fight for what we believe in, and I made a promise on the dead. I swore, even as the monster cut my father down, that I would bring every last one of these vile creatures to their knees and make them beg for their worthless carcasses even as I cut their dead hearts out. That means somethin' to me. I'll purge the old world of them single-handed if I have to, or die trying. That's why I need the magician. He can smell their dead stink on the wind. With him, I can turn defence into attack. I can hunt them down and kill them in their lairs.'

'That, dwarf, is a grudge worth having.' Lothar moved away from the door, drew his sword and knelt at Kallad's feet. He lowered his head and offered the blade out across his palms. 'My sword is yours if you would have it.'

CHAPTER SIXTEEN
The Black Library

CASTLE DRAKENHOF, SYLVANIA
Season's End

A THIN PATINA of frost rimed the stalactites dripping from the ceiling of the vast subterranean library.

Library – Nevin Kantor laughed at that.

The place was no more a library than Konrad's so-called cathedral was a place of worship. Both had all the trappings of their names, but lacked the soul that was so integral to the originals. They were little more than pale copies, like so much of the second Vampire Count's realm.

Konrad's library was a huge dome-shaped chamber hollowed out of the rock beneath Drakenhof, the stalactites hanging down like stony swords of doom some sixty feet above the magician's head while he studied, an ever-present reminder of the capricious count. The walls were lined with dusty shelves that were crammed to overflowing with books, obscure arcane texts, diaries, prophecies, codices, sacred ramblings and incantations of dark wisdom, interspersed with bell jars filled with blind eyes floating in saline, salamander skins, cockroach carapaces, pigs' bladders, spider eggs and snake venom. It was a veritable treasure trove of arcana, some nothing more than superstitious claptrap, but the rest, rare and coveted wisdom.

Unlike a real library, it was also a prison.

Thugs stood guard. Their allegiance to the clan van Carstein went beyond a simple loyalty to Konrad. The flat-headed bullies had emerged from the east with his sire, Vlad. Long-lived and yet not pureblood vampires, speculation about the swarthy thugs was rife. Clubs hung loosely in their fists. Sneers were permanently pasted on their thick lips. Their bare arms were like ham hocks, big and fleshy, and covered with a scrawl of tattoos. Hidden within the tattoos was the key to their arrogance, sigils designed to make them impervious to all but the most insidious of magics, tattooed on their flesh by Vlad himself.

The cells behind the library were filled with yokels and superstitious morons who somehow managed to tap one of the winds, with luck or latent talent, but not genuine skill. Whether or not the sigils would have actually deterred a sorcerous attack was irrelevant – few of the denizens of this dark pit had any real magical gift. They were as likely to try and club the guards to death with heavy books as they were to evaporate the water in their bodies and leave a baked pile of human paste on the stone floor.

There were few true magicians in Konrad's school. Tapping the winds accidentally was by no means the same as possessing true power. The bumpkins could coo about the mystical talents of the midwife who brought a brat out from a breech birth, and marvel at the soldier whose lucky trinket deflected an arrow tip destined for his heart. It wasn't magic, not in the pure sense. It wasn't worthy of awe.

So yes, they were prisoners, but it was the physical stature of the thugs that held them in fearful check, not the magical wards on their gaolers.

Nevin Kantor harboured no illusions: he was as much a prisoner as those poor fools were. The difference was that he was a willing prisoner. In magic, Nevin Kantor believed he would find his own immortality.

The resources that Konrad had gathered in his library surpassed Kantor's wildest imaginings. He pored over the books, absorbing every word, every mark in the margins, every explanatory diagram, every supposition and superstition.

He also heard whispers.

Leverkuhn and Fey were thick as thieves, scouring the shelves and recessed stacks for decayed pages and spineless tomes, picking through the incantations and reassembling the knowledge therein. He heard them when they thought no one was listening. At first, it had plagued him: a doubt gnawing at his skull incessantly, and so, he ingratiated himself with Immoliah Fey. The seduction was easy. It always is when you hold to one basic truth: women, even women like Fey, have the same base urges for contact and skin as men do. They need it in the same way. They want it in the same way. Kantor said things, intimate things, drawing her into his confidence with pillow talk and promises. It wasn't love, it was physical and practical, a means to an end, nothing more. The passion paid off. She told him their secret: they believed that somewhere in this vast uncatalogued horde of arcana were pages from Nagash's lost books, incantations from the *Liber Mortis*. How else, she reasoned, sleepy after their frenzied coupling, could Vlad have raised the dead?

Their reasoning was sound in one aspect, but deeply flawed in another. Kantor knew that Vlad had indeed possessed some pages from Nagash's lost books, in that much they were right, but Kantor had seen the same irreplaceable knowledge go up in smoke as the Sigmarites burned the dead Count's possessions in a cleansing fire. Only self-righteous fools like the priests would have done something so unmitigatingly stupid. Wisdom, Kantor believed, should be protected not purged – even the wisdom you disagreed with. Burning books was an act of sacrilege. It stank of smug Sigmarite stupidity.

Fey and Leverkuhn ought to have been his allies in his quest for understanding, but the two shunned him.

He shouldn't have been surprised. He had lived a life on the fringe, not accepted by the people around him. The Sigmarites had imprisoned him, intent on snuffing out his life once his usefulness to them had ended. Oh, yes, they were happy enough to bleed him dry if it suited them, and they made no secret of the fact that they were willing to sell his flesh cheaply enough – indeed, they had, for the princely sum of two vampires.

That was the value they had placed on him. Even then, the dwarf had only bought him because of his usefulness. He could sniff out the beasts, and in doing so could help the dwarf commit suicide by tracking the monsters back to their lairs. Kallad Stormwarden had talked of nobility, of the eternal struggle against evil, of buying freedom with courage. It was all hyperbole: rubbish. The dwarf was dead, killed by a stronger foe. There was no nobility in it. Death didn't consider eternal struggles and courage when it weighed out lives. It valued only strength, cunning, and power. He felt no regret over it. The dwarf would have seen him dead before the end of their shared road, so why should he shed a tear for his own would-be murderer?

He had long ago come to terms with the fact that he was shunned and reviled for what he was.

He had even come to accept the reasons. It was because he was different, because was he was attuned to the earth itself, because the music of it sang in his veins, because it bent to his will, and because he had power.

The only acceptance he felt came in the soothing caress of Shyish. The wind knew him. It savoured his flesh as he drew it into him. It delighted in his existence. It sang in his blood. It *loved* him.

In return, it was only natural that he loved it, and that he gave himself to it, body and soul.

He felt Shyish inside him even when he wasn't consciously drawing on it. The wind was a soothing presence, a calming one. A friend. A lover. It filled him: completed him.

He knew that he was changing. The flesh he wore was nothing more than an imago, a shell that he would crack his way out of to emerge as a new, beautiful, beast. He could feel the changes taking place inside him. He could feel his blood purifying, his organs being strengthened by Shyish, and the black wind making him its perfect servant. He welcomed the changes. With von Seirt dead, the only true talents were Immoliah Fey, Aloysius Leverkuhn and himself, and he would be the greatest of them all. He embraced the black wind. That, in itself, gave Kantor a position of power in the mad vampire's court.

Nevin Kantor understood Konrad von Carstein, probably better than the vampire understood himself, because they were not that different. He craved what he lacked. He coveted their magic to make up for his own shortcomings. They snickered behind his back and called him the Blood Count.

Kantor hunched over the desk, dipped the quill's nib into the inkpot and scratched out the curve of a 'C' on the vellum stretched out on the tabletop. It was painstaking work, laborious and frustrating. The ink splashed as he drew the nib down with a flourish, giving the letter 'H' an elaborate tail. Muttering a curse, Kantor took a blotting cloth and cleaned up the smear of black.

He heard footsteps, but didn't look up, expecting them to fade away into the stacks.

They didn't. They approached his desk, slow, measured, and echoing curiously in the vast vaulted room.

Kantor looked up as Konrad dropped a bloody rag on his desk. Anger flared, but the magician battled it down. Stupidity would only damage his situation. He wanted to bleed the Vampire Count dry of every ounce of knowledge that his black library possessed. The image brought an ironic smile to his lips, which Konrad mistook for gratitude.

It wasn't a rag, Kantor realised. It had the texture and consistency of vellum, but it wasn't vellum either. He touched it, spreading it thin on the desk. Black blood smeared across his work, ruining everything that he had set down over the last week. He barely noticed. The feel was immediately familiar, and yet utterly foreign. It was skin: human skin.

He looked up at the Blood Count.

Konrad's face split in an easy grin.

'A gift, my pet. Cure it. Make a book out of it. Use it as the binding for your grand grimoire.' He held up a hand, staying Kantor. 'No, no, don't thank me. It's nothing really. It belonged to a rather uncooperative fellow. He has no use for it now, so best not let it go to waste, eh?'

'I don't know quite what to say.' There was a mild edge of distaste to Kantor's voice, but his fingers played almost lovingly over the various textures of the stripped skin. The thing was both revolting and curiously compelling at the same time. He lingered over the softer areas, the undersides of the arm and the throat, and the coarse skin of the heels, the palms and the elbows.

'Tell me you'll put it to good use. You have no idea how difficult it is to skin a corpse without ruining the thing. Painstaking, well more like pain *giving* actually, but you get the idea.'

'Indeed, rather vividly,' Kantor said. He pushed the skin to the side. In his mind, he was already imagining the secrets it would bind: his first book of magic. He lifted his fingers to his lips, tasting the tang of iron that was the dead man's blood, smelling it, stark in his nose. It was still warm.

The vampire smiled, perching on the corner of Kantor's desk. 'Good, good, good. Now tell me, how goes your research, my pet? I have high hopes for what miracles you might conjure.'

'Slowly,' Kantor said, avoiding the truth. He didn't want Konrad even vaguely intrigued with his discoveries. The knowledge he'd unearthed was his. There were things he needed to do without the ever-present shadow of the vampire lurking in the background all the time. Obfuscation, that was the secret. To give a little, without so much as hinting as to its true worth. 'There is a wealth of fact and ten times as much fantasy in these books, my lord. Sifting through the dross for nuggets of gold is tiresome. So much of it is useless.'

'Ah, well, that's a shame. I had to go to considerable lengths to acquire my collection. I am sure everything my heart desires is hidden away here on one page or another. What can I say? Don't let fear of failure get under your skin.' Konrad chuckled, enjoying his own droll sense of humour.

'Given the usefulness of your latest gift, I'll make a point of it, my lord Konrad.'

'I knew you were a clever boy, even when you knocked on my door begging to be let in and allowed to serve me.'

'Shyish guided my feet, my lord. The black wind wishes to aid you in any way it can.' It was easy to lie. The vampire's vanity blinded him to anything approaching the truth. Part of the magician wanted to tell him, to whisper the name 'Mannfred' and have done with it, but another part of him enjoyed the game too much to give it up so easily. The time for revelation would come, but it wasn't now. He needed to be patient.

'Yet it mocks me, Nevin, by shutting itself off to me when all I would do is unleash its blessed darkness into the world. I would be a dark destroyer. I would bring the world to its knees, if only it would open itself up to me. If only I could be like you... You know, I could be forgiven for thinking that *you* mock me as well.'

'Who can understand the whims of magic, my lord?'

'Not I, it would seem,' Konrad said, bitterly.

The irony of it was delicious, but he didn't want to spoil the Blood Count's good humour. It was hardly surprising that since the demise of his brothers – and in Mannfred's continued absence – Konrad had been almost cheerful, but his humour was an unstable beast. One wrong word could quite easily see that goodwill vanish. Then, who knew what desk Kantor's skin would end up being deposited on as a so-called gift? The vampire owned his life and could, at a whim, snuff it out. The threat was implicit.

Oh what a tangled web we weave when first we flatter to deceive. Kantor picked up the dead suit of skin once more, turning it over in his hands. He found the face. He recognised the donor. He would not mourn the man. He would, however, make good use of his remains, crafting a book of blood and magic to rival anything seen in millennia. He also knew exactly which ensorcellment he would refine and record first: Diabolisch Leichnam.

'I am expecting great things of you, don't disappoint me, my pet. I don't handle disappointment well.' With that, Konrad left him.

Nevin looked at his hands. They were covered in blood. He was trembling, not with fear, but with exhilaration. The time was ripe. Konrad had given him the excuse he needed to assemble the incantations that he had already begun secreting in various hidey-holes. He laid his hands down flat on the table.

Let the madman posture, he thought bitterly. *Give the fool his day, for tomorrow is mine.*

That was the truth of it.

Nevin Kantor was a liar, and an accomplished one at that. It wasn't Shyish that had guided his feet to Drakenhof Castle. Mannfred von Carstein, the true heir of Vlad's Kingdom of the Dead, had bartered his life for servitude. When he could have struck Nevin Kantor down, he spared him, making a pact. It was Mannfred who owned his life, not Konrad. At Mannfred's bidding, he bent and scraped to the lunatic, but he did not *serve* him. He had bought his life with a single promise: that he would infiltrate the court of the mad count and pave the way for Mannfred's return. *Let the others fight and swagger, and ultimately destroy each other,* Mannfred's words echoed in his mind. *They are a devious backstabbing bunch of degenerates incapable of seeing the long game. Let them destroy themselves, and when the time is right, when all is said and done, then I shall return, not a moment before. You are to be my eyes and ears in the madman's court. Serve me well and you will be rewarded; fail me and we will finish what we started here today.*

As the ghost of Konrad's footsteps disappeared, the magician pushed back his chair and walked through the stacks of books and other curiosities. He knew what he was looking for, but was in no hurry to reclaim it. The place reeked of lonely death. He waited, fingering the spines of dusty books, and easing them out of the stacks to turn reverently through their brittle pages. Silence settled over the library. Still he waited. The books fascinated him. In more than half of them, the scrawl was unintelligible. In hundreds more the inks, and bloods, had faded, so much so that the words barely stained the page, but the smell as he cracked the spines and opened them was a heady rush of must, decay and genius. It was ambrosia for the hungry magician.

It took a moment to find what he was looking for, a single sheet of yellowed parchment woven out of pressed reeds, slipped inside a mildewed tome of folklore. On it, written in a flaking rust of blood was the incantation *Diabolisch Leichnam*. Beside it on the shelf lay an elaborately carved six inch-long bone case. Kantor rolled the sheet like a scroll and stuffed it inside the bone case before slipping that, in turn, inside his shirt.

Convinced, finally, that he was alone, Kantor left the stacks. He could have sneaked out, there were ways, but that wouldn't buy him long enough. He needed the best part of the night, not a few stolen minutes, so he walked towards the stairs.

Before he was even halfway there, a lantern-jawed thug blocked his way, huge ham-hock arms folded across his barrel chest. 'I don't think so.'

Kantor squared up to the man, half his size and no match for the thug's brawn, he nonetheless knew he had to play the game. There could be no fear. 'You aren't kept around for your depth of thought, though, are you? So move,' he said.

'I said I don't think so.'

'Let's put this another way, shall we? Words of one syllable: let me go or die. There, even your thick head should be able to absorb that.'

The thug didn't seem particularly disturbed by the threat, although the beginnings of a grin played across his lips. He was obviously enjoying the game. 'You ain't going anywhere 'cept back to your cell.'

Slowly and deliberately the magician withdrew the bone scroll case from within the folds of his shirt and pressed it into the guard's cheek. 'Do you know what's in here? Do you have any idea what this magic is capable of? Well, do you?'

'I'm sure it's supposed to turn my body inside out, ripping the bones right through my skin and dumping my guts on the floor at your feet, right?'

'Close,' Kantor agreed. 'Very close indeed.'

'Shame it's in that little box then isn't it? I mean, it isn't a lot of use in there is it? Especially not against my little babies.' The thug tapped the spiral of tattoos on his flexed bicep.

'It's a game isn't it? Always a game.'

'More of a dance, I'd say. You want summink I've got, I want summink you've got. We dance around it for a while, threaten to do unspeakable things to each other, and make a deal that keeps both of us sweet.'

'You're scum, do you know that?' Kantor was enjoying himself. 'Now, believe me, there's nothing I want to do in the world right now more than I want to rip your innards out in a most spectacular fashion, but I am rather hoping it doesn't come to that.'

"Cause of the mess, right?'

'Something like that, yes.'

'It's more than my life's worth to let you leave, you know that, don't you?'

Kantor nodded, taking them into the next stage of the dance.

'Damned if you do, damned if you don't. All things considered, it's not your lucky day, is it?'

'Luckier than yours, to my way of thinkin',' the thug said. He hadn't flinched so much as an inch since the bone case touched his cheek, not to twitch a smile, nor to sneer his distaste.

'How so?' Kantor asked, genuinely curious.

'Ah, it's like my old man used to say, a fool and his money are easily parted. Show me your money, fool. You want out, and me, I'm supposed to wait 'til I'm relieved, but I reckon I could meet him on the way, for the right incentive.'

That was what it always came down to with the dregs of humanity. Kantor smiled widely, pocketing the scroll case. Not, of course, that he would have wasted the *Diabolisch Leichnam* on the trollish thug.

'What, pray tell, would you consider the right "incentive"?'

The thug made a show of scratching his scalp and furrowing his brow, as if lost in thought. His eyes lit up, as if he had just stumbled upon the idea: 'Shillings.'

'Because there's a vast supply of coin down here, I suppose? Something else, perhaps? Something I might actually *have*?'

'Ah but you've got 'em, ain't ya? Show me your money,' the thug grinned, rubbing thumb and forefinger together. 'S'all about money. You pay me, I do you a favour. It's the way of the world.'

Nevin Kantor wanted, for just a moment, to flatten the leering fool all across the wall. Instead, he matched the thug's grin.

'Indeed. Well, you know, I might have something to interest you.' The magician slipped a carnelian-studded ring from his finger and palmed it. He noticed the way the gem drew the thug's eye. 'Perhaps we can come to some sort of accommodation? Let's say out tonight, back when you change shifts tomorrow? No one any the wiser that I've wandered. How much might such an accommodation cost?'

The thug shook his head. 'Cost? That pretty ring you've just hidden, but it's impossible, you know that don't ya? You'll never get away with it. The Hamaya'll sniff you out, and you'll be banged up in a proper cell without your precious books before you can say Johannes Eisblume.'

'Let's just say it is a risk I'm willing to take. So, do we have a deal?'

'It's your funeral.'

'So, we have a deal?'

'Aye, we have a deal.' The thug held his meaty hand out. Kantor pressed the ring into it and closed his fingers, making a fist.

'Sunrise,' the thug said. 'That's when I'm back. I'll be less than a quarter of an hour late, but not much less. Make sure you're back and tucked up in your cell or I'll be forced to hunt you down and break you into tiny pieces of bone and gristle. You wouldn't want that, now would ya?'

'As much as I wouldn't want to take all the fun out of your life, I think we'll try to avoid that little scenario, eh?' the magician said, turning on his heel and walking back towards the discarded skin.

CIRCUMSTANCE HAD TURNED Nevin Kantor into an expert at biding his time.

Drakenhof was a warren of disused rooms and desolate corridors that spread out like cavernous fingers into the mountain beneath the castle itself. Deep in these, Kantor had claimed his own room, utterly remarkable in every way, except one: to the casual passer-by, the room did not exist. The magician had woven a glyph around the doorframe masking it from casual discovery. Someone would have to know about the room to find it. It was a small security, but even a tiny bit of privacy was better than none.

Kantor paced the room.

A woman lay bound and gagged in the centre of the room. He had taken her from the slave pens. She wouldn't be missed, and even if she was, people would simply assume that one of the vampires had grown hungry. That was the beauty of having a ready supply of fresh meat.

'Oh, do stop whimpering, girl. You're driving me up the damned wall.'

The woman kicked and writhed, fighting against her bonds. She had woken a few minutes earlier, before he had finished preparing the incantation. Kantor walked into the centre of the bloody pentagram daubed on the stone floor and clubbed her across the side of the face with his fist.

'The more you fight the worse it will be for you, I promise you that.'

Doing his best to ignore her moans, the magician set tallow candles on the points of the pentagram, sealing them with melted wax to the stone so that they wouldn't topple during the ceremony itself.

He drew a second summoning circle for himself, pinning it out with silver thread to ensure that it remained unbroken. He harboured no illusions about the nature of the sorcery he was dabbling in. *Diabolisch Leichnam*, the diabolical corpse, was old magic, dating back, he believed, to the court of Neferata. It was magic of the blackest nature. In the common Reikspiel, it was known as *The Vessel*, an incantation capable of stripping the soul from the flesh, leaving behind an empty vessel capable of being occupied by a cuckoo, a lost spirit. It was, in a manner of speaking, a way for the necromancer to prepare a host to accept his own essence, should the need arise.

It was a fallback, an ace in the hole as the gamblers liked to call it. Kantor wasn't fond of risks and most certainly wasn't a gambler by design. The answer lay in strategy, in careful planning and forethought. It was possible to pre-empt an enemy's actions if you knew him well enough. The secret was to know your enemy, and armed with that knowledge, to minimise potential failings long before they became a problem.

Only a fool went into a fight blind.

One by one, he lit the candles. The flames guttered slightly as he began to speak, although no natural wind stirred. Excitement flooded Kantor's veins as he embraced the touch of Shyish.

The woman's eyes flared with terror. She was screaming behind her gag, but not even as much as a whisper made it through. Her back arched as she struggled to roll herself out of the bloody pentagram. It was useless of course, he had seen to it that she wouldn't be leaving the circle until he was ready to carry her empty shell out.

Kantor raised his hands in supplication, forming the words of the incantation with precision.

The light flared and almost failed, the black wind surging around the tallow candles. The sulphurous reek of brimstone filled the air, sickly sweet and cloying. It burned at the back of his throat, making it difficult to shape the words.

He sank to his knees, refusing to misshape even a syllable, threw his head back and forced the sealing line of the incantation through his lips. The skin of his hands, spreading up his arms, glowed darkly, the black wind seeping out of his veins and staining his skin.

Then the candles died.

He stopped mid-word, his heart hammering in his chest.

You dare, mortal?

He had no way of knowing if the question was in his imagination or if it was real, in the room with him.

The next line of the incantation, what was it? His mind was blank. No, not blank, filled with fear. He had to reach behind the fear, had to find the words he had spent so long memorising. There was nothing but darkness. Black.

He stared in horror at the daemon manifesting before him, drawing substance out of the air itself to make itself whole. The thing was like nothing he had ever seen: silver horns, one complete, one broken down to a stump, skin like the stone wall behind it, mould and rot shrivelling around its empty eyes, teeth like tombstones, chipped and broken and breath like brimstone.

It reached out for him, but couldn't pass beyond the barrier formed by the silver thread. The urge to run was almost irresistible, almost.

Kantor closed his eyes. Still he could see it, blazing in his minds eye.

He licked his lips.

The next word…

The next…

The last:

'Cadaver!' The word dripped from his tongue like venom. A triumphant grin split the necromancer's face.

He opened his eyes.

The daemon, half-materialised, matched the grin.

This marks you, magician. You are aware of that, are you not? This marks your soul indelibly. You are mine now, my tool to wield.

'Giving on both sides, daemon – you are mine. That is the pact of bonding, is it not?' He was shaking, adrenaline coursing through his body. He could taste the power in the air. It thrilled through him. He was alive with it.

Until I sever it, yes. Then I will feed, although there is barely enough flesh on your bones to make a decent meal. Your soul however, your soul is fat and corrupt, deliciously so.

'And you will feed, essence of the winds, I have seen to that. Take her, not her flesh mind, only her soul. You can gorge yourself on her sweet meat at another time.'

The daemon fed, stripping the woman's soul from her flesh, even as she screamed for her life, begging, whimpering and finally falling silent, lifeless, in the centre of the pentagram.

Come claim the flesh, magician, the daemon goaded, spiritual residue dribbling down its chin. It licked its talons clean, slurping up the drool with glee.

Instinctively, Nevin Kantor took a step forwards. The daemon couldn't help itself: in hunger, its eyes darted to the silver thread. Kantor drew up sharply, his toe less than a finger's width from breaching the protective circle.

Ahhh almost too easy, magician.

'But not quite. The woman is gone yes?'

No trace of her essence is left within the shell.

'Good, then your work here is done, essence of the winds, begone.' He clapped his hands and was alone with the corpse of the dead woman at his feet, the stink of brimstone strong in the air.

He had to work quickly now to bind the empty vessel to him so that it would withstand the onslaught of decay and corruption that had already begun to set in with the banishment of the host's immortal soul.

Soon, he would have a place to flee, should his master's schemes fail.

CHAPTER SEVENTEEN
Bring Out Your Dead

THE IMPERIAL CAPITAL, ALTDORF
The Birth of the New Year

THE WOLF ENTERED the capital at dusk.

Jerek moved silently, with the grace of a predator, through the darkening streets. It felt like so long ago that he had last walked amongst the living, like a man. It was a lifetime ago.

The denizens of the city lived with new caution, casting suspicious glances back over their shoulders as they walked from shadow to deeper shadow, doorway to alley to doorway, expecting at any moment the claws and teeth of death to drag them down and revel in the slaughter of their flesh. Von Carstein's war had carved this new world.

They had no idea that the wolf could dress in human clothing, that the monster could walk unnoticed in their midst, looking for all the world just like any one of them. He did not enjoy the deception.

Jerek pushed open the door to the Crooked Crone and walked into the taproom.

No one turned to stare. No one cried, 'Fiend!'

Licking his lips, the wolf called over a serving girl and ordered a pint of the house brew.

He handed her a bruised shilling and took a seat by the fire, tempted by the warmth.

Jerek didn't know where to begin. By rights, in the wake of Pieter's spectacular failure at Nuln, he should have returned to Drakenhof. He hadn't. He had come to Altdorf, city of spires, in search of von Carstein's signet ring. It had become an obsession, a disease. To his way of thinking, if he could find it, so could anyone else, and he couldn't allow them to. That meant he had to find it, and he had to destroy it.

Only it wasn't that easy.

The last glimmer of humanity in the wolf might have wanted to shatter the promise of dominion that the ring offered, but that was nothing against the hunger of the damned beast within him. The beast craved it. Inheritance: the word gnawed away at him. Like hunger, it saturated his corpse. He wanted it destroyed, yet all the while, he hungered for it.

The beast was growing more powerful by the day, demanding its right to eternity.

Soon it would be impossible to deny, and then he would be forever damned.

He warmed himself by the fire.

The taproom of the Crooked Crone was busy, women with easy smiles worked the long tables, while men with loose purse strings spent their shillings and pfennigs as if they believed that tomorrow wouldn't come, and who could blame them in these uncertain times? Let them take their pleasure when and where they could.

Men, deep in their cups, hunched over a rickety table playing knucklebones. They cursed, money changed hands, they rolled, cursed some more and more money moved across the table. Win some, lose some, the drinkers didn't seem to care. They laughed, talked of life and love, and pulled occasionally at the serving girl's skirts as she wove a path around them. Jerek sat awhile, enjoying the easy camaraderie.

Constellations of conversation moved around him. He closed his eyes and let them all wash over him. Still, he heard snippets. The shadow of the vampires hung heavy over the city. Much of the talk had moved on from the evils of war and its depravations, and grown more introverted and personal. Few had forgotten the butchery at the Sigmarites' cathedral. Those horrors were somehow more real now, given the years between the war and the fall of Vlad von Carstein at the hand of Wilhelm III.

It was amazing how humanity coped with tragedy. They could brush aside the devastation of thousands, in sympathy for the tragedy of a few. In that way, they were much like the other creatures of nature, the pack animals that put the welfare of the pack ahead of their own. Tens of thousands had died under the choking hold of the Vampire Count, through starvation and privation, rather than to more ruthless killers like steel and talons.

The conversations barely even remembered the sacrifice of the Grand Theogonist. The priests themselves might have sought to canonise the man, but the commoners had already begun to forget his sacrifice. That was another miracle of humanity, short memories.

How many years was it since he had stood on the city walls, defiant? Surely not long enough for his bravery to have become as nothing?

Jerek found himself thinking of humanity in terms of the beast that he had become, not the man he was. Years had passed, more years than many would care to remember. They hadn't forgotten. They had become removed from it. Other tragedies had befallen their lives, and gradually von Carstein had become a monster consigned to a dark time. That was the final miracle of mankind, the ability to move on.

Of course, this last miracle was as much a curse, forced on them by the fleeting nature of their lives. This second life had framed his perspective in ways he would never have been able to understand before.

He doubted that anyone here would know his sire's final resting place. He had thought they might share some kind of bond, even now, that would allow him to sense Vlad, six feet under and riddled with worms. There was nothing.

He sank back into his chair and tried to think like a Sigmarite. How would they dispose of an evil they could barely comprehend? A cleansing fire? Ritual purification? Or would they set their blessed Sigmar to watch over the fiend, even in death?

Perhaps there was a bond, after all. Jerek smiled to himself. Given the mindset of the priests, it was obvious what they had done with the vampire's mortal remains. They had buried them, and where better to inter the beast than beneath the watchful gaze of the man who slew it?

That was the truth, he was sure. It was the Sigmarite way, to cover the darkness with light as they sought to sanitise it and make it safe.

He knew where he would find von Carstein. More importantly, he knew where he would find the ring that gifted the beast his incredible restorative powers: in the dirt beneath the holy man's grave.

Jerek raised the jug to his lips and drank deeply, imagining that he could actually savour the bitter-sharp taste of the brew as it rolled down his throat.

He smacked his lips and called the serving girl over. She had her hands full, juggling mugs and tankards and sidestepping groping hands. In another life the wolf would have taught those pups a lesson in manners, but not today. Today it was important that he was one of them.

'Bonny lass,' he called, snagging the girl's apron as she breezed by. He held her firm. She looked down at him, a smile on her lips, but nothing in her eyes. 'I'll take another.' She nodded. 'And thank you for smiling for me, love. It's made this lecherous old wolf's day.'

For just a moment her eyes brightened. That was enough for him.

He closed his eyes again.

The ale came, and went down his throat. He tuned out the hubbub, even when a piss-poor minstrel struck up a ragged tune that had the locals joining in enthusiastically. He let the noise wash over him. All he needed to do was wait it out. They all had homes and beds to go to.

The singer butchered just about every tune out of his mouth, but the punters didn't care. They slammed tankards down on beer-soaked tabletops and cried out for more, joining in reels and shanties with noisy appreciation.

Finally, the landlord rang the bell over the bar, signifying the end of the revels with a call for last orders. A few of the hardened drinkers downed one last ale, but most began their wobbly journeys home to sleep off the worst effects of the drink. Jerek wouldn't envy any of them come morning.

As the last of the drinkers drifted out, the wolf left his fireside seat and joined them, stumbling slightly to mirror their own unsteady gaits.

'Which way's the cathedral?' he asked, bumping into the shoulder of the man beside him. Grinning, the man pointed off in the direction of one of the many spires.

'Had a few too many, eh?'

'Jus' enough to forget what the woman looks like 'n where she's waitin',' Jerek slurred, a lopsided grin pasted across his face.

'Ah, you knows what they say fella: ain't a woman in the world who ain't made pretty by enough alcohol.'

'Ain't that the truth! Jus' a pity us fellas need to drink to make a sows purse outta the pig's ear, eh?' Jerek agreed with a hearty chuckle and staggered on his merry way.

For the sake of appearances, Jerek walked a little unsteadily – not the exaggerated drunken lurch that would be remembered by the casual observer on his way home, but the occasional misstep that made him look like just another one of them.

He leaned against the wall on the street corner, and then pushed off again, repeating the pattern street after street until he saw the dome of the grand cathedral.

The iron railings were barred, but it didn't matter. The surrounding wall was low enough for him to scale it, easily. Jerek scrambled over the wall, his feet scuffing up the stone as he hauled himself over the top. He dropped down to the other side with a grunt.

The grounds of the cathedral were well kept. A small glade of trees sheltering a single grave caught his eye. He walked through a neatly tended rose garden to the secluded grove and into the moonlight shadows cast by a weeping willow. There was a simple stone marking the holy man's grave. A second smaller gate led through the wall to the street. The headstone was seeded over with lichen where the shadows of the willow lingered. A white rose bush grew beside the headstone, the thorns scraping against the words of the prayer carved into the stone.

He knelt at the graveside, but there was nothing remotely reverential about it. He reached out to claw at the dirt with his bare hands, but stopped, his fingers only inches from a curious metal disc set into the grass. He didn't recognise the rune embossed on it, but he felt the heat of its power even before his hand closed on it. The disc seared into his skin with shocking force, hurling the wolf back bodily from the grave.

Jerek staggered back to his feet, shaking his head. He felt the residual power of the rune in every fibre of his being, as if it was somehow attuned to his dead flesh. He turned his hand over and stared at his blackened palm and the negative image of the rune that had been branded on it. Tentatively, he reached out again. He felt the fiery pain of the burn swell, long before his hand came close to touching the dirt. He tested its limits, pushing to the point of agony, and still he couldn't lay so much as a finger on the dirt of the Grand Theogonist's grave.

It made sense, of course, that the place would be protected.

Indeed, the talisman told him all he needed to know about the dual nature of the priest's final resting place. Why else would it need a warding against dead flesh, if not to keep Vlad beneath the ground and the living dead from being able to reach down and bring him back?

It meant that he needed to exhume the holy man to get to the body beneath it and, ultimately, to the ring.

Only, he couldn't, *he* couldn't.

There was, however, more than one way to skin a cat. Just because he couldn't, didn't mean that someone else wouldn't be able to.

Jerek looked around. He knew if he didn't act quickly even this slim hope would be undone by the simple fact that his presence would be felt within the walls of the great cathedral, the sickness of unlife causing nightmares and heart tremors, stomach cramps and nausea, and countless other side effects within the holy men.

A beggar perhaps? He could drag one off the street and force him to do his bidding.

No. It had to be someone above suspicion if seen by watchers inside the cathedral.

Who then?

On the far side of the rose garden there was a small cemetery. A cemetery needed a gravedigger. What was more natural than a gravedigger abroad during the dark hours, preparing for the day ahead?

He could breathe the fear of unlife into the man, bullying him into this vile act of desecration. Could? He would have to.

Jerek knew then what he had to do. Stripping down until he was naked, his clothes folded beneath the willow, he drew on the wolf, giving himself over to the change. As the agony of the transformation took him, he screamed, the scream giving way to the protracted howl of a wolf baying at the moon.

No lights came on within the cathedral.

The wolf padded easily through the rose garden towards the lines of graves, and the small gravedigger's hovel beyond them. His skin crawled this close to so many idols and effigies of the Man-God planted in the earth. He wove a path through the graves to the gravedigger's door. Thirty feet shy of the door, the wolf sprang, hurling itself bodily at the barrier, breaking its flimsy lock open and tumbling into the small room.

He smelled the man before he saw him, cowering in his blankets, grey hair stuck up in stalks, skin sickly pale with fear.

The wolf padded slowly over to the gravedigger's bedside, jowls slack, saliva drooling around sharp teeth.

'Mercy, no,' the old man pleaded as the beast pressed its muzzle up to within inches of his face. Then he began to change, the monster withdrawing in favour of the man. The wolf's low-throated growl shifted into the more natural rhythms of Jerek's breathing. His bones shifted and re-formed until he stood naked before the old man. Instead of diminishing it, his nudity only served to reinforce the old man's fear.

'Up, gravedigger, as of now, your life is mine. You live and breathe at my whim, understand?' He baited the gravedigger.

The old man nodded so hard that Jerek almost laughed... almost.

He scrambled out of bed, his scrawny body all slack skin, bone and cavernous shadow in the moonlight, desperately eager to please the monster that had invaded his home if it meant staying alive.

'What... what?'

'What do I want?'

The gravedigger nodded again, 'Yes.' The old man was shaking uncontrollably. The last thing Jerek wanted to do was cause his heart to give out in fear.

He felt remorse for what he was about to do, but the beast was still fresh in his blood, suffocating his defiant humanity. It was a sign that the monster was winning the fight. Soon he would feel no compunction in slaughter or desecration, but for now, the bitter tang of guilt reminded him of what it meant to be alive.

He stifled it because, for once, it had no place in what he was about to do. He needed to surrender to the beast's baser nature.

'I want you to do a job for me. I want you to dig up a grave.'

It took a moment for his words to register through the old man's fear. 'You want me to dig a grave for you?'

'No, I want you to dig *up* a grave for me. The grave has already been dug once before.'

'I can't–'

'Oh, but I think you'll find you *can* and what's more, you *will*.' Jerek curled back his lip to make sure that his meaning wasn't lost on the old man. He needn't have worried, it wasn't. 'Get dressed, pick up your shovel and follow me. I don't want to hurt you, but that doesn't mean I won't. Do we understand each other?'

The gravedigger nodded again, grabbing and dropping a grubby shirt from the back of a wooden chair. He bent and picked it up from the floor, staring at Jerek the entire time as if, by looking away, he might incite the beast to attack.

Jerek walked out of the tiny hovel. The air felt good on his skin, cold enough to raise the prickle of goose pimples, but not so cold as to shrivel his skin.

A moment later, the gravedigger emerged, a bulls-eye lantern lighting the path at his feet. His expression was grim.

Without a word, Jerek set off into the graves. He wondered how long it would take the old man to realise which grave he wanted exhumed. Not long, surely. Then what? Would he resist? Fight? Raise the alarm? Or would he simply dig?

Behind him, the old man whimpered as they entered the rose garden. There was only one grave beyond this point.

'I can't…'

Jerek stopped beneath the trailing leaves of the weeping willow. 'Dig,' He said simply and with utter finality.

'I can't,' the gravedigger repeated, even as he planted his shovel in the dirt.

His suspicion had been right: the peculiar metal talisman didn't affect the old man.

'Dig,' Jerek repeated, sickened by himself even as he said it. It was easy to pretend that he felt nothing, but then lies were always believable – only not to the liar himself.

The old man dug, for his life. He turned the shovel through the soil, opening up the grave.

Jerek dressed again while the gravedigger toiled.

It took most of the long night just to reach the depth of the first corpse that the grave harboured. Tears streamed down the gravedigger's face as he dug, begging for forgiveness even as his shovel struck the wood of the Grand Theogonist's coffin. He shovelled away the dirt, until the silver clasps of the box were visible.

'Open it,' Jerek said. It was unreasonable to expect the pair to be actually buried together, but it would have been stupid not to check.

The gravedigger used the butt of the shovel's handle to crack the seals and open the metal clasps. The air sucked into the wooden box as the lid cracked open and the stench poured out of it. Time and maggots had reduced the holy man to loosely assembled bones and strings of gristle. He was alone in the coffin.

'Seal it and lift it out, we're digging deeper,' Jerek said.

The old man did as he was told. Using the edge of the shovel, he dug around the coffin, freeing it so that he could angle it upwards, and lift it out of the ground, although the task was far from easy.

Jerek had been right in his reasoning. Less then a foot beneath the Grand Theogonist's coffin, the gravedigger unearthed Vlad's remains. Without the luxury of a box, the Vampire Count had been picked clean by the grubs, his bones stripped completely of flesh, muscle and gristle. Only strips of rag remained of his once fine clothing, but the gold chains and more importantly, the ring, remained.

The Vampire Count's hands were folded across his ribcage, the extravagant signet ring on his right hand. It was gold with a garish gem set amid what looked like wings, the tips studded with precious stones.

Jerek didn't dare move.

He stared at the ornate ring with its dark gemstone setting for a full five minutes.

He couldn't believe that the Sigmarites could be so stupid as to leave the ring – the key to the Vampire Count's power – in place.

Exhilarated, he eased the ring off the finger of bone and slipped it onto his own finger. He expected to feel something, the tingle of power flooding into this tainted veins, the answering cry of immortality, but there was nothing. He held his hand up before his face, staring at the metal wings as they spread over his knuckled fist: nothing.

Did he need to cut himself? Would blood seal the bond between vampire and ring? Would he feel its power then?

That was when his stupidity sank in, finally. For all its ostentation, the winged ring wasn't the fabled von Carstein ring, it wasn't blessed with awesome powers of recuperation, it was nothing more than a pretty trinket. Why would the ring be on his finger at all? It was true: the priests had stolen it to rob von Carstein of his unearthly powers.

He couldn't bring himself to believe that.

He dropped into the hole in the ground, scrabbling about in the dirt, grunting and scraping, pushing aside the bones.

Nothing.

The ring could be anywhere.

Without knowing who took it, there was no way of knowing where it might be.

He had no choice but to return to Konrad's court, empty-handed, praying against reason that the trail ended here in this desolate garden of Morr. He knew that it didn't. It *began* with the thief who had stolen it, and even knowing that, it was beyond his ability to track it. He could only hope to wrest it from its wielder when it resurfaced, because it would, he harboured no illusions about that. An artefact so vile could not remain lost for long.

Better to let any who came looking, sniffing around and asking questions, think he had found Vlad's precious secret and made away with it.

Jerek dragged himself out of the grave and stood, dusting the dirt off his clothes.

He made sure the gravedigger knew what he had retrieved from the grave, making a fist around the winged ring, and cracking his knuckles. He reached a hand down to help the old man out of the hole, but then changed his mind, and left him knee deep in the bones of the dead to excuse his desecration.

'Your lucky day, old man. You get to live, at least until sunrise, when the priests will string you up for messing with the bones of their blessed saint.'

CHAPTER EIGHTEEN
The Taking of the Virgin and the Hag

THE COURT OF THE BLOOD COUNT, SYLVANIA
The Night of the Ravens

WOMEN LINED THE walls.

Konrad, Vampire Count of Sylvania, reclined luxuriantly in his sire's obsidian throne, savouring the heady aromas of the feast. Vlad had surrounded himself with beauty, like many beasts, drawn to the darkness within the soulless art, as if it somehow filled the void shaped by their death. Konrad despised such stupidity. There was beauty in the taking, not in admiring something unattainable: in the taking.

Konrad sighed and waved airily in the direction of a flaxen-haired beauty chained up against the wall. Her skin was as dusky as her almond-shaped eyes. She shook her head violently, writhing around against her captors' grip as they unlocked her manacles. The woman sobbed, begged, kicked and screamed. Oh yes, the beauty was most certainly in taking what you wanted, Konrad thought. The girl's fear was exhilarating. It was so much more passionate than quiet acquiescence. It was always better when they fought back. It added a sense of theft to the feeding.

One hundred and eleven women were chained, naked to the walls of the great hall, for his delectation. Their blood sang to him. He could sniff out their uniqueness, the virgins and the crones, the mothers and the whores. They all had their own unique stink. He looked at them, and at the rest of his court, coveting them.

'This,' he said grandly, 'is what separates us, what sets us apart. What you want is in my power to give. Come, let us feed!'

The woman shrieked as she was thrown down at his feet, the strength of the thralls driving her to her knees. Onursal, the Hamaya, stepped up and grabbed a fistful of her hair, tangling it in his fist as he pulled her across the floor. Her bare feet scrambled and her hands slapped at the cold stone as she tried to stop the pain, even as it soared inside her.

This was power, and it was intoxicating.

It was natural that others craved what he had, and sought to take it from him.

The beauty was in the taking.

He would have been a fool to believe that he was safe. Pieter, Fritz and Hans might be dead, but treachery still lurked in every shadow, waiting to undo him. It was the nature of the beast: he surrounded himself with predators. To show weakness was to invite death.

There wasn't a creature in the room that wouldn't have delighted in bringing him down and feasting on his corpse as a way of raising themselves up in his stead.

He looked around the room, at the naked and the dead.

He had no friends among them and could afford no trusts or confidences. They looked at him the same way, he was certain: they wanted him dead.

Well let them want, Konrad thought bitterly. He wouldn't give them the satisfaction of seeing even a hint of weakness. He would be the complete vampire, lord of his people, master of his house, cruel and callous, driven and decadent, inviolable and immortal.

He clapped his hands and the two thralls bled the woman, eager to satisfy their master's desire.

He sniffed, nostrils flared, the tang of her fresh blood was heady.

He would deny himself no more.

The pleasure was in the taking.

Konrad fed first, the thralls grabbing her hands, slitting her forearms from her wrists, deep into the hollow of her elbow, dripping the rich nectar down his throat in a luscious fountain. He savoured it as it spilled over his lips and ran down his chin.

'Another!' he commanded, even before this one was bled dry, eager for another flavour to bleed onto his palate. That was the beauty of the human cattle: they all tasted different, their blood reflecting the richness and vitality of their lives, against the youth and inexperience.

The thralls dragged the woman away to satisfy the ghoulish flesh eaters of the undead Count's hall.

A younger girl replaced her. She was barely a child, her blood innocent, and full of temptation. It was a delicacy that he had come to appreciate.

Konrad leaned back, his mouth open as the leering thrall drew a knife across her wrist.

She screamed as her blood dripped into his mouth. He nodded, and the thrall tossed the girl aside. He had barely tasted her, preferring to give her as a gift to one of his chosen ones. He knew their weaknesses, knew what they hungered for, be it young, old, boy, woman. It paid to know those closest to him, and know them intimately. Those weaknesses could always be turned against him. Onursal, the dark-skinned giant, caught and drained the girl, sidestepping her corpse as it slumped to the floor. He bowed to Konrad. 'My thanks, master.'

Konrad indulged the vampire with a wry smile. Yes, he knew his people and their weaknesses.

Around the great hall, other Hamaya feasted with their master.

Not all, Konrad amended, seeing that Jerek had not joined in the feeding.

Jerek.

The Hamaya was not himself, and hadn't been since returning from the debacle at Nuln. Konrad wanted to believe that his loyalty was not in question, that his youngest brother knew his place, but how could he know for sure? Jerek was von Carstein as much as Fritz or Pieter, or Hans had ever been, as he himself was. The taint of Vlad soiled the Hamaya's veins. How could he not crave Konrad's power? It was his blood right: his inheritance. He was von Carstein and now that, of his brothers-in-death, only Konrad remained, how could he not look at the count and crave more? In his place, Konrad knew that it would have been impossible to resist the pull of power. That left him with a problem.

The wolf was the consummate predator, ruthless with its enemies.

Was the wolf his enemy? How could he not be, given what was at stake?

The beauty was in the taking. That was the only truth to life.

Konrad turned away from the traitor, glad to see Skellan drinking hungrily. Over the course of a few minutes, Skellan gorged himself on every flavour of blood available. Konrad watched as he moved in close to an old woman, skin loose and mottled on her frail bones, and tangled his fingers in the woman's hair, yanking her head back. Seeing Konrad's intent scrutiny, Skellan laughed and called, 'Doesn't she remind you of your mother?' as he drew the hag close enough to sink his teeth into her leathery throat.

'Only in as much as she's just as dead as the bitch, otherwise no,' Konrad snarled. There was no humour in his expression as he sank his teeth into a dead-eyed blonde who had staggered too close to him for her own good. He spun her around and let her fall. 'Music!' the Vampire Count proclaimed. 'A party needs music. Someone play! I want someone to play for me!'

There were no musicians in his court. They had fed on them when he had decided their tunes did not fit his mood.

'Will someone sing for me? Jerek?'

The wolf could not mask his revulsion. He pushed past one of Konrad's thralls struggling with a fat-bellied sow of a woman. Both went sprawling across the blood-slicked floor as Jerek left the great hall.

'I think perhaps you have lost your mind, my lord,' Skellan interjected smoothly, halting Jerek mid-step. Skellan let his words hang for longer than was wise. 'The old wolf is tone deaf and is incapable of carrying a tune. Better, surely, that we make these women scream, as one, and let their terror be music to our ears as we revel in their deaths.'

'As it should be!' Konrad agreed. 'Let us savour the agonies of our fodder! Let us drink, not only their blood, for even a bug can do that, let us devour their fear! Let us lose ourselves in their fear. Truly, let us feast!'

And they did, in an orgy suffering. The screams of the dying women shook the hall, folding in on themselves in a spiralling chorus of suffering. It was delicious, dizzying.

It was a rhapsody of murder, and Konrad stood in the centre of it all, lord of his domain, master in his own house, and drunk on the music of death.

He claimed the last for his own, whispering almost tenderly in her ear as he sucked the lifeblood out of her ruined face. There was no simple death for her. He chewed off her nose and sucked the mucus and blood with equal abandon.

Sated, he held her still, surveying the carnage. This was power, here, made flesh.

Dead flesh.

This was the power of death over life.

He caressed her cheek, looking for the one face he couldn't see: Jerek's.

Skellan moved up beside him.

'He's gone, hasn't he?' Konrad asked. He didn't need to say who.

'In more ways than one,' Skellan said. 'I have marked a change in him since Nuln. Something happened to him there, I fear, and he's not the same man as a result. Not the same *wolf*. He's lost his taste for the kill. You've noticed it as well, haven't you?'

Konrad nodded. 'He didn't feed tonight. Not once.'

'That is troubling, but not surprising.'

'No?'

'No. It was something he said a few weeks ago, "A wise man does not drink from the cup of his enemy", that was it, I think.'

'His enemy,' Konrad mused. He didn't want to believe it, but all the signs were there: the shift in personality, the introspection and reclusion, the late return weeks behind the few survivors of Nuln, the unwillingness to share blood with his brothers. These were all precursors of the cold hand that was betrayal. 'No one, not even the wolf, can offer such a slight and believe himself immune from retribution. I will have his apology and his loyalty, or I will have his tongue.'

Skellan inclined his head as if weighing two equally worthy options. 'As it should be, my lord. There is wisdom to such thinking, although I wonder if it will have the desired effect on Jerek, or if your brother is too far gone for such a clean solution. I must confess I rather fear the worst.'

HE FOUND JEREK on the roof.

The wind was savage, and the night black. Jerek stood amid a murder of glossy feathered ravens, the birds flocking around him as if he was their messiah. The wolf's face was grave.

Konrad stepped out onto the roof.

'So my company offends you, wolf?'

Jerek did not deny him.

A black knot of hatred twisted in Konrad's gut. The Hamaya lacked even the courtesy to lie to him.

Jerek turned his back on Konrad, feigning interest in the chimneys of Drakenhof far below.

'Who is master here, Jerek? Answer me that.'

'I did not choose this life, Konrad, and worse, I do not like what I have become. I look about me and see life that I cannot be a part of. I see the people I fought to save from the evil I now am. I am lost, caught between two worlds, but not part of either one. Tell me where the crime is in that? It is not a slight to you. Not everything is about you.'

'You did not answer my question.'

Jerek turned slightly, his wild mane of hair streaming in the wind, 'I should not need to.'

'But you do,' Konrad said coldly.

Hatred blazed in the wolf's eyes as his lips curled into a sneer. 'You are a fool, Konrad. You see enemies where there are none. You make enemies where there were only friends. You don't know when to hold out your hand, and when others do, you slap them away.

Look around you, look at the birds, they fight and squabble over scraps. That is your kingdom, Konrad, a bloody fight for scraps. Your magical new world is built on fear, and fear is like sand, it shifts.

'You revere strength, or at least claim to, although it is obvious that it scares you. Make no mistake: strength does scare you, no matter what you would have others believe. Strength in others terrifies you, so you stamp it out, betraying your own weakness, while thinking it makes you strong. A strong man surrounds himself with strong men. A weak man postures in the centre of a circus of simpering fools.

'Believe me, *Blood Count*, there is always something more frightening to be discovered in this world, if you look hard enough. The secret is, coming to terms with the fact that the daemons you know are always less fearful than the daemons you don't know.

'You are your own worst enemy, *my lord.*'

'How dare you?' Konrad said.

There was no anger in his voice, no bluster. Indeed, it was almost a question as opposed to statement, as if the wolf's defiance bewildered him.

Jerek took a step forwards, closing the gap between them.

'How dare I? Where is the dare in telling the truth, Konrad?'

Konrad stiffened. 'You risk much, speaking to me this way, wolf. If we were not alone I would be forced to bring you into line.'

'You mean silence me, Konrad. No more lies between us.'

'I still could, wolf.'

'And in doing so, prove my point. Yes, you would be stupid enough to do just that, wouldn't you?'

Instinctively, Konrad raised his hand, ready to strike.

Jerek did not flinch. He stared at Konrad's fist as if daring him to do it, to lash out.

Konrad held himself in check, barely. A muscle beneath his cheek twitched. His fist clenched, fingernails digging into his palm. Had the stuff flowed through his veins, his fingernails would have drawn blood.

'That's what you want, isn't it, wolf? You want to goad me into attacking you. You want me to fall into a rage and throw myself at you.' A look of puzzlement spread over the Vampire Count's face. He lowered his fist slowly. 'Well, you will have no satisfaction from me.'

The wolf shook his head in disgust.

'You think I have lured you up here to fight you? You truly are a fool, Konrad. My being here has nothing to do with you, but everything to do with what you are.' Jerek laughed, a bitter, bleak sound that was ripped away by the wind. 'What we both are.' He looked over his shoulder, back towards the sheer drop down the mountainside to the jagged rocks below. 'I haven't come here to challenge you. I have come here to die, Konrad. I have come here to put an end to my own suffering once and for all, but I lack the strength to do it.'

'Oh, it can be arranged,' Konrad goaded, taking a step to match Jerek's, so there was nothing between them.

The ravens scattered, cawing raucously as they burst into the sky in a flurry of black wings that blotted out the slice of silver moon. The birds buffeted the pair, wings slapping at them, bullying them closer to the edge. Konrad took another step, unclasping his cloak. It fell behind him, only to be lifted by the wind. Billowing out, it sailed over the parapet like his own discarded wings.

'I favoured you wolf, I trusted you. I treated you like the brother you are.'

Jerek shook his head in disgust. 'You mean you used me as a tool to do what you were incapable of. You had me remove those you feared and cement your authority by becoming your personal assassin? That's no act of brotherhood in my world.'

'In your world? You talk as if we exist in different realities. We don't, Jerek. Your world is *my* world.'
Jerek shook his head, denying the truth of Konrad's words. 'You are more like me than you realise, brother. Together we could have achieved great things.'

'There is no greatness in murder.'

'At my side you could have had the world.'

'At your side I could have butchered the world, there is a difference.'

And there it was, the truth.

'So it is true what Skellan said, you have lost your taste for killing. What kind of beast have you become, Jerek? Because you are surely a wolf no longer.'

'I am not the wolf I was, but nor am I the wolf you would have me be. I am torn in two.'

'Then you are a fool, Jerek, because you can only ever be the killer, as the scorpion can only ever be the scorpion, the lamb the lamb, and the raven the raven. It is your nature just as it is theirs. To deny it is to deny your essence, to deny your soul.'

'I have no soul, our bastard of a father stole it from me!' Jerek's sudden anger was shocking.

Konrad understood. 'You hate him, don't you? You hate him for what he did, and would undo it if you could. You would renounce his gift, you would sacrifice the power he blessed you with, the life he gave you, and go back to grubbing in the dirt like some pathetic pig.'

'I don't hate him. I want to hate him, but hate is an emotion, and even something as basic as that is lost to me. I would kill him if I could. I would see the curse of his existence purged from the land, if I could.'

'You would kill me.' It wasn't a question. 'Well, wolf, I was right when I called you my truth speaker, although I have little liking for the truth that you offer now. There can be no easy forgiveness, it seems, and there can be no trust, not now. You know what it means, don't you?' Konrad's face shifted in the moonlight, his features contorting harshly as the beast within rose to the surface.

He was on Jerek before the wolf had a chance to react, tearing at his face with his claws. Jerek threw his hands up to ward off the attack, the flat of his hand – his burned hand, branded with the rune from the protective talisman that sealed the Grand Theogonist's grave – connecting with the side of Konrad's face. The Vampire Count reeled back is if he had been stung, his cry rending the night in two. He dropped into a crouch, snarling, as Jerek surrendered to his own primal monster and wore its face. Only then did the dance begin in earnest.

The birds cackled and shrieked appreciatively, circling overhead.

Konrad lashed out, driving Jerek back towards the roof's edge. Jerek met the blow and matched it, catching Konrad's fist in his own, stepping in close enough so that the mad Count's graveolent breath stung his face, and slammed his other fist into his throat. It would have killed a living man slowly, suffocating the life out of him as his windpipe collapsed in on itself and starved him of precious air. Konrad's head snapped forwards, fangs scoring across Jerek's wrist as he pulled it back.

Konrad twisted his arm, breaking the wolf's grip on his fist, and even as Jerek struggled to reassert his dominance, the Vampire Count surged forwards, cannoning his forehead into Jerek's face. The blow shattered the wolf's nose. The wolf staggered back under the sheer ferocity of the blow. Konrad followed it up with a dizzying combination of high left, to the temple, a savage low right, to the kidney, and a devastating second left in the centre of the gaping wound that had been the wolf's face.

Jerek stumbled back, his hands held up desperately in front of his face to ward off another blow.

Konrad spun and kicked downwards, his heel snapping the links between ligament and bone beneath the wolf's knee. Jerek stumbled back, perilously close to the roof's edge.

There could be no mercy for the wolf.

Konrad threw himself forwards.

The birds drove themselves into a frenzy, swarming around the pair.

The slate beneath his feet cracked and broke away, leaving Jerek's back leg hanging over nothing. Through the ruin of his face, the wolf grinned, and in a last act of defiance, took the victory away from Konrad. His smile never wavered. He looked at his would-be killer, and of all things Konrad saw pity in the wolf's eyes. Then Jerek fell back silently into the endless black and was snatched away by the battering wings of Vlad's ravens.

Rage seethed within Konrad as he moved up to the edge. He half expected to see the erratic flight of a bat trying to mask itself in the murder of birds, but the birds had all settled on the mountainside, filling every crevice and cranny. He strained to see beyond the ravens, to the teeth of the rocks below. Jerek's body was little more than a dark stain as it lay unmoving on a splinter of jagged rock. He refused to believe what had just happened. The wolf hadn't fought for his life, he had thrown it away! That last grin, the deliberate lurch backwards, giving himself to the fall instead of trying to save himself, it had been one final act of defiance, done out of spite and stupidity.

It galled him.

'How dare you?' he yelled down at his fallen brother, the manic pitch of his voice scattering a few of the more nervous birds. They circled the dark stain like vultures. Ravens were carrion eaters. Soon they would descend on the wolf and strip his carcass clean. Konrad watched for an age, while the sun rose and his rage subsided, until the remaining birds gave up their vigil. Still, the wolf lay there broken, at the base of the crag. Then and only then did a savage smile spread across Konrad's face, even as he reined in the beast and shifted back to human form. He might have been robbed of the thrill of the actual taking, but it didn't matter. What did matter was that he was alone. The Golden One, whoever the hell that might have been, was dead. He was the last von Carstein.

Triumphant, Konrad left the ravens to feed on the wolf's broken body.

CHAPTER NINETEEN
Ghost World

ACROSS THE OLD WORLD
Winter

THERE WAS NO evil that Jon Skellan was incapable of.

It was a game that offered only mild amusement, but it was a game that he loved to play just the same.

With his bare hands, he took a dark land and reshaped it into a ghost world.

His beasts ruled by tyranny. There was no justice. There was no fairness. There was no *humanity*. The world was reduced to two absolutes, pain and death, death and pain.

Skellan revelled in it. He revelled in the fear that his beasts inspired, and savoured the pain they delivered.

HE WALKED THE line of crucified corpses along the roadside. Upside down, the dead served as food for the birds and reminders to those left behind of the price of rebellion. It was a savage lesson, one the cattle took to heart.

The dead faces, drained of blood, stared back at him. More than half of their eyes were gone, pecked away by the flock of black ravens that trailed Skellan's force, scavenging carrion where the dead meat was discarded and left to rot.

They brought with them the return of the blood plague, but this time it was indiscriminate in its slaughter. Old, young, male, female, none were immune to the insidious illness, as Skellan's beasts sought to drain the Old World dry of every decent drop of blood that pumped through its veins. The pandemic spread, striking the largest cities of the Empire and wreaking as much devastation there as it did in the smallest villages. They started calling it the Season of the Dead.

The living barred their doors and windows, barricading themselves in, in the vain hope that the dead would pass them by. The dead did pass, and in their wake they left empty buildings and more than their fair share of ghosts.

Word had come that Lutwig had ousted his ineffectual father, the Pretender, Ludwig. The succession was irrelevant. Skellan didn't care who led the cattle. They existed for one purpose, to be hunted, brought down and feasted on.

With so many of Konrad's trusted Hamaya gone, it was only natural that Skellan should rise in both influence and power. Like his sire before him, he rose to be von Carstein's right hand, but unlike Posner, he would not make the mistake of getting himself slaughtered for ambition. He would bide his time. There was little to be gained by moving hastily and everything to be won by cautious strength. It was a long game, and a long game called for cunning and guile, not posturing and posing.

He watched and he learned, taking the tricks of others and turning them to his advantage. Where Vlad had offered his victims the choice of serving him in life or in death, Skellan was less prosaic. The choice he offered was an immediate death or a painful one. Few willingly chose pain. Those that did were not disappointed.

For months, the vampire's legion of the damned had savaged the land of the living, the necromancers adding fresh impetus to the sport by inventing cruel and unusual punishments for the living who were foolish enough to resist them. Skellan couldn't deny that he enjoyed their perversions, even encouraged them, but Nevin Kantor concerned him.

Even a fool could see that the necromancer was growing in strength, outstripping those around him as he opened himself up to the taint of the black Chaos wind. Death was no longer enough for Nevin Kantor. He consumed Immoliah Fey, owned her. Such was the lure of his power that even a necromancer with Fey's rare gift should fall for his fake endearments. There was no love, even he could see that, just pretty words whispered in the dark, and midnight promises, which were nothing more than midnight lies.

He took the living and violated them in ways that Skellan had never imagined possible. He experimented on them, testing the limits of their endurance, seeking to break the bonds that made them human without actually driving them into Morr's arms. He stripped flesh from bone without allowing his victims to die, forcing them to watch as layer after layer of meat peeled away before their eyes. A few, he delighted in killing, drawing every ounce of moisture from their flesh, leaving only desiccated husks. He turned others into cannibals, feeding them with their own flesh, and had destroyed them so completely that they ate it willingly.

Worse, he turned mother onto son and father onto daughter, by a dark geas, the dead being absorbed back into the family, like some never-ending serpent of consumption, the beast feeding off its own tail. He manipulated their minds, forcing visions of hell to root behind their eyes, with promises of the torments on offer should they fail him. He also raised the dead, not their corpses, but their souls, even as they travelled the long and winding road to the underworld, drawing them back, demanding to know what they saw, in detail. Demanding to know not only what they saw, but also what they felt and heard, all of it, what it was like to be dead.

The intensity of his obsession was unnerving, even to Skellan.

Kantor was a threat, potentially more so than the Blood Count. Since Jerek's betrayal, Konrad's behaviour had become increasingly erratic and unpredictable, as what was undoubtedly madness burrowed away inside him. He had come to rely more and more on Kantor's magic, more so even than

Skellan's sword. It made it increasingly difficult for Skellan's gentle nudges and sly whisperings to find their mark, although he continued to goad the unstable von Carstein into fully-fledged paranoia. To that extent, Mannfred had been completely correct when he judged Konrad: his brother possessed the fundamental insecurities of a paranoiac. Kantor had set himself up as a counterbalance to Skellan in the Count's allegiances. Skellan understood Konrad's fascination with Kantor: the necromancer manipulated the winds into miracles. More and more, Konrad sought out the human, and while Skellan had no idea what they actually discussed, it was obvious that Konrad trusted Nevin Kantor's council as much if not more than Skellan's.

Kantor was turning into a problem.

Months of manipulation were coming to fruition, a multitude of small, carefully laid plans playing out, in time for Mannfred's imminent return.

The necromancer could not be allowed to interfere.

Konrad would fall, with Skellan's help, and it would be spectacular.

He knelt beneath the upturned crucifix, scooping up a raven before the birds could frighten and scatter.

'Are you there?' He demanded. His voice was pitched low so it wouldn't carry.

The bird's yellow eyes roved and it cawed harshly, ruffling its feathers and trying to burst out of his grip.

'Always,' the raven cackled as Skellan's grip threatened to crack its delicate bones.

'Your brother's crown is slipping. The fool's slaughtered almost everyone close to him. It's only a matter of time before he turns on the last few who remain loyal to him.'

'Good, good.' The black bird preened.

'But the necromancer is turning into something of a problem.' Skellan confessed his fears to Mannfred. 'He's unpredictable, and growing dangerously powerful. He's become Konrad's crutch, making it increasingly difficult to deliver the coup de grace. I fear he may prove troublesome.'

The bird offered a single piece of advice, 'Keep the necromancer close.' Then it fell silent, its yellow eyes blinking shut.

He felt its heart race, beating hard against his hands as whatever hold Mannfred had on it was relinquished.

Frustrated, Skellan crushed the bird in his hands and dropped it in the dirt beneath the crucified man.

'Something for you to snack on if you grow hungry,' he said, but the dead man didn't laugh.

CHAPTER TWENTY
The Soul Cages

DRAKENHOF, CITY OF THE DEAD, SYLVANIA
The Season of the Dead

THEY WERE IN trouble, but then they had been in trouble from the first moment they set foot in Drakenhof, over a month ago.

It had taken the dead that long to find them, but find them they had, in a derelict corner of the city, grubbing around like rats trying to find hide or hair of the magician. Deserted buildings crowded in over them. The tight alleyway gave them an edge, but whatever hope he had had of taking advantage of it was quashed when the beasts drove them out into one of the smaller squares, pushing them towards the well in the very centre.

Lothar du Bek drew steel, ready to fight for his life. Adrenaline coursed through him.

Beside him, Kallad Stormwarden shook his head, 'No, you have to learn to pick your fights. This isn't one we can win.'

Eight of the beasts circled them: eight vampires. Three had taken the form of great dire wolves and prowled the circle's perimeter hungrily. The beasts' feral eyes never left the pair. There was a ninth, lurking in the shadows behind them, watching, waiting for the right moment to reveal itself. Lothar had seen it even before the circle had closed fully around them.

The dwarf was right, but he was damned if he was going to simply lay down and die like some sick cow looking to be put out of its misery. He would make them pay for his life. That was the very least he could do.

'You think they'll let us surrender?' du Bek asked in disbelief, steel wavering before his face as he turned and turned, unwilling to expose his back to any of the beasts, and unable to do otherwise. 'They aren't about to take us prisoner, dwarf. Soon as you lower that warhammer, they'll tear your throat out.'

'Aye, it's a gamble,' the dwarf said, 'but if we choose to make a last stand here, it's going to be a *last stand*, make no bones about it. Dunno about you, but dying's not particularly appealing, given what they do to the dead around here.'

The dwarf was up to something – he had to be. His kind didn't lay down their weapons, they fought to the death, making their enemy pay with blood for their lives. He had to trust the dwarf, but that didn't mean he couldn't vent his fear, 'They're animals! All they want to do is feed on us.'

One of the beasts broke the circle, and as he did, his face shifted back into that of a man. His smile was the only thing that gave the lie to his humanity. He was every bit the beast whatever face he chose to wear.

Lothar turned slightly to face him, keeping the blade's edge between them.

'You do us a disservice, human.' The vampire said the word 'human' as if it was a curse. 'Lucky for you, I don't take offence easily.'

'Do you think I care, animal? I'm happy to die here, and just as long as I gut you in the process I'll lose no sleep in the afterlife.'

Shaking its head, the vampire laughed easily, 'As if I'd actually allow you the luxury of eternal sleep. No, it would be much more fun to play with you for a while.' The fiend turned to Kallad. 'You, dwarf, I feel like we are old friends already. Every time I look over my shoulder, you're there. You just never give up, do you?'

'Thought I recognised your stink, even if I didn't recognise your face,' Kallad said.

'Now, now, dwarf. Practise what you preach and all that. You don't want to go getting my friends all excited now do you?'

The wolves bristled, hackles rising, their pacing growing more urgent as they circled the three of them.

The spectre of the Vampire Count's castle loomed over their backs. It sent a shiver running through du Bek, as if someone had just set a heavy foot down on his grave.

'Circumstances just changed,' Kallad growled, reaching back for the leather grip of Ruinthorn's shaft. 'You made your peace with your maker?'

'My maker is dead, no peace needed or wanted, dwarf. Have you made your peace with your own god?'

'Grimnir is ever at my side.'

'Well, he didn't appear to be at your father's side, did he? Finding out our parents aren't immortal can be traumatic at the best of times. Seeing them abandoned by your precious gods, well, that's liable to make an atheist out of even the most devout of us.'

All of the muscles tightened in Kallad Stormwarden's face. The dwarf hawked and spat a thick wad of phlegm into the vampire's face.

His lip curling into a sneer, the vampire wiped it away. 'I had hoped you would walk with me, I would know my hunter before I kill him.' He held his fingers out as if offering the phlegm back. 'I'll take this as your refusal. It matters not, your blood will tell me all I need to know when the time comes.'

'It's him, isn't it?' Lothar said to Kallad.

'Aye, Lothar, it's him,' Kallad said. The circle was truly complete, Lothar realised. Here, in a pox-ridden alleyway in a city starved of humanity. It was a soul-destroying discovery. 'The beast that the Sigmarites thought they had tamed. His name is Jon Skellan. He butchered the priests of the Sigmarite cathedral in Altdorf, murdered the family Liebowitz in Nuln, and burned his way across the western world.'

The vampire sketched a mocking bow.

'The one and only, dwarf, although, you missed out some of what I consider to be the highlights of my career. I must admit, you have me at something of a loss; your fame is not so universal. I imagine you are

Gimpy or Wazzock or some such wonderfully evocative name.'

'Kallad Stormwarden, son of King Kellus, last son of Karak Sadra.'

'Well Kallad, son of Kellus, how does it feel to know that it is all going to end like this, after so long looking for justice? I would imagine it must be galling to be so close to your revenge, only to have all hope of it crushed just like that.'

'You and me, beast.' Kallad said. 'Forget the manling, forget your wolves, you and me, last man standing.'

The vampire laughed. 'What do you take me for? Do you think I give a damn about your stupid sense of honour, dwarf? I can't think of one good reason to give you any hope of satisfaction. Do you think your grudge means anything to me? No, eight of us, two of you, those are pleasing numbers.'

'Nine,' du Bek said inclining his head towards the shadows where he knew the final beast hid.

The vampire's smile was cold. 'So you have eyes. Good for you, human.' He gestured towards the shadows. 'I believe this is something of a reunion. Come out, come out, wherever you are.'

Du Bek didn't recognise the man as he emerged from the anonymity of the dark, but Kallad did.

'Kantor.' It was barely a breath, both recognition and denial in one word, as if the world had been pulled out from under his feet.

'The magician?' Lothar asked. This was wrong. It was all going horribly, horribly wrong. They had come to this godforsaken place to free the magician, not to find him turned, and siding with the very enemy they sought to kill.

'One and the same,' the vampire said, clearly enjoying the effect that Nevin Kantor's unveiling was having on the dwarf.

Kantor walked confidently between the wolves – indeed the animals parted slightly, as if in deference to the magician.

'You just refuse to die, don't you, dwarf?'

'I could say the same about you, magician.'

'Indeed.'

'So you sold your soul, eh?'

'Don't be so melodramatic, dwarf. You were supposed to kill me. That was the only way the Sigmarites would allow us to travel together, was it not? The moment my usefulness was over, I was to be put out of my misery like some stinking mutt. Don't bother denying it, I know the truth.'

'I wouldn't have done it. I'm no monster.'

'It's academic really. Last time I saw you, you were lining up to join the ranks of the dead.'

'But as you can see, I didn't die.'

'All things considered, dwarf, it would appear that all you succeeded in doing was delaying death for a little while longer.'

'Well,' the vampire interrupted, 'as much as I am enjoying this little tête à tête, I think its time we got around to the killing, don't you?'

Lothar stiffened. He tried to look every way at once, desperately trying to cover every direction that the attack could possibly come from. It was impossible. His back was always bared to one or more of the beasts.

Beside him, the dwarf knelt, head down as he laid his huge double-headed axe down on the ground at his feet. 'Then kill me now and be done with it. I've got no fight left in me.'

'No!' du Bek yelled, throwing himself forwards. His sword speared out towards the magician's guts, and by rights ought to have spilled them out all over the cobblestones, but Nevin Kantor said a word – a single word – a harsh crack like the booming rumble of thunder answered, and a splinter ran through the folded metal of Lothar du Bek's sword. The splinter opened into a crack, splitting the sword wide open and showering him in jags of hot metal.

His hand recoiled from the hilt as the black magic chased from the sword up his arm and into his heart, sundering the organ as easily as it had the blade.

He was dead before the pieces of him hit the floor.

KALLAD STORMWARDEN CAME to in darkness.

Death would have been a blessed relief from the image of his friend's body tearing itself apart from the inside out, but it wasn't to be.

He was alone in the dark. There was no window and no light source to give even a hint of the room's size.

He fumbled around in the dark, touching stone and rotten reeds. On hands and knees, he tentatively explored the darkness. His hand found the wall and followed it. The cell was small, no more than ten feet by ten.

Kallad's knee upended the water bowl that had been left out for him, spilling its contents across the floor.

He felt out for a second bowl, reasoning that if there was water there could equally be food. There wasn't.

And they had taken his axe.

He curled up in a corner, his back pressed up against the wall.

In the aftermath of bloody ruination of du Bek, the vampire, Skellan, had stepped up and cracked him hard across the skull, turning the world to black. He remembered nothing after that. His head ached, and every time he moved it, a wave of nausea surged through him, twisting his guts inside out. Kallad moaned, the sound a dirge in the dark. He needed the wall at his back, its solidity was reassuring.

'Kallad Stormwarden, you are a fool.' His words barely touched the black. They sounded peculiar in his own ears, as if distant, muffled by a thick wadding of wool. That didn't dilute the truth of them, however. The mistake he made was in thinking that the living would protect them from the dead, when they couldn't even begin to protect themselves.

They had arrived in Drakenhof with their heads full of stories, gathered village by village, and all sharing the same disturbing similarities: housewives, midwives, gamblers, soldiers, farmers, it didn't matter who they were, anyone who owned even a hint of the uncanny had been snatched and dragged to the black castle of Drakenhof. It was more than just distance that separated Sylvania from the Empire. Centuries of oppression had taken their toll on the people. They had been stripped of even the most basic facets of personality, humour and hope. Kallad and du Bek found themselves pitying them, and along the way, they had convinced themselves that the poor downtrodden peasants of Sylvania would embrace them, rise up against their tyrannical master and bring down the beasts, once and for all. Poverty ruled the ruin of a city. The living shuffled like the dead and the damned through its filthy streets. It was stupid, naïve, dangerous, thinking that they had turned the castle itself into an icon for the evil they hunted, and it had killed Lothar du Bek.

Rather than embrace them, the peasants shunned their would-be liberators. They crossed the streets to avoid them and cast fretful glances over their shoulders as if they feared being seen even the width of the street away from the foreigners. Such was the long-reaching arm of their vile master.

It should have been obvious, given the fact that the Vampire Count's cruelty was carved into every gaunt face that stared back at him.

'TWO MEN CAN'T storm a castle,' du Bek had argued across the table in the hovel that they had found abandoned on the edge of town, even as Kallad outlined his plan.

Plan. It wasn't a plan, it wasn't even close. It was a plan's ugly sibling, a barely formed notion. The ruse meant to open the door, but after the door was open, Kallad had known that beyond that point there was nothing. 'Well, they can, but not without winding up very dead.'

'Aye, but we don't need to storm it, we just need to get inside. We don't need to take the walls down or destroy the place. It's a simple kill. Remember, we've got our man in there already.'

'You've got no intention of getting back out alive, have you?' du Bek had said, finally understanding. 'We're talking about suicide.'

'No, not suicide, my friend, it's a trade, a life for a life. Killing the monster that killed my people is enough for me, it has to be.'

'It's still suicide if you aren't planning on walking out of that place alive, dwarf, and you know it.'

NOW HERE HE was, his friend dead, trapped in the darkness deep beneath the Blood Count's castle.

He would have done anything to go back just a few days and change things. Allie's face formed in the darkness of his mind's eye. The boy had lost a father and he didn't even know it. He wondered how many days and weeks would pass before Allie du Bek stopped running to the window at the sound of a wagon, horses hooves, even footsteps and muffled conversation? How many months would it take for the lad to accept the truth: that his father wasn't coming home?

It was one thing to plan his own sacrifice, that was a price he was willing to pay if it meant his people would be avenged, but it was quite another to turn it into the murder of his friend. Too many people had died around him, good people, people who hadn't deserved their fate. Lothar du Bek was just one of many. That hurt.

The darkness only served to make the pain worse as his mind taunted him with flashes of memory, and snatches of conversations and long dead voices.

He lost all sense of time as thirst took hold and hunger gripped his gut.

Still no one came.

Was this to be his torture? To be left alone to dwell on his failings and wrestle his ghosts?

In the darkness, he saw Nevin Kantor, the magician, looking down in distaste at the blood on his clothes.

If only it was as easy to exorcise the living as it was the dead.

IT WOULD HAVE been easy to give up, to let the darkness take him, but the grudge burned brighter than ever inside him.

He would live to see it fulfilled.

THEY CAME FOR him.

They were like something out of a nightmare. Huge lumbering things that might have once been human. They dragged him between them. There was nothing comforting in the near dark. He saw things, shadows, shapes, but without the torches flickering he would have been blind to the glimpses of an underworld that didn't bear witnessing. For all that he lived his life below the surface he wasn't blessed with extraordinary sight – and the treacherous light was more than capable of playing tricks on him.

The dead lord of Drakenhof had extended his kingdom far below and beyond the foundations of his castle. The thugs bullied Kallad, stumbling and staggering, through the vast network of tunnels cut into the rock. Lichen and moss grew in the deep cracks and in places a skin of water dribbled over stone.

A familiar smell seeped into the stale air. It took him a while to place it, but when he did, the knowledge stirred the faintest flicker of hope: the Vampire Count's thralls had mined so far that they had broken into the web of deep mines that radiated out from core strongholds beneath the World's Edge Mountains: Karak Varn, Zufbar, Karak Kadrin. He breathed deeply of the air, needing its familiar tang to revitalise himself.

With that vitality came a yearning for what had been, for what he had lost. It hit him hard. He reached out and touched the rough-hewn rock. He made a promise to himself: there would be a reckoning for his people. There would be justice: retribution.

He had no idea where they were taking him until they shoved him through a door and barred it behind him as he stumbled into the holding pen.

'Welcome to the soul cages,' a wizened old man said in a voice as brittle as his bones.

Kallad could hear voices, cheering, banging and stamping feet. There was a narrow door at the far side of the pen, and a bench where the old man sat. Otherwise, the room was bare. Kallad pressed his face up against the bars, straining to see beyond them.

'Opens onto the Long Walk, and then up to the fighting pits,' the old man explained. 'The Count likes his entertainment raw and bloody.'

Kallad listened at the bars. It was impossible to gauge the size of the crowd, but its bloodthirsty nature was all too plain. They bayed for blood.

The clash of steel rang out, and then there was silence.

The sudden surge of noise from the spectators drowned out the screams of the dying man.

Kallad could picture it all too perfectly in his head: the clash of swords, savage cuts and wild slashes raining down, barely being parried in a dizzying fight to overcome death by the sheer strength of the sword arm, or to succumb to its inevitability.

There was an aura of death to the underground chamber. Men, who moments before had strode out to conquer the world, came back on stretchers, dead or dying. There was no glory in the fight. It was a lie, perhaps the greatest one of all.

The door to the pits slammed open and three ghoulish creatures dragged a body into the pen between them.

'Best get out there, dwarf. The Count don't like to be kept waiting.'

He could hear them calling for him, although they didn't know his name. The cry of: *blood, blood, blood* echoed back to him.

Let them wait, Kallad thought bitterly, and let out an abrasive bark of a laugh as he walked through the door.

It was a long walk to the surface, made longer by the haunting echo of footsteps and the muted whispers of dead men, remembered forever by the tunnels sandstone walls.

How many men had walked this same tunnel on the way to their deaths? Too many was the answer. Images of Morr, Lord of the Dead, lined the tunnel walls, whilst nameless souls dominated the floor mosaics.

The Long Walk, the old man had called it. Kallad was fully aware of the duality of the name.

Dark-skinned thralls, the life leached from their eyes, guarded the entrance to the pits.

Kallad strode out into the pit amid roars from the banks of vampiric spectators. The pit was huge, carved out of the bare rock. Stalactites hung down over the killing ground. Huge stone walls ringed the pit. There was no easy way to escape. Banks of seating scaled up the walls, climbing almost as high as the longest of the stalactites dripped low. The seats were filled. Thousands of hungry faces stared down at him as he walked into the centre of the pit.

He stopped and turned, scanning the ranks of the dead for a familiar face. He found Skellan, and beside him, a darker beast with the same mesmeric features as the beast that had slain his father. The blood of other men stained the sand at his feet. The Vampire Count, Konrad von Carstein, sat high up in the stands, most of the seats around him empty. The Count, it appeared, did not like his sycophants getting too close to him.

Kallad waited for the Blood Count to meet his gaze. The creature wouldn't.

As von Carstein rose to his feet, someone shouted, 'Death comes!' The crowd took up the chant: *'The Count! The Count! The Count!'*

Kallad let the sound wash over him. It was nothing more than bluster, meant to instil fear. He would not let it.

In the city, he had heard talk that Konrad could trace his blood back to Vashanesh, the first great vampire, and that he enjoyed thousands of years of vampiric taint in this veins.

The dwarf knew a lie when he heard one. A dynasty of aristocratic blood, or thirty-odd generations of cut-throats, whores, murderers and pirates? The truth was a curious beast in the hands of a ruler like Konrad and, no doubt, those close to him fed the flames of his mad delusion, their worm-tongues worshipping his lineage.

He shrugged it off. It wasn't his problem. He was blessedly immune to the vampire's vanities.

Von Carstein's gaze filled with sick longing as he looked towards the shadowed entrance of the pit. Kallad refused to be drawn into looking for his opponent. He would live or he would die, looking back would do nothing to alter that.

'Do you want to beg for your life, dwarf?' Konrad bellowed. His voice echoed around the subterranean pit.

Kallad hawked and spat into the sand, 'Where's my axe, coward? Frightened I might kill your pets?'

Servants of the Vampire Count moved out onto the killing floor. One of them carried Ruinthorn.

He walked slowly towards Kallad, offering the axe to the dwarf.

Kallad hefted it, felt its reassuringly familiar weight in his hands, and braced himself for the fight of his life.

He would feed them all the dead meat they could handle. As the old dwarf proverb went, 'The time will come when all gods die', and as the traps opened on the lion pits, Kallad felt doubt for the first time in years. It was a strange sensation, a quickening in his chest: the realisation that this flesh, this body, didn't belong to him, that it was a gift from the Creator. Intellectually, he knew what he was feeling: fear. Was this what the others felt when they faced Ruinthorn? He felt a surge of pity for them, the young who had fallen to his axe. Were they somewhere now, in the Halls of the Dead, pitying him in turn?

He saw Skellan smiling down on him, saw Konrad seemingly hypnotised by the creature emerging from the darkness of the pits: a naked beast-faced vampire.

The creature roared, dropping into a fighting crouch. Even as it did so, the beast's back arched and stretched as it transformed into a huge black furred dire wolf.

It was the largest wolf he had ever seen.

Is it that time, Grimna, thought Kallad? Is my life counted now in seconds? Then more bitterly: it is if you think it is, fool. Fight for your damned life!

He brought Ruinthorn to bear, kissing the rune embossed on its huge butterfly blades. His world narrowed down to the axe and the creature he had to kill. His knuckles were white. His hands were shaking.

Skellan leaned over and whispered something to the Vampire Count, but Kallad was in no position to wonder what.

Konrad laughed. His laughter, like his words before, rolled around the cramped subterranean pit, taunting Kallad as he stood down there in the middle of the killing floor.

He would not die here. He would avenge his people. He would find Kantor and wring the life from his body. He *would* live.

The assembly of vampires would not be satisfied by mere blood, had come to witness slaughter, and to a beast they were hungry for it.

The wolf circled warily, jowls curled back, nostrils flared as it smelled blood on the air. It moved slowly, a curious kind of recognition on its twisted face. Kallad studied the monster as he would any other opponent, gauging it for weaknesses, assessing its strengths.

For a second, the world froze, the beast rising out of its crouch, Konrad's mouth wide in laughter. Kallad didn't move as much as a muscle.

He had long since stopped wondering what it would feel like to die. The wolf loosed a baleful howl. Still, Kallad didn't move.

The wolf circled him.

He stood square and watched the creature as he would have watched any other opponent, facing it down, and showing no fear, despite the fact that he was suddenly aware of every drop of blood pumping through his veins and the very real mortality it ensured. It had weaknesses. Everything did. The trick was believing that, and not succumbing to the bone-freezing fear that was doubt.

The wolf circled him, its massive claws raking the wet sand. Kallad's grip on the axe tightened.

He swept Ruinthorn through a dazzling combination of sweeps and arcs, but showmanship had no noticeable effect on the creature, and only served to tire the dwarf. The wolf continued its relentless circling, claws churning through the sand.

A deathly hush settled over the crowd.

Kallad held his ground, content to let the wolf exhaust itself going around and around in circles.

He lunged forwards, shifting his weight onto his front foot and swept the butt of the axe forwards, reversing the blow to test his foe. The wolf swatted the steel blade away as if it was an irritating fly. Still, the force of the impact reverberated down the length of Kallad's arm, giving him a very real idea of the sheer brute strength of the thing he faced.

The wolf let out a roar of rage, reared and lunged forwards. Its claws raked across Kallad's cheek before he could spin away. The wound stung unnaturally as the taint of unlife burned itself into his skin.

Kallad spat at the dirt. Ignoring the fire beneath his skin, the dwarf threw himself at the wolf, Ruinthorn's twin blades ripping into the creature's thick hide. The wolf shrieked: a distressingly human sound as it lost focus on its bestial form and began to shift back into its human guise. The crowd roared, a shockingly animalistic sound.

He looked up at Konrad, and beside him Skellan. The Blood Count's smile was vicious. Kallad spat another wad of bloody phlegm onto the wet sand.

Wounded, and caught between forms, the wolf-man was more dangerous than ever. The echo of human cunning blazed behind its eyes. Somehow, it retained the natural abilities of both forms, making it twice as deadly.

The wolf-man slammed its half-formed fists against its chest and leapt.

Kallad threw himself to the floor as the thing's claws raked through the air where his head had been a second before.

It launched a second desperate attack, before Kallad could scrabble to his feet.

The crowd was screaming.

The beast came down on top of Kallad, its powerful jaws closing like a vice around his nose and the side of his face. The pain was incredible. Fifty wounds punctured his ruined face. Kallad screamed, a real full-bellied desperate scream, as he fought the all-consuming blackness that threatened to engulf him. He felt his own piss run down the inside of his legs. This wasn't how he wanted to die. There was no honour in it, no restitution for the dead, and no price for Grunberg, for Kellus, for Sammy and du Bek and all of the others.

He owed them more than this.

Kallad's head swam with sickness.

There was joy in the creature's eyes, Kallad saw, right until the last when he brought Ruinthorn around over its back and split it open at the spine, parting hide, bone and flesh in a killing blow. In that last second of life, a flicker of recognition passed between them, killer and victim, and then the beast was slain. Kallad pushed the monstrosity to the side and struggled out from beneath it.

Struggling to his feet, Kallad felt their sickness wash over him.

He found the beast that had killed his father, met his gaze and did not flinch as he said, 'And now I am coming for you.'

Konrad von Carstein did not look happy, but beside him, Jon Skellan looked positively delighted by Kallad's victory.

Then a wave of dizziness took him. He staggered, but he did not collapse.

Kallad turned away from the Blood Count and walked back towards the soul cages.

The vampire's thralls swarmed over him as he entered the tunnel. They pulled at him, trying to tear Ruinthorn from his grip. Kallad snarled and cracked one of the men's skulls off one of the many images of Morr decorating the wall. The thrall twitched as he slumped to the floor. A bloody red rose blossomed just below his receding hairline. Kallad stepped over the man's legs.

'Who's next? No need to all rush at once, there's plenty to go around.' His grin was manic as he thundered an unforgiving fist into the side of a second thrall's head. He made the mistake of getting in the dwarf's way.

Three more thralls stood between him and the cage door.

Kallad dropped into a fighting crouch. Ruinthorn, held level at his waist, rested easily in his hands. He turned the blade over and over.

'You want to die, lads, then take one step forward, otherwise get the hell out of my way.'

They gave him no choice: as one they charged.

Fighting at close quarters in a cramped tunnel was far from ideal, but against unarmed men with no skill for the game, it was little more than butchery.

They were unarmed and underfed. They didn't stand a chance.

In less than half a minute, Kallad was stepping over their corpses.

The old man looked up as he pushed open the door. He smiled. There was genuine warmth to it, 'You made it back, then, eh? I bet that pleased the Count no end.'

'He didn't look too happy,' Kallad agreed.

'What happened to the guards?'

'Had an accident. It's slippery back there. Stupid buggers fell right on my axe. Made a hell of a mess.'

'They'll send more,' the old man said.

'Then let's hope they're just as clumsy, eh? Now, I dunno about you, but I'm just about ready to get out of this place. Are you with me, human?'

'Look at me, I'm an old man. I can barely make it across this cell without having to sit down for twenty minutes to catch my breath.'

'Then I'll carry you on me back, laddy. I'm not leaving you.' It was guilt, of course, survivors' guilt, as if by helping this one old man he could make up for all the others that he hadn't been able to help.

The old man ratcheted himself up from the bench. 'Sebastian,' he said, holding out a liver-spotted hand. Kallad shook it.

'Kallad.'

The dwarf heard footsteps coming up the Long Walk. He slammed the door and wedged it with the wooden bench that Sebastian had just vacated.

'Well come on, Sebastian, wouldn't want to outstay our welcome.'

The passage divided into three smaller passages, each lined with identical heavily barred wooden doors.

'The soul cages,' the old man said. 'You didn't think you were alone down here, did you? There must be fifty or sixty more just like you, fighters who are thrown out to fight for their lives for the Blood Count's amusement.'

Without a word, Kallad strode purposefully towards the first door and threw back the bolt barring it. He pushed the door open and stepped into the doorway. 'On your feet,' he called into the cell. 'We're going home.'

He moved on to the next cell, and the next, and the next, the message the same for each and every one of von Carstein's prisoners. 'We're goin' home.'

SKELLAN STOOD BETWEEN the dwarf and freedom.

The dwarf had a small army of starving prisoners behind him. Desperation might have made them dangerous, but malnutrition and abuse, and the constant promise of unlife hanging over them had stripped them of spirit as well as strength. They stumbled into each other, stumbled and fell, and lacked even the strength to drag themselves back to their feet before the next one had stumbled over them.

'Going somewhere?' Skellan asked.

He was not alone. The last four of Konrad's loyal Hamaya, including Onursal, backed him up. He raised his hand and was met by low-throated growls as they unleashed the beast within.

Too easy, Skellan savoured the thought. He fully intended to enjoy the killing now that the time had come. The bones were cast, the endgame was playing itself out and, all things considered, there was no way he could lose. It was beautiful watching all of his plans come to together into one perfect glorious whole. That Konrad had demanded Onursal come with him to kill the dwarf was just a delicious irony, and so convenient. It would save hunting the beast down later.

'Out of my way, vampire,' the dwarf barked.

Skellan chuckled. 'Given the circumstances I am not sure you are in any position to be giving orders, little man.'

'I killed your friend back there, and I figure I can kill you just as dead, if I have to. Now move, Ruinthorn is getting thirsty.'

'You really are quite tiresome, dwarf.' Skellan turned to Onursal. 'Kill him.'

He moved aside so that the Hamaya could charge.

The dark skinned beast pounced, throwing himself at Kallad. Onursal staggered the dwarf back into the shambling pack of wretched human beings that were far beyond saving. They scattered, and the dwarf went down beneath the ferocity of the Hamaya's attack.

Skellan grinned and watched for a moment as the dwarf gave every bit as good as he got, battering the beast back in a flurry of blows. It looked as if the dwarf might actually have it in him to kill the Hamaya, the contest was that evenly matched. Skellan held back the remaining Hamaya.

'The fight is his. If he is incapable of killing the dwarf he has no place among us.'

That wasn't the truth, or at least not the whole truth. It was only an aspect of it. Excluding Skellan, Onursal was the strongest of Hamaya, and he was fiercely loyal to Konrad; stubbornly so, even in the face of the Blood Count's madness. His death would be a bitter blow for Konrad.

'Never tasted dwarf blood,' one of the Hamaya said petulantly.

Skellan shook his head. 'Blood's blood. Goes down just the same.'

'So you say.'

As Skellan watched the struggle, his face slipped, the daemon rising to the surface. Cold black anger roared through his veins. He harnessed it.

Satisfied that the dwarf would not fail him, Jon Skellan turned on the three remaining Hamaya.

'You want blood so bad? Here,' he tore out the throat of the beast nearest him in a shocking display of naked savagery. 'Drink this.'

He tossed the corpse at the gaping Hamaya and spun, lashing out. His claws eviscerated the second Hamaya before the creature even saw the danger.

The third, Massika, was more difficult to kill. The creature backed off and turned to run. Skellan surged forwards, arching his body so that he hit the side wall at a run, using the sheer force of his momentum to carry him up it, and propelled himself into the air, arms and legs pistoning as he hammered into the back of the fleeing Hamaya and brought it down.

Skellan grabbed a fistful of hair and yanked the creature's head back.

He hooked the claws of his other hand into the vampire's eyes and ripped the top of its skull away from the bones of its neck. The beast's cries were pitiful. Skellan pulled again, tearing the head free of the spinal column, and a third time, until the skin tore and the head came away in his hands.

When he stood, Skellan saw Kallad Stormwarden staring at him, perplexed by this sudden turn of events. Onursal lay dead at his feet, the dwarf's axe still buried deep in the Hamaya's spine. The first of the twin blades had actually torn open the vampire's chest cavity and spilled his black heart and a rope of greasy intestines across the tunnel floor.

The dwarf planted a boot on the Hamaya's back and wrenched his axe free.

His footsteps echoed chillingly as he advanced on Skellan, ready to kill again.

'Don't make the mistake of believing you know everything, dwarf,' Skellan said, still holding the dead Hamaya's head in his right hand. 'I've bought your life here, make no mistake about it. You wouldn't have lasted another day fighting in the pits. You aren't stupid. You can work out why I'm helping you. I want the monster dead, just as much as you do, but it is about more than that – more than him. You have to understand that, dwarf. The fates of nations of the living and nations of the dead rest in your hands.'

'You don't own anything, least of all my life. The only thing I'm interested in is killing your wretched Count and laying my people's ghosts to rest finally and forever, the rest is going to have to be someone else's problem 'cause it sure ain't mine.'

'Stupid grudges. Do you think it matters if one vampire dies? One bloody vampire? Do you think it will save a hundred other villages? A thousand young girls? You're a bigger fool than I took you for if you do. Cut down one and another arises. You might avenge a few dead, but you'll damn a hell of a lot

more living. Is that a price you want to pay, dwarf?
Can your conscience live with sacrificing hundreds,
thousands, of souls just to satisfy your bloody
grudge? Right now you need to live. That's why I'm
putting my own throat on the line. You need to get
out of here and convince Emperor Lutwig and the
Otillia, and whoever else will listen, of the threat
Konrad von Carstein and his necromancers pose.
You've seen a little of it here. You have an idea of
what he is capable of, but this is just the beginning.
The damned that marched to Vlad's drum are nothing compared to the nightmare that this madman is
raising. He intends to turn the Old World into one
vast Kingdom of the Dead, and he won't rest until
everyone is rotting and risen into his brave new
world.'

Skellan didn't move. He couldn't afford to make a
mistake.

He had to work a way around the unreasoning
stubbornness of the dwarf's grudge and convince him
that there was more to be gained by pushing the
boulder that would start the landslide that would
bury Konrad von Carstein. Rather than succumbing
to the instant gratification to be had from striking
down one enemy, with a little patience he could
bring down a damned dynasty.

The dwarf shook his head. 'No, I don't buy it.
You're selling me a lie. You're a cold-blooded killer,
like your master. There's no reason for you to help
me, less it helps yourself, too. And let's face it, you
being dead helps me a lot more than you being alive.
I think we finish this here.'

'You being dead doesn't help either of us, dwarf, and believe me, that's how this little charade would play out. Go, now, get word to your people. Warn the Empire. Tell them what you have seen. Impress it upon them. They *must* be ready when the Blood Count marches!'

The dwarf shouldered his axe and Skellan knew, through all the bluster, his message had found its mark. The dwarf wouldn't just carry the message, he would ensure that the living were prepared.

Skellan turned and walked away, knowing that the dwarf wouldn't strike him.

The dwarf was one of a rare breed: a hero.

Skellan could smell his bleeding heart.

CHAPTER TWENTY-ONE
From The Mountains of Madness

THE WORLDS EDGE MOUNTAINS
Dawn of the Dead

KALLAD LED THE survivors through the endless subterranean world of the deep mines, miles beneath the surface, beneath the light and the air. They stumbled along blindly behind him.

They had no food and no water.

They were dying by the day. The fifty he had rescued were reduced to thirty.

Twice already, Kallad had felt the draught of fresh air leaking into the mine, tasted it, but every turn seemed to lead them deeper into the claustrophobic depths of the Worlds Edge Mountains.

They stumbled on.

A few wanted to scavenge meat from the dead, arguing that the sustenance would keep them alive, buying them precious time to find their way out of this purgatory.

Kallad would have none of it.

For each of the fallen, he delayed, building a makeshift cairn from broken stones littering the tunnel.

The echoes of von Carstein's men ransacking the tunnels, hunting them, haunted them. The sounds of running feet, distant taunts, wolves baying and ringing steel kept them from sleeping, driving them on beyond the point of exhaustion.

Still they stumbled on.

'We're going home.' Kallad said it like a mantra, repeating it over and over.

They had long since stopped believing him.

They had christened the deep mines Sorrow's Heart, and resigned themselves to dying in its depths, but they didn't die, these last few.

Kallad led them out of Sorrow and into daylight for the first time in weeks, months, and for some of them, years. Stepping out into the air felt like being reborn from the darkness of despair into the light of freedom. He threw his head back and laughed, savouring the irony of a dwarf being happier out under an open sky than beneath a mountain. He saw the way they looked at him, but still he laughed. Let them think him mad.

Freedom came at a price. The sky was thick with snow, blowing a blizzard. The cold tore through their scant rags, but still it was the most beautiful moment of release. They gasped and sucked in air, fell on their backs, the snow crusting and powdering around them, and tried to embrace the sky. They were free of Sorrow. They were out of the godforsaken maze of tunnels, and they were going home to wherever home was. It was a long walk, but even Kallad welcomed the snow-laden sky over his head and the wind in his hair. Beside him, Sebastian swore that he would never complain about being stuck outside in the middle of nowhere again, knowing even as he made the vow that he would break it. He was an old man. Complaining about the elements was his lot in life. The day he stopped complaining about the blasted snow or the blessed rain was the day he died.

Kallad looked at the few men he had led out of hell and smiled. He had come to think of them as his lads.

'We're going home,' he said, and this time they believed him. Their cheers could have been heard in von Carstein's grand hall, with the Blood Count himself rooted to his obsidian throne by the ragged jubilation. Every one of the men facing him had resigned himself to dying long ago. Now, they were going home, and it was because of him.

It was a small counterbalance for his Indic scale, lives saved to weigh up against lives lost.

They were going home.

One of the men knelt and scooped handfuls of snow into his mouth, another rolled in it, and others sank down and kissed the ground. More than a few cast a last lingering look back in the direction of Drakenhof, invisible in the distance.

Kallad knew that it wasn't just because of him that they were going home. They owed their freedom to one of the beasts: Skellan.

He didn't understand why the vampire had turned on its own, or why it would want von Carstein toppled, but that didn't matter. The beast had bought their freedom. Kallad was determined to use it to pay Skellan back by wiping his kind off the face of the earth.

He saw that the old man, Sebastian, had moved away from the group and lay, propped up awkwardly against a boulder. The dwarf walked over to sit beside him. Drawing nearer, he could tell that there was something wrong. It was the angle of the old man's head, the way it lolled on his neck. Kallad had seen enough death to recognise it close up.

It wasn't fair, after everything, having made it out, for Sebastian's heart to give in here, now, when they were free. There was no justice in it. Kallad bottled up the sudden surge of anger that he felt rising inside. They were going home.

Kallad knelt at Sebastian's side.

'At least you died free, looking at the sun,' Kallad whispered, his breath conjuring wraiths of mist that hung like a veil between the living and the dead. It was a small consolation. The failing sun was a sickly yellow eye on the horizon. Small mercy that it was, the old man had died with the gentle warmth of the sun on his face.

Kallad closed the old man's eyes.

It was a last act of kindness. Already, the old man's skin was colder than death. His sweat had become a brittle frost that clung to his face like a second skin. A fine dusting of snow had settled on his rags, now that the heat of life had left his body.

Kallad stood, ignoring the icy chill worming its way into his heart.

Behind him, the Worlds Edge Mountains and their snow-capped peaks reared, reaching into the grey sky. Beneath him lay a sweeping bank of forest, the white-laced leaves rustling like living things, while the north wind whispered fragments of the wood's darkest secrets, hints of the hearts it had stilled, the dreams it had buried in its rich soil. The nearness of the forest was oppressive.

The wind cried traitor in his ear. He ignored its mocking voice, knowing that the whispers would be endless and unforgiving. 'I haven't forgotten you,' he promised his ghosts. Guilt was one of the many burdens that came with being a survivor. Guilt and ghosts. He had ghosts, ghosts that whispered and taunted with the voice of his own guilt, ghosts that could never forgive him for being alive, because he couldn't forgive himself.

'I COULD LIE down now.' He barely breathed the words, knowing that he couldn't. That he didn't have it in him to give up. 'I could close my eyes like Sebastian, sleep and never wake up. The cold would take me before dawn. Is that what you want?' But the wind had stopped listening to his lies. It knew he could no more lie down and die than the sun could cease to shine or the seasons stop turning. It was a survivor's nature to survive, to go on living no matter the costs to those around him. A survivor would find a way.

Kallad Stormwarden was a survivor.

He would carry the message to the living.

Von Carstein would be stopped.

He wiped the sweat from his brow before it could freeze there. His lips were chapped from the wind's perpetual kiss. The others were feeling it too, the intense cold that came with their freedom. Their rags were no defence against it. The cold was their enemy, just as lethal and immediate as the soul cages had ever been. Kallad hadn't realised just how thirsty he was until he knelt and brushed away the thin coating of snow from the surface of a small frozen tarn. Quickly, he used the wooden handle of his axe to crack the ice. Kneeling over the tarn, he scooped a handful of water to his lips. It tasted heavily of minerals and dirt, but it could have been wine to the lips of a drunk. He drank deeply, wiping at his beard where the water ran down his chin, and scooped up another mouthful.

'OVER HERE, LADS! Water!' he called. Those desperate enough came running, staggering over the mountainside, stumbling, falling and pushing themselves on for fear that they would be too late and the water would have run dry by the time they arrived.

In the distance, movement caught his eye. He pushed himself to his feet and squinted towards a thin line of picked-clean trees that spotted the horizon. Shapes moved across the whiteness. He counted three figures. They moved with the surety born of life on the mountain. It took a moment to realise that they were dwarfs: a scouting party.

'Grimna's balls, we're saved!' Kallad said, slapping one of the few survivors on the back.

The youngster grinned back at him.

* * *

THEY WALKED AWHILE to shelter: an abandoned bear cave beyond the trees. Despite the blizzard and the blinding snow, many of the survivors were reluctant to re-enter the earth.

Kallad didn't have the heart to bully them back underground, so those that wanted to freeze were left to shiver and huddle up against the trees as they tried to light a fire with damp wood. Truth be told, he wasn't too enamoured of the idea of going back underground either, but he wasn't about to freeze to death out of stubbornness.

It wasn't merely pragmatism. He *had* to survive this final ordeal. He had no choice in the matter. He had to deliver his warning to everyone capable of standing against the vampires, and convince them that their only hope of survival lay in putting aside their arguments and joining together. By dying here, he would damn them all.

The dwarfs were a short range scouting party from a nearby stronghold, Karak Raziac, although it still served under the aegis of Karak Kadrin far to the north.

The cave was stocked with game that had been skinned and dried, and it was obviously something of a permanent base for the dwarf scouts.

'Hunting greenskins,' Grufbad Steelfist explained. 'The beasts have been causing hell over the last few months. Getting braver and braver with their raids. Stealing cattle, burning down homesteads. Razzak wants them stamped out good and proper, so we're out looking for the rat hole they crawled outta.'

Steelfist was the leader of the small troop, an unflinching soul hewed out of the very stuff of the mountain he ranged.

Kallad knew the story well enough. He could have been listening to his father, Kellus, declaring that the greenskins had gotten out of hand and needed to be put in their place. He nodded.

'What about yerself? By the sounds of it you're a long way from home, Kallad son of Kellus.'

'Aye, long way for sure, Steelfist, and I'm just talking about distance,' Kallad said sourly. 'We got thirty refugees from the dungeons of the Vampire Count here, and barely a lick of grub between us. The manlings have been through hell and back, and instead of being safe, now they're up against the elements. I doubt even half of them will make it back to their families.'

'That's them, I asked about you.'

Kallad looked at the hard-faced dwarf. Twin scars ran down Steelfist's cheeks where he had been in an argument with a wicked blade and lost, badly. He was perhaps twice Kallad's age, if not more, but then, in eyes of his people, Kallad was little more than a child, for all that he had lived more than sixty years.

'There are things I have to do,' Kallad conceded. 'For my people, and for others.'

Steelfist nodded, 'You have the mark of a grudge bearer.'

'Aye, but I'm coming to understand that the grudge isn't all, that there's more I have to do to earn my rest.'

'It never ends,' Grufbad Steelfist agreed. 'So, for now, share the burden a while. Tell me your story, Kallad Stormwarden.'

And so he did.

Kallad talked of abandoning his home, the march to Grunberg, the fall of Kellus and the suckling baby dead in its mother's arms, feeding off her like some ungodly parasite until he killed it a second time. He couldn't remember her name, and it hurt him that she had slipped from his memory so easily. He talked of the slaughter of the Sigmarites in Altdorf, hunting Skellan and his unnamed master, the death of his companions at the hands of the beast, and his own bitter wounds. He told Steelfist of the villages with their barred windows where fathers locked out their own sons because the plague of unlife had claimed them, the traitorous vampire who had freed them in return for the promise that they would raise a force to stand against the Blood Count, and he painted a bleak picture of the days to come.

'We must get word to Razzak,' Steelfist said, 'convince him to dispatch emissaries to Karak Kadrin, Zufbar, Karak Varn and every stronghold the length of the Worlds Edge Mountains. It won't be easy, he's dour at the best of times, but he's not stupid. This threat goes beyond the manlings. The undead curse is one that even a thickhead like him cannae ignore for long.'

'You think he'll march?'

'Aye, if you plead your case like you just did, youngling. I think he'll answer the call, and the dwarfs of the deep will march to war at the side of the humans once again.' There was an edge of pride in Steelfist's voice as he wrapped a fatherly arm around Kallad's shoulder. 'Come on, let's round your boys up for a feed, and then get on our way. Time's running out. It'll be day after the morrow before we're in sight of Karak Raziac. 'Nother day after that before you can talk to Razzak.'

Kallad felt the uncomfortable sensation of eyes watching him. He twisted. There was no one there. Then he saw a black raven, perched on an overburdened bough less than ten feet beyond the mouth of the cave, studying them intently. He trusted his instincts. The bird was unnaturally curious. Kallad knelt and picked up a rock, throwing it at the carrion bird. The stone whistled past the raven, cannoning off the tree trunk and causing a flurry of snow to spill. The raven cawed once, a deep guttural sound, and took flight.

Something about the bird disturbed Kallad Stormwarden profoundly. He sensed, in fact, that he was witnessing the first rumblings of the storm of the century.

CHAPTER TWENTY-TWO
Torn

THE RAVEN TOWER, DRAKENHOF CASTLE, SYLVANIA
The Winter of Discontent

JON SKELLAN JUGGLED the knife easily, tossing it from hand to hand, the silver blade turning end over end lazily as it passed through the air.

Konrad was raving.

He wasn't listening. He didn't actually need to, he had heard it all before: the paranoia, the deep-seated insecurity, and, surprisingly the suspicion of all animals around the castle. He had ordered all of the dogs butchered, cats gutted and nailed up around the city, drove the ravens from the tower and had poisons laid down to kill any foolish enough to return. He did the same with people he grew suspicious of, gutted them, poisoned them or drove them off.

The Blood Count went off on these random rants regularly, losing all sense of self in his tirade, and one was very much like another.

'Konrad doesn't like it! Oh, no he doesn't. Not at all. No, can't trust them. No. They would destroy Konrad if they could, but they can't. No, they can't.'

'No,' Skellan agreed, 'they can't.' Whoever they were, Konrad had developed a wonderful habit of railing against imaginary foes recently, seeing conspiracies where there weren't even people to conspire. He liked to take credit for the mild erosion of von Carstein's sense of self. He had wormed his way into the Blood Count's confidence, dislodging the others he trusted, those who supported his reign.

The prize was the necromancer, Nevin Kantor. The magician had been a thorn in Skellan's side ever since his arrival at the black castle. He had worked his way close to the Count, ingratiating himself into Konrad's favour by reinventing himself as the Blood Count's pet.

For a while it had worked. Kantor offered Konrad the gift of magic.

It was something Skellan couldn't hope to compete with. The hunger for magic had, for years, been the Blood Count's obsession. The secret was to turn the magic itself into something sinister and untrustworthy, like the Hamaya who had betrayed their master, like his treacherous kin, like all who had a reason to covet Konrad's power. It was as ingenious as it was simple. He had to play on Konrad's ignorance and turn the magic into something to be feared instead of adored.

The whispers were simple enough at first, snatches of gossip overhead below ground, in the subterranean necromancer's library, from the soul cages and the fighting pits. Magic had been used in the dwarf's escape. Skellan hinted that he believed the necromancers had engineered the whole thing, after all, the dwarf had been Kantor's travelling companion. They had a shared loyalty, a bond older than Kantor and Konrad's. The web of lies he spun was almost believable, and the beauty of it was that with Konrad's mind so torn, there was far more material than necessary.

He told Konrad that his precious necromancers were looting his gold, using his own coin to raise armies of their own, loyal to the black magicians, merging their skeletal horde with ghoulish humans.

In the end, Skellan had broken Kantor's hold over von Carstein with the simplest of arguments: the magician could not be trusted. It was in his nature to manipulate the truth of the universe and reshape it in the guise of one of his lies. It wasn't that Nevin Kantor manipulated the winds, it was the nature of magic itself to corrupt the practitioner. If it were natural, honest, then Konrad would have been able to do it, but he couldn't. So it wasn't Konrad's failing. On the contrary, it was Konrad's strength. The winds could not twist him.

Skellan also promised him protection, of course.

He looked around the room, at the gibberish that he had forced a peasant to scrawl in a tight spidery hand across the walls. He lied to Konrad and told him that they were wards against incantations, shields against the evil thoughts of those who would do him harm, and that the peasant was actually a hedge mage. He cemented the lie with another, promising Konrad that if he fed on the blood of the mage he would make the gibberish unbreakable. Konrad drank greedily and fed the corpse to his dogs, the same dogs that he butchered a week later.

The delicious irony was that the protection itself terrified the Blood Count. He paced the room, never at rest, never able to relax for fear that there was more to the scrawls than the dead hedge mage had admitted – that perhaps the peasant had actually been in the employ of the necromancers, and that it was no protection at all, rather a form of entrapment.

The Blood Count turned to Skellan, his anchor in a sea of chaos.

'But you love Konrad, don't you Skellan? You are loyal to him. You understand that Konrad is great.'

'I worship him,' Skellan said, knowing that the wry humour was lost on Konrad, 'for Konrad is the most monstrous and powerful of all the children of the night. Konrad is Vashanesh reborn.'

Konrad is also stark raving mad, he added silently.

'Yes,' Konrad said. 'Yes, yes, yes. You understand Konrad. You are loyal. You are the only one, Skellan, the only one that Konrad can trust.'

'I am the Golden One,' Skellan said.

The secret was in the way the web supported itself with its own fabrications. Enough lies had been proven true in the Blood Count's eyes to make even the most outrageous new ones seem plausible.

The Hamaya were his now, freely given by Konrad. With Onursal implicated in the escape from the slave pens – he had, according to Skellan, turned on his fellow vampires. It was only good fortune for Skellan that the dwarf's axe had brought the dark-skinned Hamaya down before he could turn on him. Konrad, at Skellan's insistence, demanded the Hamaya purged. Then, summoning the remainder of the vampiric aristocracy to the subterranean cathedral, he urged Skellan to fulfil the role of father to the Hamaya, as the wolf, Jerek once had, and choose only those that could be implicitly trusted, so that once more the Hamaya were proud to serve Konrad, the Blood Count.

This winnowing gave Skellan the perfect opportunity to cull the few lynchpins of Konrad's precarious Empire, isolating Konrad in his own court.

It was all so subtly perfect. There was a synergy to the lies. They fed off one another.

Where others trod on eggshells around the madman, Skellan masked his own role in the dwarf's escape with the confession of failure. He begged Konrad's forgiveness for his own shortcomings. He hadn't seen the traitors in their midst. He had allowed himself to be gulled by them and as such it was his fault as much as it was Onursal's and Kantor's.

It was a stroke of genius. His own cowardice had allowed the dwarf to escape. Indeed, he was only alive because the dwarf chose to allow it. In confessing his own failings, Skellan showed himself to be the true inheritor of the wolf's place at Konrad's side. With one beautiful lie, he became Konrad's new truth speaker.

In a court of lies and paranoia few would own up to failure for fear of bringing von Carstein's wrath down upon their own heads. It was a self-preservation instinct. Skellan set himself apart by owning his failure.

He had knelt before the Blood Count, asked forgiveness, and awaited judgement. It had been a risk, but he had played it right. By offering up his own head, Skellan had proved, beyond a shadow of a doubt in the madman's torn mind, that he was the only one that Konrad could truly trust.

The improbability of the dwarf sparing the vampire never occurred to him.

'Konrad will see them now,' Konrad said, suddenly. Finally.

'You understand what you must do?'

'Konrad is not a fool. Oh, no, no, no. Konrad is not a fool. He will not allow them to treat him like one. They will learn their lesson well today. Konrad will teach them with steel.'

'Well said, my lord.'

Skellan sheathed the knife.

It had taken little prodding to convince Konrad that the time had come to go to war, it was all part of the web of deceit that he had spun. The beauty of it was how it all came together so flawlessly to support itself. The dwarf, freed by the faithless necromancers, was out there, warning the humans, galvanising them into resistance. Because of the necromancers, the Empire's defences would be strong, stronger perhaps than anything his sire had ever faced. It was fitting that the traitors should lead the line. The necromancers should be made to fight, not merely raise zombies to hide behind. They must fight, *and die*.

Skellan opened the door to the necromancers, Fey, Leverkuhn and Kantor.

He was looking forward to seeing their faces as he delivered their death sentences.

CHAPTER TWENTY-THREE
Ruinthorn and Runefang

THE BATTLE OF THE FOUR ARMIES
The Season of Rot

THE RELENTLESS STAMP of ten thousand feet reverberated around the hills. The sound folded in on itself, becoming an endless rolling thunder that washed across the Empire. Hammers and axes banged on shield bosses, and gruff song drove the dwarfs on. They were a tidal wave of righteous fury to come crashing down mercilessly on the heads of the dead.

They bore the weight of vengeance on their shoulders.

The world had suffered enough.

It ended here, with the coalition of the living, ready to purge the land of the unnatural plague of von Carstein's kith and kin.

'We'll not fail you, Kellus,' Kallad Stormwarden swore, hoisting the banner of Karak Sadra. He bore the burden of the banner himself, proud to bear it into battle one final time. He fully intended to plant it in the Blood Count's skull and make his final stand beneath the pennon as it tore in the wind. 'Not while there's breath in our lungs and iron in our arms.'

The dwarfs marched to war united under the banners of the great strongholds. They had mustered six moons ago, in the shadow of the blighted towers where the Stir crossed the Silver Road. Five thousand was less than Kallad had hoped for, but more than he had dared expect. He prayed it would be enough.

At the muster, King Razzak and his counterparts from Karak Norn and Karak Hirn had urged Kallad to claim his birthright and allow them to name him king before the great battle so that he might march towards whatever fate Grimna held in store for him as the last ruler of the fallen karak.

'Nay, your kingship, it isn't right,' said Kallad. 'Kellus was the last king of the stronghold. There is no Karak Sadra now. I'll not be proclaimed king over a pile of rubble and ghosts. It's not right.'

That had ended the discussion, and the royal line of Karak Sadra would end with Kellus, last true King of the Karak, slain by the very monster that they were marching to fight. It was a fitting tribute that his son should carry the banner of Karak Sadra alongside the banners of Karak Raziac, Karak Kadrin, Karak Hirn and Karak Norn.

The vampire's evil had spread deep into the Empire. Instead of uniting, the forces of the Empire were in complete disarray. Runners had returned at dusk with stories of bitter conflicts amid the forces of the living, with both Lutwig and the Otillia claiming the right to lead the army. Helmut of Marienburg, on the other hand, strove to council patience and cooperation, arguing that in fact each of the three of them should be figureheads for their own forces, as Razzak should be for the dwarfs, in a grand army of equals.

They shouted him down as an idealistic fool.

So, all three declared themselves master and commander of the four armies, and retreated to discuss tactics with their own men, ignoring emissaries from the other camps. Instead of cooperating, they were tearing their armies apart, issuing conflicting orders, preparing conflicting contingencies, and expecting non-existent support.

It would be a massacre.

'Fools!' the dwarf king spat. 'The Blood Count won't need to defeat them, they'll do it for him.'

The stars hung radiant silver in the darkening sky, casting their pure light down onto the cracked and broken path that led to the battlefield. Most of the bloodsucking flies of the mountain's moss had retreated into the night, but Kallad felt the sting of the occasional stubborn insect feeding on his flesh. He slapped his neck, bursting the bloodfly between his fingers.

The winds blew incessantly down the Silver Road, funnelling down between the mountains and along the path of the river.

'The curse of power, Razzak. Much wants more,' Kallad said, shaking his head sadly.

'It was ever the way,' the king agreed. 'Your few years have brought you wisdom, Kallad son of Kellus. That's a rare thing.'

'In worse things, aye,' Kallad agreed, accepting the compliment. He scuffed his feet. The brittle grass had been worn away by trampling boots. 'But in other things, in better things, I'm woefully ignorant, your kingship. It is my curse. I know peace only with my axe in me hand.'

'Such are the times,' Razzak agreed.

Far to the south, the camp of the pretenders' three armies was a wall of glowing light against the backdrop of night. It was impossible to judge how many souls camped out under the stars, making their peace with Morr before the dawn's early light banished the little respite they knew.

Kallad had faced enough battles to know what was going through the mind of each and every manling down there: thoughts of home, faces and smells, making connections inside their heads, bringing back memories of childhood and first love, of intimacy, and beneath them all, a black undermining undercurrent: fear.

Fear was the hidden enemy, capable of infiltrating even the stoutest heart. Stark cold fear brought on by the sure and certain knowledge of what they faced across the field, by the inhuman nature of the enemy.

Fear could make even a strong man weak.

There would be desertions as fear got the better of some men. The lull before the storm broke was always the worst time, when fear was at its most deadly. Things would happen in the glow of the night's fire that would be regretted, should the participants live long enough to have the luxury of regret. Mistakes would be made. All they could do was pray that they would not prove fatal.

Kallad made his excuses and withdrew, choosing to walk alone for a while. He sought the calm centre of his being, the pacific core where he was the rock around which the storm broke. There was no peace. He could hear his own heart, the steady rhythm of it, so absolute was the calm here, removed from the killing ground. There was a mindless quality to it, an eternal reminder of mortality.

There, alone on the mountainside, surrounded by his kin, it began to haunt him.

THE BATTLEFIELD WAS littered with wasted life.

The dwarfs had turned the tide of the skirmish, the Hammerers and Ironbreakers charging down from the low lying hills and crashing into the bones and lichen-smeared carcasses being puppeted across the field of death by von Carstein's necromancers. Kallad planted the standard in the dirt and threw himself into the thick of the fighting, his double-headed axe hewing through rotten flesh and brittle bone with ruthless efficiency. He was a tightly controlled whirlwind of death on the battlefield, Ruinthorn hacking and slashing, cleaving limbs, stoving in dead skulls and gutting his ghoulish foes. He fought with the manic intensity of a true slayer. The dead lay in pools at his feet. He cut down fifty, sixty, more, losing count to the endless press of the enemy surging forwards, wave after wave of the dead and the damned.

He took a battering, was dragged down twice by clutching hands, and twice managed to fight his way back to his feet and drive the dead off.

The dead relinquished the field only when Razzak ordered the full might of the engineer's war machines to be wheeled into the fight. The war machines were huge chariots, equipped with bolt throwers and fire breathers that belched a cocktail of liquid fire, and of rolling artillery flankers and organ grinders that fired silver shot instead of arrows, burning the dead where it sizzled into their flesh. Ballistae launched fragile demijohns of blessed water into the front ranks of the dead and huge stones that skittled through the skeletons.

The legions of the dead restrained themselves. The winds rose, biting and blowing hard across the field. Thick storm clouds drew in, heavy with the threat of rain.

The next few hours saw several small, relatively ineffectual raiding parties driven off by the living. It exposed them for the shambles they were. Twice the Otillia and Lutwig clashed, their own men turning on each other in frustration. The Blood Count was testing their mettle, gauging the effectiveness of their response. Already, after only a few days of trying to coexist, the living were in disarray. They undermined each other at every turn.

Chirurgeons tended to the wounded, but the living were too late to reclaim their dead. The necromancers wove their dark magics, breathing black life back into the fallen and drawing them into the ranks of the dead, swelling von Carstein's unnatural horde with dwarfs and humans. Kallad took a savage blow to the side, crushing the plates of his mail shirt. His breathing was laboured, drawing a fresh breath was an effort. The dour faced chirurgeon poked and prodded the wound.

'You've bruised your lungs and it feels like you've cracked a couple of ribs. Y'll live.' He pressed a poultice up against the wound. 'Keep this in place for an hour, it'll ease the swelling from the ribs and take the pressure off your lungs.'

'Aye, if you know who gives us a minute's respite,' Kallad said. He left the chirurgeons' tent and headed towards the dwarf encampment, away from the bickering manlings. He saw Lutwig, the Altdorfers' pretender to the Imperial throne, deep in conversation with two unsavoury looking sorts. He was whisper thin, with lank, greasy hair that spilled over the right side of his face, and gaunt cheeks. The stresses of the war were taking it out of the man. The last time he had heard speak of Ludwig's successor he had been deemed striking, handsome and commanding, but none of these adjectives suited the tired man that stood across the field from him. Kallad's sharp eyes spotted a pouch changing hands. It was surreptitiously pocketed.

'Tonight,' one of the others said, his voice just loud enough to carry to where Kallad stood, rooted to the spot. To make sure there was no misunderstanding, the solider drew a finger across his throat, signing the execution order with the promise that it would be done.

Who would Lutwig want dead so badly that he would pay soldiers to be assassins?

That of course was only half of the question, the full question was slightly different: who *here* would Lutwig want dead so badly that he would pay to have him killed?

There was only one answer: the Otillia.

The Otillia directly opposed Lutwig's every move and was making a mockery of his leadership. That kind of slight would burn a man of singular ambition.

Was this so-called hero of the Empire such a coward that he would resort to assassination?

'There's a storm coming,' Grufbad Steelfist said, coming up behind Kallad.

Kallad looked at the thick rolling thunderheads in the sky, and then back at Lutwig and the assassins.

'You're not wrong, my friend. You're not wrong.'

THE CRIES RANG out before dawn:

'The Otillia is slain!'

'Murder!'

Her throat had been cut while she slept. Her chamberlain had found her in a bed of blood-soaked sheets. The old man had been roused by the sounds of struggle from within her pavilion.

The fiends had not escaped justice, one lay dead, slumped over her magnificence as if in worship, and the other had stumbled into a dawn patrol, her blood still on his hands. The assassin had denied nothing, he had merely smiled and looked at the rising sun. 'It is not over,' was all he would say for an hour. Then, with the sun high in the sky, he changed his statement, 'It is over now. The day is lost, the day is found, and bodies there are, all around.' They executed the assassin at noon, during the highest point of the sun, but not before he had confessed his sins and named his paymaster. Few could believe it, even when Kallad Stormwarden came forward and confirmed that indeed, the assassin was one of the pair he had seen trading gold for promises with the Pretender, Lutwig.

Gossip was rife. Lutwig of Altdorf, Pretender to the Imperial Throne, had sanctioned the assassination of one of his greatest political rivals, the Otillia of Talabecland. Fears rose for Helmut of Marienburg, the third pretender. Could Lutwig be so bold as to shatter their fragile peace now of all times, and push his claim for sovereignty?

Talabheimers declared the murder a vile act of cowardice, yet still there were whispers from certain quarters to the contrary, that it was a stroke of genius and would have taken great courage from Lutwig, as, finally, the forces of the four armies could be united under one commander, and two deaths would assure thousands of lives saved. Talk of the greater good was a dangerous thing.

Shockwaves ran through the camps. Driven by fears of resurrection, those loyal to the Otillia hacked her corpse to pieces and burned it. It was far from a fitting burial for an empress. Even as her pieces burned down to embers, tempers rose and fights broke out. At close quarters it was turning ugly. Vigilantes seeking their own justice turned on stragglers from other camps who had wandered too far from their own people, bludgeoning them to death with sticks and stones. It wasn't enough for them. The Talabheimers demanded restitution. It was like a sickness within the mob.

From one raised voice came the cry, 'Death to Lutwig!' and the hatred of the others was inflamed. They marched on the Altdorfers' camp, intent on ramming the pretender's head onto a pike, turning the man who would be Emperor into food for the ravens.

Torches blazing, they raised arms, turning on their allies as they forced their way through the tent city to Lutwig's pavilion.

They were greeted by an angry mob, armed with hatchet, axe and sword, and equally hungry to taste the blood of their master and commander's murderers. There were two murders that night, but Helmut of Marienburg was not the unfortunate second victim, Lutwig of Altdorf was.

Physicians emerged from Lutwig's pavilion, faces grave. The pretender had succumbed to the poison on the assassin's blade. There was nothing even their considerable skills could do, Lutwig was dead.

'The pretender is dead!'

'Murderers!'

The Altdorfers surged towards the Talabheimers, demanding their own bloody justice.

In a bizarre twist, King Razzak's dwarfs and Marienburg's men found themselves between a rock and hard place, trying to keep the peace and root out the truth among so much wild speculation and flared tempers. Two of the three pretenders to the Imperial Throne were dead, that much was undeniable. The uneasy peace was shattered. The four armies were disintegrating, and now, of course, was the perfect time for the dead to rise up and destroy what little remained of their resistance.

They came quietly, fiends rising from between the trampling feet to claw down the mob, dragging them down into death. They came loudly, on nightmare steeds, brandishing unholy blades, banshees shrieking in their wake as they charged.

Even the threat of extinction couldn't reunite the armies of the living.

It was cold-blooded slaughter.

Without the dwarfs it would have been so much worse.

As it was, thousands fell in the hour that turned the field into a Morr's paradise on earth.

Razzak ordered the organ grinders to spray bullets of silver across the field, indiscriminately. The engineers used up every last flake of metal in their arsenals to drive off the dead and earn a few minutes of respite.

The screams of the dying were hideous. The screams of the living were worse.

The necromancers pulled every last corpse from the mud and threw it at the living.

Kallad stood in the middle of it, swamped by the press of humanity as it strove to tear the throats out of its traitorous allies, while it all but succumbed to the crush of the dead.

In resisting the dead, the dwarfs bought the living precious time to unravel the treacheries of the night before. Too exhausted to fight, and drained by having to dismember friends and sword brothers to save them from a fate far worse than death, the men rallied around the banner of Helmut of Marienburg so that the third pretender could impose some kind of order.

The truth, when it emerged was as bitter as it was ironic: Lutwig had ordered the Otillia's murder, hoping to rise himself up as rightful leader of the armies of the living, and likewise, the Otillia had paid good coin to assassins to dispose of Lutwig, who she saw as nothing more than a thorn in her side.

In one way the whisperers had been right, however, with only one figurehead to rally behind, the living were more than fit to match the dead on the field of combat.

They buried their dead and their hatreds with them, and clung to Helmut of Marienburg, as they would have to Sigmar himself had the Man-God descended from the clouds to fight beside them.

THE BATTLE RAGED on day and night for a week.

There was no give on either side: no weakness.

The dead fought for dominion.

The living fought for salvation.

THE DEAD HAD called a parlay and come out under the flag of truce. It was unexpected, and not welcomed by the survivors.

The soil steamed, the rocks and dirt hissing with heat where the liquid fire had burned itself out.

Kallad stood in the middle of the scorched earth, the banner of Karak Sadra gripped firmly in his hand. He forced it deep down into the sizzling soil, ramming the point home, and shouldered Ruinthorn, keeping the faithful axe close to hand should he need it.

The carnage was laid bare across the killing ground, skulls set on sword pommels, carrion birds haunting the skulls. Ravens circled overhead, swooping low to pick worms of flesh from the newly dead. They were a numbing reminder of war's cost and its futility. Kallad knew that in a few hours those bones would begin to stir again, twitching back into unnatural life as the necromancers reanimated them.

Only Morr himself could take any satisfaction in this day's work, and only then if the necromancers didn't succeed in robbing him of the souls that were rightfully his.

The contempt this enemy had for life was staggering.

Four vampires walked across the steaming earth. They squared up to the living. He recognised Skellan as one of them. One of the creatures was female, but that was not the only difference that marked her as special in this group of the dead. Indeed, despite her chalk-white complexion and red red lips, there was something distinctly *alive* about her.

Helmut of Marienburg, his son Helmar, Kallad, and the dwarf king, Razzak, met the dead halfway across the burned earth. They were all that remained of the leaders of the four armies.

The woman spoke: 'Our master wants to speak with you.'

A distant howling caught Kallad's attention: wolves.

'He would now, would he?' Helmut said, his voice thick with utter contempt.

'It is not a request, human,' the second vampire interceded smoothly. 'Konrad *commands* an audience with the leaders of the living. There will be no discussion.'

'Your master's arrogance is outstanding.'

'As is your stupidity.'

Kallad studied Skellan's face during the exchange. A flicker of a smile touched the vampire's lips as insults were traded. He was enjoying himself. He obviously hoped to provoke the pretender into saying or doing something rash.

'Konrad would speak with von Holzkrug as he believes the Untermensch witch and the pretty pretender are no more,' the fourth vampire said, stepping forwards. He swept his cloak aside, resting his delicate fingers on the wyrm-hilted blade at his side. 'Konrad gets what Konrad wants, always.'

'Konrad does,' Skellan said, speaking up for the first time. 'Gentlemen,' He inclined his head slightly to Razzak, 'and dwarfs, may I present von Carstein's rightful heir, the Blood Count himself, Konrad, Vashanesh reborn.'

It burned Kallad to be so close to the beast that had murdered his father. He tugged unconsciously at the standard, lifting it six inches out of the dirt.

'Konrad gets what Konrad wants,' the Blood Count repeated, the wyrm-hilted sword singing as it slid clear of its sheath, 'and Konrad wants...' He turned in a circle, pointing the tip of the blade at each of the living in turn. It passed over Kallad and stopped on Helmut of Marienburg. Konrad's grin was sly. 'You! Or are you craven?'

'What are you talking about, man?' Marienburg blustered. 'You want me for what?'

Kallad could feel the rain on his face as the skies broke: a drop at first, then harder, more insistent.

'Konrad would make a king of you. Yes he would, a true king, not some petty pretender. Konrad would raise you up and honour you, as you deserve. Konrad would have men worship you. Konrad would turn you into a legend among the dead. A dead king. Yes, that is what Konrad wants with you, Helmut of Marienburg. Konrad wants to make you immortal, human. Konrad wants to bless you.'

The ground beneath their feet sizzled as the first raindrops evaporated.

'Konrad is mad,' Helmut barked, drawing his sword and slapping away the Blood Count's blade with it. For a moment, the two swords locked. The steel serration along the edges of Marienburg's monstrous Runefang caught Konrad's bone blade. The last of the pretenders rolled his wrist and drew his blade back with a smooth tug. It was a simple manoeuvre that would have disarmed a weaker foe with ease, but von Carstein's grip never wavered. His blade slipped free of Runefang's teeth.

Kallad launched himself into the fight, only for Skellan to intercede. 'This is not our fight, little man,' Skellan hissed, catching hold of Ruinthorn with both hands and forcing the dwarf back.

'Konrad is glad you have decided to accept his offer, your majesty. Konrad is delighted.'

'Father!' Helmar cried as Konrad launched a blistering attack that finished with his sword slicing

Helmut's chest. His ring mail saved him from having to scoop up his entrails. Marienburg staggered back under the frenzied attack, barely getting his sword up to deflect three more staggering blows aimed at removing his head from his shoulders.

Steel clashed loudly with steel-hard bone.

Still, Skellan would not release his hold on Ruinthorn. 'Stop the boy from getting himself killed,' the vampire said, pushing back and sending the dwarf sprawling.

Helmut stumbled over a smouldering chunk of rock protruding from the steaming mud.

It was all Konrad needed.

The vampire threw himself into a forward roll, coming up on his left shoulder, sword snaking out like some pit viper's tongue. The wyrm-hilted blade slipped easily through the muscle of his calf and up into his hamstring. Konrad came out of his roll, towering over the fallen pretender.

Negligently, he cut the ties binding Helmut of Marienburg's soul to his flesh.

'Now Konrad is as good as his word. Yes he is. So to make you a king! Immoliah!'

Kallad was back on his feet quickly enough to restrain Helmar.

'Now's not the time, man. Fight when you can kill them. Don't make the mistake of giving up your life cheaply,' he rasped, clamping a hand on the newly orphaned boy. Helmar shook it off and stumbled forwards, his legs buckling as his body betrayed him. He didn't scream or cry as he fell to his knees. He collapsed in on himself. His grief was absolute. He opened his mouth to moan and sickness swept over him. Helmar threw up as the woman moved easily to her master's side.

The rain streamed down her face, matting her luxuriant raven black hair flat to her face. She looked up as if to savour it, raising her hands above her head. The wind swarmed around them. At the far sides of the battlefield the dead stirred, pulled closer to the necromancer by her silent call. She breathed the wind in, Shyish merging with nature's own cold, wet wind, in her lungs, and she breathed out magic.

The corpse of Helmut of Marienburg shuddered as unlife touched it.

The dread Kallad felt was all too real. Around him, he saw dark shadows moving on the battlefield and heard the low, keening moan, of the dead shuffling forward, effectively isolating them from the rest of the armies of the living.

'Rise!' Konrad screamed. 'Rise my new king of all the dead, rise!'

The corpse rose, gracelessly. Its legs betrayed it, collapsing where there was no muscle to support the bone.

Immoliah Fey reached out a hand to steady the newly risen corpse, bleeding the black wind into its bones to give it the strength to stand.

Neither Immoliah Fey nor Konrad saw Helmar of Marienburg gather up his father's Runefang, and lurch forwards, sobbing. The first they saw was the wicked teeth of the sword cutting into his father's neck. It took Helmar three swings to decapitate his father's corpse.

CHAPTER TWENTY-FOUR
Sometimes They Come Back

THE BATTLE OF THE FOUR ARMIES
The Season of Rot

SKELLAN FACED THE dwarf, Kallad Stormwarden, across the mutilated corpse of the third pretender, Marienburg.

'This is better than I could have dared hope, dwarf. You have excelled yourself.' Skellan kicked the corpse at his feet, 'So much death, so meaningless in its brutality. The Blood Count could never have wrought so much destruction alone, but you know that, don't you, dwarf? You understand the sickness of the living, don't you, dwarf? But, as with all good things, it must come to an end. All those cravings, all those personal weaknesses, greed, ambition, lust and other base hungers. Humans are the worst sort of monster, so dwarf, my thanks. You have served your purpose admirably, but now that you've served, I regret to say that you're nothing more exciting than a loose end. It's time to tie you off.'

'You talk too much, vampire. Shut your yapping and fight. I'll kill you first, and then I'll take your damned master into the dirt if that's the way its gotta be.'

Beside the dwarf, Marienburg's son turned on Konrad, brandishing the bloody sword, Runefang.

'I'll have your head, murderer!'

'Oh, Konrad likes this. It's grand. Lots of blood to be spilled, lots indeed, starting with the little man's.' The vampire's smile was quite mad.

Helmar lunged forwards, but again the dwarf restrained him.

'This is not the place. Go, your people need your leadership. A lot depends on you. More than just your anger is at stake here, manling. You have your people to think about. You're theirs now, not your own. Be the man you have to be.' The dwarf levelled a finger at Skellan, singling him out. 'This here is my fight. Me and the vampires. This is what it comes down to: payment of old debts. It was you on the wall at Grunberg, beside your sire. You killed my father that day, you butchered my people, those're debts that need accounting for, Konrad von Carstein. It's time for the reckoning, a life for a life.' Kallad stepped forwards, axe in hand.

'Konrad killed your father as well?' the Blood Count asked, relishing the thought. 'How delicious. Well Konrad has killed a lot of enemies in his life, so why not two fathers? You have a bond now, you two. Thank Konrad, yes, thank Konrad for making you brothers through grief. Konrad is irresistible. Konrad is Vashanesh reborn. All should tremble before his might. Fall at his feet and beg for Konrad's mercy. Yes, beg!'

'Oh, shut your yapping, your madness,' Skellan growled, mimicking the dwarf's colourful dialect and economy of words. His patience for the mad Count's ravings had long since worn thin.

'You serve a fool, Skellan. In my books that makes you the bigger fool,' Kallad said. The dwarf pumped himself up and swung his huge axe in an explosive arc aimed squarely at lopping Skellan's grinning head from his shoulders. The axe screamed through the air. Skellan didn't move until the wicked silver edge was less than a foot from his throat, and even then he barely moved. Rocking back on his heels, he watched the axe slice through the air a fingertip's width from this nose. His grin didn't falter for a moment.

'Predictable, dwarf,' he said, stepping in close and thundering a clap off the side of Kallad's helm that would ring in his ears for hours to come.

The dwarf launched three successive scything attacks, the third of which stung Skellan across the left arm as he turned his ankle on a jag of stone, causing him to miss-step and almost not make the dodge.

The wound smarted. He backed up a step further, feeling out the gash.

'You'll pay for that, little man,' Skellan promised, and the world exploded with violence.

Skellan hurled himself forwards, unleashing the beast within, his face contorting with rage as he roared at the dwarf, hammering him back step after brutal step. The dwarf had no defence for it. His axe flashed and cut, wide of the mark. Skellan drove him back, slamming a fist into the dwarf's nose and shattering the gristle, and again above the eye, spilling blood.

Around them, the battlefield came alive with the sounds of war. The living had seen von Carstein's treachery, seen their last liege lord fall, and had united, turning their combined fury on the dead. The Blood Count's necromancers matched their might with black magic. The clouds parted, but instead of a brilliant beam of light shining down from the heavens, they unleashed the might of Shyish, the black wind leaching all light and colour out of the world. Thunder cracked and the rain came down. There was no first drop, it was a deluge, turning the field into mud, and drawing sheets of steam from the scorched earth.

Next came the flies.

Thick clouds of bloodflies swarmed over the living, getting into their noses and eyes, into their mouths and down their throats, choking them and making it impossible to see, as the dead descended. The armies of the living stumbled on blindly into the shambling dead, rotten claws tearing at their armour, dragging them down as they slipped and slithered in the oozing mud.

Konrad was swept up in the fighting and carried away on a rising tide of death as his wyrm-hilted blade hacked a path of blood and steaming entrails through the living. Immoliah Fey was at his back, her whispered incantations bringing them back in time to see their own guts unravel in their hands painlessly.

Bubbles of mud burst as the ground roiled, coalescing into straining arms and the curves of skulls as the long dead crawled back up from far below the battlefield, the bones of animals and men answering the necromancers' call. Broken antlers breached the surface, followed by the black sockets of a wolf's elongated snout and eyes, and the skeletal remains of a horse's fetlocks. More beasts rose with the remains of the men, most rotten and incomplete, but that did not stop the dead animals from trying to answer the call back to unlife.

Skellan's world narrowed to just the two of them, the dwarf and him. The rest could go to hell, blazing every inch of the way with brimstone and the very stuff of the earth, the rocks, the dirt and the grasses melting beneath the intensity of the unholy fire as they went.

He threw himself at Kallad, driving the dwarf to his knees with the fury of his blows, jumping and seeming to hang suspended in the air for half a second before arcing his spine and delivering a massive kick to the side of Kallad's head. He felt the bone give beneath his foot. The dwarf slumped in the mud, axe spilling from his hands. The fight left his eyes as he looked up, dazed and beaten.

Steel sang as Skellan drew his sword and stood over the dwarf, poised to deliver the killing blow.

He drew back his arm and swung, but the blow never landed.

A crippling blow slammed into the base of Skellan's spine, and a second one into the nape of his neck. The sword tumbled out of his hand as his fingers sprang open. Before he could turn, a fourth and fifth blow had crunched into his spine and ear with crippling force. Pain exploded behind his eyes.

He staggered away and fell, his legs buckling. He sprawled in the mud beside the dwarf and slithered around onto his back so that he could see the face of his attacker.

He saw a ghost looking down at him.

Although the ghost's face was ruined, it was still hauntingly familiar. For a moment, the only thing Skellan could think was that the dead had truly answered the necromancer's call. A rush of doubt filled him. It was an emotion that he had almost forgotten the taste of, and he didn't appreciate being reminded of its bitter tang.

He tried to rise, but the ghost pressed him back down into the mud with an all too substantial foot.

'I should have known your being dead was too good to be true, wolf.'

'Go,' Jerek urged the dwarf.

He didn't allow himself the luxury of seeing if the dwarf heeded his advice. He kicked Skellan hard, hammering a blow into his side that almost lifted him out of the sucking mud.

In the long months of his exile, Skellan's had become the one face that haunted the wolf, not Konrad's, not Vlad's: Skellan's. His evil was subtle and far-reaching.

He kicked Skellan again, in the face this time, below the right eye. A brutal blow that split the skin and cracked the bone, sending a sliver into the milky orb.

Skellan pitched sideways and fell back. Jerek lifted him bodily and slammed him down again in a back-breaking crunch.

'Nice to see you too,' Skellan coughed between gasps, his hand pressed up against his ruined eye.

'Give me a reason, Skellan, just one, to finish you and it is done.'

'You're going to keep an eye on me, are you?'

The unnatural darkness hanging over the battlefield slowly dissipated as the living drove back the dead.

'You mock me at your peril, Skellan,' Jerek said coldly.

'I know, but what can I do? It is in my nature. Why have you come back, wolf?'

Skellan started to rise, only to have Jerek's heel crunch into the bridge of his nose. He sprawled backwards in the mud, head cracking off a jagged edge of rock. 'I've killed men for less, wolf, remember that.' His face was a mess, his nose smeared halfway across his cheek, and the twin white bones of his brow exposed where the flesh had curled away from it. The splinter lodged deep in his blind eye completed the ruin.

'Him,' the wolf said, inclining his head to indicate the manically laughing Blood Count cutting a red swathe through the scattering humans. 'He must be stopped.'

'Couldn't agree more,' Skellan said. He picked at the bone in his blind eye, 'but time and again that isn't enough, is it? We cling to our foolish ideas that simple solutions exist. You want him gone, I want him gone, and yet here we are, enemies once more.' Skellan drew the sliver of bone out of his right eye, the jelly of its vitreous humour spilling down his cheek. 'So while I work quietly to destroy everything that he is, you disappear only to return claiming that our mad Count is your sworn enemy? It's all very… melodramatic, isn't it, wolf?' He held the jagged splinter of bone between thumb and forefinger, examining it with his good eye. 'Have you learned nothing from the von Carsteins? There is beauty in all things, even betrayal. A little more forcefully and you could have really hurt me, you know. As it is, I think it will leave a nasty little scar.'

Skellan tossed the bone away.

Jerek looked at the man he had come to hate. Until that moment, he truly believed that he had gone as far into the vampiric aspect of his nature as it was humanly possible to do.

He was wrong.

'Show me your hands.'

'What?'

'Just do it. Show me your hands.'

Skellan held out his hands.

There were no rings.

Frustration consumed Jerek. He surrendered totally and completely to the black surge of anger, channelling it through his fists as he pummelled them into Skellan's face, wiping the grin off it by destroying the vampire's mouth. Over and over, he pounded his fist into the smug grin, ruining Skellan's mouth by shredding his lips against his teeth.

He didn't stop until Skellan was incapable of fighting back. He kicked and beat Skellan into the ground and then stood over him. It would be so easy to finish it, to slay Skellan and rid the world of his taint, but he couldn't do it. He wanted to, there was no doubt about that in his mind, but he couldn't physically do it. Skellan's words stayed his hand. What if it was true? What if Skellan truly wanted Konrad dead, and not merely to usurp his throne?

What if for all the crimes the man had committed, for all the atrocities carried out by his hand, he had come to realise the unnatural threat the dead posed to the very fabric of the world itself? What if? What if? What if? He couldn't answer any of the questions flying round like blind ravens inside his head, colliding, crashing, falling into and over each other, wings flapping desperately, the cacophony of caws drowning out all hope of rational thought. What if Skellan offered the most unlikely alliance?

He couldn't do it. He couldn't deliver the killing blow, even though he knew that if the roles were reversed, Skellan would have suffered no compunction in his place.

Jerek left Skellan in the dirt.

The battle raged on.

He didn't know where to turn. So much of his life had been given over to the hunt for von Carstein's signet ring. After the fight with Konrad, it had been easier to disappear than to go home.

Home? That was a joke. He had no home.

He was trapped between two worlds, human and undead, and not welcome in either.

Jerek was a ghost, cursed to haunt the Old World until he found the damned ring and could finally rest.

Until then, he could only torment himself by haunting the living and the dead, lurking on the outside of their realms, looking in.

He saw the dwarf staggering back towards the safety of the pavilions and felt the pull of the necromancers' magic. He didn't know which way to turn. Neither camp would welcome him. He cursed himself for a fool for being drawn to this foreign field, but he had always known that he had no choice but to be here. He had to walk amongst the dead. He had to find the ring. It had to be destroyed. He couldn't allow it to fall into a madman like Konrad's hands, or worse, an amoral killer like Skellan's.

Jerek walked away from the killing.

He followed the dwarf towards the chirurgeons' tents. War was not one battle: it was continuous attrition, grinding down the enemy over and over again. Von Carstein would surrender the field. The signs were there to be read. A sunburst of light threw its yellow glow across the fighting, scattering the shadows. They returned a moment later to smother the light, but it didn't matter, the darkness had shown weakness, vulnerability. That in turn gave the light hope. The living rallied, throwing themselves at the dead.

Then, from between the cracks in the hillside, came salvation: a long rippling snake of movement coming out of the valley of darkness and spilling out onto the plain, dwarfs bearing the banner of Zufbar, another thousand at least.

Wooping around them, human riders bore the banner of Marienburg, their burnished armour catching that fleeting burst of light and magnifying it. They swarmed onto the field, lances levelled, skewering the mindless dead who were too slow or too clumsy to get out of their way. Their chargers' hooves crushed skulls beneath the stampede, and the dwarfs cleaned up after them.

The dead were routed.

This day, at least, was won.

Drive a foe from the field one day and he returns the next, renewed, more desperate to be your doom.

As much as he was loath to involve himself, to expose himself, Jerek knew that his only hope lay with the dwarf and his people. They were committed to exterminating his kind, in that common cause they were united. They were his best chance of destroying Konrad, even if it meant sacrificing himself.

Cheers went up from the living, but they were not the exuberant cheers of victory, they were the desperate cries of relief. They had been saved; they hadn't won. There was a difference, and they knew it.

JEREK WATCHED THE dwarf. He haunted the camp. It was surprisingly easy, considering his nature, to move unnoticed.

He wasn't sure exactly how he was going to befriend the dwarf. He had thought about claiming that he was owed a life debt for saving the dwarf from Skellan, and while it might be enough to keep him alive, it wasn't exactly something that he *wanted* to do.

Would the dwarf throw his lot in with the dead, trading one evil for another? Moreover, when the deed was done, would the dwarf turn on him?

The surprising truth of it was that after living through the torments of this unlife, Jerek welcomed the prospect of that final rest. It held no fear for him, even if dying again did mean the destruction of all that he was. Here, now, he would have welcomed a complete cessation of existence with arms wide open. If the ring was destroyed, then it was a price worth paying.

Years of fighting against his nature could finally end here, on this field.

That was why he had returned, that was the truth he was hiding from himself.

He knew this was the first move in the endgame.

He knew that by saving the dwarf and making his presence known to Skellan, he had accelerated everything. He *could* have lurked in the shadows, hunting for clues, following the path of the ring, but by coming forward, he had chosen to become a catalyst. Things would happen around him. Mistakes would be made, hands played too early, secrets betrayed. One of them would lead to the ring, he felt sure. One of them *had* to.

As the dwarf passed, Jerek stepped out of the shadows and grabbed him from behind, pressing his hand over the dwarf's mouth and hissing, 'Shhhhhh,' before the dwarf could fight back. 'I am a friend.' He removed his hand.

'You're no friend of mine, freak.'

'Then let's hope that by the end of the night I am,' Jerek said.

* * *

THE DWARF HEARD him out.

'Why in hell should I trust you?'

Jerek had wondered that himself and the truth of it was far from convincing. 'Because of who I was, not who I am,' he said, hoping it was enough. 'Because, as the White Wolf of Middenheim, I gave my life trying to protect the same thing that you are trying to protect, and because, for some reason, a spark of whatever it was that made me *me* still burns inside me. How long it will last, I don't know, but while it does I am a ghost, trapped between the land of the living and the nations of rot and decay. I am nothing in either world, and because of that, I can pass unnoticed in both. I can get where you can't, close enough to Konrad to kill him if that is how it must end. I do not want to end up like *them*.'

'And what are you proposing I give you in return?'

'Help.'

'Go on.'

'You know the story of the first war?'

'I was there, yes.'

'Then you know that it was won by guile, not force. Von Carstein had a talisman of incredible power that enabled his dead form to regenerate. The talisman was stolen during the Siege of Altdorf, allowing the Sigmarite priest to slay him once and forever.'

'I know the story,' the dwarf said. 'The Vampire Count's ring. The thief stole it and gave it to the priests.'

'Yes, the von Carstein ring – only I don't for one minute believe that the thief gave it to the priests. Put it this way, it wasn't in either grave and I can't see them leaving it in a jewellery box on a nightstand, can you?

I need to find the thief who took it. I need to make sure that the damned thing is destroyed. That is what I need your help for.'

'And who told you I know anything about any ring?'

'You did, just now. I said talisman, you said ring.'

'I could have heard that in a taproom just about anywhere in the Empire.'

'Yes, you could have, but you didn't, did you?'

'No, I met the thief. I saw with me own eyes the price he paid for his heroics. He ain't got that ring though, you can take my word for that. One of your kind took it. Cut his hands off in the process and left him for dead, only he didn't die.'

Jerek didn't say a word for the longest time. When he finally spoke, it was as if he hadn't heard the dwarf's words. 'I saw the banner you bore into battle. I recognised the device: Karak Sadra. I know what happened to that stronghold, dwarf. I know who was responsible for destroying it. That means I know what you are, or who you are, rather. You are the last of your clan.

'Knowing that gives me the key to you, how you work. I know what drives you. I understand the anger festering inside you, the need for vengeance, better than any other you will meet. You bear a grudge against the monster that slew your people.

'I bear one as well, against the monsters that made me into what I am. I will not lie down and let them swallow my world whole. I will not stand by and watch it plunge into eternal night. I will not watch it become a place of blood and sorrow. No, dwarf, that cannot be allowed to happen, but it falls to people like us to prevent it. That is what will happen if what you say is true. That ring cannot be allowed to adorn the finger of a vampire. It cannot. The world cannot withstand another dread lord of my sire's ilk.'

That confession went against every instinct the wolf possessed, still it felt important to have no lies between them, not if he was going to sway the dwarf to his side.

'You're saying you and him... you and the mad one... you're brothers?'

'Of a sort, dwarf, but not in any meaningful way, there is no kinship between us, no bond. He is vermin and should be treated as such.'

'You're brothers though, in blood. Brothers with the monster that killed my father.'

There was no way he could deny the truth so he didn't.

'You see a beast gone rabid what do you do?' Jerek asked.

'Put it out of its misery.'

'That's my brother, dwarf. A beast that needs to be put out of its misery, that is all he is.

'Now, guile won the last war, not strength of arms, not the supreme sacrifice of one man. That stinks like the effulgence it is. The thief won the war by taking away the one thing that von Carstein had – his invulnerability. Once he was stripped of it and made mortal, the war was as good as over. Any blade could have struck him down. It didn't have to be Sigmar sent or Ulric blessed. This war could be won the same way.

The Blood Count has no talent, and so long as the von Carstein ring hasn't found its way into his possession, he isn't blessed with that infuriating knack of coming back and coming back and coming back. All he is is a madman who demands that his few pet magicians raise his armies for him. He is a shadow of his sire and he knows it, self-loathing and doubt consume him. He strives to reinvent himself as more than he is. He is trying to build a legend, but those men he relies upon, well, they have no such immortality – in other words, they aren't particularly difficult to kill. Hit them and the war is essentially over.'

'I've got no liking for this and I don't mind saying,' the dwarf grunted, cracking the bones in his neck as he twisted, 'but there's no denying what you're getting at. Well, it makes a fair deal of sense.'

'You don't need to like it, dwarf, just accept that it is so. I am less than human, more than vampire, something else entirely and nothing completely. I have no loyalty to the dead. I would do what I have always done, all my life. I would protect the living. I'm not claiming the life debt you owe me for saving you from Skellan back there, although I could. I know your culture. I know what it means to save a dwarf from certain death. I know that you are beholden to me, but I don't care. I want your help given willingly or not at all. I cannot risk you suffering a change of heart. No, what I am asking for is nothing more than your help in preventing a dark and hungry god from arising in our time, in our children's time. I am asking you to do the right thing. You have already proven that you know more about this thief and the ring than

I have unearthed in long months of searching. Together, we can do things that alone we can't. So, dwarf, do we have a pact?'

He studied the dwarf, saw him struggling to get past his natural hatred of the beast he had become, the betrayal he felt knowing he faced a blood relative of the beast that had slaughtered his people, trying to grasp that something of the man he was still remained, and that he could in fact be trusted.

Finally, the dwarf nodded.

'Aye, you hold up your end, get close to the necromancers and kill them if you can, but the mad vampire is mine,' Kallad Stormwarden said, spitting on his palm and holding his hand out. 'When that's done we'll turn our attention to that damned ring of yours.'

They shook, sealing the bargain.

CHAPTER TWENTY-FIVE
To Kill The Mocking Birds

GRIM MOOR
The Season of Decay

DEATH COMES TO all living things, there is no escaping it: death, the great destroyer; death, conqueror, liberator, defiler, despoiler.

Death. It was his gift to the living.

Konrad von Carstein's mind was in turmoil. Thoughts he didn't recognise as his own pulled him every which way. He was torn. He heard voices: they weren't externalised, they were inside him. They taunted him and jeered at his failings. He knew the loudest of them. It belonged to a head from his rotten gallery. Although the head of Johannes Schafer was far, far removed, the man's voice was an incessant yammering in his head, going on and on and on.

He screamed. He hammered at his temples, trying to drive the voices out, but they wouldn't leave him, and they wouldn't leave him alone.

Schafer was dead. Konrad couldn't remember how he had killed the man, only that he had and that the rogue had been a screamer. That he remembered. Now, as penance, he carried the ghost around inside his head.

'Leave Konrad be, leave him!' Konrad yelled, spinning around violently. He tore the map from the table and shredded it. His sword lay on the tabletop beside a goblet of dark liquid. In anger, he lashed out and sent the weapon clattering to floor. His necromancers, Immoliah Fey and Nevin Kantor, backed off a step from his madness. 'Not you! You!' They had no idea whether they were supposed to stay or go. 'You will obey Konrad! You will serve him with your heart or he will feast on it, Understand?'

Neither said a word.

In truth, they had no idea whether the Blood Count was talking to them or raving at some invisible speaker whose words filled his head.

There was an uneasy balance in the room: they could not trust him and he could not trust them. He knew they were scheming behind his back. Skellan kept him informed. Skellan, his last loyal soldier. Skellan, poor, pitiful Skellan. The war had all but destroyed him, but he refused to die.

It was only pity that stayed Konrad's hand, pity for himself, not for Skellan, pity that the wretched beast was the closest he had to a friend, family, or a lover; pity that all around him sought to topple him from his lofty perch. Pity that it had come down to this: kill or be killed.

He had never been afraid of bringing death into the world. Death was his one true talent, his gift.

Konrad heard a cough and turned.

'Whistle up the daemon,' he said as Skellan moved awkwardly into the room. The Hamaya dragged his left leg, and his right arm hung uselessly at his side. The muscles showed signs of atrophy. It had set in with surprising speed, as if Skellan had lost the will to heal himself, and had given in to the natural entropy of all things flesh. The bones twisted around on the shoulder joint, hunching his back uncomfortably.

For all that, it was his face that betrayed the full extent of the toll that the war had taken. It was barely recognisable: a ruin of scars closed up his right eye, the flesh itself merging into a flat plane from nose to brow with only the narrowest slit where his eye had once been.

He refused to say who had done this to him, although Konrad harboured suspicions. There were few great heroes allied to the forces of the living, certainly no more than a handful of men capable of standing up to a vampire of Skellan's lethal cunning.

'You wanted me?' There was no deference in Skellan's voice. His battering had knocked the respect out of him. Konrad would deal with it, in time, but not today. Today, he needed Skellan's devious nature to undo the forces of the living that had rallied behind Helmar of Marienburg's banner. He knew Skellan was devious, that Skellan plotted his own schemes, that his Hamaya desired nothing more than to usurp him, but Konrad was no mere beast, Konrad was Vashanesh reborn. Konrad was supreme. Konrad was immortal!

'Yes, yes, yes. Konrad wants you. Konrad wants to pick your brains. These two pretend loyalty, but they refuse Konrad.'

'Then make them. It is as simple as that. Take something of theirs and threaten to destroy it. What do they love more than anything?'

'They love nothing,' Konrad said, exasperated.

'Wrong, your madness, they love their books. They love the trinkets and treasures you gave them. They love their power. Take it away from them. Take it all away from them unless they do as you demand.'

'You can't!' Fey cried.

Kantor slapped her across the face, hard. She wheeled around on him, her snarl feral.

Skellan laughed harshly. 'See, Konrad. Threaten to take their toys away and they turn on each other fast enough. You didn't need me for this.'

'Konrad would hear the truth, and you are his truth speaker, Jon Skellan, so speak to him. When you look at the field what do you see?'

'What do you want me to say? Bloodshed, devastation, suffering? I see a world of hurt.'

'But is it enough? Does it satisfy you? Will it open the way for the Kingdom of the Dead? Will it?'

'You want the truth?' Skellan asked, shuffling awkwardly to one side so that he could draw the tent flap back. The cold air, heavy with the taint of blood and urine, blew into the pavilion. The sounds of battle rushed in behind it. The sounds of death and dying, the low moaning keen of the zombies, the creaks and groans of the skeletons, the shrieks of the ghouls and the howls of the dire wolves a haunting counterpoint to the agonies of the living, the clash of steel on bone and the wet tearing of flesh.

'Yes, Konrad would hear your truth.'

Skellan stared at him, his one good eye blazing hate. 'I think you are finished, Konrad. I think your pets are turning against you and you can't do a damned thing to stop it. I don't think you even see it, you are that blind. Kantor here, and Fey, have dreams of dominion. They see the world you are carving out and think to themselves: but this is all our doing, not his. And they are right, because without them you are nothing, and out there, on that blasted moor, I think you are being destroyed bit by bloody bit.' His words came out slurred because he couldn't curl his lips around them properly when he grew angry. 'They will not write glorious histories of your life, and they will not fall for the drivel you had Constantin scribble in your honour. They will remember you for what you are, a poor deranged fool. That is my truth.'

'You seek to anger Konrad? You seek to drive him to violence, yes? Konrad understands your pain, understands that you are less than a man, so you lash out at his greatness to appease your own pain. Konrad understands, but Konrad does not forgive. Oh, no, Konrad does not forgive such slights.'

Skellan smiled, as best his ruined mouth would allow.

'It isn't for Konrad to forgive. Konrad matters nothing to me.' He shook his head, as if irritated that the Blood Count's affliction of referring to himself in the third person had transferred itself to him. 'Who controls your Hamaya, your madness? That's a rhetorical question, by the way. I do. We both know it. Every one of the second generation was hand-picked by me. Where does their loyalty lie? You can answer this one, go on, have a guess.'

'You,' Konrad rasped, the beast roaring out from beneath his skin. His brow split, his nose thickened and elongated, stretching his mouth up to bare cruel fangs.

'Me,' Skellan agreed.

He didn't unleash the beast.

'Who is loyal to Konrad? WHO?' the Blood Count raged, spinning around the confines of the tent. He grabbed Immoliah Fey by the throat and drew her close. He saw fear in her eyes and revelled in it, rasping into her face, 'Are you loyal to Konrad, bitch?'

For all her magic, she had no answer for him. She feared him.

That in itself was condemnation. Who had need to fear but a traitor?

He threw her aside and wheeled around on Kantor. The weasel threw up his hands and spat an oath that hit Konrad in the gut, twisting his insides. He didn't understand what he was feeling at first, didn't grasp the seriousness of it as the necromancer continued his malicious incantation. He felt a fire in his blackened heart, felt it spreading out through his left arm and down his left side. He didn't wait to see what was happening to him, he lashed out, sending the necromancer sprawling back over the table and into the pavilion's canvas wall. He stood over Nevin Kantor, poised to deliver judgement.

'You will swear loyalty to Konrad, spirit of Vashanesh reborn. You will swear it or you will die here.'

'I will bring your army to its knees first,' Kantor rasped. 'You ignorant fool, harm me, and your hold over the dead dies. Can you be so far gone that you don't realise it? Your army exists through me, not you. You are not the lord here, Konrad. I am, and she,' he inclined his head towards Immoliah Fey, 'is my dark queen.'

'Build an empire on dust, Konrad, and you have to expect it to sink eventually. It is the way of all things.'

'No,' Konrad said, refusing to believe the truth of his own ears. 'No, no, no, no.'

Kantor struggled to his feet, a contemptuous sneer pasted across his face. 'Do you hear that, Konrad?'

'Konrad hears nothing.'

'Exactly, that silence is ominous isn't it, considering this is a battlefield. Where are the screams of the dying? Where is the clash of sword on sword?'

'What have you done?'

'Only what I promised – I have taken my dead back. They do not fight for you. They await my will, and sense that my anger is directed inwards, focused on you, Konrad. Can you hear them coming? Can you hear the grind of bones, the shuffling feet? They are coming for you.'

Konrad pushed past Skellan and staggered out of the pavilion and into the harsh light of day. The sun burned his skin. He looked up at the sky, at the golden orb hanging above his head, and screamed, 'Where is the darkness? Konrad commands it be night!'

The necromancers emerged from the tent, faces impassive. Skellan came up behind them, something gleaming in his right hand.

'You truly are a fool, aren't you, von Carstein?' Kantor spat. 'You bluster at the heavens and don't even look at the earth. Look, damn you, see your doom as it nears.'

'Betrayal,' Konrad whispered, seeing the dead fighting amongst themselves, the vampires struggling against the endless press of Kantor and Fey's automatons. The dead were coming for him: the dead, his dead. 'Fight!' Konrad roared. 'Butcher the living!' But it was useless.

'Your time of blight is over, Blood Count,' Kantor said smugly.

It was the last thing he ever said. Skellan rammed a thin-bladed dagger into his back, between the third and fourth bones of his ribcage, and buried it deep into the necromancer's heart. His lips moved, but he didn't make a sound. A white mist leaked from Kantor's mouth, coalescing into a wraith-like shadow, gathering form. It was a vile beast. Konrad knew what he saw, just as he knew that he couldn't be seeing it. Kantor's essence, Kantor's soul, and then, even as the winds around the battlefield howled and a massive thunder-clap split the clear blue sky, the mist dissipated and an unerring calm settled over Grim Moor.

Then his body collapsed.

The dead under Kantor's thrall echoed his collapse as one, the black thread of Shyish that bound them back to this life cut.

Ravens circled the battlefield, settled on the roofs and guide ropes of the pavilions, on the corpses of the dead and on the stones, and cawed, their mocking cry taking on an uncomfortably human aspect: *he is coming... he is coming...*

Konrad ran at the nearest ravens, scattering them.

They swooped low overhead, cawing, cawing, ceaselessly cawing: *he is coming...*

Immoliah Fey struggled to rally her own zombies while hissing incantations to raise Kantor's dead from the dirt of the field, but the vampires had turned on them.

The dead were destroying themselves. All the living had to do was bear witness.

'Kill them. Kill them all!' Konrad raged, running around the battlefield like a madman possessed, flapping his arms at the black birds.

Skellan allowed himself a satisfied smile.

THE FORCES OF the living rallied, given new strength by the sight of their enemy's collapse.

They brandished swords and spears, and charged into the mud of the field, stumbling and falling, and picking themselves up to charge on, their war cries terrible to hear.

True death came to the dead on the field that day.

KONRAD STOPPED, FROZEN in the act of strangling a raven.

Out of the bloodshed and devastation of Grim Moor strode a face from his past, a ghost.

'Konrad killed you,' he said, even as the bird broke in his hands.

Jerek von Carstein stood before him.

At his side were two grim faced dwarfs and the boy-man, Helmar, clutching his father's sword, Runefang.

Fighting raged around them, the living banishing the dead.

Skellan moved to stop the dwarf, Kallad. Beside him Grufbad shook his head.

'Out of my way, ugly, this is between me and the man that killed my father.'

'Kill him!' Konrad yelled, but to his horror, he saw Skellan shake his head.

'You have to own the consequences of your own actions, Konrad,' Skellan said, grinning. 'Looks to me a lot like the world has come to pay you back.'

'You say no? Konrad will kill you if Konrad must, you will die just the same, little man.' The Blood Count reached down for the wyrm-hilted blade at his side, but it wasn't there. It was inside the pavilion, beneath the table. His anger swept him away. 'Konrad has no need of steel!' He threw himself at the first dwarf, Kallad, who met his charge head on, butting his head full into Konrad's face. Rage deadened all feeling. Konrad lashed out, clawing at the dwarf's face. The dwarf took it without flinching.

Konrad felt fire, in his chest, and looked down to see the blade of a huge double-headed axe buried in his chest.

His scream, as the dwarf yanked the axe clear, was terrible to behold.

His scream, as the dwarf slammed the axe home a second time, was worse.

But still he didn't fall. He caught the dwarf's axe and hurled it away, backhanding a massive blow across the side of Kallad's temple. He roared, pure animalistic rage, and then felt arms take him. He couldn't break the grip. He writhed and twisted and shrieked but there was no way out of these bonds.

Kallad stepped up again, ready to cleave skull from shoulders but Helmar stayed his hand.

'He killed my father as well, dwarf. I would finish this. For me, for my people.'

Kallad looked at the young warrior. There was something in the young pretender's face that told him he needed it more, to find peace, than Kallad did. 'Aye, lad, justice is done whoever lands the blow. Do it.' The dwarf stepped back.

Helmar stood over Konrad while Grufbad held him down.

He raised the Runefang…

KONRAD'S VISION BLURRED. He saw Skellan. He saw the ghost of Jerek. He saw Immoliah Fey dead at his feet, the wolf holding her heart in his fist. He saw the dwarf.

His legs buckled beneath him.

All around, the ravens mocked him. He saw them everywhere, a murder of black birds, and in their eyes, he saw the true source of his betrayal, and knew at the last that he had been undone by one of his own.

'Konrad is betrayed,' Konrad breathed, darkness closing over him. He reached out for the wolf, for his truth speaker.

He never felt the blow that claimed his head.

EPILOGUE
Grim Moor

KALLAD STORMWARDEN STOOD over the corpse of the Blood Count.

He had his revenge. He had justice for his father. He had retribution for his people. And yet… and yet he felt nothing.

There was no satisfaction in delivering death. He was hollow.

'Time to leave this place,' Jon Skellan said, and seemed to unfold his crippled body. He stretched and bent, manipulating his muscles. He drew himself to his full height, forcing his leg to obey him. He gasped, pressing his shoulder back into place. His arm still showed the rigor of atrophy and his face bore all the marks of mutilation from Jerek's beating, but his bearing was powerful once more as he shook off his helpless disguise. 'I am not one for lost causes, eh wolf? I delivered my end of the bargain, now you deliver yours.' He turned to leave and then stopped. 'You did well, dwarf, surprisingly well. I wouldn't have thought you had it in you. Go back to your hole in the ground. The greatest of them all is coming. You do not want to be here when he returns.'

Ravens settled on Skellan's shoulder, one on his left, one on his right, and though the wind tore away their mocking cries, he could have sworn he heard a name:

Mannfred.

ABOUT THE AUTHOR

British author Steven Savile is an expert in cult fiction, having written a wide variety of sf, fantasy and horror stories, including Star Wars fiction. He won the L Ron Hubbard Writers of the Future award in 2002, and has been nominated three times for the Bram Stoker award. He currently lives in Stockholm, Sweden.